The fiery brilliance of the Zebra Hologram Heart which you see on the cover is created by "laser holography." This is the revolutionary process in which a powerful laser beam records light waves in diamond-like facets so tiny that 9,000,000 fit in a square inch. No print or photograph can match the vibrant colors and radiant glow of a hologram.

So look for the Zebra Hologram Heart whenever you buy a historical romance. It is a shimmering reflection of our guarantee that you'll find consistent quality be

GOLDEN CAPTIVE

"I hate you!" Trista swore, tormented by her own weakness and her betrayal of Michael.

"It matters little to me what you think or feel, my golden captive." Lance's expression didn't change as he knelt down beside her and brushed her hands away from their feeble attempt to hide herself from him. "All that matters is that I have made you mine." Boldly he let his hands roam over her, deliberately fondling those places she'd tried to hide.

"I'm not yours, and I never will be! Never!" Trista denied her shame as she tried to twist away from him and block his caresses.

He gave a sharp laugh. "You already are. You can say what you want, but your body does not lie, Trista. Does Michael's touch make you feel this way?"

"Michael has never touched me so!" Trista gritted her teeth against her body's betrayal as she continued to try to evade his touch.

It filled Lance with pleasure to know that no other man had ever been so intimate with her. And he vowed she would never know love from another — never. . . .

TEXAS SPLENDOR
BOBBI SMITH

ZEBRA BOOKS
KENSINGTON PUBLISHING CORP.

FOR THE "I SURVIVED THE ALAMO IN THE RAIN GANG"—EVELYN, JIM, JASON, EMMA, PAUL, SYLVIE, AND JOHN.

ALSO—A SPECIAL NOTE OF THANKS TO DORETHA ELIZABETH PEDIGO SMITH, THE WORLD'S BEST LITERARY CRITIC.
HAPPY 80TH BIRTHDAY MOM!

ZEBRA BOOKS

are published by

Kensington Publishing Corp.
475 Park Avenue South
New York, NY 10016

First Printing: February, 1988

Printed in the United States of America

Prologue
Central Texas, 1850

Somber-faced, the warrior reined in his foam-flecked mount on the low rise above the Comanche camp. Below, the scene was peaceful as the dogs who guarded the encampment had not yet picked up his scent and were still dozing in the warmth of the afternoon sun. Warriors, young and old, lounged lazily near their tipis, trading stories of their hunting prowess and bravery in battle. Scantily clad children raced happily about the village as their mothers, ever close and watching, labored over the multitude of tasks that filled their days. Usually the cheerful sound of the young ones' carefree play would have lightened the warrior's mood, but not today. Today there was no flicker of emotion, gentle or otherwise, reflected in his eyes at the sight of his tribe. His expression remained inscrutable, betraying none of the tension within him. Finally, the importance of the news he carried driving him on, the warrior knew he could delay no longer. Kneeing his exhausted mount into motion, he guided the weary steed down the incline.

The ferocious sound of the dogs' barking always signaled an arrival in camp. Lone Elk, war chief of the tribe, emerged from his tipi to see who was returning. Tall and cleanly muscled, he carried himself with an arrogant male grace that reflected not only his superior athletic ability but also his authority

5

within the band. The position of war chief was earned, not inherited, and Lone Elk had achieved his rank through outstanding bravery and by leading many successful raids against the whites. He was well known for his fearlessness in combat, and more than a few of his warriors held in him awe. An astute leader, little escaped Lone Elk's notice, and he wondered now, as the lone rider approached, why the brave had felt it necessary to push his mount to near exhaustion to reach the village. Whatever the warrior had to report, he knew it would not be good.

"Shrieking Eagle," Lone Elk greeted him as he drew near.

Ignoring all those who clamored about, excited by his arrival, Shrieking Eagle stopped before his chief and agilely dismounted, sliding quickly to the ground. He faced Lone Elk, his heart heavy with the message he was about to impart. "I have news, Lone Elk."

The chief's black eyes became piercing in their potency, glittering dangerously at his tone. "What is it?"

"Your sister . . ."

"Shining Star? What of her?" He was instantly alert as his gaze searched Shrieking Eagle's face for a clue as to his meaning. "What is it you know of my sister?" he demanded.

"She is dead," the young brave supplied, not wanting to risk his wrath by hesitating. "A fever took her . . . *a white man's fever.*" He added the last in a derogatory sneer.

Lone Elk stiffened visibly at the news. As much as he would have liked to deny it, he knew Shrieking Eagle would never lie to him about such a matter. It was the truth. His sister, the one person he loved above all others, was dead! Wailing his grief in an agonized cry, he turned from the messenger and the

6

rapidly gathering crowd of onlookers to mourn the loss of his beloved sister.

Shrieking Eagle's mother, a portly, gentle woman named She Who Speaks the Truth, approached her son cautiously and asked, "What word have you brought us that has caused Lone Elk such pain?" She had known Lone Elk all of his life and had never seen him so deeply affected.

Shrieking Eagle glanced down at his mother. "Shining Star is dead, Mother."

She Who Speaks the Truth nodded slowly as her gaze followed Lone Elk. "Only her death could affect him so," she remarked sagely, knowing of the chief's devotion to his only sister. "What of her child? Is there news of her son?"

"I know nothing of the child."

"Lone Elk will go for him."

Shrieking Eagle's expression was filled with loathing as he turned on her. "The child is a white!"

"Only half-white," she countered. "A part of him is Comanche, too."

"It would be dangerous . . . foolhardy . . ."

She Who Speaks the Truth shrugged as she started to walk away. "Lone Elk will go."

It was late, the night moonless and very dark. Though campfires burned brightly in the village, the flickering light did not help to dispel the gloom, but served only to cast weirdly distorted shadows upon the surroundings. It had been four days since Chief Lone Elk had received the news of his sister's death, yet his mourning had not lessened. The sounds of his grief echoed almost continually through the camp as he remained prostrate in his tipi. It was only as the first rays of dawn brightened the eastern sky on that

7

morning of the fifth day that he rose from his bed and drew out his knife. In silent tribute to Shining Star, Lone Elk sawed at the thickness of his braided hair until his left braid was cut completely off. Another cry of misery broke from his lips as he stared down at his severed pride. Forever he would mourn her. . . .

Hatred for George Barrett, the white rancher who had taken Shining Star from him, seared his soul anew. Lone Elk knew he should have forbidden her to go, that he should have denied her any contact with the man, but even as he thought it, he realized it would have been pointless. His sister had been like no other woman. She had been proud and beautiful and stubborn . . . oh, so stubborn. Had he forbidden her her love, she would have defied him and gone to Barrett anyway, so he had not tried to stop her when she left the village and took the white man as her husband.

For the past eight years, Shining Star had lived the life of a white woman on the Barrett ranch, the Royal Diamond, and Lone Elk had purposefully stayed away. Though his love for her was strong, his hatred and distrust of whites was stronger.

Lone Elk shook his head sadly. He had known her future would not be happy with the whites, and he had been right. It was not happiness she'd found in their midst, but death. Forever he would feel the punishing weight of knowing she had been lost to him because he hadn't forced her to remain with the tribe. Lone Elk's grief, rage, and helplessness all combined to fill him with bitter viciousness. He hated the white man who had stolen his sister's heart, and he held Barrett responsible for her death.

It was then that he thought of the child . . . her child, Lance. Lone Elk realized that a part of Shining Star was still alive in her young son. His enmity for the husband ran deep, and a firm resolve took root within him. There was no way he was going to allow Barrett to raise Shining Star's son as a white. The boy was blood kin to Lone Elk. The boy was Comanche, and he belonged with his people. The white man's ways were not for him.

A surge of fierce determination filled the chief then, and he strode from his tipi once again master of his emotions. He would honor his sister. He would raise her son as his own and see him a great warrior in the tribe. Before the sun had cleared the treetops, Lone Elk and five other warriors were headed for the Royal Diamond to claim Lance Barrett, son of Shining Star, and bring him back to live as one of them and learn the ways of the Comanche.

Chapter One

"But I want to see my father, Rosalie! Why won't you let me see him?" seven-year-old Lance Barrett demanded.

"He's not feeling well right now, Lance," Rosalie Chavez, the longtime housekeeper of the Royal Diamond, told him in her no-nonsense tone as she sat at the table in the kitchen of the ranchhouse. "Perhaps he will be better later." Her last statement was more of a prayer than a positive belief as she thought of George Barrett and how, for several days now, he had locked himself in his study alone with his whiskey. . . .

"But, Rosalie," Lance protested in childish confusion as he stared up at her, 'I haven't seen him for two whole days! Is something wrong? Is he sick like Mother was?" His vivid blue eyes widened as he considered the possibility. A tremor of fear shook his small, sturdy body, and he ventured hesitantly, "Is Father dead, too?"

Rosalie could read the terror in his expression and quickly took him in her arms to reassure him. Drawing him onto her lap, she hugged him to her ample breasts. Her dark eyes misted as she tried to ease the little boy's agony. "No, little one, your father is not sick with the fever. Have no fear on that account, muchacho."

"Then what's the matter?"

11

"It is a sickness of the heart, Lance." Rosalie attempted to explain his father's withdrawal from life since the death of his beloved wife, Shining Star, several weeks before. "He misses your mother."

"But I miss her, too, Rosalie!" Lance gazed up at her, tears brimming in his troubled gaze.

"I know, I know." Rosalie patted him comfortingly, her heart aching for him.

"It's not fair! Why did Mother have to die?" he asked tormentedly, struggling to control his need to cry. He had been brave for so long, ever since the funeral, but suddenly it seemed almost too much for him . . . the loneliness . . . the desolation.

She rocked Lance tenderly, crooning to him to ease the pain within him. "If you need to cry, go ahead. You will feel better if you let it out."

Lance stiffened in her embrace and pulled himself free. Standing almost defiantly before her, he angrily dashed away the tears that had started to trace down his cheeks. "No! I won't cry! Father says men don't cry!"

"Lance . . ." Rosalie's voice reflected her misery as she opened her arms to try to hold him again, but he backed away.

"I won't cry! I won't!" Turning his back on her, he fled the room and the house.

Rosalie watched Lance race away knowing that, no matter how far he ran or how fast, the sorrow and bewildering pain would still be with him. Right now he needed his father more than he ever had before, yet Rosalie realized that George Barrett was in no condition to help his son. The wealthy owner of the Royal Diamond had lost all interest in his son and his ranch and was taking solace in the forgetfulness of drink. Without his wife, he saw no reason for living.

Having been a witness to George's unfailing devotion to Shining Star, Rosalie knew that their love for each other had been great. Still, she could not understand his complete disregard for the devastation his own child was feeling over her death. Lance had adored his mother. They had been as close as any mother and son could be, and he, too, had lost her. Truly the boy was suffering greatly, yet there was precious little she could do for him. It was his father's love and consolation he needed right now, not hers.

The sound of George drunkenly bellowing her name interrupted Rosalie's thoughts, and she shook her head in sorrowful understanding as she got slowly to her feet. During the past two days, the only time he'd called for her had been when he'd been out of liquor and in desperate need of more. She longed to deny him, to force him back to soberness so he could see what he was doing to himself and his son, but she had no right or authority to do so. Pausing only long enough to retrieve another bottle of whiskey, she started from the kitchen. As she went, she couldn't help but wonder just how long this could go on before tragedy struck the family again.

George Barrett sat alone and miserable at his desk in the darkened confines of his study. He rubbed at his throbbing temples with a shaking hand as he waited for the servant to come to him.

"Rosalie! Damn it, woman, where are you with my whiskey?" he shouted, and then cringed at the loudness of his own voice. Leaning heavily on the desktop, he got drunkenly to his feet intending to search out his wayward housekeeper and reprimand her for taking so long to answer his summons. A wave of nausea flooded through him, and his already pale color worsened as he lurched unsteadily toward the door.

Rosalie tried to let herself in when she reached the study, but to her dismay, the door was still locked.

"Señor George!" she called out as she rapped sharply on the portal. "The door is locked. Open the door."

George was relieved that she'd finally come. He managed the last few steps and then, with difficulty, unlocked the door and threw it wide.

Glaring threateningly at his servant, he demanded in slurred, angry tones, "Where have you been?! Did you bring—" He stopped when he saw the fresh bottle of whiskey in her hand. "Ah, yes . . . I see that you did."

Like a greedy child, his glazed eyes alight at the promise of another drink, he reached for the liquor with both hands. Eagerly he tore off the cap and lifted the bottle to his lips, thirstily downing a sizable portion of the potent drink.

When he'd opened the door to face her, Rosalie had almost taken a step back as the sour smell of human sweat mixed with the stale scent of liquor had assailed her senses. Her lips curled in disgust as she stared at her boss for a long moment and then looked around the room. The study was dark and gloomy, the shutters deliberately drawn against the brightness of the day. Within the heavy shadows, Rosalie could make out books and papers scattered haphazardly about the usually neat room. Numerous empty whiskey bottles littered the floor and desk, giving silent testimony to George's current state.

It was then that Rosalie knew a moment of true concern. All along she had believed that George would eventually pull himself together and put aside his grief. Now, however, she was beginning to have her doubts. He had to get a grip on himself soon or risk losing everything. Determined to help in whatever way she could, Rosalie brushed past him into the room. Stalking purposely to a window, she made short order of opening it. Unaware that Lance was in the

14

yard right outside, within earshot, she threw wide the shutters.

George was so engrossed in drinking the whiskey that he paid little attention to Rosalie. When the sunlight flooded into the room, he was startled, and he turned on his faithful housekeeper with an uncharacteristic snarl. "Close the damn window, woman!"

Summoning all her strength of will, Rosalie faced George, her hands planted firmly on her wide hips. In the harsh brilliance of the afternoon sun she stared at him, and it took an effort on her part not to let the shock she felt at his appearance show in her expression. The man standing before her was not the George Barrett she knew—tall, handsome, and self-confident. Clad in rumpled, stained clothing, the man clutching the liquor bottle firmly in hand was a mere shadow of himself. The darkness of several days' growth of beard, combined with his shaggy and unkempt brown hair, gave him a wild, almost savage look. George's blue eyes, blue like his son's, usually mirrored his intelligence and good humor, but today they reflected nothing in their dull and bloodshot depths. It was as if all life, all joy had been drained from him.

"No. I will not. You've been in here alone far too long. It's time for this to stop. You are needed and—"

"Shut up and do as I say!" he snapped.

"No," Rosalie answered firmly, glowering at him.

At her reply George looked up, his face a mask of fury. "Need I remind you that you are but a servant here?"

"I know my place," Rosalie managed, hurt. In all the twelve years she'd worked for him, she'd never known him to threaten or bully any of his servants. Now all that had changed.

"Do as you are told or I'll fire you!"

"Señor George . . . please," she ventured hopefully. "Lance needs you."

"I don't care! I don't want to hear about Lance and what Lance needs!" he shouted, interrupting her savagely. His words, yelled so forcefully, carried out to where the boy stood in silence. "Without Shining Star my life is over! I have nothing left to live for . . ."

"You have your son!" Rosalie countered.

George was oblivious to the fact that his young son was listening in total confusion to his every word. Swigging from the bottle again, George then wiped his mouth with his forearm.

"My son!" George snorted in drunken derision. "Don't you realize that every time I look at him I see the Indian in him? It's like a damn knife in my heart! I can't stand it!"

Lance was devastated by his father's declaration. It seemed obvious to him that his father hated him . . . hated his Indian blood. Why else would he be unable to stand the sight of him? Why else would he have refused to see him all this time? More agony assailed the boy, and again tears threatened. It had been terrible to lose his mother, but now to find out that his father hated him . . . it was almost more than he could bear. Lance rushed toward the stables and his horse, needing to escape the abyss of misery that threatened to engulf him.

"But Lance is lonely and frightened. . . ." Rosalie was saying, not realizing what damage his last statement had done to the child she was trying so ardently to protect.

"I don't want to see him or talk about him!" The agony in George's voice was apparent. "Every time I see him . . . every time I hear his voice, I think of Shining Star!" Despite the liquor's insulation, pain still ripped through his vitals at the thought of his beloved wife's death.

"You should cherish him. . . ."

"Cherish him? When the very sight of him brings me nothing but pain?"

"But he is suffering Shining Star's loss, too."

George brushed past her and dropped wearily into the chair at the desk. "Close the shutters," he directed in a tired, defeated voice as he guzzled from the bottle.

Frustrated, she moved to draw them closed once more.

"Now, get out of here. I want to be alone," he told her when the room was dark again.

"Shall I bring you something to eat? You haven't eaten for several days. . . ."

He stiffened at her continued intrusion and pointed toward the door. "I said get out! If I want anything, I'll call you."

"And what shall I tell Lance? He keeps asking for you."

"I don't care what you tell him! Just keep him away from me!"

Heartbroken and defeated, Rosalie nodded. "Yes, Señor George. I will do as you wish."

George looked up as he heard the door close, and he stared at the closed portal with unseeing eyes. *How could it have happened? Just a short time before his life had been perfect, and now* . . . In agony he buried his face in his hands and wept. His beloved Shining Star was dead, and without her by his side, his life held no meaning. She had been everything to him, and now she was gone. Sobs wracked him, and it was a long time before the storm of his turbulent emotions subsided.

When the tears were spent, George sat up and grabbed for the bottle once again. Silently he cursed

17

Rosalie for her intrusion. He was sure that, given time, Lance would be all right. The boy was a Barrett. He was tough. He would handle it. Beyond that, George didn't want to think about his son, for he was too vivid a reminder of Shining Star. Tilting the whiskey to his lips, he drank deeply, and as the fiery liquor burned a trail to his stomach, he prayed that forgetfulness would soon follow.

Ignoring the direction of Sam, the elderly stable-hand, to stay close to the ranchhouse, Lance put his heels to his mount's side and, leaning low over the horse's neck, gave the mare her lead. As one entity, they tore away from the stables and out across the low, rolling hills of the Royal Diamond. Lance was un-mindful of the scorching heat of the afternoon sun beating down upon them as they raced across the countryside. Instead, he concentrated solely on the freedom of the ride, forcing from his mind all the wretchedness that had become so much a part of his life and pretending just for a short time that nothing had really changed.

Time ceased to exist for the pair as they continued their desperate escape, and at long last, only the scent of water tempered the mare's breakneck pace. Slowing to a brisk trot, they altered their course and headed toward the stand of cottonwood trees that bordered the creek some distance ahead. Lance reined in on the tree-shaded bank and then dismounted, dropping the reins so his horse could drink her fill.

The creek had always been his favorite place to play. Lance had hoped that returning there would ease his pain, but to his great disappointment, it did not. As he stood beside the sparkling, gurgling waters, all he could think of was his mother. She had often accompanied him there and taken as much delight in the fresh babbling brook as he had.

At the memory, his denied agony returned full force, and Lance felt completely overwhelmed . . . totally lost. The desolation he had fought so long and so hard to control finally won out, and he dropped to his knees, surrendering at last to his need to cry out his sorrow. In wretched despair, he gave vent to his anguish. As he grieved alone there in the wilderness, he ached for the warm, loving arms that had always hugged him when he'd been sad, and he longed to hear the soft, gentle words of comfort that had never failed to soothe his hurts and take away his pain.

The sun was low in the western sky, and darkness was just beginning to extend its possessive grip across the Royal Diamond as Lone Elk stealthily approached the ranchhouse. He had instructed his companions to await his return at a secluded rendezvous point some distance away and had traveled the last miles by himself. Lone Elk knew that it would be far easier for him to gain access to the house if he went alone. There was far less chance of being discovered that way. He had no desire for a confrontation with the whites this night. He wanted only to meet with Barrett and then leave with the boy as quickly as possible.

Lone Elk topped the hill that overlooked the ranch and was filled with icy fury at the sight of the main house and outbuildings spread out before him on the valley floor. The neatly laid out house and grounds represented all that he hated about the whites. A burning desire grew within him to attack the unsuspecting settlement and destroy all vestiges of the white man's presence, but the solemn pledge he'd made to

Shining Star years before not to raid the Royal Diamond held him back. He had promised her that he would never raise a hand against Barrett, and he was still bound by his word.

With the utmost of caution Lone Elk began his descent toward the main house. He was not looking forward to facing George Barrett again, but he knew it was something that had to be done. He could not allow Shining Star's son to grow up completely under a white man's influence. The boy was his flesh and blood and, as such, deserved to know his heritage.

Slumped at his desk, his head resting on his arms, George vaguely became aware that the window was open again and that there was someone in the room with him. Annoyed that anyone had dared to breach his strict order to be left alone, he lifted his head slowly and growled, "Damn it, Rosalie! I told you I didn't want to be disturbed!"

"So, Barrett, you are awake after all."

The well-remembered sound of Lone Elk's deep, mocking voice cut through George like a knife. Sitting bolt upright in his chair, he stared across the darkened room to where his brother-in-law stood in shadowy concealment. When he finally found his voice he croaked nervously, "Lone Elk!? How did you get in here?!"

"It was simple. Your guards are fools, white man," the chief sneered.

His senses liquor-numbed, George groped about the desktop struggling to find a match so he could light his lamp. When at last he located one and struck it, the flickering flame bathed the room in a muted glow. With fumbling fingers, he managed to put flame to wick and then turned to face his longtime adversary.

Tall and sun-bronzed, his powerful arms folded across his sleek, hard-muscled chest, Lone Elk stood unmoving in the far corner of the room. The sight of him was enough to send a paroxysm of fear racing down George's spine, for Lone Elk was the epitome of the fierce Comanche warrior. His face painted in a hideous design of vermillion and black, the aura about the chief was one of confident arrogance as he returned George's regard.

"Why have you come?" he demanded. Then, after a long, uncertain pause, he ventured, "You know? You've heard of Shining Star's—"

"I have heard of my sister's passing." Lone Elk's reply was flat, his obsidian eyes and stony expression mirroring nothing of his thoughts.

George's mind was fogged by the whiskey's potency, and he could not fathom Lone Elk's reason for returning to the ranch. They had never made any secret of their animosity toward each other, and he found his sudden appearance at the Royal Diamond disconcerting.

"Why have you come now, after all this time?"

"I have come for the child, the son I know to be Shining Star's."

"What?" George blinked in stunned surprise.

"I have come for Shining Star's son. He is flesh of my flesh, and now that his mother is dead, I must be the one to teach him the ways of his people."

"You want to take Lance?" he was dumbfounded by the thought. At the chief's curt nod, George panicked. "Lance isn't going anywhere with you! I will not see him raised as a filthy savage!"

"I see that the years you lived with my sister did not change you, Barrett. You are still as much of a fool now as you were eight years ago."

21

"Why, you ignorant bastard!" George somehow managed to get to his feet.

"My sister should never have married you! It is because of you that she now lies dead!" Lone Elk told him brutally.

"You bloodthirsty cur!"

George lunged at him, wanting to murder Lone Elk for having accused him of hurting his own wife, but he was so drunk, his efforts were totally futile. Though George was not a small man, Lone Elk brushed him aside like a troublesome gnat. George stumbled and then pivoted unsteadily to glare at him with baleful intent.

"You know I speak the truth, Barrett," he sneered.

"It was the fever that took her!" George protested as guilt swept through him at the thought that he might somehow have been responsible.

"It was a *white man's* fever! Had she never left her people, she would still be alive today!"

"Shining Star was my wife! The Royal Diamond was her home! It was her choice to marry me and come here to live."

"It was her choice," Lone Elk agreed, barely keeping himself in control as he stalked predatorily forward to stand directly before him. "You remember that I did not stand in her way, Barrett. I could have stopped her. I could have forbidden your joining."

George raised his fevered, tormented eyes to meet Lone Elk's. "I know."

"I allowed Shining Star to choose, and now you must let her son choose."

"Never!"

"I did not prevent her from marrying you, and it is that burden that I carry with me to my grave. If I had kept her from you, she would still be alive!" A flicker of emotion shone briefly in Lone Elk's eyes, but he quickly disguised it.

"Don't you think I know that?! Now that she's dead, I have nothing left! My life is over!" George's expression was despairing as he tore his gaze away from the chief's knowing one.

"Then since you do not want Shining Star's son, let him come with me."

"No . . ."

"The boy has the right to choose. You would not deny him that right, would you?"

George floundered helplessly before Lone Elk's maddeningly logical argument. He thought of Lance, and a shaft of pain tore through his heart. He was so like his mother that, ever since her death, the very sight of him had meant nothing but pain and agony to George. That was why he couldn't bear to be with him right now. That was why he'd refused all contact with the child. Even so, he wondered if he could allow his son to go to live with his mother's people.

Lone Elk could sense his bewilderment and pressed his point. "Lance is all that is left of Shining Star. You cannot deny that he is half-Comanche, and you know that my sister wanted him to learn our ways."

George knew he was right, for Shining Star had spoken of Lance's future many times, and she had always insisted that he be raised with knowledge of both ways of life. Staggering defeatedly to his desk, he picked up the whiskey bottle and drank from it once more.

"All right," he acknowledged in a slurred voice. "If Lance wants to go with you, I won't stand in his way, but there is one condition."

Lone Elk's eyes narrowed suspiciously. "What?"

"If he chooses to go with you, I will allow him to on the condition that he'll be free to return whenever he wants."

"The decision to stay with us or to leave will always be his." The chief nodded in agreement. "Now, where is the boy? I want to see him. He must make his choice tonight."

"Tonight?"

"You know I cannot stay here, Barrett. There are those among your neighbors who would kill me on sight. Where is he?"

The Lance who rode slowly back toward the stables at sundown was not the same Lance who'd ridden out earlier. His time alone at the creek had stripped away his innocence, and he was no longer trusting and dependent. The truth of his father's feelings coupled with the final, painful acknowledgement of the irreversibility of his mother's death had robbed him of his naiveté. During those hours alone in the wilderness, Lance had aged emotionally. Much of his youthful enthusiasm was gone, buried now beneath the grim acceptance of the realities of life.

Relieved that there was no one around to reprimand him for disobeying orders to stay close by, he dismounted and almost mechanically set about bedding down his horse. When his work was finished, he started toward the house, feeling more alone than he ever had before.

Lance had half expected Rosalie to be watching and waiting for him, but the house was seemingly deserted as he entered. He was pleased at the prospect of being left alone and was just starting up the stairs to seek out the solitude of his room when he heard voices coming from the study and noticed the light shining from beneath the study door. Lance knew that his father hadn't wanted to see anyone, and he grew bitterly angry at the thought that someone else had been admitted into his sanctuary. Pausing by the closed portal, he frowned in concentration as he tried in vain to identify the deep voice of the man speaking with his father. It was difficult for Lance to hear the conversation clearly, but when the tone of their dialogue became heated and their voices were raised, snatches of it were unmistakable.

"Why, you ignorant bastard!"

"My sister should never have married you! It is because of you that she now lies dead!"

Sister? Lance stared at the door. His mother had often spoken of her brother, Chief Lone Elk, with pride and love. The thought that the brave Comanche warrior was actually at the ranch left him stunned.

"You bloodthirsty cur!"

His father's furious statement affirmed that it was indeed his mother's brother. Lance knew a moment of excitement at the thought of finally getting to meet Lone Elk, but along with that anticipation came an edge of caution, for he remembered clearly his mother telling him of the bad blood that existed between husband and brother. Listening now, he realized that she had not been exaggerating, for the argument going on within the confines of the study was vicious and ugly.

". . . she's dead, I have nothing left! My life is over!"

The excitement of the moment died within Lance as he heard his father again claim that there was nothing of importance left in his life, and Lance hardened his heart even more against him.

"Then since you do not want Shining Star's son, let him come with me."

"If Lance wants to go with you, I won't stand in his way."

When he'd been alone by the creek, Lance had forced himself to accept the reality of his situation, but even so, he had clung desperately to the hope that

25

his father hadn't really meant his earlier declarations. Now, however, he knew it was true. His father no longer cared about him. Despair settled over him like a heavy mantle.

The study door suddenly opened then, and for the first time, Lance came face-to-face with his uncle. Unwaveringly, he met the chief's black-eyed gaze.

When Lone Elk had asked George where Lance was, George had waved him toward the door, directing him upstairs to the boy's bedroom. Eager to be gone from the hated white man's home, the Comanche had not hesitated but had hurried across the room, anxious to find the child who was the fruit of his sister's womb. Throwing the door wide in his haste, Lone Elk had been surprised to find Lance standing there in the hall. A surge of fierce, loving pride filled the chief as he gazed down at his nephew.

"You are Lone Elk." Lance's remark was more a statement than a question, and Lone Elk nodded.

"I am."

"I'm Lance."

"I know." And he did. Though Lance was all boy, there was no mistaking Shining Star's part in his parentage. His hair was coal-black like his mother's, and his complexion was darker than that of his father. Only Lance's blue eyes and slightly refined features revealed Barrett's influence.

"Why have you come?" Oddly, Lance felt no timidity with this warrior who towered above him.

"I have come for you." Lone Elk knew a growing respect for Lance. Confronted with this situation, the boy was exhibiting none of the fear he had expected from a child raised in white society. *Shining Star had taught him well*, he thought with satisfaction.

"Why?" Lance challenged again.

"Because it is as your mother would have wanted it."

Lance considered this and knew that his uncle was right. His mother had always emphasized the importance of learning about his Comanche background. Past the point of caring what his father's reaction might be to his presence, he moved into the office.

"Pa?" he spoke up, and was more than a little surprised when his voice held steady.

George was sitting at his desk, his head buried in his hands, the empty whiskey bottle beside him on the desktop. At the sound of Lance's voice, he turned to regard his son through bleary eyes, seeing before him not a little boy in need of reassurance, but a painful, excruciating reminder of all that he'd lost. "What?" His tone was slurred, yet sharp with irritation.

"What do you want me to do?" He longed desperately for his father to suddenly declare that he loved him and couldn't live without him, but it was not to be.

"Lone Elk wants to take you to live with him so you can learn about your mother's people. The decision is yours, Lance," George said emotionlessly, looking away.

His noncommittal answer extinguished the final flicker of hope that had nestled deep within Lance's battered heart. Lance silently berated himself for having been foolish enough to hope that his father would declare his love. Hadn't he already heard the truth of his father's feelings?

"Is it what your mother would have wanted," the chief spoke up. He had seen the sudden, slight droop of the boy's shoulders and had known that he needed some form of reassurance.

At his words, Lance looked up at him. "I will go with you."

The chief did not smile, but a light of approval shone in his eyes. "It is good. We will leave as soon as

27

you are ready."

"Now? Tonight?" Lance's eyes widened in shock.

"Tonight," the chief confirmed.

"Pa, I—" Suddenly frightened at the enormity of what was happening, he turned quickly to say something to his father, only to find that George had passed out at the desk.

"Perhaps it is best this way," Lone Elk said slowly.

With an effort, Lance tore his gaze away from the sight of his drunken parent. Pushing aside the fear that threatened to overwhelm him, he reasoned *If his father didn't want him anymore, at least his uncle did. Perhaps he could find happiness again with his mother's people.*

"Maybe you're right." He turned his back on his father and walked from the room. "It will only take me a few minutes to pack my things."

As Lone Elk watched Lance disappear up the stairs to his bedroom, he remained silent. His heart filled with emotion as he reflected on how bravely the boy was handling the situation. He knew the next few months would be very difficult for him as he adjusted to a totally different way of life, but he also knew that Lance would do well. He was, after all, his mother's son. With one last disparaging glance at Barrett, who was still slumped at his desk, Lone Elk moved out into the hall to await his nephew's return.

Chapter Two
1869

It was a balmy night in late spring, and at the Royal Diamond Ranch the party in honor of young Michael Barrett's engagement was in full swing. Neighbors and friends from miles around had made the trek to the ranch to join in the celebration and to meet Michael's fiancée, who'd just arrived from her home back East. The house was alive now with music and laughter, the sounds of which were echoing mutedly across the rolling hills.

Alone and on foot, having left his mount some distance away to avoid detection, the tall, lean Comanche warrior crept soundlessly toward the crest of the hill that overlooked the ranchhouse. The moon was but a sliver of silver, providing little in the way of illumination, but instead of cursing the darkness, the Indian was grateful. The night's shadowy cover effectively shielded him from discovery, and that was just the way he wanted it. Lured onward by the sounds of the whites' merriment, the warrior cautiously moved closer until he finally reached the top. The brave crouched motionlessly and silently amid the rocks, his stony features revealing nothing of his inner turmoil as he watched and listened to all that was taking place.

Lance hadn't meant to come here. If anything, he'd wanted to avoid the Royal Diamond. Yet when the wild golden stallion he'd been tracking and chasing for days had led him onto the Diamond land late that afternoon, he had been helpless to do anything but follow. He wanted that horse. For months now many of his tribe had been trying to capture it. The others had all given up, but Lance was determined to succeed, and he knew that his standing among the warriors would be greatly enhanced if he could bring back the prized, elusive golden one as his own.

As a tall, trim, silver-haired man appeared on the porch of the main house below accompanied by a rather tall, buxom, dark-haired woman, Lance suddenly tensed, and all thought of the stallion fled his mind. Though some distance away, he recognized the man immediately as his father. Bile rose sour and bitter in his throat at the sight of the white man who had denied his very existence so long ago. His blue eyes narrowed to lethal slits as he watched them standing there in the moonlight. When the older man slipped an arm about the woman and bent to her to press a gentle kiss to her lips, his hands clinched into fists of frustrated rage.

The power of his reaction to that simple gesture both surprised and puzzled him. Lance thought of himself as a man with total control of his feelings and emotions. He thought that he'd put all the turbulent memories of the time he had lived as a white at the Royal Diamond behind him, but as he stood there now watching the man and woman below, unbidden remembrances flooded through him.

Lance grew angry with himself. He did not want to remember his life on the ranch or the death of his mother or his subsequent departure to live with Lone Elk. He did want to think about the time when, desperate to see his father again, he had decided to leave his loving uncle and return to the Diamond. Yet

30

these images were playing in his mind as if it had been yesterday instead of nineteen years ago, and he was powerless before their onslaught. He had been a mere child then, an innocent in the ways of white men and their kind, but he had learned quickly.

At the time, Lone Elk had not stood in the way of his leaving. Instead, in his wisdom, he had sent him on with the knowledge that the Comanche were his people and that he would always be welcome to come back. Lance realized now that he had been a fool to ever imagine that he could resume the idyllic life that had been his before his mother's death. A sneer of disgust twisted his lips as he remembered what had happened the last time he'd come here. His father had not even been at the ranch. He had been on a trip to town . . . a trip that had included taking along his new *white wife* and the *son* she had borne him. The hot, searing pain of his white father's betrayal had branded him forever that day. He had fled to his mother's people, *his* people, and he had never looked back . . . until now.

Filled with loathing, Lance suddenly felt the need to get away. He turned and was about to move off when the light, lilting sound of feminine laughter spilled through the night. The sound entranced him, and Lance pivoted to glance back down toward the house.

Lance stood transfixed, his gaze riveted on the woman who had just emerged from the house on the arm of a tall, dark-haired man. Whoever she was, she was the most beautiful woman he'd ever seen. Her hair was the color of sunlit spun gold. It had been styled up and away from her face at the sides to emphasize the perfection of her features, before being allowed to tumble freely down her back in a mass of errant curls. It was a hairstyle that instinctively

31

begged for a man's touch. Lance found himself wondering how it would feel and wondering if it would be as warm, lustrous, and silken as it looked. He regarded her hungrily, taking in the firm swell of her bosom and the trimness of her small waist beneath the impractical white woman's dress she was wearing.

Never before had he found himself so attracted to a woman. For the briefest of instants he let himself imagine what it would be like to strip the cumbersome full-skirted garment from her and gaze upon her naked flesh. Desire, powerful and unexpected, surged through him at the thought and took him completely by surprise. Frowning into the darkness of the night, he cursed himself for his weakness. This woman was white, and no doubt just like all the others of her breed. He was certain that it was only the unusual color of her hair, so like that of the stallion he was pursuing, that had drawn his interest — nothing more.

"Well, darling, what do you think of the Royal Diamond so far?" Michael Barrett asked his fiancée, Trista Sinclair, as they joined his parents outside on the porch for a cooling, restful moment away from the excitement of the celebration within.

Trista gazed up at him happily. "Your home is lovely, Michael, and the ranch itself . . . why, it's almost impossible for me to imagine that it's actually as big as you say."

George Barrett chuckled good-naturedly at his future daughter-in-law's observation. "It's an average-size spread by Texas standards, Trista. The Diamond's only a hundred thousand acres or so."

"And you love every inch of it," she remarked with knowing fondness. Though she had only been there for a few days, she was already very aware of the depth of George and Michael's dedication to the ranch.

"I've always dreamed of the Royal Diamond being the best spread in Texas," Michael told her.

"Well, if it isn't already, I'm sure it soon will be," Trista said, her admiration evident in her tone.

"We're working on it." George's smile reflected the pride he held in the ranch. "Now that Michael's completed his education and come back home . . . well, things should work out just fine." George's gaze was warm and loving upon his son. Yet even as he considered Michael, the memory of another son . . . so long unseen . . . intruded.

Lance . . . George paled at the thought of his long-lost older son. Why had he thought of him now? This was a night of happiness and celebration, not morose regrets. He was grateful that the semidarkness on the porch hid his expression, for he had no desire to explain his sudden shift of mood.

"We're glad you didn't object to coming here to live," Eleanor Barrett remarked sweetly to Trista.

"I did have a few nervous moments," Trista confessed. "I wasn't quite sure what living on a ranch here in the middle of Texas would be like."

"And now?" Michael asked with real interest. He had no idea that she'd been put off by the thought of leaving Philadelphia to come west with him, and he awaited her answer with some concern.

"Now I think I'm going to like it here," she answered with confidence. "Everyone I've met has been so warm and friendly. I feel as if I belong here already."

"You do, my love. You do," Michael assured her, his dark brown eyes meeting and holding her blue ones in an intimate, unspoken exchange.

Eleanor sensed that they needed a moment of

privacy, and she spoke casually to her husband. "George, why don't we go back in? I'm sure our guests are wondering what's become of us. . . ."

He immediately took the hint and held the door wide for his wife. "Of course, dear. Michael, Trista, we'll see you inside."

Michael was only barely aware of his parents' departure as he gazed down at Trista. Lost in thoughts of how lovely she was, he reflected, not for the first time, on how lucky he had been to win her. They had met while he was attending school in Philadelphia. He'd heard rumors about the fabulous Trista Sinclair long before they'd ever been introduced. According to the talk, she was comfortably wealthy, absolutely gorgeous, and totally unattainable. Rumor had it that many men had paid the cool blond beauty court, but that she had disdained them all.

Michael had anxiously anticipated their meeting, and when they were finally introduced at a society ball, he had discovered that the gossip had all been true. Trista was the most beautiful woman he'd ever seen, with her sun-streaked golden hair, flawless figure, and perfect features. He had been immediately smitten and had grown determined not to suffer the same fate as all her other ardent suitors. To this day he wasn't quite sure what he had done differently from the other men to win her heart, but he didn't care. All that mattered was that she had accepted *his* proposal, and she had agreed to become *his* wife.

Michael suddenly felt a desperate, possessive need to kiss her, and he drew her away from the lamplight shining through the windows. "Come here . . ." His voice was husky with desire.

"Michael . . . where are we going?"

"Shhh . . ." he whispered conspiratorially as he maneuvered her quickly into a shadowy corner of the porch where they would be safe from any prying eyes. "Alone at last." His tone was melodramatic as he pulled her into his embrace.

"But what about the others? I mean, your mother and father both know that we're out here alone." Trista glanced worriedly toward the front door. "Won't we be missed?"

"Yes," he admitted regretfully, "but not for a minute or two . . ." His mouth sought hers in a sweet, cherishing exchange.

"Oh, Michael . . ." Trista gave a soft sigh as she looped her arms about his neck to bring him closer. As always, his kiss was warm and affectionate, and she responded openly, enjoying the feeling of closeness between them.

Absorbed in the pleasure of the embrace, Trista let her thoughts drift back to the first time she'd met Michael at a society ball in Philadelphia. She had seen him from across the room and had known immediately that there was something innately different about him. Certainly he was good-looking, but no handsomer than any of the other young men who had paid her court. It was just something about the way he moved and the way he had returned her regard that had left her with the impression that he was so controlled and so overwhelmingly masculine. She'd found herself growing curious about him and, after several discreet inquiries, had discovered that he was a Texan, born and bred, who was attending school in town. One thing had led to another, and soon they were seeing each other.

From the very start, her relationship with Michael had been different, and because of that difference, she had seen him as the answer to her dilemma. Her father was determined that she should marry—and soon. Ever since she had reached her eighteenth birthday, her widowed father, Randolph Sinclair, had been pressuring her to marry and settle down. He had introduced her to every suitable young man in Philadelphia, and at first she'd found his efforts amusing. After a while he'd grown frustrated with her refusal to marry any of the suitors, and a tension had developed between them that had not eased.

Trista had not been against the idea of marrying; she'd just wanted to pick her own husband in her own way. She'd found Michael attractive, and of all the suitors she'd ever had, she got along with him the best. Many successful marriages had been built on less, and so, when he'd proposed she'd accepted.

Initially, her father had been less than pleased with the idea of her marrying Michael, for he was not from one of "the families" in Philadelphia society. However, once he'd discovered the vastness of the Barrett wealth, he had quickly changed his mind. He had given them his blessing and had even agreed to allow the wedding to be held on the Barrett ranch in Texas.

Now here she was, living happily on the Royal Diamond and soon to become Mrs. Michael Barrett. The thought pleased her. She liked Michael's family, and she was falling in love with the vastness of this beautiful western state. *Yes,* she mused as Michael ended the kiss, *she could be very happy here.*

"I can hardly wait for the wedding, love," Michael uttered almost painfully as he held her close, enjoying the feel of her softness pressed against him. "This next month is going to pass real slow."

"I know," she agreed, "but Father couldn't get away any sooner. I hope you don't mind too much. . . ."

"I mind, all right, but I guess you're worth the wait." His brown eyes twinkled devilishly as he gave her a measured look.

"Michael!" Trista feigned outrage.

Michael gave a soft laugh as he silenced her mock protest with another kiss. When they broke apart long moments later, his passion for her was clearly mirrored in his eyes. "Yes, love . . . you're definitely worth the wait."

"Thank you." She smiled up at him tenderly. "I think you're worth waiting for, too."

As they stood wrapped in each other's arms, the music began again, penetrating their sanctuary and bringing them back to awareness.

"As much as I hate to say this, I guess we'd better rejoin the party."

"I know, but I almost wish we didn't have to," Trista sighed, moving reluctantly out of the protective circle of his arms.

"Me, too." With a guiding hand at her waist, Michael started to escort her into the house.

As they started across the porch, Trista suddenly had the eerie feeling that someone was watching them. The sensation was so powerful that a shiver of awareness frissoned down her spine, and she glanced back over her shoulder into the darkness of the Texas night.

Michael felt her shudder, and he drew her closer to his side. "I guess it's a good thing we're going in. It wouldn't do for you to take a chill. . . ."

Trista wanted to explain to him what she was feeling, but when she couldn't see anyone around, she dismissed her fear as ridiculous. Not wanting to trouble him, she replied, "It is getting a bit cool out here. . . ." Yet even as they entered the house, she still couldn't shake the feeling that someone had been out there.

Lance stood unmoving on the hilltop, his features frozen into a mask of anger and resentment. Emotions to which he could put no name twisted tormentedly within him, leaving him troubled and confused. He didn't want to care about this ranch or his father or anyone else connected to the white man's world. Yet the fact that he was reacting this way revealed a vulnerability in him that he wanted to, but could not, deny.

Furious with himself, Lance turned his back on the peaceful scene in the valley. He realized now that he had been foolish to come. Logic told him that there was no future for him in the white man's world. His future was with his people. Still, as he made his way back to the solitude of his camp, he couldn't help but wonder why a part of him still longed to be accepted and acknowledged by the very father who had so long ago denied him.

Chapter Three

As flame-haired Sukie Harris watched Michael Barrett squire his newly acquired fiancée about the dance floor, her demeanor seemed nonchalant. Only her longtime friend, Emily Warren, who was standing beside her, realized that her calm expression was an elaborate act. Emily knew that Sukie had been devastated by the announcement of Michael's engagement to this easterner, *Trista Sinclair*.

"She's certainly beautiful," Sukie agonized as she tore her gaze away from the sight of Michael holding the other woman in his arms. She had been in love with Michael since she was ten years old and had always dreamed of becoming his wife. Now that dream was over. He had found Trista during his time back East in Philadelphia, and she was the one who owned his heart.

Pain ripped through Sukie as she tried to understand how this had happened. They had been so close before he'd left. . . . She fought back the urge to cry as the memory of all the parties they'd attended together and all the kisses they'd shared haunted her. They had meant so much to each other then. . . . And now . . .

"I know," Emily agreed, not immediately noticing her friend's distress. "And that gown she's wearing! Have you ever seen anything so beautiful? It's as gorgeous as a wedding gown. Why, it looks like it

39

came straight from Paris." She sighed in admiration of Trista's white tulle evening dress.

Sukie listened miserably to her comments and then glanced up again at Trista, noting the slimmer skirts and flowing design of the exquisite dress she was wearing.

"It is lovely," she managed. Self-consciously, she smoothed the unfashionably full skirts of her own dress, which, while not unattractive, was definitely not of the same updated styling or quality as the eastern woman's.

Emily heard the strain in her voice and quickly apologized. "Sukie, I'm sorry. . . ."

"It's all right, Em. I think I'll just go outside for a little while. Maybe if I just get a breath of fresh air . . ."

As Sukie started from the room, Emily hastened to follow. They didn't speak again until they were standing alone on the porch in the cool, encompassing darkness of the night.

"I know how you feel about Michael, Sukie, and I'm sorry things haven't worked out the way you'd hoped."

"So am I." Though she felt numb inside and out, Sukie couldn't keep the bitterness out of her voice. "I don't know what I'm going to do, Em. . . . I love Michael so much. It seems like I've always loved him."

"I know it's been a shock to find this out, but I'm sure things will work out. You'll find someone new, and then you'll forget all about him."

Emily's advice was the last thing Sukie wanted to hear. "I don't want to forget him, Em! He's been a part of my life since I was ten years old."

"But, Sukie," her friend soothed, "this is something you're just going to have accept. Michael and Trista *are* engaged. They're going to be married real soon."

"I won't accept it! I won't!" Sukie choked, her emerald eyes sparkling with unshed tears as she faced Emily defiantly. Memories of the times before he'd gone back East assailed her . . . memories of when she had been the girl in Michael's arms. She had always believed that he would come back from Philadelphia and propose to her, but now all her dreams were shattered.

"You're going to have to. You've seen the way he looks at Trista. He can't keep his eyes off her, Sukie."

"But I love him, Em. . . . I always have, and I always will." She gave a small sob. How would she ever manage to survive his marrying someone else? Emily made it sound so simple . . . *just accept it* . . . but she couldn't. She couldn't just stop loving him because it was the right thing to do.

"Those are your feelings, though, not Michael's," Emily was saying, trying to make her face the inevitable.

But Sukie would have none of it, and her temper flared in frustration as some of the stunned numbness began to wear off. "You know, Emily, things may not be as bad as they seem. . . ."

Emily was caught off guard by the abrupt change in Sukie, for she had gone from being completely devastated to suddenly being cool and almost composed. She knew a sudden feeling of misgiving, and she eyed her friend suspiciously. "What do you mean?"

Sukie faced her, her expression enigmatic. "Well, you know Michael isn't married *yet*."

"You can't mean—" Emily paled at the thought of Sukie interfering in Michael's life.

"Oh yes I can!" For the first time since she'd learned of Michael's engagement earlier that evening, she felt there was still hope for her. "There's still plenty of time for me to figure out a way to get him back."

41

"But, Sukie! Is this fair? He loves Trista, and Trista loves him."

Sukie glanced at Emily, her gaze unyielding as her thoughts raced ahead trying to dream up a strategy to win him back. "All's fair in love and war, Emily. . . . And this is both!"

Leaving her friend standing on the porch, Sukie forced a pleasant smile and returned to the party. Step number one was to make sure Michael didn't find out she was upset. Step number two was to attract as many suitors as she could tonight to make herself look popular. Though she did not desire the attention of other men, she knew the best way to attract them was to act as if she was having the most wonderful time in the world . . . even if she wasn't. With her head held high, she swept back into the parlor. One way or the other, before this night was over Michael was going to have noticed her.

"Eleanor, your dress is just lovely," Mary Lou Harris complimented her hostess as she admired the fashionable evening gown she was wearing.

"Thank you, Mary Lou," Eleanor Barrett preened. She was most pleased that the other woman had commented on its exquisite style, for she had taken great care in choosing it.

"Did you get it back East?"

"Yes. I bought it while I was in Philadelphia visiting Michael," she offered, knowing that the silk gown fit her lush figure perfectly and that the deep gold color complemented the rich darkness of her auburn hair.

"Well, it's simply beautiful on you."

"Thank you, dear."

"Speaking of Philadelphia, we really haven't had

much time to talk about your trip. How was it?"

"Marvelous," Eleanor answered, eager to impress Mary Lou with the news of her travels. "It has been years since I was there last, but little seems to have changed."

"Do you have family there?"

"Some," she replied, "but they're only distantly connected. The truth of the matter is, I made the trip because Michael wrote to me about Trista. He wanted me to meet her before he proposed."

Mary Lou glanced up to watch the newly engaged couple dance by, her penetrating gaze hardening a bit as she watched them. Despite her best efforts, her expression soured slightly at the realization that this woman, and not her daughter, was going to become Michael's bride. She'd always hoped for an alliance between their two families, because their ranches adjoined. Michael and Sukie certainly would have made a handsome couple, but observing Michael now, she knew it wouldn't be happening. It was quite obvious that he was in love with his fiancée.

"How thoughtful of him," she finally remarked as she turned back to her friend.

"Michael has always been most solicitous of my opinions," Eleanor told her with cool confidence, knowing how Michael never failed to heed her advice.

"And I take it you approve of Trista?"

"Completely."

"What's she really like?" Mary Lou inquired, wondering at the woman who had captured Michael's heart.

Eleanor smiled almost condescendingly at her friend. It pleased her that Michael was the center of such attention, and she was feeling quite proud of her only offspring. "Trista is a lovely person."

Mary Lou looked decidedly grumpy at her bland

answer. "There has to be something special about her, Eleanor. Why, you know every girl in this county tried to get your Michael to the altar. Even my own precious Sukie had her hopes . . . But now he's passed them all by to pick Trista." Mary Lou's gaze was critical as she stared at the young blond woman. "Tell me the truth. What's she like?"

"Well, she's beautiful," Eleanor supplied with deliberate coyness, and her comment drew a low groan of impatience from her companion.

"Of course she is, but then, so is my Sukie," she replied defensively.

"Sukie is very pretty, Mary Lou," Eleanor soothed, "but Trista is the woman Michael loves. Who can explain love? It just happens. . . . And judging by all that he's told me, he fell in love with her the first time they met."

"Well, there's certainly no denying she's attractive, but she looks rather fragile. Do you think she'll adjust well to living out here? Michael isn't planning to move back East, is he?"

Eleanor had never considered that Michael might forsake everything and go back to Philadelphia just to please his bride, and the thought unnerved her for a moment. As quickly as the doubt entered her mind, she dismissed it. He was her son, and she knew him well. He would never give up his life on the Royal Diamond.

"I'm sure Michael plans on staying," she assured her confidently, "and as for Trista adapting . . . well, knowing her as I do, I'm sure she'll be quite happy here."

"But she was born and raised in Philadelphia, wasn't she? Living on a ranch is going to be quite a change for her," Mary Lou pried.

"Trista looks upon it as a challenge. She was quite

excited about coming to Texas to live. Since we arrived earlier in the week, she's become even more enthusiastic, so I don't think we have to worry on that account."

"Well, I can hardly wait for the wedding. It'll probably be the social event of the year for the county."

"Indeed it will be," Eleanor replied with arrogant certainty. She had waited all her married life for Michael to marry, and she was determined that the wedding would be a huge success. She felt quite fortunate that Trista had proved as malleable as she had originally thought she would be and that the younger woman had acquiesced to all her suggestions.

Mary Lou listened dispiritedly as Eleanor described all the plans that had already been set into motion for the upcoming nuptials. There could be no doubt about it. The wedding was definitely on.

As the music ended, Michael gave Trista a wry smile. "Shall we face the well-wishers again?"

"I suppose we have to, don't we?" she responded as he ushered her slowly across the room to where his mother stood.

"There's no escaping it tonight, I'm afraid," he confided before greeting his mother and her friend. "Hello, Mother . . . Mary Lou. Mary Lou, have you met Trista yet?"

"No, Michael, I haven't." Mary Lou's welcoming smile was strained, but no one seemed to notice.

"Mary Lou Harris, may I present my fiancée, Trista Sinclair. Trista—this is Mary Lou Harris, our neighbor." He made the introductions quickly.

"It's nice to meet you, Mrs. Harris." Trista greeted the older woman respectfully, wondering at her pinched expression.

"Thank you, dear, but please call me Mary Lou. Everybody does," Mary Lou replied, trying not to let the truth of her feelings show. "Michael, it's so good to have you back. We missed you while you were away."

"I'm glad to be back, Mary Lou." Michael's reply was honest, for though he had done well in his studies during his time in Philadelphia, he had always felt stifled and uncomfortable there. Now that he was back in Texas, he felt alive again.

"I'm glad you're home, too," George said gruffly as he joined them, affectionally clapping his son on the shoulder. "It was too quiet around here without you. And now that you've brought Trista back, too . . ." His blue-eyed gaze was warm and approving upon his future daughter-in-law as he asked her, "Are you having a good time?"

"Wonderful," Trista answered, giving him her brightest smile. She had only met Michael's father upon their arrival at the ranch earlier that week, but she had been immediately fond of the older man. He seemed a silver-haired duplicate of his son, except for his eyes—George's being a light, piercing blue while Michael's were a warm, mellow brown like his mother's.

"Good," he responded, pleased that she was enjoying herself.

As Eleanor gazed at George and Michael, she, too, was thinking about how much they resembled each other. Both were tall, broad-shouldered, and lean, their easy manner and soft-spoken ways making them perfect Texas gentlemen. Only George's gray hair and his deeply tanned, weathered complexion revealed that he was older than Michael. Though she'd had her doubts at the time, Eleanor knew now that she'd done the right thing when she'd married him all those years ago. Her son was certainly proof of that.

Her heart swelled with love as she studied Michael. To her, he was perfect in every way. During his formative years he had never given her a moment of grief, being always eager to please and most concerned with her wishes. She had doted on him always, and she loved him now more than life itself.

Since learning of his love for Trista, Eleanor had known several jealous moments at the thought of sharing him. But she'd managed to keep those feelings carefully controlled, for she felt certain that sweet, docile Trista was in no way a threat to her position of influence in Michael's life.

"Everyone's made me feel so welcome. I was telling Michael a little while ago that I feel as if belong here already," Trista was telling George.

"That's good to hear." Though he'd only known her for a few days, George was already inordinately fond of Trista. Not only was she the prettiest girl Michael had ever shown any interest in, but she was intelligent and witty, too. He was glad that she was fitting in with their lifestyle so well.

"Have you seen much of the Royal Diamond yet, Trista?" Mary Lou asked. "It's the biggest ranch in these parts, you know."

"Oh, yes. Michael told me all about it even before we came. He's been taking me out riding to a different section every morning," Trista told her.

"So you ride?" Mary Lou seemed surprised by the news.

"Oh, yes. I've been riding since I was old enough to keep my seat."

"She's quite knowledgeable, too," Michael added, proud of Trista's way with horses.

"You're an expert on horses?" Mary Lou's eyes narrowed in frustration. Trista seemed almost too good to be true.

"Now, Michael . . ." She colored faintly at his praise. "You know I'm no real expert. I just love them, that's all. Our stables at home are quite extensive, and I always spent as much time as I could there."

"Speaking of horses, Michael . . ." George interrupted their chitchat as he remembered the news he'd heard. "I was talking to Ben earlier this evening, and he told me that the golden stallion is back in the area again."

Michael's attention suddenly riveted on his father. *"Fuego?* Are they sure?" he asked quickly, his dark eyes glowing fervently.

"Yep. Ben caught sight of him near Eager Creek on his way from the Lawsons'."

"Did he try to catch him?"

"No, he was too far away."

Michael nodded in complete understanding. "There's no way that stallion will ever be caught in a straight rundown. He's too smart, and he knows too many tricks. It's going to take some kind of luck to trap him."

"This stallion—Fuego, did you call him?—sounds very special," Trista ventured, intrigued by the change she'd noticed in Michael the moment the stallion had been mentioned.

"That he is, love." Michael smiled down at her as he went on to explain. "Fuego is a legend in these parts."

"Is that his real name . . . Fuego?"

"No one knows his real name or if he even has one. We just call him Fuego because of his coloring," George told her.

"He's no run-of-the-mill palomino, that's for sure," Michael added. "He's fiery gold, and his markings are outstanding."

"He's just about the most beautiful horse I've ever seen," George commented, but he knew she wouldn't completely understand their fascination with Fuego until she'd seen the flame-and-gold-coated horse for herself. "He'd be worth a pretty penny if anybody ever did manage to catch him." George cast his son a teasing look.

"I still don't know how he was able to break that rope." Michael shook his head sheepishly in remembered consternation.

"You mean you actually got close enough to him to get a rope on him?" Trista's blue eyes widened in curiosity.

Michael looked a bit shamefaced. "That's about all I did, too."

"I don't understand."

"It was about three years ago. I was out riding herd and had gone off to check for strays when I accidentally came across him at a watering hole. I don't know who was more surprised, him or me. Anyway, I reacted quickly enough, I guess. I did manage to rope him." He paused in his recounting of the incident to remember how glorious and powerful the stallion had looked as he'd fought for his freedom against the strangling lariat. "But somehow that devil snapped it."

"He's that strong?"

"He's that strong and that smart. I vowed then that one day I was going to be the one to catch him and brand him for the Royal Diamond. I don't like being outsmarted by a horse."

"Maybe this time you'll catch him," Trista reassured him. "Does anybody know where he came from?"

"No. He just showed up on the range one day," George answered. "One thing's for sure, though. He's got no use for people. The minute he catches sight of anybody, he's gone."

"Is he very old?" she asked.

"Hard to say," Michael replied. "He was already full-grown when I had my 'run-in' with him, so he's at least five or six . . ."

"But if he's that old, and he's run wild all his life, why would you want him?" Trista looked from George to Michael. "Isn't he what you'd consider a rogue?"

"Possibly, but what a rogue!" George smiled. "He's faster than any horse we've got, and with his intelligence . . ." He gave an eloquent shrug. "Just keep a lookout when you're riding. If we could find out where he's holed up, maybe we can figure out a way to corner him."

"George . . . Michael . . ."

The sound of someone calling from across the room drew their attention, and George looked up to see Sam Frederickson and Ben Madden motioning for them to come and join them. "Michael, I think they want to speak with us. If you ladies will excuse us for a minute?"

"I'll be right back," Michael promised Trista.

"Of course."

As they moved off to visit with the other guests, Trista turned to Eleanor, her eyes sparkling at the thought of the infamous stallion. "Perhaps tomorrow Michael and I can ride out to where Fuego was last spotted. I'd love to get a look at him."

"I'm sure Michael won't be taking you there," Eleanor replied almost too quickly, and then added self-consciously, "It's much too far away."

"Oh, I don't mind an all-day ride or . . ." she went on, gaily anticipating a great adventure in tracking down the elusive rogue.

"What Eleanor is trying to say is that you don't want to go riding out toward the Lawsons', Trista." Mary Lou's remark sounded ominous as she joined the conversation.

Trista could not fathom the reason for the cryptic responses. "Why not?"

Eleanor gave Mary Lou a stern look, but the older woman ignored her as she answered, "Because some Comanche have been raiding up there. The Lawson place was attacked just a little over two weeks ago." She had been looking for the chance to test Trista's true mettle, and she knew this was the perfect time.

"Mary Lou!" Eleanor scolded in annoyance. She had wanted to shield Trista from the ugliness of the current Indian situation.

"If she's going to be living here, she might as well know the truth," Mary Lou huffed.

"The truth?" Trista turned to Eleanor questioningly. "I thought all the Indians were on reservations."

"Most of the Indians are on reservations, dear. . . ." Eleanor began evasively.

"But there are some who are not?"

"That's right, Trista," Mary Lou affirmed. "The government would certainly like them to be on the reservations, but there's no way to contain some of them. It's as my John always says, *'The only good Indian is a dead Indian.'* "

Trista had read about such sentiments in the news accounts back home, but she had never really believed that people actually felt that way. "Surely you don't mean that, Mary Lou."

Mary Lou pinned her with a glacial glare as she gave a short, derisive laugh. It was not a pleasant sound. "I most certainly do mean it, Trista. After you've been here awhile, you'll come to feel the same way, too." At the younger woman's doubtful expression, she added, "You see, I lost my only brother and his family in a raid about ten years ago. The Comanche are nothing but cold, cruel killers. Why, when I think of how they tortured poor Harry . . . and the things they did to Kate—"

"Really, Mary Lou," Eleanor spoke up, "this is hardly the time or the place for such a discussion."

"I think it's important that she know just how wild and vicious they are." She was undaunted by Eleanor's comment. "There are whole raiding parties that sneak off the reservations just to terrorize the countryside, Trista. It's almost like they get some kind of perverse pleasure in maiming and killing decent white folks," Mary Lou recounted with relish. "So you and Michael should be real careful when you go out riding. If they've come as close as the Lawson spread, who knows where they'll strike next."

"Mary Lou!" Eleanor cut her off sharply as she saw the sudden fear in Trista's eyes. "Trista, dear, you mustn't concern yourself with these things."

"But is it true?"

Eleanor knew better than to try to make light of such a serious subject. "Yes, I'm afraid raids are a fact of life here, but the Royal Diamond is very well protected."

"I see." Trista's pleasant expression wavered only slightly as every horror story she'd ever heard about Indian attacks came to mind.

"You'll be safe as long as you stay close to the ranch."

"Of course." Trista forced herself to relax. Since Eleanor didn't seem overly worried about the possibility of a raid at the ranch and Michael had never mentioned it, Trista decided firmly to put the thought from her mind. She had come to Texas to make a life with Michael, and that was exactly what she was going to do.

She glanced up then, wondering just where Michael had gone with his father. To her surprise, she found that George was deep in conversation with several older men across the room, but there was no sign of Michael. Suddenly feeling the need to be alone with him, she excused herself from the ladies and went in search of her fiancé.

Sukie had been watching and waiting all evening for the chance to maneuver a moment alone with Michael. Her frustration had run rampant as he'd spent almost the entire evening at his fiancée's side, giving her absolutely no opportunity to approach him. It was only when Michael moved off with his father to speak with a group of men that she thought she might finally get the chance to be alone with him.

Having bolstered her fading spirits with several cups of punch, she was ready when Michael excused himself from the discussion and left the parlor. Sukie didn't know where he was going, but she knew this was the only chance she was going to have to speak with him privately. As casually as she could, she set her half-empty cup aside and followed him from the room.

The empty hall that greeted her sent her hopes plummeting, and she sagged defeatedly against the wall. A moment later the sound of Michael's deep voice coming from the study buoyed her. Straightening, she quickly arranged her skirts and then squared her shoulders as if preparing, subconsciously, to do battle. With an effort, she managed a festive smile as she started forward.

"Good evening, Sukie," Frank Madison greeted her as he left the study on his way back to the parlor.

"Evenin', Frank," she returned calmly. Her pulse quickened at the thought that Michael was now by himself in the study. She waited until Frank had disappeared back into the parlor before venturing in. "Michael . . . good evening . . ." Sukie used just the right amount of surprise in her voice to insure that he believed their encounter was accidental.

"Sukie . . ." Michael looked up from where he stood at the liquor cabinet pouring himself a glass of bourbon. "It's good to see you again."

Her heart ached with the thought that he didn't really mean it . . . that he was only being polite.

"It's good to see you, too," Sukie told him, her gaze hungrily devouring the sight of him. How handsome he looked to her! Desire surged powerfully through her. She longed to throw herself into his arms and kiss him madly . . . passionately. Sukie wanted to tell him of her love and beg him to make her his. "I missed you while you were gone."

If Michael noticed the suddenly husky tone to her voice, he gave no indication of it. "Well, it's certainly good to be back." He finished pouring his drink and came to stand near her. The faint, elusive scent of the perfume she used touched a warm chord within him, and memories that had long been buried stirred to life—memories of the good times they'd shared together . . . of picnics and dances and kisses stolen in the dark.

"How was Philadelphia?" Sukie asked. Before he'd gone away, they'd had many heart-to-heart talks about the fact that it was his parents' idea that he go back East for school and how he really did not want to go. She hoped she could encourage him to talk with her now, just as they had before.

"Philadelphia was—" he paused as if searching for the right word "—very civilized, I guess is the best way to phrase it." His dark-eyed gaze dropped to her upturned features. Sukie . . . he had forgotten how sweet she was and how easy it was to talk to her. He'd

54

forgotten the glory of her red hair and the beauty of her emerald eyes. A faint frown creased his brow.

"Did you enjoy it?" She had noticed his slightly puzzled look and wondered at the cause.

"Let's just say that I did finally get used to it." Michael smiled wryly. "But it certainly wasn't home."

"I know what you mean," Sukie agreed, not wanting the conversation to end. "I spent a month with my Aunt Lea in New Orleans last year. It was nice enough, but I was really homesick most of the time. I guess we're two of a kind. . . . We've got Texas in our blood."

Michael nodded. "I know I never want to leave again."

"I'm so glad. . . ." she said breathlessly, the fear she'd been harboring that he might return to Philadelphia with Trista relieved.

The unexpected urgency of her tone created a tension between them. Michael felt a sudden, overwhelming urge to reassure Sukie that he was, indeed, home to stay. His gaze met and locked with hers, and an almost palpable current of awareness passed between them.

"So am I," he said gruffly, caught up in the mood of the moment.

To Sukie's complete frustration, the fragile thread of intimacy between them was broken by the sound of voices just outside the study door.

"I don't know where Michael's gone, Trista, but perhaps he's here in the study," George was saying as he led Trista into the room.

Though Trista was a little surprised to find Michael in the study alone with another woman, she thought nothing of it. This was, after all, his party, and all these people were his friends.

The mood broken, reality descended upon Michael,

55

and giving an imperceptible shake of his head, he moved to greet them. "Pa . . . Trista . . ."

"See, I told you he was here somewhere, Trista," George remarked good-naturedly as they joined them.

"Trista. Is something wrong?"

"Oh, no, Michael. I was just wondering where you'd gone," she told him easily as he came to her and pressed a soft kiss on her lips.

Sukie had managed to keep her expression carefully guarded until she witnessed the kiss, and then she could no longer hide the hurt and anger that were filling her. The truth of her emotions flashed in her eyes for just the briefest of instants, but in that moment, Trista looked up. It happened so quickly that Trista was not really sure she'd seen the look of utter outrage cross the other girl's face.

"Trista, Sukie . . . have you two met yet?" George asked.

"No, we haven't," Trista answered.

"Trista, this is Sukie Harris, Mary Lou's daughter. Sukie, this is Trista Sinclair." George casually made the introductions.

"It's nice to meet you." Trista smiled warmly at the other girl.

"It's nice to meet you, too, Trista," Sukie said with an ease she little felt.

Trista could detect no trace of venom in her greeting and immediately dismissed her earlier impression as imaginary. "Have you and Michael been friends for a long time?"

"Yes, we have," she told her, managing to give Michael a fond look.

"Then I'm sure we'll be seeing a lot more of each other. I just met your mother, and she's a lovely woman."

"You'll have to have Michael bring you for a visit as

soon as you get completely settled in."

"I'd like that."

"You two had better get back to the party," George prodded. "There are still some guests who haven't had the chance to meet Trista yet."

"We'd better go. Sukie, we'll see you later," Michael said as he slipped an arm possessively about Trista's waist and guided her from the room, leaving George to follow.

Lost deep in thought, Sukie stared about the now deserted room with unseeing eyes. For a moment during her time with Michael, she had felt the closeness they had once shared. Though he hadn't responded overtly, she was certain that he had felt it, too. Tonight he had remembered how close they had been before he'd left, and her hopes brightened at the thought. Maybe, just maybe, she did have a chance to win him back. Encouraged, Sukie was smiling as she left the study to rejoin the party.

Chapter Four

Alone and magnificent, his golden coat glistening in the morning sun, Fuego stood atop the bluff surveying the surrounding countryside with regal disdain. The danger of the day before seemed to have gone, and once again his territory . . . his domain . . . was quiet. He gave an arrogant toss of his head as he savored the peace of the moment.

The light breeze shifted then, and with its changing direction came a revealing hint of something hidden . . . something unseen. Fuego moved restlessly, suddenly on alert. He was an animal who survived strictly on his instincts, and though he had passed a good night here, and food and water were plentiful, his innate impulses were telling him that all was not as safe as it appeared.

An uneasiness settled over Fuego, and as if sensing a closing danger, he swung abruptly about. It was that moment that saved him from Lance's carefully set trap, for in that instant, Fuego caught the true scent of his presence. Across the distance they spotted each other. Both paused . . . man and horse . . . frozen into immobility as they studied each other with measured interest. It was the stallion who broke first. Nostrils flaring, his eyes wild, Fuego bolted and raced away in a streak of golden splendor.

With a furious curse, Lance watched the powerful, surefooted Fuego bound from the bluff at breakneck speed. Though he was annoyed at his own ineptitude in allowing the stallion to escape, Lance could waste no time on self-recrimination. The horse was escaping *again!* Charging forth from his place of concealment, Lance ran to where he'd left his own mount securely tethered. Snatching up the reins, he vaulted onto his horse's back and put his moccasined heels to its flanks.

Frustration filled Lance as he gave chase. He had thought the plan he'd devised during his long, sleepless night to capture the horse to be nearly perfect, but he had not counted on the golden one's uncanny instincts. In spite of the fact that he had taken every precaution when approaching, the stallion had managed to elude him yet another time.

His respect for the stallion's intelligence growing, Lance knew that this was no ordinary rogue. It was as he'd always suspected. There was something very special about this animal, and it was that very "specialness" that made him such a treasured prize. The thought of how proud he'd be to return to the village with the stallion fed his need to conquer, and Lance's expression grew grim with determination. It was only a matter of time now. Today's escape would be his last. The golden one would be his.

Trista was growing more than a little nervous as she reined her mare, Sheba, in near the crest of the hill. Tipping her low-crowned western hat back, she shaded her eyes against the brightness of the sun and scanned the area in hopes of finding a familiar landmark. To her frustration, she recognized nothing . . . not the distant grove of cottonwoods or the creek that ran through them.

She silently reviled herself for having been stupid enough to ride out on her own that morning. How foolishly confident she had been to think that she could find her way around the Royal Diamond alone after only a few days! Trista realized now that she should have waited for Michael to finish meeting with his father so he could come with her, but her need to be out riding on this glorious morning had overruled her common sense. Now here she was, quite lost and quite disgusted with herself. She knew the only thing left to do was to backtrack and try to follow her own trail to the house. As tired as her mount was, though, Trista decided to ride down to the creek first to let the mare rest and have a drink.

From the distance Trista had thought the stream nondescript, but as she drew nearer, she discovered it was far more. Hidden behind the natural hedge of trees, the babbling creek fed a small, crystal-clear pool whose banks were shaded by a stately stand of cottonwoods. Dancing beams of sunlight dappled the grassy ground in a kaleidoscope of changing patterns as a faint breeze stirred the leafy branches of the guardian grove.

Enchanted, Trista dismounted and led Sheba down to the water's edge. As the horse drank her fill, Trista closed her eyes and put all thought of her predicament from her, allowing herself to be enveloped by the complete serenity of the moment. *This was what heaven will be like*, she thought in blissful contentment . . . clear, splashing waters, soft breezes, the scent of wildflowers blooming, and the warm touch of the sun. She could have remained that way for hours had Sheba's sudden restiveness not broken into her reverie.

"What is it, girl?" Trista patted the mare's neck comfortingly. "What's troubling you?"

Sheba quivered, every muscle in her body taut and ready for action, as her attention focused on a rocky ridge across the valley. Though Trista could neither see nor hear anything unusual, she grew uneasy as all the talk of Comanche raids the night before came to mind. Tightening her grip on the reins, she quickly swung up into the saddle, ready to take flight if need be.

It was then that he burst into view. His muscles bunching and straining, his coat foam-flecked from the ordeal of his flight, Fuego cleared the top of the hill and streaked down the slope, heading in Trista's direction.

Trista recognized him immediately. Excellent judge of horseflesh that she was, she knew that this had to be the elusive golden stallion Michael and George had been speaking of at the party.

"Fuego . . ." She whispered his name in awe, understanding now why George had been so interested in having the rogue for his own. He was gorgeous . . . and he was heading her way.

The last realization incited her to action, for she knew she'd never have a chance like this one. She grinned as she imagined what Michael's and George's reactions would be if she returned with Fuego in tow. Taking up the rope that was attached to her saddle, Trista prepared to intercept his headlong flight. As the stallion raced ever closer, she put her heels to her mare and darted out directly into his path.

Fuego knew a moment of panic. He had just managed to evade the one who had been hounding him for days, and now here was another . . . waiting and ready. In desperation, the frightened horse changed course. Angling away from the more level terrain in Trista's direction, he headed toward the rockier, less surefooted country to the north.

Lance watched the stallion disappear over the hilltop and leaned low over his own horse's neck, giving the pinto his full lead. Though not as fast in a dead run as the golden one, Lance's mount's capability for endurance was proving an effective weapon. The stallion had never been stalked this tenaciously before, and Lance hoped that the days of constant pursuit had taken their toll on his strength and judgment.

Rope in hand, Lance topped the hill hoping to find that the stallion was slowing down. Instead, what he discovered pleased him even more, and a feeling of triumph engulfed him. The fleeing steed had changed course and was now veering off toward a rock-strewn area that would hamper his breakaway speed. Lance did not have time to consider the stallion's reason for altering his direction. He only knew that this was the moment of reckoning. The pinto was surefooted and agile and more than capable of keeping up in the rocky terrain. His concentration complete, he focused only on the stallion.

Guiding Sheba with a firm yet knowing hand, Trista gave the mare full rein as they chased after Fuego.

"We're going to get him, Sheba . . . Just a little bit farther and—" Out of the corner of her eye, she caught a glimpse of another horse and rider racing after Fuego from a different direction. Trista automatically assumed that it was someone from a neighboring ranch, and so she didn't break her stride as they continued to give chase. She wanted to capture Fuego and show everybody on the Royal Diamond just how perfectly she could fit into ranch life. Her gaze never wavered from the rogue as she refused to back off.

Lance was closing fast, and his heartbeat quickened at the prospect of finally attaining the prize. Soon the golden one would be his. He could see himself in his mind's eye now, returning to his village with the stallion and receiving everyone's congratulations and admiration. The imagining was a good one, and it filled him with confidence as he drew ever nearer to the slowing steed. Lariat in hand, Lance directed the pinto with pressure from his knees only as they galloped steadily closer.

It was then that Trista broke into Lance's line of vision. It was a moment of confusion for him, and the pinto, reacting to his master's sudden bewilderment, faltered slightly in its stride. Lance's gaze was anxious as he looked back in the direction from which she'd come, wondering if there were others with her. Relief filled him when he discovered that she was alone, for the last thing he'd wanted or needed was a confrontation with any whites.

Recovering quickly from the intrusion, Lance swore silently over his loss of momentum, and he goaded his mount on. The pinto responded quickly and surged forward once again, picking up the pace. Lance couldn't help but wonder who the white woman was and what she was doing out riding alone, but he firmly dismissed the thoughts. Right now only the golden one mattered. He would capture him, and then worry about the white woman.

The scrub oaks and mesquite trees faded to a blur as they raced onward. Trista grew even more excited as she closed on Fuego. Nervously readying her lariat, she hoped that the little she knew about roping would not fail her. The sound of the other rider gaining on her from behind convinced Trista that she had to make her move now if she was ever to have a chance at the stallion. As steadily as she could, she rose up in the stirrups and threw the rope.

Lance and his pinto moved as one as they bore down upon the stallion. With fierce determination, he drove himself and the pinto to the brink, passing the woman without a glance just as she threw her rope. Fury, mixed with an immediately denied admiration, swept through him as he saw her lasso land accurately over the golden one's head. The stallion was his!

As Lance charged past her, Trista saw him clearly for the first time. The shock was numbing. Her grip on the rope slackened, and the lariat slipped from her fingers as she stared after him in mute surprise. *Dear God . . . the other rider is no ranchhand . . . The other ridre is an Indian! A Comanche!* Her concentration was lost as fear shot through her at the sight of his longish black hair and near naked, sun-bronzed body. Knowing she had to escape while she could, Trista sawed back on the reins in a desperate motion. The unexpected change in command startled Sheba, and the faithful mount stumbled and lost her footing, falling heavily.

Lance wasn't aware of exactly what happened when the woman's rope went slack, and he didn't have the time to concern himself. All that mattered was that at last he was certain that he had the golden one! With cool precision, he threw his own rope and then watched with intense satisfaction as it collared the fleeing steed.

The struggle between man and beast was long and hard as Fuego fought with all his might to retain his freedom. Rearing and pawing the air in frustration, he battled fiercely against this man's domination, but to no avail. The days of unending chase had taken their toll. The nooses choking him into submission, the stallion was quivering in exhaustion as Lance kept his rope taut and maneuvered his pinto ever closer. In one final strategic move, the wild steed was thrown to the ground.

The feeling of victory that possessed Lance was heady as he stared at the subdued horse. There had been times during the past days and nights when he'd wondered if the agony of the pursuit had been worth it, but he knew now that it had. The golden one was as beautiful up close as he had been from a distance.

Lance secured his rope and then dismounted. He approached the horse with caution and quickly slipped a hackamore over the stallion's head. Fuego grew fearful at the feel of yet another noose about his neck, and only the man's subtle crooning kept him from struggling to his death. He found something soothing in the deep, dulcet tones, and although it made no sense to him, he did not fight against the feel of the man's hands upon him.

Feeling the horse's surrender, Lance knew his success was complete. Rising, he stood victoriously over the vanquished horse. Lifting his eyes to the sky, his arms spread wide, he cried out his joyous triumph.

The sound of his pinto whickering drew his glance, and it was then, when he noticed the black mare disappearing riderless over the far ridge, that he remembered the woman. A frown creased his brow as he scanned the area but could see no sign of her. After checking to make sure that the bonds on the stallion were still secure, Lance set out to look for the woman.

Though the fall had knocked the breath from her, Trista knew she had to run away as quickly and as quietly as she could before the Indian had time to come back for her. A shudder of fear shook her as she remembered all that Mary Lou Harris had told her about Comanche raids the night before. With an effort, she pushed herself into a sitting position intending to flee, but she immediately regretted the action when waves of dizziness assailed her. Groaning, she lifted a shaking hand to her forehead and closed her eyes against the throbbing pain.

Trista would never know whether it was the chill his shadow cast upon her or an intuitive knowledge of his nearness that caused her to look up just then, but she did, and the sight that greeted her struck terror to the depths of her soul. *It was the Comanche! He'd found her!* She had hoped to have time to escape, but now it was too late.

Her mouth went dry, and her eyes widened in horror as she stared up at him. She had heard all the tales of how hideously ugly the Indians were, but even the most outlandish of the stories had not prepared her for this.

Still dazed from the force of her fall from Sheba, she had only a vague impression of sun-bronzed nakedness as she stared up at him. Her gaze moved to his face, and she hoped for some sign of kindness or friendship, but what she saw there made her recoil in terror. Streaks of red and black paint slashed across the warrior's face, giving him the appearance of a hideous demon straight from hell.

Lance had been cautious as he combed the area for the woman. He'd had no idea if she'd been armed or not, and so he had moved slowly . . . carefully . . . his tread catlike and silent. He had come upon Trista just as she'd managed to sit up. He did not recognize her at first, for the glory of her tawny hair was confined in a thick braid that hung down her back, and her face was turned away from him. It was only when she looked up that he felt the totally unexpected jolt of recognition. The woman was none other than the beautiful female he had seen the night before at the ranch.

Lance kept his expression implacable as he regarded her. His gaze may have seemed cold as it raked over her, but his reaction to her nearness was anything but indifferent. He thought she looked just as lovely up close as she had from a distance. As she was sitting, braced back on her arms, the soft white material of her blouse was pulled tautly across her breasts, hinting at their fullness. Lance felt an urge to release the strained buttons and see what delights were hidden from his view. Her split riding skirt was in disarray, its modest length now hiked up past her knees, revealing long, shapely limbs. His desire to touch her grew unbounded.

Trista could sense a sudden tension in him, and she shifted nervously, trying to avoid looking at him and frantically trying to think of a way to escape. From all that she'd heard, she knew the reality of the situation, yet she refused to give in without a fight. Had Sheba not run off, her chance to get away would have been better, but it was too late to worry about that. Right now she had to save herself by whatever means possible.

There was no more time to think, only to act. In a lightning move, she grabbed up a handful of the sandy soil and threw it in the warrior's face. His guttural grunt of agony as the sand seared his eyes pleased her, and she took advantage of his momentary blindness to scramble away. Trista ran blindly. She didn't know where she was going; she just knew that she could not remain there and face certain death . . . or worse.

Lance had not been expecting her attack, and though she took him briefly by surprise, he reacted quickly. Angered, yet respecting her daring, he wiped the grit from his stinging eyes and started after her.

Dashing madly across the rocky, uneven ground, Trista grew desperate as she looked back and saw the warrior already following her. She changed directions and dodged between some scrub brush and rocks in hopes of eluding him. She had never before had to run for her life, and she found herself shaking uncontrollably as she made her way across the rugged landscape. On gut instinct alone, she headed for higher ground, ignoring the cockleburs that tore vi-

67

ciously at her clothes and hair.

As Trista reached the top of the incline, she was near collapse but knew she could not rest. A quick glance back filled her heart with even more terror, for the Comanche was nowhere in sight. *Had she managed to escape, or was he playing some kind of perverse cat-and-mouse game with her?* Her breath was a strained sob in her throat as she struggled mindlessly on, refusing to give in.

Trista started down the hillside but lost her footing and tumbled the rest of the way to the bottom. She landed jarringly against a boulder, its sharp-edged hardness bruising her ribs and knocking the breath from her. It took Trista several long minutes to pull herself together. Excruciating pain shot through her as she staggered to her feet, and she doubled over, clutching her side.

A pebble fell. Though the noise it made as it bounced down the incline was minimal, to Trista it sounded like a death knell. Her blue eyes wild with fright, she slowly looked up. Her heart seemed to miss a beat as she saw the warrior standing silently atop the hill, his arms folded across the powerful width of his bare chest, his expression seeming both mocking and murderous at the same time. She swallowed nervously as she forced herself to action. Unmindful of the agony of her injured side, she started to run again.

Trista had managed only a few tortured steps before it was over. She cried out in pain, horror, and frustration as her braid was caught in his unseen hand, and she was yanked forcibly backward. Losing her balance, she twisted as she fell, landing on her knees before the warrior. The thick, ropelike length of her hair was wrapped around his wrist, and he held her pinned there in submission.

Terror struck at her heart, yet Trista fought to keep her fear from showing. She remembered someone telling her that the Comanche respected only strength and that cowards were held in the lowest contempt, so she bravely raised her eyes to meet his. It was then that she noticed the startling color of her captor's eyes against the black and blood-red paint on his face. Rather than the dark color she had expected, his gaze was a riveting, vivid blue.

The discovery shocked her. A blue-eyed Comanche? How could that be? Remnants of tales she'd heard raced through her mind, and she vaguely recalled stories of how the Indians often took children captive when they raided ranches. At the time when she'd heard the tales she hadn't believed them, but now . . . the thought gave her a measure of hope, however small. If this warrior was perhaps one of them, then it might be possible for her to appeal to that side of him and earn her freedom.

Her brief instant of hope was soon destroyed when he reached out to grasp her by her right arm and haul her to her feet. He said nothing as he twisted her right arm behind her back and pulled her full-length against him, trapping her free left arm between them.

"NO!" she screamed, determined not to give in.

With what little strength she had left, Trista began to fight him in earnest, struggling against his near-ness. She pushed against the rock-hard wall of his chest with all her might and kicked out at him with her booted feet. Trista knew her blows connected, yet her captor gave no outward indication of experiencing any pain. His only reaction was to tighten his grip on her braid, forcing her head back and exposing the length of her throat. Fearing that he was about to kill her, she pulled her left arm free and swung at him, hoping to strike him in some way that might incapacitate him. Her efforts were all to no avail, though, as Lance quickly released her hair and snared her left wrist just as she would have hit him.

His hands were unyielding cuffs of steel, and the pressure he was exerting threatened to snap the delicate bones of her wrists. His hold upon her was so cruel that Trista was forced to grit her teeth to keep from crying out.

Lance, however, was unaware of the mercilessness of his grip as he stared down at her left hand in anger and confusion. On her ring finger was a ring that bore the crown insignia, and on the four points of that crown were four perfectly matched diamonds. It was the Barrett brand made into a ring, and the sight of it filled him with furious fascination. He glanced at her head, bowed meekly now in resignation, and wondered coldly at her connection to the Royal Diamond and the Barretts.

Only when a low moan escaped her and she sagged against him did Lance realize just how heartless his hold on her had been. For some reason, her helplessness touched a chord of response within him, and he loosened his grip.

Trista had noticed the wicked-looking knife the warrior was carrying in the waistband of his breechcloth. Knowing it was her last and only hope for salvation, she pretended to be close to a faint and swayed weakly against him. She found it difficult to believe that her ruse worked, but when the warrior slackened his hold, she reacted instantly, wrenching herself free and grabbing the knife at the same time. Trista faced him then, knife in hand, the blade glinting in the brilliance of the mid-morning sun.

The Indian was watching her as she backed away from him, and when his lips curved into a dangerous imitation of a smile, Trista was completely unnerved.

What was this savage thinking? What was he planning to do to her? She tried not to let her desperation show. Brandishing the weapon threateningly, she retreated.

"Stay away from me!" Hysterically, she wondered if he even understood what she was saying, and when he continued to stalk her slowly, she assumed he did not.

Trista grew tense and jittery as she kept angling away from the savage. She knew that if she let her defenses down for even a split second he would be upon her, and so she watched his every move, waiting for that fateful moment when he would attack. His attack came and instinct took over. Fighting for her life, she lashed out with a knife to protect herself.

Lance felt the blade slice through his upper arm with something akin to amazement, and he silently cursed himself for having underestimated this woman. She was as wild and spirited as the golden stallion, and just as beautiful. He was determined to master her.

Lance ignored the throbbing pain of his wound as he kicked out and knocked her off balance. As she fell, he launched himself at her, pinning her to the ground and grabbing the wrist of her knife-wielding hand. In a vicious motion, he forced her to drop the weapon and then trapped both her arms above her head with one hand.

"Unless you plan to kill a man, you should never pull a knife on him." Lance's smile was fiendish as he retrieved the bloodstained weapon and held it up before her face.

Trista gasped at his cool command of English, and then blanched at the sight of the knife. A chill of impending doom shook her. He was a Comanche . . . a murderous savage. Trista felt certain that he planned to kill her. She began to fight him again, bucking and squirming in an effort to twist free of his oppressive weight.

"Let me go!"

Lance shifted his position lower to stop her from fighting him. Suddenly what previously had been a restraining hold became an intimate caress as his legs entangled with hers and his hips pressed hers to the ground. The contact was shocking in its sensuality.

The surge of excitement that rushed through Lance at the feel of her moving restlessly beneath him was near to overpowering, and took him by complete surprise. He was no stranger to women, yet never before had one affected him so strongly. Dropping his gaze to her face, he kept his expression dispassionate as he studied her. She was flushed in her agitation, and her heightened color made her appear all the more beautiful. Her blouse had been torn during her flight from him, and now one smooth, creamy shoulder and the beginning swell of one round breast lay exposed. He longed to touch that tempting flesh.

Trista felt the new tension, too, but in her innocence was unable to understand it. All she knew was that it frightened her. "Leave me alone! I'm Michael Barrett's fiancée! He'll kill you if you hurt me!"

Her words penetrated Lance's thoughts, freezing the desire that had stirred in his loins. Lance went perfectly still. That was the meaning of the ring! She was engaged to Michael Barrett . . . the half brother he'd never met . . . the man he'd seen with her the night before. Lance gave a harsh, hollow laugh. "He'd have to find me first, and I don't think he'd want to do that."

Trista read into his words a threat, and tried not to show her fear. "Michael would track you down! This is Barrett land! Why don't you just go on and leave while you still can? You don't belong here!"

Her statement stung him more than the blade of

the knife. "You and your Michael are the intruders here, not me."

Trista thought he was referring to the fact that before the settlers came, the Comanche had once roamed this part of Texas freely. "Michael's family has lived here for years! The Royal Diamond is their home . . . and mine, too, now!"

Abruptly Lance released her and stood up. His movements were barely controlled as he slid the knife back in its sheath. His blue eyes were glacial as he regarded her. "Get up." It was an order.

Trista wondered at his sudden withdrawal and knew a moment of profound hope. Maybe he was letting her go! Maybe her mentioning of Michael and the Barretts had saved her life. Favoring her injured side, she got to her feet.

Lance noticed her discomfort. "You're hurt?"

"No," she denied, turning slightly away from him. "I'm all right. Am I free to go?"

Impatiently, Lance snared her arm again and pulled her to him. As he started to push her shirt up, she tried to break loose.

"Be still," he commanded, and for some reason, she obeyed. His hand was gentle as he lifted the blouse to examine her injury. The lower side of her back was scraped raw and bruised. Lance knew it had to be painful for her. He thought of her fearlessness in fighting him and of how she was bearing such a wound without complaining. "Come with me." His statement was dispassionate.

"No! I don't want to go with you!" She pulled back. "I want to go home to the Royal Diamond!"

Lance's expression didn't falter. "Your home will be with me now. Come."

Chapter Five

Trista refused to budge and tried once more to pull her arm free from his firm, possessive grip. Her expression was mutinous as she demanded, "Let go of me! I'm not going anywhere with you!"

"You'll do what I tell you to do." Lance's tone was terse as he faced her, and had she known him better she would have realized the danger of pushing him any further.

"I will not! If you're going to kill me, then do it here! Now!"

Again Lance's smile had a chilling effect on her. "Killing you was not what I had in mind."

Trista's eyes widened at his remark, revealing for the first time the depth of her terror. "I won't go with you . . . I won't!"

At her continued defiance, Lance's mouth firmed to a hard, grim line. He had had enough. While he'd admired her spirit in the beginning, he found now that he was growing quite weary of her protestations. Without uttering another word, he pulled a leather thong from his waistband.

"What are you going to do to me?" She recognized a subtle change in him and grew fearful of his intent as she glanced from his face to the length of leather in his hand.

Lance didn't bother to answer as he caught up her other wrist and quickly tied her arms together.

Alarmed, not knowing what he was doing, Trista kicked out at him, but this time he easily avoided her frantic efforts. As he hoisted her unceremoniously over his shoulder, she gave vent to her feelings of desperation.

"Put me down!" she cried out, pounding on his back with her bound fists.

"You will learn to do as I say, golden one, or you will pay the price," Lance commented dispassionately, paying no attention to her pummeling.

"You aren't going to live long enough to get me to do anything you want!" Trista snapped as she furiously continued her struggles. "When Michael finds out—"

The mention of his half brother's name hardened his heart even more, and Lance clamped a restraining arm about her legs to still her writhing motions. "By the time your Michael discovers what's happened, you'll be far away from here."

"Michael will come for me!" Trista raved on. "The Barretts won't let you get away with this, you filthy savage!"

Abruptly Lance stopped and, without a word of warning, dumped her to her feet. Trista staggered, then managed to regain her balance. Filled with fright and hatred, she glared at him defiantly, but he displayed no emotion as he returned her regard.

"My people have ways to silence captives who speak too much," he said brutally, already sick of hearing the Barrett name.

Trista had wanted to keep fighting him, to never give in, but she recoiled visibly as he drew his knife from its protective sheath. Was he going to kill her here . . . now? Or, as she had heard in some horror-filled Indian torture tale, was he going to cut out her tongue? Both possibilities struck terror in her heart, and she began to quake.

Wildly Trista glanced around, seeking a way of escape, searching for someone to save her, but she realized that it was useless. Helpless humiliation washed through her. There would be no flight to freedom, to rescue. She was now a captive . . . the slave of a Comanche warrior.

A depressing resignation set in. Trista had heard the whispered stories about the white women who'd been taken by Indians and later freed by the army. Their tales of survival had been filled with misery and abuse. She faced him silently now, trying to control her nervousness and praying that she was strong enough to live through whatever it was he planned to do to her.

Lance had witnessed the play of emotions revealed so plainly on her face, and while he found himself filled with hatred for her and all she stood for, he could not deny that he admired her courage. As he reached out toward her, she tried to block him with her bound forearms. Lance brushed her attempt aside and seized the hem of her blouse. Cutting a length of material from the already ruined garment, he moved behind her and gagged her with the cloth.

Trista's imagination had been wreaking havoc on her nerves as she'd envisioned all the torturous misery the Comanche could inflict with his knife, but when the warrior only gagged her, her knees went weak in relief. This time when he lifted her over his shoulder, she did not protest or fight, but hung limply in his controlling grip.

Glad that he had quieted her, Lance headed back across the rugged terrain, his mood bitter. He had wondered in the beginning exactly what he was going to do with her, but now that he knew the truth of her identity, he was filled with a grim resolve. She was the future bride of his half brother, and since Michael had taken all that was really his—his name, his birthright, his father's love—Lance felt no hesitation in taking something of Michael's. He would keep this woman for his own. Though he knew she would not be the easiest, most malleable female, she would be his.

Trista's bruised side was aching miserably as she hung uncomfortably suspended over Lance's broad shoulder, but she was too filled with anger and fright to care at the moment. The tales she'd heard of the women who'd been taken captive were haunting her thoughts. Not many details had ever been given, but it had been widely understood without saying that torture and rape had been common.

Trista thought of Michael and his gentle ardency and wished desperately to be safe in his arms right now. Again she chastised herself for her foolishness in riding out alone, and her heart ached when she realized how worried he would be about her when she turned up missing. Though she knew that without a horse or a weapon, escape was impossible right now, Trista vowed to herself never to give up hope. Somehow, someway, she would return to Michael, and then they would have the wonderful future together they had planned.

"Mr. Barrett! Mr. Barrett!"

The sound of Poker Bradley's frantic call drew Eleanor from the front parlor, where she had just settled in to enjoy a quiet moment and drink a cup of tea. Throwing wide the front door, she stepped out into the shadows of the front porch to meet the ranchhand who was running to the house.

"What is it, Poker? What's happened?"

Poker, a tall string bean of a cowhand with thinning

blond hair and a protruding Adam's apple, whipped off his hat and faced the mistress of the ranch as politely as he could in the urgency of his distress. "I need to see Mr. Barrett right away, ma'am."

"Why, they're not here right now, Poker. They rode out about fifteen minutes ago. Is there anything I can do to help?"

"It's Miss Trista, Mrs. Barrett," he began nervously.

"Trista? What about her?" Eleanor frowned. She had slept in later than usual this morning because of the party the night before and had been unaware that her future daughter-in-law had ventured out alone.

"Well, ma'am, her horse just came back without her."

"She was riding alone?" She was incredulous.

"Yes, ma'am. She went out an hour or so ago by herself, but she promised to stay close . . ."

"Good heavens!" Eleanor concern was very real. "Send a rider out to find my husband and Michael. They were heading out to the south range to check on the herd there."

"Yes, ma'am."

"And get a group of riders together yourself. We can't waste any time waiting on Michael and George. Trista could be in trouble."

"Yes, ma'am," he replied, jamming his hat back on his head and racing off to do as she'd ordered.

Michael and George had only gone a short distance when they heard someone hailing them. Reining in, they turned in their saddles to see a lone rider racing in their direction.

"Mr. Barrett! Wait up!"

"It's Whitey. . . ." George frowned as they waited for the short, heavyset ranch foreman to catch up with them. "I wonder what's happened."

"I don't know," Michael added, "but it must be something important if Whitey's the one coming after us."

"What is it, Whitey?" the owner of the Royal Diamond called out as his most trusted hand drew near.

Whitey sawed back on his reins and brought his charging steed to a strangled halt. "You're needed back at the ranch. . . ." he related quickly.

"What happened?" Michael asked.

Whitey slanted him a judging look before he spoke. "It's your fiancée, Michael."

"Trista?"

"Yes, sir. Seems her horse came back without her."

Michael felt as if he'd been kicked in the stomach. He had not wanted her to go out riding alone, but when she'd promised not to go too far from the house, he'd finally assented. Guilt swept over him at the thought that she might have been hurt in a freak accident, and he prayed fervently that she was all right. Without a word, Michael put his heels to his horse's sides and took off at a run back toward the house, leaving George and Whitey to follow.

George gave Whitey a worried look as they watched Michael ride off. "Were there any signs of trouble?"

"Sheba was limping. She might have just taken a tumble and unseated Miss Trista." Whitey tried to reassure his boss. "Why, Miss Trista's probably waitin' for us right now."

"I hope you're right. . . ." His troubled gaze met his foreman's.

"So do I, boss."

Without another word they put their heels to their horses' flanks and set out after Michael.

* * *

Time seemed suspended as the search party from the Royal Diamond combed the area north of the ranchhouse. With Michael and George in the lead, they managed to locate Trista's trail and track her as far as the creek. But once her path ventured onto the more rocky terrain, they lost it. The sun reached its pinnacle and then began to dip westward, signaling the lateness of the hour as they continued to seek some clue as to her whereabouts.

Eyes squinted against the brightness of the sun, Michael never paused in his efforts as he fanned out away from the group. Though he kept up a brave, unflagging front for the others, as the hours passed, he grew deeply worried. When they had first begun the search, his concern for Trista's well-being had been real, but his confidence in her riding abilities had led him to believe that they would find her close to the ranch, a bit shaken up by the experience. But now . . . now that they were trekking farther and farther out away from the house, that sense of security had been completely destroyed. As much as he didn't want to admit it, Michael was beginning to suspect that something terrible had happened to Trista. . . .

"Yo! Michael . . ." George's call echoed across the countryside.

Looking up, Michael caught sight of his father anxiously beckoning to him. Urging his weary mount forward, he hurried to where George stood, intently studying the dusty ground.

"Look here. . . ." George spoke solemnly as he knelt beside the maze of hoofprints. "Two horses . . . neither one of them shod . . . and footprints . . ."

"Footprints . . ." A cold grip of fear seized Michael, and his vitals lurched violently. Unshod horses could only mean one thing . . . Indians. He was out of the saddle, kneeling beside his father in a split second. As he stared at the moccasin imprint, he noted the mark of the fringe in the dust and knew immediately that the wearer had been Comanche. Michael groaned, "Dear God . . . no!"

"Now, don't go jumping to any conclusions." George tried to calm him. "There's nothing here to say that Trista was here."

Michael raised dark, tormented eyes to his father. "I'll circle about and see if there's anything else."

George nodded his agreement. They both took up their reins to lead their horses as they continued to search on foot. It was Michael this time who found the damning set of tracks that led to the scene of the abduction.

"Pa! Here . . ." His voice was strangled with emotion as he stared down at the sight of Trista's booted footprints.

George was some distance away and could not see exactly what it was Michael had found, but from the sound of his son's voice, he feared that he'd located Trista herself. He rushed to his side and was slightly relieved to discover that Michael had found only the tracks.

"She *was* here. . . ." Michael stated numbly as the last vestige of hope he'd clung to vanished. He frowned as he looked up. "I don't know. . . . He must have carried her off since there's only the one set of tracks leading back to where the horses were."

Silence hung heavily between them for a long moment.

"It's my fault, Pa. . . ." Michael choked. "I should never have agreed to her riding out alone. . . . I should have forced her to wait for me. . . ."

"Michael, I heard you and Trista talking this morning. She's a very persistent young woman when she sets her mind to something. She wanted to ride, and she did promise you she'd stay close." George could imagine what he was feeling and wanted to comfort him. He rested a warm hand upon his slumped shoulder.

"I know, but—"

"Trista's not dead, son. If the Comanche had wanted to kill her, he would have done it here. She's still alive, and we're going to find her and get her back."

"But God only knows how much of a head start they've got on us. . . ."

"All the more reason to get going. I'll call the men together, and we'll get on back to the ranch."

"I'll leave now . . . from here. . . ." he began, thinking to tear off after the bastard who'd captured the woman he loved.

"No," George was firm.

"But, Pa!"

"You want to find her, don't you? You been back East too damned long, boy," he growled, trying to talk common sense to his offspring. "You head out now, and you'll be on foot by tomorrow. Your horse needs rest, and you need supplies. We'll go back, gather what we need, and set out at first light tomorrow."

"That'll give them almost a full day on us," Michael argued hotly.

"I'm sorry, Michael." George's refusal was firm. "There's no other way."

Clasped tightly against the unyielding width of her captor's bare chest, her thighs and buttocks cupped by his unclad hard-muscled thighs, Trista bore the humiliating familiarity in silence, wondering all the while just how much longer they were going to ride.

The sun had set long before, and yet the warrior had shown no sign of stopping for the night. Despite the darkness of the hour, he'd continued to press, driving them ever onward across the miles of seemingly endless countryside.

Though every inch of her body ached from the abuse she'd suffered that day, Trista refused to make any protest. She had no intention of letting her Comanche captor know of her discomfort. If he could stand these hours of endless travel across wickedly rugged territory, then so could she. She had had a lot of time to think since they'd ridden away from the Royal Diamond, and she knew that the only thing that mattered was that she survive until Michael could come to her rescue.

Fearful uncertainty plagued her as she wondered what the future held. Captives were often traded to other tribes, and Trista worried that Michael wouldn't find her soon enough to save her from that fate. And if she wasn't traded, she knew she would have to be subservient to this half-dressed, wild brute. Even in her fright, the thought rankled. He was nothing but an animal . . . an uncivilized, dangerous savage. She fought to suppress a shiver as she remembered the feel of his body pressed so tightly to hers as he'd pinioned her to the ground during their struggle, and wished that she could wake up and find that this was all a nightmare.

All Trista wanted to do was to get away, and she longed for just one chance to relive the day. *If only she hadn't gone out on her own. . . . If only she hadn't gotten lost. . . . If only . . . if only. . . .* The words tormented her until she was ready to cry out in despair just to banish them from her mind. There was to be no quick release from either her guilt-ridden misery or her captivity, though, and as the miles and the hours passed, only exhaustion managed to dull her senses enough to ease the anxiety.

Lance was tired, and his injured arm, which he had treated quickly before they began their headlong flight across the hill country, was aching, but he knew the necessity of putting as many miles as he could between himself and the Royal Diamond. He had no doubt that a search party had been sent out as soon as the woman had been found to be missing, and he had every intention of being as far away as possible before their trail was discovered.

A smile that could only be described as cruel curved the grimness of his mouth as he imagined the chaos among the whites once they'd determined that she'd been taken captive by Indians. Wanting to reassure himself that he did indeed have her within his power, Lance tightened his grip on her, his arm banded about her waist bringing her back more fully against his chest. She resisted only slightly, keeping herself stiff against him. Lance was pleased that the fight seemed to have gone out of her. He considered removing the gag, but then decided against it. She was his now to do with as he pleased, and it pleased him to keep her silent. He didn't want to hear any more of her threats about what the Barretts were going to do to him when they caught up with him. There was nothing the Barretts could do to hurt him. Nothing.

Lance dragged his thoughts away from the woman and her relationship with the Barretts and back to the present. His pinto seemed to be holding up well even under the additional weight of his captive, and he gave silent thanks for the steed's hardiness. Had his mount had less endurance, they would have been forced to rest by now, and their risk of discovery would have been greater. As it was, the pinto's energy had held steady and its pace had not slowed during the grueling hours. Even the golden stallion seemed to be holding up under the strain, and though the wild one was definitely not docile, he had not protested Lance's lead too vigorously.

Lance considered the similarities between the horse and the woman, and smiled a smile of pure pleasure. He was going to greatly enjoy the taming and mounting of both. He knew both would fight his domination, but in the end he would prevail. A perverse satisfaction surged through him at the prospect of taking his half brother's woman. He would use her as it pleased him and then trade her away when he'd had his fill. Lance thought it quite lucky that she was pleasant on the eye, for she would bring a good price when he decided to get rid of her.

The moon had long ago begun its downward trek when Lance spotted the shadowy outline of a small grove of scrub oaks in the distance. Knowing that the pinto was straining, he quickly headed toward the shelter to seek some much-needed rest. Reining in, he quickly slipped to the ground and then reached up to clasp the woman by her waist and pull her off the horse. Even with her hands tied, Lance did not trust her not to try to escape.

Trista couldn't believe that they were finally stopping. She blinked in tired confusion at her surroundings as the warrior took her by her waist and helped her down from the horse. A part of her told her to fight his touch, and Trista did try to hold herself rigid as she slid along the hard, lean length of his body. Her legs felt lifeless as he set her upon her feet, and she could not prevent herself from leaning weakly against him for support.

Lance wasted no time wondering at her ploy. The last time she had pretended to be weak, she had stolen his knife from him, and he had no intention of falling for any such female trick again. Coldly, he pushed her away from him.

"Sit there," he ordered curtly, pointing toward a protected area beneath one tree before turning his back on her to see to the horses.

Trista staggered to the place he'd indicated and dropped to her knees on the ground. Just the thought of being able to lie down filled her with relief, and she was about to collapse upon the hard earth when the sound of his voice drew her attention. His words were indistinguishable but his tone had changed; it was soft now and crooning, as opposed to the brusque, emotionless tone he used with her. She glanced up and saw that he was approaching Fuego, his hand outstretched toward the wild stallion in a gesture of openness.

Trista wished the horse would attack him, so she could make a break for freedom, but as she watched him work his wiles on the untamed steed, she knew it would not happen. This brave evidently had a way with horses. His manner . . . the coaxing sound of his voice . . . the gentleness in the way he stroked the quivering, nervous stallion's neck . . . all showed that he knew exactly what he was doing.

She bitterly resented his expert handling of the horse. Many men had tried to capture Fuego, and yet this Comanche was the one who had succeeded. Trista glared at him across the distance, wondering at his abilities.

In the shadowy blackness of the night, she could not make out the ugliness of the vivid paint on his face, and it eased her reaction to him. She found without the shock value of the hideous red and black paint, she could appraise him as a man, not a murderous warrior. As the moonlight touched him, it sculpted his body in muscular hollows and curves, etching him forever in her mind as a silvered memory. He was tall and broad-shouldered. He wore a head-band ornamented with several eagle feathers, and his hair, she noticed now for the first time in puzzlement, was not in the usual shoulder-length braids she'd been given to understand Indians wore. Black as midnight, it was cropped bluntly short, skimming just at the nape of his neck.

His breechclout fit snugly about his trim waist, and Trista felt a flush stain her cheeks as she stared at that minimal garment. The memory of his body fitted so intimately to hers . . . his legs—so well muscled, long, and straight—entangled with hers, sent a surge of some unaccustomed emotion through her. She didn't know what it was. She only knew it made her feel ill-at-ease and very self-conscious. Trista was grateful that her confusion was hidden by the cover of darkness.

She lifted her gaze to his face and found it a study of angles and planes in the stark contrast of the moon's light. His nose was straight, his cheekbones high. She had already learned that his mouth, full and mobile as it was, could be a grim line of determination one minute or a threatening leer the next. His brows were dark, expressive slashes over his eyes. His eyes . . . they were his dominant feature, and again she wondered at their color. That he was part white was obvious, but whatever his relationship had been with the whites, Trista felt certain that he claimed no connection. He was a Comanche.

As she continued to watch him work with Fuego, soothing the beast's frazzled nerves, Trista recognized that he was a man who exuded power and control. He wasted no effort, his every movement orchestrated toward his goal of gentling the stallion to human

87

touch.

Identifying with the captive Fuego, Trista grew annoyed when the horse seemed to mellow a bit under the warrior's ministrations. Angrily, she swore to herself that she would never give up her struggle for freedom. She might bide her time and adapt herself to the circumstances of the moment, but she would never surrender herself completely to this man's domination.

Lance stroked the stallion's neck, all the while murmuring soothing words of assurance to him. He had feared that the golden one would balk at being so handled, and he was pleased by the horse's reaction. Many in the tribe had scoffed at his dream of capturing and taming him. They had claimed that a horse as wild and accustomed to freedom as this one would be beyond breaking, but Lance knew he was going to prove them all wrong. By the time they arrived back in camp two days from now, he would be riding the golden one.

Reverently, he touched the small pouch he wore tied to his waistband. Within its soft buckskin folds was the source of his power, the magic of his medicine . . . a nugget of gold. It had been during his first vision quest, before he'd become a full-fledged warrior, that it had been revealed to him that his future would be tied with gold. From the moment Lance had first seen the stallion, he'd known that the horse was destined to be his.

Running his hand over the horse's back one last time, he turned away from the golden one to see to his other captive. His gaze fell upon her then as she knelt beneath the protection of the trees, and he stopped, frozen in mid-stride. Caressed by the moonlight, she was a vision of ethereal blond beauty. An electrifying shock of recognition bolted through him as he stared at her, but he denied it. She was a white woman, and she was connected to the Barretts. She meant nothing to him. She was only his captive. He desired her as he would desire any woman. That she was as golden as the stallion meant nothing.

Irritated by his thoughts, he snatched up his blanket and the few supplies he carried with him. He noticed that her eyes widened in fear as he drew near and for some inexplicable reason, he found that that disturbed him. Without a word, he dropped to the ground beside her.

Trista shivered at his nearness. When he moved behind her she held her breath in frightened expectation, but drew a deep sigh of relief when he united the gag.

"Thank you," she managed to croak through parched lips.

"If you do not hold your tongue, I will use it again," he threatened.

"I'll be quiet," Trista hastened to reassure him, not wanting to suffer the misery anymore, and he only grunted in reply as he moved to sit beside her.

"Eat," Lance directed, handing her a small piece of dried meat.

Having never partaken of such before, Trista almost refused the unsavory-looking fare, but the gnawing pangs of hunger in her stomach convinced her to take whatever was offered. She chewed the tough meat in silence, all the while warily watching the warrior's every move out of the corner of her eye.

"What is your name?" Lance finally asked as he finished his own piece of meat.

"I'm Trista . . . Trista Sinclair," she told him hesitantly.

Lance nodded, thinking it a most unusual, yet attractive name. "You will call me Lance."

Trista turned to look at him then . . . at the fierceness of his painted features and the corded muscles that rippled beneath his bronzed skin. Lance seemed a far too civilized name for him.

"Lance," she began, "when will you let me go?"

"I have already told you. You belong to me now, just as the stallion does."

"I'm not a piece of horseflesh! You can't own me! I'm a person with feelings and thoughts of my own!" Trista was stung by his casual assumption of ownership of her.

Lance's gaze hardened as he regarded her. Though he knew she was right, his determination to keep her captive didn't waver. By taking her, he'd struck a long-delayed blow against the Barretts, and it gave him a great sense of power.

"You will not find it so bad being my captive," Lance told her slowly as he reached out to cup her cheek.

Trista went still at his touch. His unexpected gentleness left her unnerved and bewildered.

"You are mine, Trista Sinclair." He traced his hand down her cheek to her throat, where he felt her pulse pounding madly. "Your body knows it even as your mind denies it."

"No! That's ridiculous!" She shivered violently at his words.

Lance slipped his hand lower to caress the softness of her bared shoulder. "Is it?" His tone was low and insinuating as he felt her tremble.

Trista tried to jerk away from the scorching heat of his touch. "Michael's the only man I'll ever belong to."

At the mention of his half brother, Lance tightened his grip upon her shoulder for the briefest of instants before letting his hand drop away. With a casualness he was far from feeling, he took up his buffalo paunch of water. He drank deeply before holding it out to her.

"Drink."

Trista eyed him and the paunch skeptically. The fact that he hadn't pressed her left her confused. She had been prepared to fight him tooth and nail to save herself, and his sudden indifference left her off balance. *Did he have some more terrible torture in mind for her? Surely there could be nothing more terrible than suffering his touch. But since she was completely under his power, why hadn't he taken her, even against her will?*

"Drink now," Lance ordered brusquely, "or you'll get no more until morning."

Resentfully, she snatched it from his hand and drank her fill as Lance stretched out beside her and wrapped the blanket about him.

"Come here." He lifted an edge of the blanket to accommodate her.

"No . . . I . . . ." she protested, not wanting to be anywhere near him.

"I said come here, Trista," he commanded.

Again she balked. Exhausted from the ordeal of the day, his patience wearing thin, Lance sat back up and grabbed her by her bound wrists. With one forceful tug, he pulled her sprawling against him.

"You would do well to learn to do as I say the first time, woman," he growled in her ear as he turned her to her side and fitted her against the curve of his body.

Trista tried to move away from him, but he slipped an arm about her waist.

"Be still. There is little enough time to rest."

She swallowed nervously as he drew her close. The firm masculine length of him seemed to burn against her back, and she quaked at the intimacy of their position. Trista meant to stay awake. She meant to stay on guard against his overpowering nearness, to show him that she would not be pliant to his will. Just because he'd told her to rest didn't mean she'd do it. But somehow the exhaustion of the day won out. Despite all her intentions to resist, she slept, nestled there in the protective warmth of his embrace.

Chapter Six

Michael reined in at the crest of the hill and tilted his hat back on his head. Wiping a forearm across his sweat-beaded brow, he said bitterly, "Nothing, Pa . . . there's not a sign of them."

"There's still a couple of more hours before sundown." George tried to reassure him.

"It's almost like they disappeared into thin air!" he returned in frustration.

"Stay in control, Michael," his father advised, for he sensed his son's growing desperation.

Michael swung around in the saddle to look at him. "It's a little hard to stay cool and calm when all I can think about is Trista in the hands of some bloodthirsty savage!"

"And that is exactly why you have to keep a tight rein on your emotions. We're going to find her, and when we do, she's going to need you to be strong."

"When we find her?! Don't you mean 'if?'" he shot back harshly.

"Michael! I don't ever want to hear you say anything like that again. She's still alive, and that's all that matters," George declared with a firm conviction he little felt. Though his dealings with Lone Elk all those years ago had not been violent, he knew full well just how brutal the Comanche could be when it suited their purposes.

"How can you be so sure that she's still alive? She's

been a captive and at his mercy for over a day now. . . ." He shuddered at the thought of what might have happened to her during the previous night. Trista was such a lovely, gentle woman. . . . She didn't deserve this horror.

"Believe me, son, I know the Comanche. If this warrior had wanted her dead, he wouldn't have bothered to take her along with him. He would have killed her long ago."

Michael fell silent, his thoughts solely on the woman he loved. Trista was out there somewhere, and she needed him; yet he was stymied in his effort to help her. He felt impotent and useless, and he cursed himself again for not having stopped her from riding out alone that morning.

"Michael . . ."

The sound of his father's voice penetrated his self-incriminating thoughts, and he glanced over at him questioningly.

"Let's check out the area north of here. It's rugged, but not impassable."

Michael was willing to try anything if there was a chance that it would lead him to Trista. "Whatever you say."

The others in their group were searching to the west, and George signaled them to expand their hunt in a northerly direction as he and Michael rode out to lead the way.

Trista had always known that she could be stubborn when the occasion called for it, but she'd never suspected that her sheer grit could get her through a day like the one she'd just experienced. Lance had awakened her abruptly an hour before dawn, and she had been embarrassed to discover that she'd fallen asleep so easily while lying in his arms. Despite the fact she'd been exhausted and desperately in need of rest the night before, Trista had not been able to forgive herself the weakness. Though Lance's closed expression had revealed nothing of his true thoughts, she'd sensed he'd somehow been amused by it all. Humiliated and angry, she had silently vowed to herself to sit up all night if need be, rather than surrender to his wishes again.

Still stiff and sore from the previous day's exertions, Trista had moved slowly when Lance had curtly ordered her to mount the pinto. Seated once more on its sturdy back, she'd waited for him to join her, watching as he'd skillfully erased all signs of their presence at the campsite. When Lance had finally swung up behind her and encircled her waist with a restraining arm to resume their positions of the previous day, Trista had held herself stiffly away from him again. Lance had put his heels to his mount and had urged it to action, the pinto's sudden movement forcing her back against the hardness of his broad chest.

"Stay," he'd commanded when she'd tried to push away, and he'd tightened his hold on her. "Haven't you learned your lesson yet?"

There had been no mistaking the mockery in his tone, and despite her fury, she'd been forced to ride resting fully against him.

As often as she could, Trista had glanced back in the direction from which they'd come, hoping to see some sign that Michael was coming after her. To her dismay there had been none — no pounding of distant horses' hooves, no dust rising in telltale betrayal on the horizon. Forced to endure the long, arduous hours on horseback without hope of imminent rescue, her spirits had fallen, and she'd wondered at the need to push themselves to such limits since there was obviously no one even close on their trail.

As the day had progressed they had not spoken to each other beyond the few words that were necessary. Trista had longed to try to convince Lance of the mistake he was making in keeping her with him, but his continuing silence had made him seem so unapproachable and forbidding that she'd wisely kept quiet, not wanting to risk being gagged again. It was bad enough that he still kept her wrists bound. She certainly didn't want to suffer the other indignity again.

They had stopped to rest only twice during the long, grueling hours of their trek. They'd taken the time for a cooling drink and a small piece of dried meat near mid-morning when they'd come upon a small, clear-running creek. Later in the afternoon they'd paused in the shady shelter of a massive boulder formation, but had not eaten.

Though she'd been ravenous, Trista had been too proud to reveal her need to her captor. If he wasn't going to eat, then neither would she! She had suffered in silence. Yet when they'd mounted up again to continue on, instead of feeling pleased with herself for not having wilted under the stress, all she'd felt was gnawing hunger.

Trista was beyond exhaustion as the late afternoon blended into dusk, and as the sun dipped low in the western sky, she wondered just how much more she could take.

Lance guided the pinto up a steep hillside and then paused at its crest to look back over the territory they'd just covered. In the fading light of sunset, his blue-eyed gaze combed the horizon for any sign of trouble. When he was satisfied that there was no one close behind them, he kneed the pinto on down the incline.

It pleased him to know that he'd managed to elude the search party he was certain was following them. But even as confident as he was, Lance was no fool. The horses were in need of rest, and so he decided to make camp early tonight. He knew of a small, secluded pool located nearby, and he headed his mount in that direction.

The last rays of the setting sun bathed the sky in streaks of cranberry and gold as Lance drew the pinto to a halt at the water's edge. Ignoring Trista, who was slumped wearily on the horse's back, he took up the stallion's lead rope and jumped lightly to the ground. Lance led the rogue to the bank and set about tying its lead rope to a low-hanging tree branch so it could drink its fill.

It dawned on Trista that for the first time she found herself in a situation where escape was possible. She felt her weariness disappear as a surge of energy tingled through her. Since Lance had negligently dropped the reins to the pinto, all she had to do was grab them up and ride off. Trista tensed, watching Lance's every move out of the corner of her eye. The moment he turned his back completely on her, she snatched at the fallen reins and dug her knees and heels into the pinto's sides. As tired as the pony was, it still responded to her command. Trista tugged at the reins, wheeling the steed about, and leaned low over its neck in an effort to urge it quickly through the maze of bushes and trees that surrounded the pool.

Lance heard the pinto moving and turned from his task to see what was happening. He watched in stunned disbelief as Trista yanked on the reins and spurred the horse to action. Fury consumed him, and he responded as a warrior to the threat of someone

97

stealing his mount. At a dead run, he gave chase and then vaulted onto the pinto's back just as Trista would have made her break to freedom.

There was no mercy in Lance's grip as he wrapped an unyielding arm about her waist and hauled her viciously against him. Her breath was knocked from her by the power of his steely grasp, yet she continued to fight to be free of him. Violently, he jerked the reins from her hands.

"You little fool!" he snarled, struggling to control both her and the horse.

Never before had Lance ever encountered such a stubborn, exasperating woman. Comanche women knew their place and stayed in it, but Trista was completely different. She challenged him at every turn. He tightened his grip on her even more in his frustration.

"Let me go!" she gasped as his fingers bit into the tender flesh of her bruised side.

Lance sawed on the reins trying to still the shying horse as Trista struggled against him. As she continued to fight against him, the pinto danced nervously about. Lance realized that there would be no controlling the horse while both of them were on his back, and so pulled Trista from in front of him in hopes of sliding her to the ground.

Trista, however, misread his intentions. She was certain that he was so angry that he meant to throw her to the ground to be trampled beneath the horse's hooves. She clung to him for dear life at the thought, and her tenacious hold only succeeded in throwing him off balance. Her arms locked around his neck, Trista fell, and as she tumbled to the ground, she drew him with her. They sprawled awkwardly in the dust, Lance landing heavily atop her.

Realizing the precariousness of their position,

Lance reacted instinctively, quickly shielding Trista's prone body with his own to protect her from the thrashing hooves. The danger lasted only an instant, but the shock waves of sensual awareness that came with that moment of peril branded them forever.

Lance lay intimately upon Trista, chest to breast, hip to hip, thigh to thigh. The heat of desire welled up within him at the feel of her soft, unresisting body beneath his, and he felt his loins tighten in expectation. Angrily Lance recognized his growing desire for her. When she'd fallen asleep in his arms the night before, he had been tempted to take her then, but had decided against it. There had been little time, and rest had been more important. Yet rest had not come as he had lain awake all night obsessed with the thought of burying himself deeply within her and claiming her — Michael's woman — as his own.

Vaguely he became aware that the pinto had quieted, but it didn't seem to matter anymore as he levered himself up on his elbows to stare down at Trista. Her braided hair had come loose and was spread out in a golden tangle about her in the dust. Streaks of dirt marred the loveliness of her pale features, and the rip in her blouse that before had bared just a smooth ivory shoulder and the hint of a breast now had torn further. There, completely exposed to his probing gaze, was the sweetness of one firm breast. His breath seemed to catch in his throat at the sight of that tender orb. Since he'd seen her at the ranchhouse he had wondered at her hidden beauty, and a fire of need consumed him as he imagined what it would be like to caress that delicate pink-crested flesh with his hands and lips.

Lance glanced up to find her blue eyes upon him, their expression troubled as if she sensed his turmoil and worried at it. His desire to touch her, though, pushed him past any conscious caring, and he lowered his head to press a heated kiss to the succulent fullness.

Trista had been watching Lance nervously as he'd risen above her. His blue eyes were glinting strangely with some emotion she was at a loss to define, and when he lowered his head toward her, she stiffened, not quite sure what to expect. The intimate touch of his lips upon her naked skin startled her, and she bucked wildly beneath him, wanting to dislodge him from her. But Lance seemed to take no notice of her movements as he continued to plunder the softness of her breast with his lips and tongue.

Trista had never felt anything like it before. While on one hand she fought to be free of his disturbing touch, still a curling thrill of excitement tightened in her most secret places. A low moan escaped her as he caught the taut peak in his teeth and nipped at it gently. Shudders of unbidden desire ravaged her as he laved the sensitive point with the moist warmth of his tongue before drawing it within his mouth to suckle. The rhythmic draw of his mouth sent her passions spiraling out of control. Never had she felt such ecstasy! Never had she known such bliss!

Her conscience cried out to her—*Think of Michael! This Lance is a savage!* She tried to picture Michael in her mind, but her body was responding to Lance's masterful touch, striking all logical thought from her.

When he loosened her bonds and freed her hands, she had no desire to fight him; instead she welcomed him. Trista found that she was moving restlessly against him now, seeking rather than evading, and she gloried in the lean hardness of his big male body. He was so different from her, and yet at the moment she was not frightened by that difference. If anything, she was intrigued by it. Of their own volition, her hands

100

began to move over him, caressing his broad shoulders and exploring the rock-hard muscular ridges of his arms.

Lance lifted his head, and his blue eyes glittered in excitement as he gazed down into her passion-flushed face. He bent to claim her moist, parted lips.

The kiss was explosively erotic as Trista found herself caught up in the spell of his sensuality. Her mouth opened to his possession, and though she reacted timidly at first to the bold thrust of his tongue, eventually she met him in that most intimate exchange.

Lance savored the honey-sweet taste of her, and as the kiss continued, he cupped her breast to tease the peak with a knowing touch. Pressing his hips more tightly to the cradle of hers, he let her know of his desire for her. Trista gasped at the sensation and innocently surged upward against him in natural invitation.

In the throes of passion, Lance was trying to ignore the persistent, annoying sound that was treading the edges of his consciousness. Caught up in the excitement of Trista's heated response, it was long moments before the reality of the warning finally penetrated his thoughts. Recognition dawned. He stilled all motion, abruptly ending the kiss, and as slowly as possible he raised his head to glance about them.

"Lance?" Trista, completely at a loss as to why he had stopped kissing her, reached up to him to draw him back down.

"Don't move!" he ordered viciously through gritted teeth.

At his cold, imperious tone, reality returned with a vengeance, and she was filled with shame. She had been reaching out to him, wanting more of his kisses and caresses. Why, Trista realized in horror, she had

101

almost made love to this . . . this Comanche! Angrily, she began to squirm, trying to get away from the now oppressive weight of his body on hers.

Lance realized too late that he'd been stupid to expect that she would obey him. Knowing that there was no point in trying to subdue her, he wasted no time in making his move, for the danger was very real. In one smooth effort, he drew his knife, and then, rising up to his knees, he sent it slicing through the air. His expert accuracy was reaffirmed as the blade sank deeply into the body of the coiled, ready-to-strike rattler, killing it instantly.

Trista had seen Lance go for his knife and had frozen in terror, expecting the worst. When he'd shifted position to throw it, she'd quickly scrambled completely free of him, wondering at his actions. She'd caught sight of the snake then, and a shudder of fear quaked through her. It had been so close, and it could have struck them both. Trista knew little about snakes, but she'd heard talk of rattlers and how big and dangerous they were. Gauging from this one's size, she had no doubt that this was one of them.

Dragging her gaze away from the sight of the bloody carcass, Trista looked to Lance and thought again of what a savage he was. His expression was fierce in concentration, the paint he still wore emphasizing the basic wildness of his nature. His corded muscles were taut beneath the sheen of sweat that glistened on his deeply tanned chest and shoulders. She realized that there was nothing even remotely civilized about him.

The thought of his untamed ways made Trista wonder how she could ever have considered allowing him to touch her. She had never even allowed Michael the liberties that Lance had taken, and she loved Michael! It was with a definite feeling of guilt that she admitted to herself that she had responded physically to Lance's touch. Disgust at her own actions chilled her, and she glanced at him once more, her expression clearly revealing her emotional turmoil.

The tension ebbed from Lance as he stared triumphantly at the unmoving snake. Shaking himself mentally, Lance brought his focus back to Trista, who had escaped his embrace. She was now crouched several feet away from him, clutching the remnants of her blouse over her one exposed breast and watching him warily. His gaze turned stony as he looked from her distrustful expression to the breast she was so desperately trying to cover and then back up again. He understood in frustration that, though his body was still demanding fulfillment, the moment of passion between them had been lost. Any attempt to recapture that blatantly sensual encounter would be useless, and he was definitely in no mood for another fight. He got slowly to his feet.

"Do not think that you can escape me, Trista. I have already told you that you are mine," Lance stated arrogantly.

Determined to put her in her place and keep her there, he picked up the leather thong and moved to tie her hands again. As she tried to keep her breast covered from his view, he mercilessly pulled her hand away. His gaze went coldly over her bared flesh as he held her bound wrists in one of his own powerful hands. Trista flushed in embarrassment at his bold appraisal. She lifted her eyes to his but could read no emotion in their icy blue depths. Without another word, Lance rose. Ignoring her completely, he turned his back on her and went off to retrieve the skittish pinto.

Trista found herself both relieved and annoyed at being so summarily dismissed, and she pondered that feeling of irritation as she watched him stalk his mount and recapture it with little difficulty. She knew she should have been completely ecstatic that he hadn't taken her and that her virtue was still intact for Michael. Certainly, considering Lance's strength, it would have been no problem for him to overpower her and take what he wanted. She had been prepared to fight him, and he hadn't given her the satisfaction. Why should it bother her that he'd left her alone?

Feeling quite defeated, she got slowly to her feet and made her way down to the pool's edge. Cupping her hands, she dipped them into the water and drank thirstily of the refreshing liquid. As the cool drink eased her parched throat, Trista gazed out across the night-shadowed waters and drew a measure of serenity from the quiet dusk. She tried to push all memories of what had just happened with Lance from her mind and make Michael the center of her thoughts. Michael would be coming for her soon. Everything would be fine once he'd rescued her. Only the gnawing doubt that hovered in the back of her mind concerning how she would react should Lance approach her again disturbed her inner peace. Though she attempted to deny it, it remained . . . a faint, disturbing threat from which there was no escape.

"We're camping here for the night."

The sound of his voice so close behind her surprised Trista, and she wondered how he could have moved so quietly that she had not heard him coming.

"All right," was her only answer. She refused to face him, expecting him to say more. When no further conversation ensued, she gave up and turned toward him only to find, to her strange disappointment, that he'd already walked away.

* * *

Michael's mood was solemn as he sat alone before

the crackling campfire. Though they had finally managed to pick up Trista's trail, it had been too late in the day to make any real progress toward finding her. The Indian now had over a full day's lead on them.

Michael was seriously beginning to doubt that he would ever see Trista again. He knew what happened to captive white women, and most of it wasn't pretty. His grip tightened on the tin coffee cup he was holding, and his jaw set in anger. *Why Trista?* he raged inwardly. His life had been almost perfect, and now all his hopes and dreams had been shattered.

"Michael . . ."

He stiffened as his father's call interrupted his thoughts. "Yeah, Pa?"

"You know we're riding out at first light. Don't you think it's time you turned in?" George was well aware of the direction of his son's thoughts, but he also knew that there was no point in dwelling on the terrible reality of what had happened. All they could do was to keep up the search and pray that they weren't too late when they finally caught up.

Michael didn't respond verbally. He only cast aside the cold dregs of coffee and stood up to make his way to his bedroll. Michael doubted that he would get any sleep that night, but he knew it couldn't hurt to at least attempt to rest. Tensely, thoughts of Trista still haunting him, he stretched out in his bedroll. With all his heart, he hoped she was alive and well somewhere out there in the wilds, staring at the same star-dusted sky he was. As he restlessly turned to his side and closed his eyes against the fading flames of the fire, he willed morning to hurry so he could be up and on his way to find her once again.

Chapter Seven

His arms folded across his massive chest, Lance stood apart from the campsite, staring out across the moonswept countryside. It was late, and yet, even as tired as he was, he hesitated at the thought of bedding down with Trista. Trying to sleep the night before with her resting in his arms had been torturous enough. Tonight, he knew, would be far worse. The powerful explosion of desire that had erupted between them had caught him totally unawares.

Lance found he was cautious of the potency of this attraction he was feeling for Trista. He did not want to harbor any warmer feelings for her. She was his captive, taken in vengeance and hatred. That was all.

Lance turned his gaze toward the place where Trista awaited him. The thought of her wrapped in his blanket, anticipating his return, sent a flash fire of excitement through him. Why should he deny himself? He would have her this night. She was his. He would use her as all Comanche warriors used their captives. There would be no more to it than that. As he headed back, he was almost regretting that she wouldn't be willing, and then grew annoyed with himself for even caring what her feelings were.

The moon passed slowly behind the shadow of a night cloud, and the sudden darkness that covered the land hid much. As Lance approached the campsite, he was confident that Trista would be there. Surprise, then shock, and finally anger gripped him as the moon slipped from behind the cloud and cast its unforgiving brilliance on the scene, revealing clearly that Trista was not there.

Blood lust filled Lance as he looked around. Never before had a woman dared so much with him! Yet even as his fury raged within him, worry intruded. It struck him as odd that there was nothing missing from the camp. Trista hadn't taken the blanket or any food or water. So unprepared, he knew that she wouldn't be able to survive long, alone and unarmed in the wilds.

Lance was about to begin to search when he noticed for the first time that her boots were lying on the bank of the pond along with what looked to be her riding skirt and blouse. Cautiously he moved nearer, and the sight that greeted him left him stunned to immobility. Trista had not run away. . . . She was there, gloriously unclad, her arms untied, bathing in the pool.

Mesmerized by the sight of her standing at the center of the pond with the moonstruck water swirling gently about her slender hips, Lance remained motionless as he watched her. Trista seemed a goddess of the night—innocent, yet sensual. Caressed by the silvery light, her ivory flesh glowed like the finest porcelain. Though her back was to him as she bathed, Lance found this view of her most enticing. The glorious tumble of her now-unbraided golden hair, the inviting curve of her tiny waist, and the gentle swell of her hips all seemed to beckon to him.

For a moment Lance hesitated. A part of himself that he'd long denied argued that Trista had been right the night before when she'd proclaimed that she could not be owned. Logically, he knew that he had no right to take her, and yet, even as he realized he shouldn't, he couldn't deny himself. His desire to possess her body was as overpowering as his desire for revenge. All other thoughts fled. He would make her his.

Like a man possessed, Lance quickly divested himself of his weapons and breechclout. Without making a sound, he moved out into the pond. Silently, he slipped beneath the water and swam smoothly in her direction.

Trista had tried her best to rest after Lance had stalked away from their campsite some time before, but sleep had proven elusive. As tired as she was, the guilt she felt over her earlier encounter with him and the thought that he was going to return and share the same blanket with her again had left her nerves on edge. After tossing restlessly for what seemed like hours, she had finally given up the effort. It was then that she'd started to think of how wonderful it would feel to scrub away the trail dust and, hopefully, the memory of Lance's arousing touch. Trista had known that Lance might return at any time, so she'd had to hurry. It had been difficult, but using her teeth, she'd managed to untie the thong that bound her wrists. She'd quickly stripped off her clothes and boots then and had waded out into the pond to begin her ablutions. Trista planned to be back, dressed and wrapped in the blanket, before Lance reappeared.

Trista lifted cupped hands filled with water and delighted in the sweet caress of the soothing liquid as it spilled down her body. She longed to linger in the small pool but knew time was of the essence. Nervously glancing over her shoulder back toward the campsite, she was greatly relieved to see that Lance had not yet returned. Trista submerged herself one last time and then stood up to make her way back to the bank.

Lance's powerful strokes brought him quickly to her side. Trista felt the unexplained current in the water and knew an instant of soul-chilling fear as she tried to imagine what kind of creature could be in the pool with her. With the run-in with the rattlesnake still fresh in her mind, her imagination ran wild. She tried to hurry, to flee to the bank and safety, but the water slowed her, dragging at her legs and holding her back.

Lance surfaced directly behind her. As she attempted to run, Trista heard something break the surface near her, and she struggled even harder to reach the side. Lance saw how desperate she was to get away and immediately assumed that she had seen him and was running away from him. Angered by her actions, he grabbed her roughly by the arm and hauled her backward.

Trista had no time to react as his hand closed painfully around her upper arm and jerked her backward. As she lost her footing on the slippery bottom of the pool and started to fall, she caught sight of Lance, and what had been terror in her heart was replaced by relief. There was no horrible monster in the water with her, only Lance.

Lance responded instinctively, as she lurched unsteadily in the water and moved quickly to scoop her up into his arms. Turning her in his arms, he brought her against him, and when Trista's pale, wet nakedness made sudden, intimate contact with Lance's hard, sun-bronzed male frame, all time seemed suspended. The moment was tension-filled as their gazes met and locked.

Trista was stunned by the sudden turn of events. Her relief at discovering that it was Lance in the pool with her momentarily sapped her will to fight him.

She felt strangely disassociated as she stared up at him in the moon-kissed darkness, studying the hard planes and angles of his paint-streaked face. His underwater swim had erased some of his black and vermillion camouflage, but Trista suddenly longed to see what Lance really looked like beneath his ferocious disguise.

Almost without conscious thought, she lifted her hands to slowly wash away all traces of the paint he wore. The action was innocent, but the intimacy of her gentle, yet cleansing caresses somehow heightened the already sensually charged encounter.

As she wiped the last vestige of color from his face, her expression grew rapt. Her breath seemed to catch in her throat at the sight of Lance without the hideous mask of paint marring his features. For the first time Trista saw Lance as a man. As the water had washed away the harsh color, it had also washed away much of her fear. No longer the barbarous savage, he somehow seemed almost familiar to her, and she marveled at the handsomeness of his features.

Lance had remained perfectly still as Trista had cleansed him of his warrior's markings. He had intended to wear the paint until he had returned to the village as a symbol of his struggle and conquest over the golden one, but now, suddenly, it didn't matter anymore. All that mattered was the naked woman who stood before him in seeming surrender.

Trista looked ethereally beautiful in the moonlight's loving caress. The silvery light touched upon her every feminine curve, emphasizing the glorious beauty of her rounded breasts and the shapeliness of her slender waist. Droplets of water glistened upon her body, and he knew a sudden, burning desire to kiss the pearling liquid from the sweet-satiny texture of her skin. Her pale hair, unbraided now, hung down her back in a cascade of wet gold, and Lance lifted one strong hand to the back of her neck to tangle in its silken thickness. Exerting a gentle pressure, he drew her head slightly back so he could see her more clearly. Trista arched toward him to accommodate his urging, and in doing so her breasts thrust against his chest. The contract was electrifying to the both of them.

There in the secret quiet of the night they stood. The warm waters of the pool lapped gently about their hips, and the evening's cooling breeze drifted delicately about them, but they took no notice, for they were caught up in the splendor of the moment.

Trista was vaguely aware of the danger of their position, but she was helpless to summon the strength to move away from Lance. She was entrapped by a web of her own making. Captivated, she stared up at him transfixed.

Lance, too, was spellbound. Slowly he lowered his head, until he could capture her lips in a sweet-soft exploration. His mouth moved gently . . . enticingly over hers. Trista remained unmoving in the circle of his arms, wondering at the rapturous feelings that were soaring through her. Their earlier torrid embrace had not prepared her for this . . . this subtle, tender seduction.

Faintly, Trista knew she should struggle to be free. She was Michael's fiancée and planned to marry him soon! Yet all thoughts of Michael fled before the persuasive pressure of Lance's mouth. Her eyes fluttered closed as he deepened the kiss, parting her lips and delving within to taste of her exquisite sweetness. A myriad of wild new emotions coursed through her as their tongues met and dueled in love's age-old erotic dance.

Crushed to his chest, her breasts tautened in aware-

111

ness. Trista's breathing grew strained as Lance lifted his free hand to fondle that burgeoning flesh. A whimper of arousal sounded deep in her throat, and it was all the encouragement he needed. Breaking off the kiss, he lifted her slight weight higher to seek the fullness of her bosom with his lips.

The ecstasy of his mouth upon her flesh lit a fire of passion in her veins, and she caught at his shoulders to support herself. So braced, she threw her head back in ecstasy as he plundered her breasts with heated kisses. Her unrestrained response to his caresses urged Lance on, and he lowered her in his arms so his mouth could meet hers again.

This time when their lips met, there was nothing gentle about it. They embraced hungrily, each seeking more from the other. Trista's legs intertwined with his as she slid down the length of his body. The power of his arousal pressed against her with heated urgency, and the foreigness of that part of him, so different from her own supple, yielding flesh, frightened her a little. She tried to pull away, but Lance understood her hesitation and murmured his reassurance.

"Don't be afraid, my golden beauty."

It wasn't so much his words as his tone that soothed Trista's fears. As Lance stroked her back with long, rhythmic caresses, gentling her and easing the tension from her, she succumbed to his expertise. They kissed again in passionate abandon, and when he shifted her weight to lift her into his arms, she did not protest. Willingly, she locked her arms about his neck and lay her head upon his shoulder as he started back across the pool.

Trista was aware of nothing except Lance's nearness as he carried her up the bank to their campsite. Cradled against his chest, she gloried in his warm embrace. As he knelt beside the blanket to lay her upon its welcoming softness, Trista kept her arms looped firmly about his neck, bringing him down with her. A fire of desire was burning deep within the womanly heart of her, and instinctively she knew she needed the answering fulfillment only he would be able to give.

Lance's long, lean body fit perfectly to hers as he lay full-length on top of her, and Trista knew an overwhelming sense of rightness at being with him. When he bent to kiss her once more, she eagerly responded. There could be no denying that she wanted him, for his every touch set her senses reeling.

Her hands restlessly explored the broad expanse of his back, holding him near as she met him in kiss after passionate kiss. Their hunger for each other grew with each caress. As Lance trailed burning kisses down the arch of her throat to the throbbing peaks of her breasts, Trista began to move beneath him in primitive, sensual invitation. There seemed to be a vast emptiness consuming her and filling her with a yearning for completeness she didn't understand.

His hand found her then, probing her tender womanflesh, and she bucked wildly trying to escape him.

"Easy, my golden love." His voice was hoarse with excitement as he continued to caress her. "Easy . . ."

Trista willed herself to relax as he lowered his head to the sweetness of her bosom once more, but the tug of his mouth at her breast coupled with the erotic massage of his hand teased her to a peak of excitement she'd never known existed. The fire within her loins grew to unbearable proportions, and Trista knew a moment of fear as her arousal soared unchecked.

"Lance . . ." She cried his name out loud as the pulsing ecstasy of passion's peak threatened to take her to the mystery of love's pinnacle and beyond.

With the masterful touch of a man well schooled in love's ways, he caressed her to the heights of pleasure, initiating her to the power of ultimate delight. Trista stiffened as the unfamiliar waves of rapture swept through her, and when they had passed, she lay mindless and quivering in his arms. Lance shifted his weight to raise up above her and press a soft, almost cherishing kiss upon her parted lips.

Trista lifted a wide-eyed, questioning gaze to Lance. "I didn't know. . . ."

"You still don't love. There is more, much more. . . ." His voice was husky with desire as once again he began to touch her in her most sensitive places.

Trista was completely astonished to find that her body was responding. "There's more?" Her breathing quickened as he nudged her legs more widely apart and then settled fully between the soft valley of her thighs. She could feel his alien hardness trapped against her, and she stiffened.

"It is time to love you, Trista. To make you mine in the fullest sense of the word," he was saying as his hands traced paths of magical, sparkling arousal over her.

Something in the back of her mind balked at his statement, and she wanted to protest, but his mouth closed over hers, preventing her from speaking. His lips and tongue coaxed her to forgetfulness, and she found herself lost to all but the glorious sensations that only he could create in her.

Lance's restraint was but a slender thread, and when she returned his kisses with ardent abandon, he was lost. There was no thought of stopping as he lifted her hips to fit more tightly to him. All he could think of was the joy of being buried deep within her velvet heat. He had conquered her resistance. He had given her pleasure, and now it was time to take his own.

Slipping a hand between them, he sought and found her welcoming wetness. This time she did not protest his caress, but arched up to his touch, hungrily seeking the release he offered. So encouraged, Lance positioned himself at the portals of her womanhood and slid deep within her, breeching the slight barrier of her innocence and mounting her fully.

Trista gasped at the unexpected pain, and tears stung her eyes. Reality crashed through the sensual haze he'd created with his lovemaking, and waves of agony and shame washed through her. Thoughts of Michael entered her mind, and she bit down on her lip to keep from crying out.

His eyes closed as he savored the joining, Lance held himself still once he'd entered her, giving her time to adjust to his possession. The ecstasy of being held, sheathed by her heated sweetness, drove him to move, though, and he began his rhythm . . . giving then taking . . . giving then taking . . . until he felt her begin to respond.

Trista had not wanted to feel the excitement building within her again, but the hard-driving press of his hips created a new fire of need. It was different, yet the same as what she'd experienced before, and though she hated herself for wanting him, she could not stop. His mouth claimed hers in a deep, hungry kiss, and all thoughts of right or wrong were forgotten. There was only Lance, and the starburst of feeling that was overpowering her.

The explosion of her desire shocked her. More powerful than the pleasure he had given her before, she crested in a surge of heart-stopping rapture, her body taut as a bowstring as he rode her, playing upon her senses and driving her to the heights even as he sought his own end. The knowledge that she was so

115

wildly responsive to him severed Lance's control, and his own passion peaked in hot, shuddering excitement. Sated, he collapsed heavily upon her. Neither moved or spoke as they lay together in silence.

Lance's thoughts were confused when he finally rolled away from her. He had never experienced such pure joy in joining with a woman before, and the discovery troubled him. He had known that he wanted her physically, but he had never expected to find such rapture in her embrace. It angered him that he felt strangely threatened by what he had just experienced, but at the same time, he was pleased. He had taken his half brother's woman and made her his own. It was what he had set out to do, and he had done it. Lance knew a particular moment of pleasure in thinking of her response. This had not been rape. Trista had eagerly sought his touch. He *had* made her his. There was victory and a certain smug self-satisfaction in his eyes as he got to his feet and gazed down at her.

Weak with contentment, Trista lay with her eyes closed, overwhelmed by the pure sensuality of their lovemaking. Never, not even in her wildest dreams, had she ever imagined that any man's touch could bring so much pleasure. Caught up in the newness of what had just happened to her, she lay quietly, savoring the memory of Lance's every kiss and touch.

Only when Lance rolled away from her did she open her eyes to look up at him. It was then, seeing the terrible, degrading look of triumph in his expression, that the starkness of her situation hit her full force. She was filled with sudden, almost violent self-loathing. How could she have given herself to him? How could she have been so weak? Chills of disgust trembled through her, and a tear of remorse trailed forlornly down her cheek. Quickly, she moved to cover herself with her hands.

"I hate you!" she swore, tormented by her own weakness and her betrayal of Michael.

"It matters little to me what you think or feel, my golden captive." Lance's expression didn't change as he knelt down beside her and brushed her hands away from their feeble attempt to hide herself from him. "All that matters is that I have made you mine." Boldly, he let his hands roam over her, deliberately fondling those places she'd tried to cover.

"I'm not yours, and I never will be! Never!" Trista denied her shame as she tried to twist away from him and block his caresses.

He gave a sharp laugh. "You already are." Lance cupped one of her breasts and teased the peak to hardness. "You can say what you want, but your body does not lie, Trista. Does Michael's touch make you feel this way?" he taunted.

"Michael has never touched me so!" Trista gritted her teeth against her body's betrayal as she continued to try to evade his touch. "Don't! No . . ."

Lance had known she was a virgin, but it filled him with pleasure to know that no other man had ever been so intimate with her. He needed suddenly to caress the very center of her again and slipped a hand lower to claim what was his.

Trista fought against this new encroachment, keeping her legs pressed tightly together and trying to push his hands away. Lance grew weary of her protestations and grabbed her wrists in a viselike grip, drawing her arms away and leaving her body open to his scathing gaze. "It would not trouble me to bind you, Trista," he threatened coldly, his blue eyes raking over her.

All the fight went out of her at the thought of being bound again. "No . . . please . . . don't."

"Then remember, and know that I'll do it if you give me cause," he told her dispassionately.

Hatred and frustration were reflected in Trista's eyes as she ceased her struggles. She held herself rigid and lay still before him. She expected him to press his point and take her again, but to her surprise, Lance merely stared at her impassively for a long moment and then released her. The relief that had washed through her at being freed was quickly erased, though, as he lay down beside her, pulled her into his arms, and drew the blanket over them.

"Sleep. We'll be riding out before dawn," he commanded.

Trista lay tensely against him, thinking that he was going to force her to make love to him again, but to her surprise he made no such overtures. After a while, it became too much of an effort to keep her eyes open, and for the second night in a row, curled intimately in her warrior's embrace, she slept.

Long after Trista had drifted off, Lance lay awake, staring off into the darkness and wondering at the conflicting emotions this woman could arouse within him. He had been tempted to take her again just to prove to her that she did indeed desire him, but the look of pure hatred she'd given him had put him off. He didn't know why it bothered him that she hated him; he only knew it did.

Logically, Lance knew he hated her and all she stood for. She was a white woman. She was engaged to a Barrett. Nothing could be more damning in his eyes.

He drew some satisfaction from his seduction of her. The remembrance of her willing surrender sent a shaft of heat through his loins, and he stroked the silken curve of her hip as she lay sleeping against him. A restlessness possessed him as he thought of having her again. Though the desire to take her was strong, he controlled it with an effort.

Extricating himself from her side, Lance got up and stood silently over Trista. He stared down at her sleeping form for a long moment, his expression curiously blank. Then, knowing that dawn would be coming all too quickly, he moved off into the darkness away from Trista's disturbing presence to seek out his own rest.

Chapter Eight

As the sun dipped low in the west, signaling the end of yet another day, a slender, young Comanche maiden stood apart from the rest of her tribe near the edge of the Indian village staring off across the countryside. Her expression was searching and her manner anxious as she gazed out across the deserted land. She was consumed with worry for the man she loved, and her dark eyes mirrored that concern. *Where was Lance?* Not for the first time, she cursed the golden stallion that had taken him away from her. He had been gone for weeks now on his solitary quest, and she was beginning to wonder if he ever would return. Agitated by that final thought, she turned away from her vigil and made her way slowly back toward the tipi she shared with her mother.

Wrapped warmly in a brightly colored blanket to ward off the night's growing chill, She Who Speaks the Truth was sitting before a small campfire, watching her daughter approach. She marveled once again at the beauty of her youngest child and wondered how such a vision of loveliness had sprung from her loins. Her own shortcomings were many. She was short and fat and plain of face, her hair quite gray now in her old age, while her daughter, Night Lark, was the complete opposite of her. Tall and willowy, with shining black hair and a curving figure, Night Lark was thought by many to be the most beautiful maiden in the village. It was praise that She Who Speaks the Truth did not deny, for she knew that no other maiden in the tribe came close to matching her daughter's loveliness.

She Who Speaks the Truth knew that Night Lark's beauty would serve her well, too, for she already had many young bucks eager to claim her for their own. It dismayed her somewhat that Night Lark showed interest in only one warrior, Lance, the nephew of Chief Lone Elk, and that he had no interest in taking a wife.

She thought of the half-white nephew of their chief and frowned slightly. Ever since Lance had come to live with them all those years ago, he had been accepted as one of the tribe. He had proven himself to be an able hunter and warrior many times over, but She Who Speaks the Truth had always felt that there was a part of himself he was holding back. She had no proof of it. It was just something she sensed, and her reputation for knowing what couldn't be known was almost legendary within the tribe. Perhaps it was the way that he had always kept his hair cut short as a sign of mourning his mother's death, or perhaps it was the memory of the time he'd attempted to return to his white father's home only to come back to Lone Elk and the tribe a few days later. She had never learned what had happened to him on that last trip. Neither he nor Lone Elk had ever spoken of it. All she did know was that whatever had happened had affected him deeply. He had departed the village a young boy, but he had returned a man. He matured almost overnight and from that point on had given his utmost to becoming the best among his peers — to becoming a full Comanche in every way that he could.

She Who Speaks the Truth had always wanted only

the best for her child, and so she had no objection to Lance as her daughter's choice. He was a fine warrior. Still, she knew that Night Lark would have much to deal with should Lance decide to take her for his wife, for he was a man with many demons inside of him.

"There is no sign of him yet, Mother," Night Lark complained as she folded her long, slim legs beneath her and sat down opposite her mother at the camp-fire.

She Who Speaks the Truth suppressed a smile and shook her head in dismay at the impatience of youth. "You waste your time mooning over him, Night Lark. Lance will return when he has captured the golden stallion — not before."

"I am not mooning over him!" she replied testily with a toss of her head. It had always annoyed her that her mother could read her thoughts so readily.

"You speak to the wind, daughter. Who knows you better than I?" She chuckled good-naturedly at her offspring.

"I love him, Mother," Night Lark stated simply, hoping for some sympathy from her parent.

"He is a fine warrior," She Who Speaks the Truth agreed, "but he is also a man driven."

Night Lark looked puzzled at her statement. "I don't understand. . . . What do you mean?"

"I am not sure of the cause. I only know that Lance is not completely happy."

"Why would he not be happy?" she argued, blind to any but her own feelings. "What more could he want? He is the nephew of the most powerful chief. He is a great warrior in his own right. He is respected by all. . . ."

She Who Speaks the Truth shrugged. "As I have said, I do not know."

"I grow tired of your vague statements! You are

only making up tales to try to change the direction of my heart, but you will not succeed," Night Lark scorned.

"Only you can control the desires of your heart, my daughter," she responded knowingly. "I can advise you to happiness, but you must make the choice yourself."

"My choice is made!" She stood up angrily. "I will take Lance for my husband."

"But first he must want you for his wife," She Who Speaks the Truth pointed out.

The painful truth of her remark brought a deep flush to Night Lark's cheeks, and she answered haughtily, "Lance wants me. When he returns I will tell him of my love."

"Sometimes, daughter, there are more things involved than we know. Do not leave yourself open to be hurt beyond measure," she counseled.

Night Lark, however, was in no mood to listen to her sage advice. Instead, she was lost in the remembrance of the passionate embrace she had shared with Lance the night before he'd gone off in search of his stallion. "Lance will be mine, Mother," she proclaimed with confidence, never doubting her ability to attract him. "You will see."

As She Who Speaks the Truth watched her daughter disappear into their tipi to retire for the night, she said quietly to herself, "I hope you prove me wrong, but I have the feeling that all is not as simple as you would have it."

Trista sat huddled against the cool night air, watching Lance work with Fuego. The day had passed uneventfully for them as they'd continued their flight across the endless Texas countryside. He had not bound her wrists after last night, and she was determined not to ever give him any cause to tie her up again. That little bit of freedom had taken on enormous importance in her current state of captivity, and so she had been quick to obey his every command since rising this morning.

They had had little to say to each other about what had happened between them the night before. Trista had known defeat, pure and simple. She had tried to resist him but could not. She wanted to believe that she had fought his possession with all her might, but she knew in her heart that it had not happened that way, and the realization sickened her.

Trista had never considered herself a weak woman, but now she was beginning to have doubts about her own character. She loved Michael. She planned to become his wife. Yet she had given herself to this Comanche warrior! Her feelings of having betrayed Michael were great, but she was at a loss as to what to do. She was helplessly under this man's control and had no alternative except to make the best of the situation.

A shudder of expectancy quaked through her as she thought of the long hours of darkness to come. Would he come to her again? Trista knew she would be forced to sleep in his arms again, and she worried about what would happen should he try to take her again. Firmly, she swore to herself that she would defend her honor and try to fight him off. Yet even as she was girding herself for a confrontation, the memory of his overpowering strength and his threat to bind her and take what he wanted anyway left her confused and frightened.

Lance offered the golden stallion a drink of water from his cupped hands, and he smiled to himself as the horse drank thirstily. After the initial challenge of the chase and capture, the rogue had proven to be much less arduous to tame than he'd expected. He had responded nicely to all his techniques, and when they reached the village tomorrow, he would begin breaking the stallion for riding.

His thoughts drifted to Trista as he mentally compared the two. Both were his captives, and both, he knew, would bring him much praise and glory among the other warriors. Whereas the stallion was becoming more and more easy to handle and would soon be broken and willing to do his bidding, he had a feeling that Trista never would. Despite the submissive demeanor she had presented to him today, he did not believe for a moment that he had completely conquered her. Briefly, he had known the pleasure of her surrender, but as soon as their moment of passion had faded, she had been on the defensive again. He wasn't sure why it bothered him — she was, after all, his prisoner — but it did.

A fierce surge of determination took him, wiping away any bothersome thoughts he was having about her. Trista might be fighting him now, but one way or the other he was going to bring her totally under his control. Then, when he did, she was going to learn, just as the golden one was learning now, that he was the master and she was the slave.

Lance glanced back toward their campsite and decided confidently that tonight would be the perfect night for another lesson. Stroking the stallion's powerful neck one last time, he murmured a soft word of praise and then headed back to where he knew Trista sat awaiting his return. First they would eat. Then he would set about taming her.

Trista had been watching for him, and she tensed when she caught sight of him returning. Her eyes were round and wide with uncertainty as he came to stand before her. His inscrutable expression gave no clue as to his intentions, and so she stared up at him nervously, wondering at his mood.

Trista had never learned how to disguise her own true feelings, and Lance easily deciphered the sense of dread that was assailing her.

"We will eat now," he pronounced as he sat down comfortably upon the blanket. "Bring the food."

Trista was so stunned by his order that for an instant she could only stare at him in surprise. She was so pleased that he wasn't going to try to make love to her right then that she hastened to do as he commanded. Having watched his every move the past two days, she knew exactly where everything was, and she soon was handing him the water bag and the dried meat. Unsure as to what he wanted next, she remained standing hesitantly before him until he looked up at her with something akin to annoyance.

"Sit down."

At his direction, she sat down beside him, taking extra care not to come too close to him. Hunger was gnawing at her. When he handed her a piece of meat, she took it without comment and ate quickly. When she finished she was startled to find his blue-eyed gaze intently upon her.

"Put these away," he ordered.

Again she jumped up to do as he'd directed, glad to be away from his prying eyes. Somehow it seemed to Trista that Lance could read her very thoughts, and the idea of it chilled her. She didn't want him to learn of the confusion his nearness wrought in her soul.

Wanting to stay away from him for as long as she could, Trista dallied too long at the task assigned. His sharp call forced her to return, and she found him already stretched out on the blanket waiting for her to join him there.

"It's time to rest. We must ride again tomorrow."

It was the moment she'd been dreading all day, and she knew there could be no avoiding it.

"I'll sleep over here tonight," she answered quickly, moving to sit some distance away from him.

There was a steely quality to Lance's tone when he responded to her show of defiance. "You have no choice, Trista. Have you not learned yet?"

"I won't run away," she offered, hoping that that was what he was concerned about.

"You are running away now," Lance claimed coldly. "You will sleep with me, for that is what I want."

"But what about what I want?" Trista demanded, suddenly angry in her fear.

"Shall I show you what you want?" Her words were a challenge to him, and he was on his feet in an instant, stalking slowly toward her like a panther after its prey.

"NO!" She backed desperately away from him, knowing what his touch could do to her resistance, knowing that she wouldn't be able to keep up any semblance of a fight once he caressed her in *that* way.

Lance moved so quickly that Trista didn't have a chance to run. Before she had time to realize what had happened, she was trapped against his chest, held firmly in the circle of his arms. Her throat went dry, and the sound of her own heart pounding thundered in her ears.

"Please, don't make me do this again. . . ." She was reduced to heartbroken pleading.

"I have made you do nothing, my golden one." His eyes burned into hers searching for the truth. "Have you forgotten so quickly how aroused you became when I touched you here . . . ?" His hand slid to her breast. "And here . . ." He then sought the juncture of her thighs.

"No . . . don't . . ." Trista struggled against the

explosion of feeling that rocketed though her when he caressed her most sensitive place.

"Oh, yes, my captive," he growled in satisfaction as he felt her weaken against his continuing sensual assault. "You are mine in *all* ways, love."

"No . . . I love Michael. He's the only man I want."

Her words cut at him like a knife, but only served to increase his resolve to prove her wrong. "You speak, but your body does not listen," he taunted. He unfastened her riding skirt and let it drop unheeded as he sought the damp heat of her arousal.

As his hand claimed hers, Trista found herself no longer struggling to get away, but instead, moving with his caress. Her legs were threatening to buckle beneath her as he stroked her in a manner that both calmed and excited her at the same time. She felt her head swim with the forbidden ecstasy of it. *How was it that his touch could bring her to this mindlessness so easily?* she wondered vaguely through the mist of her passion. When Lance swung her up into his arms, she could only cling to him, and when he lay her upon the blanket, she could no longer physically resist him.

Trista's gaze was pleading as he came to her. A part of her wanted him so wildly that she arched with it, but another part of her was fighting to retain her own self-respect.

"Lance . . . please . . ."

Lance, past the point of stopping, thought that she was begging him to hurry in his possession of her. "Please what, Trista?" He wanted her to tell him that she desired him. He was not expecting the answer he got.

"Please stop. . . . Surely you remember some of the white man's ways and know—" She got no further.

A hot rage of fury possessed him, and he stilled, staring down at her. *The white man's ways* . . . "Yes, I remember the white man's ways!" His answer slashed coldly across her protest. "I remember all too well the betrayal, the deceit, and the hatred."

Without another word, Lance kissed her, his mouth savaging hers in an exchange meant to conquer and to punish. He had wanted to be gentle with her as he had been gentle with the stallion, but all thoughts of tenderness were lost. Over and over he pressed devouring kisses upon her lips, forcing a response from her. He stripped off the rest of her garments then and began to caress her, each stroking touch calculated to arouse and stimulate. His lips trailed fire over her writhing body, evoking passion-filled cries of ecstasy from Trista.

"Tell me that it's your Michael you want, Trista," he snarled at her as he ceased all motion and loomed over her in the darkness.

Trista was on fire with desire for Lance. All thought of denying him had disappeared as he'd plundered her silken curves with masterful kisses and caresses. Michael . . . Michael . . . She tried to bring him to mind, but all she could see was Lance, poised and waiting motionlessly above her for her answer. His eyes were glittering with his triumph over her senses, but she suddenly didn't care. She wanted him. Her body was aching with the need to be one with his, and she wanted only to surrender to him and take the pleasure he was offering.

"Tell me, Trista!" he commanded, rubbing his hips in intimate offering against her.

"Lance . . . Lance . . ." She breathed his name, her eyes telling him what he wanted her to put into words.

"Say it, Trista. I want to hear you say that you want me . . ." He bent to explore the fullness of her breasts as she hesitated.

The heat of his lips pushed her past the point of

caring about anything but fulfillment. "Yes . . . oh, yes, Lance. I want you. . . . I want you. . . ." She was sobbing then, the admission wrenched from her.

Lance's feelings of rage and hate disappeared at her confession. No longer did he want to punish her. Suddenly he wanted to show her that she had lost nothing in telling him the truth of her desire.

Trista was defeated, but her subjugation was also her victory as Lance pierced her body with his, giving her the gift she so desperately longed for. The sweet agony of his driving possession took them both to rapture and beyond. Together they surged and blended, wrapped in each other's arms, their legs intertwined in the throes of passion. Each movement, each touch, each kiss took them higher and higher in their pursuit of perfection. Lost in love's madness, oblivious to the past or the future, their bodies melded until they reached the heights and soared as one.

The night passed in a torrent of desire, and no further protests were spoken. The hours seemed as minutes as Lance and Trista came together over and over again. Each joining grew more fervid than the last as they learned each other's pleasures and tested sensuality to the limits. The first pale light of dawn found them sleeping, locked in love's most perfect embrace.

With Lance's arm familiarly around her waist holding her tightly against him as they rode, Trista endured yet a fourth day of racing across the wilds of the Texas countryside on horseback. Her spirits were at their lowest ebb as she stared dully down at Michael's ring upon her finger. What had happened the night before had shattered her dignity, and she felt more lost and alone than ever before.

How could she have let it happen? She had vowed after her first surrender to Lance never to allow him to have his way with her again, and yet, when he had touched her last night, all had been lost. The memory of her blatant response to him brought a flush to her pale cheeks. His kiss . . . his caress . . . had set fire to her senses, and she had been helpless before the heat of her desire.

Trista wondered if there could be a worse fate. She was a captive and completely subject to him. She did not doubt that Lance would take whatever measures he considered necessary to insure that she obeyed his every command, and it was that very fear that forced her to do his bidding. Her only hope lay in rescue, and as the days and miles passed, that hope grew more and more dim. Silently, she prayed that Michael would find her, and soon.

Wind Rider reined his pony in at the crest of the small rise and lifted one hand to shield his eyes from the glare of the late-afternoon sun. Intently his black-eyed gaze searched the southern landscape.

"Striking Snake . . . look!" he called to his companion. "There are riders coming. . . ."

Striking Snake urged his horse to the hilltop beside Wind Rider to get a better look. Side by side, the two fierce-looking warriors paused to determine who would be stupidly daring enough to cross their territory. Wind Rider was the first to recognize Lance.

"It's Lance, and it looks as if he's caught the golden stallion!" With an ear-splitting war cry, he put his heels to his horse and raced off in Lance's direction, leaving his companion to follow in his dust.

Trista saw the warriors coming across the flat

stretch of land, and even from this distance she could make out the bright, hideous markings of red and black on their faces. Their ponies running at top speed, the two Comanche hurled toward them, rifles in hand, their bloodcurdling shrieks shattering the quiet of the afternoon.

"Lance!" She could not prevent a cry of alarm at the sight. It had been one thing dealing with Lance one on one, but to face two near naked, vicious-looking savages was almost more than she could bear. Terrorized, she clutched at Lance's arm about her waist, and she wondered why he was pulling the pinto to a stop when he should have been making a run for it.

Lance recognized his friend Wind Rider right away and fought down the urge to smile too widely as he approached. Sitting easily on his pinto, he tightened his grip on both Trista and the stallion as he waited.

Wind Rider had always thought Lance the best warrior and hunter in the village, but as he drew nearer to his friend, his respect for him grew even more. Not only had Lance caught the golden stallion, but he'd found a beautiful, golden-haired white woman as well.

"My brother!" Wind Rider called out in the Comanche tongue as he reined in beside them. "You have returned!"

Striking Snake rode up in a cloud of dust, and his horse reared in protest as he sawed tightly back on the reins.

"Hello, my brother," Lance returned in the same language. He grinned broadly at Wind Rider before turning to the other warrior. A rivalry of long standing existed between Striking Snake and him, and Lance knew a moment of pure pleasure at the other Comanche's jealous expression as he stared at both the girl and the horse. "Striking Snake. It is good of you to come out to welcome me. Have I been so missed in the village?"

"Of course, Lance. Your uncle has missed you greatly," the other warrior sneered.

Wind Rider was excited over Lance's obvious success and wanted to know more, but he was in no mood to listen to the terse verbal exchanges these two usually shared. "Everyone has been waiting to hear of your success, Lance," he assured him. "It looks like you have snared more than just a good piece of horseflesh. Surely your tale must be an interesting one, my friend.

"Indeed," Striking Snake agreed, maneuvering his horse in closer. He was fascinated by the pale color of Trista's hair, and he reached out to caress the curling lock that rested on her breast.

Trista thought the end had come. She could not understand what they were saying, but she could understand the glint of lust in the ugly Comanche's eyes. She thought he was going to fondle her intimately right there, and she panicked at the prospect. Was this to be her fate? Was she to be shared with these other men? Her heart was in her throat, and as Striking Snake's big hand came nearer to her, she slapped at him as hard as she could.

Striking Snake was surprised by her attack, but found it more amusing than annoying. Leering at her hungrily, he brushed her hands aside as if she were no more than an insect. Undeterred, he reached out and touched the pale, lustrous curl, letting his knuckles rest against the swell of her bosom. Looking up at Lance, whose expression was carefully blank, he said, "She is a wild one. Perhaps I will help you train her."

Using his knees, Lance urged the pinto to take a step backward, freeing Trista from the lecherous Striking Snake's touch. His tone was carefully controlled as his frigid blue eyes met and challenged the other warrior's black ones. "I have no need of your help. Can you not see that I have already trained her? She is mine, Striking Snake, as is the golden stallion."

Striking Snake was infuriated by his insult, but Wind Rider quickly interrupted them to stave off possible trouble. "We must hurry if we are to make the village before sundown, Lance. You can tell us of the stallion's capture as we ride."

Trista was unaware of anything except the one savage's eyes upon her. She had never thought she would turn to Lance for anything, but the terror the other barbarous-looking warrior aroused in her left her feeling helpless and afraid for her very life.

Relief flooded through her as the big, brutish warrior wheeled his horse about and charged off. As they began to follow in his direction at a slower pace, she sagged weakly back against Lance, almost savoring the warm protection of his arm about her waist. She was unmindful of the continuing conversation between Lance and the other warrior, for all she could think of was the fear that someday she might have to face that other Comanche alone.

Chapter Nine

"Lone Elk will be surprised," Wind Rider remarked in the Comanche tongue as he rode alongside Lance on their way to the village.

"Why? Did my uncle not have faith that I could capture the golden one?" Lance frowned at the thought.

"Few doubted your ability to trap the rogue," he explained as his gaze dropped to Trista, who was riding so quietly before Lance on the pinto's back.

"Then why do you think he will be surprised?"

"You have ridden with raiding parties many times, but never before have you taken a captive." Wind Rider lifted his dark gaze to Lance's.

Lance gave his longtime friend a knowing smile as he bantered, "Could you have left this one behind?"

Wind Rider chuckled. "She is a prize of great worth. What do you call her?"

"Her name is Trista," he answered.

Trista had been trying to hold herself aloof from all that was happening. At the sound of her name being mentioned, though, she stiffened against Lance. She longed to be able to interpret their conversation so she could have a clue to her fate, but the words they uttered were totally foreign to her ears.

Although she could not understand what they were saying, Trista somehow sensed a kinship between these two men. Their manner together now was a far cry from the tension that had possessed them earlier when the other warrior had been present. These two were at ease with each other, and she knew that they must be friends.

Trista cast a sidelong glance at the warrior who was riding with them. Though this Comanche was not as fearsome-looking as the one who had ridden off ahead of them, he was still a frightening sight. She had no idea what he really looked like, for his face was disguised with the ugly red and black paint in the same manner Lance's had been. His hair, however, was worn differently from Lance's. It was much longer and was plaited into two long braids that hung down far past his shoulders. Both braids were adorned with feathers and fur. He was dressed as Lance was in just a breechclout and moccasins, and she could see that he was strongly built. He rode his horse with the same easy control, almost as if he were one with the animal.

"Striking Snake would pay you handsomely for her. What do you plan to do with her?" Wind Rider was saying, unaware of Trista's silent appraisal.

"I have not decided yet," Lance replied evasively.

"Well, should you decide to sell her, I will take her off your hands," he offered graciously, his eyes twinkling with good humor.

For some reason, Wind Rider's joking words irritated Lance. Though he laughed with his friend, it was forced merriment. "If I sell her, she will be yours."

"What of the stallion? Tell me of the capture."

Lance told him of the endless days of chase, carefully avoiding any reference to the Royal Diamond, for his friend knew all about his early childhood. "Trista appeared just as I was about to run him down."

Wind Rider was amazed, for he thought white

women were the most cosseted of creatures. "She was riding on the range alone?"

Lance smiled in remembrance as he nodded. "She was chasing the golden one just as I was."

Wind Rider looked at Trista with a new respect. "She is a special woman."

"Yes."

"How did you manage to catch them both at the same time?"

"I took the stallion first."

"I had thought you would." His friend grinned, knowing how obsessed Lance had been with the golden one.

"Trista's horse had fallen. I found her later."

"She seems a calm one, easily tamed. She will serve you well until you tire of her."

At Wind Rider's remark, Lance laughed deeply. "All is not as it seems. Trista appears subdued, but she is as wild as the rogue."

At his laughing reference to her, Trista grew angry. It was bad enough that they were speaking in the Indian language, but to make her the butt of what she was sure were jokes was just too humiliating. She wished for some way to could prick his overblown warrior's confidence.

"It will be entertaining to watch the taming of both, then."

"It will be entertaining to tame them both," Lance countered, his eyes alight at the challenge. "I will begin breaking the golden one for riding in the morning."

"And your woman?"

"Her taming has already begun."

Night Lark was helping her mother prepare the evening meal when she saw Striking Snake ride back into the village alone. She knew that he had ridden out with her cousin, Wind Rider, and she thought it most unusual that they had not returned at the same time. Leaving her mother to the cooking, she hurried off to try to find out what had happened. She saw him stop to speak with Chief Lone Elk and maneuvered herself just close enough to overhear their conversation.

"Where is Wind Rider? Has there been trouble?" Lone Elk was asking Striking Snake as the bull-like warrior dismounted from his pony.

Striking Snake knew he could not refuse to answer the chief, but it irked him to be the bearer of such news. "There has been no trouble, Chief Lone Elk. Wind Rider is following behind with Lance."

"Lance is returning?" Lone Elk's lined, weathered face lit up in delight at the news.

Night Lark heard his pronouncement, and her heart began to beat excitedly in her breast. Lance was returning! He would be there soon! Thrilled, she raced back to tell her mother and to make herself more attractive for him.

The two Comanche paid no attention to Night Lark as she hurried away.

Chief Lone Elk glanced out in the direction from which Striking Snake had just come. "Why did you not ride in together?"

"He was traveling slower than I wished to travel."

"Has he been injured in some way?" He knew his nephew well and found it unusual that Lance would not be riding into camp at top speed.

"No," Striking Snake replied, sorry that that wasn't the case. "He is leading the stallion and is also riding

138

double."

Chief Lone Elk pierced him with an impatient glare. "Do not tease me. Who rides with my nephew?"

Insulted by the chief's sharp words, the warrior stiffened as he answered, "Lance has taken a captive."

This truly surprised Lone Elk. He and Lance had ridden on raids together many times, but whereas the other warriors had often taken captives as booty, Lance had not. Lone Elk thought it most unusual that his nephew was returning with one now, especially since he had ridden out alone with no intention of raiding.

"Tell the women to prepare a feast for tonight. I will be in my tipi. Send Lance to me when he arrives. I would hear of this captive." Intrigued, the chief returned to his lodge to await his long-absent nephew's return.

Wind Rider smiled as the village came into view. "I know of one who will be particularly glad to see you, my friend."

"Oh?" Lance glanced at him questioningly.

"Night Lark has made no secret of her yearning for you while you were gone. Many dusks she waited and watched for you until the darkness claimed the land."

The news surprised Lance. Though he had shared a few passionate embraces with the lovely young woman, he was not in love with her and had never given her any hope that he would make her his wife. "It will be good to see her again."

"She wants to do more than see you, I'll wager," Wind Rider remarked knowingly.

"What Night Lark wants does not concern me," Lance answered arrogantly.

139

"She has turned away many suitors in hopes of capturing your heart."

"No woman will ever capture my heart." Lance was firm in his declaration. "When I marry, it will be because it is time to father children. Nothing more."

They fell silent then as they entered the village. The sight of Lance returning with the elusive stallion and a white woman brought most of the villagers rushing out to greet him. As he rode slowly through their midst, they called out praises of his prowess in capturing them both and questioned him boldly about where he'd found the golden woman to match the stallion. Lance easily avoided answering their questions as he made his way toward his lodge. Only when Striking Snake blocked his path did he stop.

"Chief Lone Elk would see you," the warrior told him as his black eyes settled hungrily on Trista. "He waits in his tipi for you now."

"Thank you, Striking Snake," Lance answered. He started to turn to Wind Rider to ask him to take Trista and the stallion on to his own lodge when the other warrior offered first.

"I will take care of your horses and your captive while you see to your uncle."

There was no way Lance could refuse his offer before all of the tribe without insulting him gravely. He slid slowly out of the saddle.

"I will go along to help, too." Wind Rider spoke up quickly, for he knew how little Lance trusted Striking Snake.

Lance nodded and smiled quixotically. "Perhaps he will need your help. Both are still quite wild." With calm determination, he handed the reins over to Striking Snake.

Trista had no idea what was being said, and she

140

was growing more frightened with each passing moment. She had kept her fears under tight control as they'd entered the village, enduring the open, leering stares of the Comanche men and women as they'd swarmed around her, but now her icy calm was threatening to shatter. The protective circle of Lance's arm about her had kept her feeling almost safe, or at least it had until she'd come face-to-face with the other big, ugly brute of an Indian once again. Trista hadn't meant to show her fear, but when Lance dismounted and handed the reins over to the other warrior, she'd grown distraught.

"Lance . . . ?" Her voice was a frightened squeak, and she started to slip from the horse's back to follow him.

"Trista. Stay where you are," he commanded in English. His tone blazed with an authority she'd never heard before, and she froze.

"Don't give me to him. . . ." she whispered hoarsely, terrified of what the big Comanche would do to her once they were alone. "Please Lance, don't do this."

Lance's expression didn't change as he regarded her dispassionately. "Striking Snake will see to you for now."

Trista wanted to cry out and beg him to take her with him, but a quick glance at the sneering faces of the villagers stiffened her. She knew she could show no weakness to them. Sitting more proudly in the saddle, she said nothing further as Lance turned his back on her. Trista watched as he strode purposefully to a brightly painted tipi, called out a greeting of some kind, and then disappeared inside.

Striking Snake did not take his eyes off of Trista as he said something to the crowd gathered around them. His comment drew a murmur of approval from all the men who stood nearby watching. Keeping a firm hand on the reins, he started off in a different direction, leading the horses behind him. Trista could only keep her seat and stare straight ahead as she was led away.

Night Lark heard the sounds of Lance's return and dashed forth from her tipi ready to seek him out.

"Dawn Blossom!" she called out to one of the other young maidens she saw standing at the fringes of the crowd. "Is it true? Has Lance returned at last?"

The plump, normally cheerful Dawn Blossom groaned inwardly as she saw her coming her way. Of all the other single young women in the village, only Night Lark stirred this dislike within her. Dawn Blossom wasn't sure exactly why she didn't like the slender, doe-eyed Night Lark. It was just an instinctive thing. She sensed a certain female ruthlessness within her that was sometimes almost frightening in its intensity. When Night Lark wanted something, she got it. Right now, Dawn Blossom knew that Night Lark wanted to marry Lance.

"Yes," she answered, "Lance has just ridden in and is with Lone Elk now."

"Oh." Night Lark's disappointment at having missed him was obvious.

"He did not return alone," Dawn Blossom offered, eager to impart the news of his captive.

"Yes, I know," came the other woman's dismissing reply. "He rode in with Wind Rider."

"Wind Rider is not the only one who accompanied him," she taunted.

At this, Night Lark looked up questioningly. "There was someone else riding with him?"

142

"Evidently Lance did some raiding while he was gone. Not only did he capture the golden stallion, but he has brought a white woman back with him. She is most beautiful."

"Lance has taken a captive?" She was stunned, for never before had he ever shown any interest in such things.

"Yes," Dawn Blossom confirmed, "and judging from the way the men looked at her, I think Lance will be able to get many horses in trade for this one."

"Yes . . . of course," Night Lark replied distractedly. The news had disturbed her greatly, for she did not like the thought of sharing Lance's attentions with anyone, much less a lowly white woman. "Where is this captive now?"

"Striking Snake and Wind Rider took her and the stallion to Lance's lodge."

Before Dawn Blossom could say another word, Night Lark was gone.

Striking Snake halted the horses before Lance's tipi and then handed Wind Rider the reins to the stallion. "Take care of the horse while I see to the woman."

Wind Rider nodded and led the golden one away to the place where Lance kept his own herd of horses penned, leaving Trista behind.

Alone with the savage who struck terror within her heart, Trista kept her seat on the pinto's back and concentrated on staring straight ahead. Not quite sure what to expect, she was prepared for the worst. She longed desperately for a weapon of some kind to protect herself from this beast of a man.

Seeing that Wind Rider had disappeared from sight, Striking Snake dropped the pinto's reins and walked around to the side of the horse to stare salaciously up at Trista. Casually, he rested a hamlike hand on her thigh and squeezed.

"You are a delicious one, white woman, and one day very soon you will be mine," he told her confidently.

Though Trista couldn't decipher his words, she could plainly read the lust in his expression. As forcefully as she could, she kicked out at him. She managed to land one blow to his chest.

Without Lance's presence Striking Snake felt no compulsion to tolerate her defiance. His grip on her leg tightened to bruising proportions, and he forcefully jerked her from the horse's back and dumped her heavily on the ground.

Trista lay sprawled at his feet, tears of pain and indignity stinging her eyes. She glanced quickly around, hoping to see Lance or even the other, less savage warrior coming for her, but they were nowhere in sight. It was then that she noticed the small cooking fire a short distance away, and a plan began to form in her mind. If this animal tried to lay another hand on her, she knew what she would do.

"Get up, woman," Striking Snake ordered in English as he stood over her with his brawny arms folded across his massive chest.

Knowing that there was no alternative, Trista struggled to her feet and stood before him.

"Perhaps you are not as wild as Lance would have me believe. . . ." He smiled lasciviously as he reached out to touch the swell of her breast exposed by the tear in her blouse. "Perhaps I will taste of you before I buy you, white woman. . . ."

Striking Snake made the mistake of speaking in English, and his words pushed Trista to the limit. It had been difficult enough for her to suffer Lance's sensual torment, but she knew she could not survive this man's possession. He was an animal. He would take his own pleasure from her body and care nothing for the destruction he wrought while doing so. She bolted, preferring death to his touch.

The warrior's confident laughter followed her panicked flight. With the pace of a man accustomed to dominating, he followed after her. Only when Trista grabbed a burning stick from the fire and turned to confront him did his expression turn deadly.

Trista stood before him, braced for a fight. She did not want to die, but would do so to save herself from this man. Lance, even at his most cruel, had been kind compared to what she was sure this one would be like, and she silently cursed him for deserting her.

Striking Snake moved with all the stealth of the reptile for which he was named. His obsidian eyes revealed nothing of his plan of attack as he circled the defiant Trista. It irked him that she had been so subdued with Lance, and he was determined to bring her under his control, too. He was a better warrior than Lance. Certainly no woman was going to show him up! He lunged for her, but to his surprise she darted quickly to one side. Trista swung out at him with her makeshift weapon as she evaded him, and the burning stick struck him a glancing blow on the arm.

Howls of raucous laughter filled the air, and Striking Snake looked up to find that several of the villagers had gathered to watch. The fact that she'd just made a fool of him enraged him, and he knew he would make her pay for her resistance.

Trista read the murderous glint in his eyes, and she backed away, suddenly truly frightened. She swallowed nervously, knowing that her meager strength was no match for this warrior's. She would now pay the price for her actions.

Striking Snake lunged. Trista would have been able to avoid his tackle again had she not tripped. She had thought the area behind her clear, but suddenly she found herself falling backward. Her one weapon flew from her grasp as she tumbled. She lay in the dust, the breath knocked from her, her gaze fastened on the warrior who was coming toward her, his expression black.

"You are stupid, white woman," a feminine voice taunted from above her.

Twisting, Trista looked up to see a young Comanche woman standing over her with a knife in her hand.

"I cannot see why Lance bothered to take you. He should have killed you where he found you. Perhaps I will save him the trouble now. . . ." Her smile had a feral quality about it that sent a shiver of apprehension down Trista's spine.

"I did not need your help, Night Lark," Striking Snake snarled as he drew near.

The maiden shrugged. "That is true, Striking Snake. She is as stupid as she is ugly. Why, she tripped right over my foot. . . . I do not see why either of you would want this one."

"It is not important that you see anything," he snapped, dismissing her. "All that matters is that she be tamed. Obviously Lance hasn't managed to learn how to control her yet, so I will teach her obedience."

He reached down then and grasped Trista by the front of her blouse, hauling her to her feet. With his other hand, he slapped her viciously, and he smiled as her lip split beneath his assault. As he was about to hit her again, Wind Rider reappeared and shouted out to him in Comanche.

"Striking Snake! Do not lay another hand upon her. She is not your property. She belongs to Lance and Lance alone." He moved forth boldly to take Trista by the arm and pull her free of the other warrior's threatening hold.

Trista had never been so glad to see anyone in her life. She did not know what the other warrior had said, but she was grateful for his rescue.

"She was fighting me!" he argued, lapsing into his native tongue as he tried to justify his actions.

Wind Rider gave him a scathing look and jeered, "She is not fighting now, Striking Snake. Perhaps you do not know how to treat women!"

His statement drew another round of laughter as those who had been standing around began to drift away to see to their own business. Striking Snake gritted his teeth in anger but knew it was best not say anything more. He would get this female from Lance one way or the other, and then he would show her the cost of humiliating him before his tribesmen.

"I will tell Lance of her defiant ways," Wind Rider assured him as the warrior stalked away. He thought about how bravely Trista had acted. She was a rare female to have so fiercely defended herself against Striking Snake's brute force, and she probably would have done much better had Night Lark not interfered. He turned to the Indian maiden then. "If you have come in search of Lance, he is with his uncle."

"I know where he is, my cousin. I merely came to see the captive he brought back." Night Lark's tone was nasty, for she resented Wind Rider's defense of this pasty-faced female. "She does not look very strong," she remarked as she circled Trista, studying her critically.

"Lance did not bring her back because he thought she was of sturdy stock, Night Lark," Wind Rider told her derisively. "She is as beautiful as the sun, and I'm sure she can create as much heat."

The maiden flushed angrily at his words. Jealousy consumed her at the thought of Lance making love to this white woman. "She is as pale as the snow and probably as cold!" she returned. "He will find no comfort between her thighs."

Night Lark's hostility was an almost tangible thing, and Trista wondered at it as she watched the other woman warily. She had heard that the Comanche women were sometimes more vicious than their men, and looking at Night Lark, she believed it. Her raven hair was wild about her shoulders. Her eyes were narrowed and reflected clearly her hatred. Trista didn't doubt for a moment that, if they had been alone, the other woman would have attacked her.

"Where Lance seeks his comfort is none of your business, Night Lark," Wind Rider told her bluntly. "He is not your husband. You have no claim on him."

She flashed her cousin a knowing look. "Not yet, but I will. Lance will be mine, and then I will see this bitch sold to the highest bidder." With that, she stormed off.

"Come. We will wait here for Lance's return." Wind Rider spoke in English as he led her to a place before the tipi.

Trista drew a deep, shuddering sigh of relief at his mention of Lance. He would be returning. . . . He hadn't given her away to Striking Snake. She wiped at the blood on her mouth as she followed him. "Thank you."

Wind Rider gave her an appraising look but said

nothing as he directed her to sit down before Lance's lodge. She was a fiery one, this one. Having seen her in action, he knew his friend definitely had his hands full in trying to tame her. Suppressing a smile, Wind Rider couldn't help but think what an exciting challenge it would be to bring this blond beauty under control and how great the rewards would be once she was. He hoped Lance would sell her to him soon.

"Striking Snake has told me that you returned with more than just the stallion," Lone Elk remarked to Lance as they sat facing each other in the privacy of his lodge.

Lance immediately resented Striking Snake's having borne the news to Lone Elk that should have been his own to impart. "He has spoken the truth, my uncle."

Lone Elk's dark eyes probed deeply into Lance's blue ones seeking answers to questions he had not yet posed. "This white woman . . . why did you bring her to our village? You have never done such as this before."

"Perhaps it was time for me to claim that which is my right," he answered, thinking of the Barrett ring Trista wore.

Lone Elk nodded but did not speak. He knew Lance better than any other living soul, and he sensed that there was much more to this than just the taking of a white captive. He changed the subject for the time being, knowing that eventually he would find out the real truth behind his actions. "You captured the stallion as you said you would."

"Yes. Did you doubt me?"

"Never," the chief told him, and then paused as one

of his three wives entered to bring them cooling drinks. When the woman had served them and then gone, he spoke again, a smile curving his usually stern mouth. "When you set your mind to a challenge, you do not fail. I do not think you know the word."

Lance was pleased by such praise from his uncle. "I merely try to imitate your example."

Lone Elk chuckled at his obvious flattery. "I am growing old, and such words are like the joy of children's laughter to my ears. Tell me of the horse. Was he worth the struggle?"

"He is magnificent," he confirmed. "He is smart, too. Already I have him drinking out of my hands. I will mount him for the first time tomorrow."

"I will watch this mounting," the chief proclaimed.

"I hope it is only one," Lance said wryly, wondering just how difficult it was going to be to break the rogue to riding.

"Many sought the golden one. Only you succeed. We will celebrate tonight when the moon rises."

"I am pleased by the honor."

It was almost nightfall as Lance made his way back to his tipi, and he was feeling quite pleased by his uncle's planned tribute. He could see Trista sitting before the campfire with Wind Rider. In the semidarkness he did not immediately notice her bruised face and puffy lip. Only as he drew closer did he see the telltale sign of Striking Snake's blow. A surge of chilling rage that he didn't understand swept through him at the sight of her injury. His expression was wooden as he looked from Trista to Wind Rider and back.

"You will tell me what happened," he demanded of his friend coldly in their native language as he stood

150

before them.

"I do not know exactly what happened. When I returned from taking care of the stallion, Striking Snake was beating her. He claims she attacked him."

"You stopped the attack?"

"We both know that Striking Snake would think nothing of killing a woman. I merely reminded him that Trista was your property, not his."

Lance nodded as he spoke with distaste. "I find he is much like his name. I do not trust him. Thank you, my friend."

There was a sparkle in Wind Rider's eyes as he got to his feet and answered, "Do not thank me. I was merely protecting what I hope will soon be mine."

Chapter Ten

Trista had seen Lance coming toward them, and her gaze had not wavered from him as he drew near. She had never in her wildest imaginings thought that she would ever be glad to see him, but at this moment she was. The fact left her confused and resentful. Lance had kidnapped her and had dragged her across miles of rugged, treacherous terrain against her will. He had forced her to make love to him, taking from her the precious gift of her innocence, and then, to humiliate her further, had forced her to confess that she had enjoyed his touch and had wanted him. . . .

Staring up at him now, Trista knew she should have felt shamed and abused. Instead, all she could think of was how wonderful it was to see him and how relieved she was that he had not given her to Striking Snake, but had kept her for himself. As he continued to talk with Wind Rider, her gaze clung to him hungrily, and again she wished that she could translate the words they exchanged in the complicated Comanche tongue.

"Have you arranged for a place for her to stay?" Wind Rider was asking. He knew it was bad medicine for a woman to live in a warrior's tent if she was not his wife, and he wondered if Lance had given any thought to the problem.

"I was hoping you could convince She Who Speaks

the Truth to take her in," Lance suggested.

Wind Rider knew how fond his aunt was of Lance and quickly agreed to check with her. "I will ask her right away. I'm sure she will have no objections."

"Good. Tell her that I will bring Trista to her soon, before the celebration begins."

"I will do that," he told him as he started off to seek out his aunt.

When Wind Rider had gone, Lance stood towering over Trista. He regarded her in silence for a long moment, his expression inscrutable. His feelings for her were ambivalent, and it troubled him greatly. His near violent reaction to the thought of Striking Snake hitting her had stunned him. Lance generally prided himself on being coolheaded and in control, and the power of the emotion that had surged through him upon learning of the warrior's cruelty to Trista had left him slightly shaken. That, plus the reluctance he was feeling over sending her to sleep at She Who Speaks the Truth's tipi, left him exasperated. He knew it would not be acceptable for her to share his lodge, yet he found himself, for the first time in all his years with the tribe, wanting to break with tradition.

Lance told himself that he hated Trista. She was representative of everything he despised. She was white. She was to marry his hated half brother. He had only taken her captive to use her to seek revenge against the Barretts. Yet despite all the anger and bitterness he felt toward Trista, when he touched her a madness seized him, and it was a madness that only oneness with her could cure. He had had desirable women before, but no one had affected him as she did. His expression hardened at the thought that he might be feeling more for her than just lust, and he thrust the possibility from him. She was a white woman captive, nothing more. He would treat her as

153

such.

As tired, sore, and mentally exhausted as she was, Trista had hoped for at least some peace now that Lance had returned. But her pleasure at seeing him was rapidly diminishing as he stood over her, scowling blackly.

"Lance?" she ventured hesitantly. She was unsure of his mood and wondered if her struggle with Striking Snake had angered him. He had ordered her to go with him and warned her many times previously what he would do to her if she did not obey his commands.

Without a word, Lance abruptly turned away from her and stepped inside the tipi, leaving her to follow.

Not quite sure what to do, Trista hurried after him. Her gaze quickly swept the tipi's interior, and she was surprised by the practicality of the simple furnishings. In the center of the floor was a small fire pit, cold and dark now because of the warmth of the day. A single bed of skins lay at the back of the lodge, opposite the door, and upon the walls hung several parfleche bags and some cooking utensils. To one side, resting against the tipi wall, was his shield. The design upon it was the image of a horse painted in varying shades of yellow and gold. It was the sight of what was tied to the shield by sinew thongs that made her gasp in terror . . . . white, gleaming animal teeth and what looked to be scalps.

Lance looked up at the sound of her distress, and noting the direction of her gaze, he laughed mockingly. "Do you like my shield? It has great power, you know."

Trista did not answer, but retreated even farther across the tipi away from it.

When she didn't respond, he continued derisively, "As brave as you were with Striking Snake, I did not think the sight of a few bears' teeth and horses' tails would trouble you."

"Horses' tails?" she repeated dully.

"Among my people the bear teeth tell of the warrior's hunting skills, and if a warrior's shield is adorned with horses' tails, it tells of his great abilities at raiding."

"So you've stolen many horses?"

"I have taken many," he confirmed confidently, "but the golden one is the one of which I am most proud."

"Fuego . . ."

"Fuego?" Lance looked at her questioningly.

"That is what the stallion is called. Michael and his father referred to him as Fuego because of his unusual coloring. It's Spanish for fire and—"

"I know what it means," he cut her off brutally. For a moment they had been talking together almost civilly, but her mention of Michael and his father had stirred the turmoil of his feelings again.

"Oh . . ." Trista was puzzled by the sudden change in him.

"You will not be staying with me. It is not allowed. You will stay with She Who Speaks the Truth."

Trista's heart plummeted at his declaration. With Lance she felt protected, but now she was to be thrust off on someone else . . . a stranger who probably didn't even speak English. Judging from the way the one girl had treated her earlier, Trista knew it would not be easy for her.

"It is only for you to obey. You will do whatever She Who Speaks the Truth asks of you. As long as you do as you are told, you will be given the free run of the camp. But know, Trista, that I will not hesitate to punish you should you cause any trouble."

Trista realized that her joy in seeing Lance again had been miserably misplaced. She meant nothing more to him. She was his slave, bound to do as he ordered. She was his property and completely at his mercy.

A fleeting thought of Michael and possible rescue crossed her mind. The spark of hope must have shown in her eyes, for Lance immediately reacted.

"Do not think about escaping or being rescued, my golden captive." He crushed her hope with his cruel words. "Those who would have followed us were lost after the first day, and I made certain to erase all signs of our trail."

His arrogant assurance struck a nerve with her, and she could no longer control the roiling, twisting emotions that were seething within her.

"I hate you, Lance! I hate you with every breath I take! Somehow, someday, I'm going to see you pay for what you've done to me!" Trista cried, throwing herself at him and pounding on his chest with both her fists.

Lance pinned her arms to her sides with little trouble and pulled her against him. "If you ever physically attack me again, Trista, your punishment will be severe," he ground out, his blue eyes flashing dangerously.

"What more could you do to me that you haven't already done?!" She glared up at him mutinously.

Lances grin was evil. "I don't think you want to find out."

"Why, you . . . !!!"

"Your temper is fiery, Trista." Lance tightened his grip upon her, holding her more tightly to him. "You will learn to keep it under control," he taunted, and then grew serious. "Perhaps you should be called Fuego, too. Fire and passion . . ."

As Trista stood, crushed against his hard, manly frame, something wild exploded within her. Her body was suddenly alive with excitement at being held so intimately to him. Her breasts swelled at the contact with his chest, and to her shame, she could feel her nipples hardening in invitation. She wanted to deny it. She wanted to break free of his hold, to run from here and never look back, but it was too late. As she lifted her stricken gaze to his, she saw his knowledge of her weakness reflected there.

When Lance had pulled her into his arms, a rush of heated desire had swept through him, taking him completely by surprise. He looked down at her, mesmerized, as he felt her own response to his nearness. *What was this thing that ignited between them at a single touch? This reckless, desperate blaze of emotion that rendered them both insensible to anything but their need to be one?"* Lance had no answer to the dilemma, except one.

His need was fierce as he bent to kiss her, and he was pleased when Trista resisted only for an instant before surrendering fully to his savage embrace. His mouth plundered hers with a carefully controlled violence. He hated her for the power she had over his senses, yet he could not, would not, stop. His was a need that had to be satisfied, and only Trista could satisfy him. Hungrily, his lips sought the sweetness of her throat and then skimmed lower to the thrust of her breasts. With impatient fingers, he stripped off her shirt and bared them to his questing caresses.

The kisses Lance pressed upon her silken flesh were hot and arousing, and Trista grew weak with desire. She clung to him, wanting more than just these few heated touches. When he moved to his bed, she went willingly. Her clothing cast aside, she welcomed him to her. Her arms reached out to hold him close as he tantalizingly stroked every inch of her satiny curves.

There was no thought, only a driving need to possess and be possessed. At his urging, Trista spread her thighs, and then there were no barriers between them as Lance moved deep within her. He gloried in the feel of her holding him tightly in her womanly depths, and he lay still for a moment savoring the velvet heat.

Trista did not understand the reason for his quiet, and she moved restlessly beneath him, wanting him to continue. Her senses were crying out for him to release her from this sensual bondage he'd created, to slake the hunger that his touch had aroused.

No words were spoken as he began to move. Driven to the brink by her encouragement, Lance thrust deeply within her, claiming her as his own, branding her forever as his. His desire mounted with each potent stroke of his hips, and he sought his pleasure, taking her with him to the ecstasy of paradise.

Trista crested, the throbbing excitement pulsing through her in a rainbow of rapture. Mindless in the aftermath of her passion, she lay with him, cradling him to her.

The beat of the drums penetrated the haze of contentment that had momentarily engulfed them both. The harshness of their savage rhythm brought Lance back to reality, and he moved quickly away to pull on his clothing.

Trista was startled by his sudden withdrawal from her, and as the coolness of the night's air chilled her previously heated body, the mist of satisfaction that had clouded her thinking vanished. A tremendous sense of remorse filled her. It had happened between them again, and she had been powerless to stop it! Stricken, she grabbed for her own clothing and hastily began to dress.

Lance did not look at her until he was heading out the door. "Do not leave my lodge. I will send someone for you."

"But Lance, I—" she began, but it was too late. He

had already gone, and she was alone with only her bitterness and her regrets.

Clad in his finest buckskin clothing, his face painted in honor of the celebration, Lance sat with his uncle before the huge bonfire, enjoying the evening's events. Dancers moved about the flames in time to the pagan, pulsing rhythm of the drums, singing out their joy at his accomplishment.

"It is a fine celebration, Lone Elk," Lance thanked him as he watched the dancers before him.

"It is only worthy of your success. You alone caught the elusive golden one," his uncle told him proudly. "I am looking forward to watching his taming."

"I am looking forward to having him tamed, although I do not believe he will ever be completely docile. His pride is fierce."

"He is much like his master then." Lone Elk smiled at Lance. "This is good. His offspring will strengthen your herd."

"His foals will bring much in trade," Lance agreed.

"Where is your captive tonight?" Lone Elk asked, wondering at her absence.

"I have left her with She Who Speaks the Truth," he replied.

"I would see this woman you brought back."

"Tomorrow I will bring her to you."

Lone Elk grunted his approval and turned his attention back to the dancers.

Night Lark danced feverishly to the rhythm of the drumbeat. All night she had done her best to try to attract Lance's attention, but so far she had met with little success. Her frustration was growing.

Night Lark knew a moment of disquiet as she thought of his white captive. Wind Rider had made no secret of his desire for her, and he had also indicated that Lance wanted her, too. The possibility jarred her. She was the most sought after maiden in the tribe, yet she disdained all offers in favor of Lance. She had loved him for a long time now and had waited patiently for the time when he would take her as his wife. If he chose the white woman over her, it would be a blow to her esteem from which she might never recover. She would become the laughing-stock of the village! A sneer curved her full lips at the thought. There was no way she was going to let the pale, ugly white woman have Lance. He was hers!

What she'd been angry about before, she now considered a blessing. Wind Rider had convinced her mother to allow the captive, Trista, to stay with them. At first it had disturbed her, but Night Lark knew now that it was the perfect situation. With Trista at her beck and call, she could keep an eye on her at all times and make her life a living hell. The thought pleased her, and a smile of pure delight curved her mouth. Lance would never belong to the white woman! Never!

The savage beat of the music drawing her on, Trista crept closer to the center of the village. The ways of the Comanche were a mystery to her, and so she stayed hidden in the shadows as she watched the festivities. She stared in fascination at the dancers as they moved to the frenzied, haunting rhythm, their painted, sweat-streaked bodies gleaming in the flicker-ing firelight.

She searched the crowd for Lance. His appearance was so different because of the paint he'd used and the change in his clothing that it took her a minute to recognize him. No longer was he wearing a simple breechclout. Instead, he'd donned a buckskin shirt and leggings that were decorated with colored beads, bits of silver, and long, flowing fringe. His face was painted in several different colors this time, but Trista still found that she hated the Comanche disguise. She could find no kindness in him when he looked so fiercely alien.

It was then, as she was watching Lance, that she noticed the woman dancing directly before him as if offering herself to him. Trista recognized Night Lark almost immediately and knew a great desire to trip her now, just as Night Lark had tripped her earlier during her confrontation with Striking Snake. Their situations might not be the same, but she knew she would derive great pleasure from embarrassing her.

Trista did not hate many people, but Night Lark was definitely one of the few who had earned her enmity. Their first encounter had been galling enough by itself, but the thought that she now had to live in the same lodge with her made it even worse. When she had come for her at Lance's lodge with her mother, She Who Speaks the Truth, Night Lark had wasted no time in making her lowly position in their household known. Trista sensed that Night Lark would be incredibly cruel to her if the opportunity arose, and she knew she would be hard put to tolerate the other woman's viciousness should it come to that.

Her gaze drifted back to Lance. She noticed that his full attention was now directed to Night Lark and that he was smiling widely at her. The older man sitting beside him said something to him, and Lance laughed good-naturedly at the remark though his eyes did not leave Night Lark's swaying body.

A surge of aggravation shot through her, though

she did not know why she should care if he found the other woman attractive. She hated Lance! Hated him with all her heart and soul! Turning her back on the revelry, she disappeared into the night, refusing to put a name to the emotion that was tugging so painfully at her heart.

It was much later when Lance left the celebration. The day had been a long one, but though he was tired, he was feeling well satisfied with his life. He had attained what had amounted to almost a lifelong goal for him in capturing the golden rogue, and tomorrow he would begin training the stallion to accept a rider. The thought that soon he would be regularly riding the once elusive horse filled him with great pleasure. He smiled widely at the thought as he made his way through the quiet of the camp heading in the direction of his tipi.

"Your evening has been a happy one, Lance?" The sultry female voice came to him through the darkness of the night.

Lance paused and turned toward where he knew Night Lark stood. "Your voice is as sweet as your name, Night Lark, and yes, my evening has been a happy one."

She stepped forth to confront him, her eyes sparkling with desire, her pulse beating rapidly at the thought of sharing his heated embrace. "I would like all of your nights to be this special."

"It would be more than even the bravest of warriors could bear," Lance returned lightly, for the celebrating had lasted long into the night, with food and drink flowing freely.

"Then we will speak only of tonight," Night Lark murmured as she moved toward him, pressing herself completely against him and linking her arms around his neck, "and tonight is not yet over."

With a slight tug of her arms, Night Lark drew him down for a flaming kiss. When Lance accepted her kiss, Night Lark moved sinuously against him in a deliberate effort to try to arouse his passions.

Despite all of Night Lark's sensual efforts, an image of Trista intruded in Lance's thoughts. It was a vision of Trista lying naked on his bed . . . her golden hair spread out in a pale halo about her . . . her rounded, silken breasts begging for the touch of his lips . . . her slender thighs wrapped tightly about his waist as he plumbed the depths of her womanhood.

It angered Lance that Trista had the power to haunt him even when he was kissing another woman. It had been bad enough that Trista had slipped into his thoughts on several occasions during the celebration and that numerous times he had found himself scanning the crowd, to no avail, for a glimpse of her. But for her to barge into his consciousness as he was holding another woman in his arms, that was too much! She was nothing but his slave.

Even so, to his frustration, Lance was finding Night Lark's nearness more suffocating than exciting. Though her mouth was hot with promise and her body lushly curved and pliant against his, Lance felt no thrill as she moved her hips in wanton suggestion. Knowing that he did not desire her and that it would be a mistake to take her under these pretenses, Lance encircled her waist with his hands and held her gently away from him.

"Lance?" Night Lark tried to go back into his arms, but he kept her at a distance.

"Go home to your mother, Night Lark."

"But Lance . . . I want you . . . I love you. . . ." she proclaimed shamelessly. "You know that, don't you?"

"But I do not love you."

"I can make you love me! Let me show you the unending pleasure I can give you. . . ." Night Lark offered brazenly.

"No," he refused as he released her. "One day you will find a warrior who returns your love. I am not the one."

Stunned and humiliated, she stared up at him with pain-filled eyes. "Someday you will want me, Lance! I know it!" Then, fighting back the anguish that threatened to destroy her composure, she fled into the night.

Lance watched her go, feeling relief more than anything. Wearily, he continued on his way to his lodge. When he entered his sanctuary, he fell exhausted upon the bed, eagerly courting sleep.

To his surprise, though, sleep did not come. Erotic thoughts of what had last happened on the bed assailed him. Trista . . . an image of her swam before him in the darkness, and he suddenly realized that he missed her warmth beside him. Though they had only slept together for three nights, he felt somehow very alone without her near. As he recognized the direction of his thoughts, he cursed his weakness and rolled over, more determined than ever to put her from his mind.

Trista lay wide awake on her small pallet in She Who Speaks the Truth's tipi. The hours of the evening had seemed endless since she'd left Lance's celebration. Alone and miserable, she had wandered the camp, taking care to avoid any contact with the villagers. Eventually she had found herself at the rope corral that housed Lance's horses and had spent a long time watching Fuego.

Trista felt a certain kinship with the golden rogue. They had lost the freedom of their lives at the same time, and both were now expected to be subservient to Lance. As if aware of her commiseration, Fuego had approached her. At her softly murmured encouragements, he had edged closer until, in time, he had allowed her to touch him. In a tentative truce, they had remained together . . . golden woman and golden horse . . . throughout the long, lonely hours of the night, until the music had stopped and Trista had been forced to return to her new home.

She Who Speaks the Truth had retired shortly after Trista had returned, but there had been no sign of Night Lark as the night had progressed. Now, as dawn cast red and purple streaks across the eastern horizon, Trista lay restlessly upon the hard mat that served as her bed, wondering at the other woman's absence. Where was she? Had Lance taken her up on what she had been so obviously offering him during the dancing? The thought sickened her even as she rationalized that she didn't care what Lance did.

There was the sound of muted footfalls, and then Night Lark slipped quietly into the lodge. Taking great care not to disturb her mother, she moved about the tipi to her own bed near Trista's.

Since running away from the misery of Lance's rejection, Night Lark had had time to think, and she had come to the conclusion that the white woman was responsible for her plight. Before he had returned with his captive, he had never refused her embrace, but now . . . it was probably as Wind Rider had suggested. Lance was seeking his comfort with this pale, blond bitch. Night Lark was sure that he would tire of her sooner or later, and when he did, she would be there for him. Until that happened, she would just

165

have to bide her time.

When she saw that Trista was lying there still awake, her pride insisted that she convince her that she had been with Lance all this time. As she sat upon her own bed, she gave her a smug smile as she stretched in a catlike motion.

"It was a wonderful celebration," she said softly, her sensual movements giving extra meaning to her words.

Her insinuation sent a shaft of unexplainable pain through Trista, but she said nothing. What was there to say? She knew that the revelry had ended a long time before. Lance had no doubt made love to her and then spent the rest of the evening in Night Lark's arms. Her hatred for him grew unbounded.

Night Lark settled comfortably on her own bed. "Lance and I will be married soon. When we are, I will find great joy in giving him many sons."

Trista lay still as the other woman's words haunted her. . . . *Lance was to marry Night Lark.* Staring blankly off into the night's enveloping darkness, she wondered at the ache that clutched at her breast.

Chapter Eleven

Lance's mood was black. As badly as he had needed rest the night before, he had been unable to get any real sleep. Every time he had managed to drift off, dreams of Trista had disturbed his slumber. Desperation had finally driven him from his bed, and seeking diversion from his thoughts of her, he had gone down to the corral to check on Fuego.

Seeing the golden stallion, however, had not provided the distraction he had hoped. Even as he watched the rogue, his golden coat gleaming in dawn's early light, thoughts of Trista invaded. It would not have troubled him so badly had his thoughts been of her connection to the Barretts and his need to seek his revenge through her. But instead he was obsessed with the memory of her lovemaking and the joy that was his when he was buried deep within her body, possessing her to the fullest.

Lance knew he could not afford to feel anything for Trista. She was but a tool for him to achieve some measure of vengeance on the father who had deserted him and the half brother who had taken his place. He had already made Trista his, Lance told himself logically. He had taken her innocence, which by rights had belonged to Michael, and he would continue to take his pleasure with her. When he grew tired of her, he would sell her to Wind Rider.

For some perverse reason, the thought of her belonging to Wind Rider or of his friend touching her infuriated him. He shook his head in confusion, disquieted by the strength of his reaction to the prospect.

Pushing all disturbing thoughts of Trista from his mind, Lance took up a hackamore and entered the corral. Cautiously, he approached the still-untamed stallion. In his usual controlled manner, he carefully coaxed Fuego closer until he was able to slip the restraint on him. So in hand, Lance led the rogue from the pen and began making his way to the sandy-bottomed creek that ran along the far side of the village.

As he passed through the camp, he stopped briefly at Lone Elk's tipi to tell him of his plans, for he knew his uncle wanted to watch the first mounting. He then paused at Wind Rider's lodge to seek his help. Though his friend grumbled at being awakened so early, he hurried to join him.

Word spread quickly that Lance was about to begin the breaking of the golden one. Despite the hour, many came to watch, knowing that it would be a great challenge for Lance to bring the elusive rogue under domination.

Fuego could sense the excitement in the air. He grew edgy as Lance led him to the stream and then down into the water. Skittishly, he balked, trying to pull free of Lance's grip, but Lance merely talked to him softly and calmed him with his crooning words.

"Shall I hold his head while you mount?" Wind Rider was afraid that the rogue might bolt should he come near, and he waited until Lance signaled that it was safe for him to approach.

"Yes. Hold him tightly until I'm completely on his back," Lance directed, "then let him go."

Though they had broken many horses together in

the past, this first actual mounting of Fuego was special, and they were glad they were sharing it together. Lance took a quick glance around at those gathered on the bank, waiting excitedly to watch the taming, and then handed the restraint to Wind Rider.

Fuego stood quivering and uncertain as he eyed the two men skeptically. Though he had come to trust Lance somewhat, his previous bad experiences with men had scarred him deeply. The tension in the growing crowd brought back many memories of pain and danger, and even Lance's gentle strokes and melodic words did not ease the tense knot of fear that filled him.

Lance vaulted onto the stallion's back in one easy move, and for a moment all was quiet. Then, as if exploding, Fuego bucked, his back arching, his eyes rolling wildly in his desperation to be free of Lance's oppressive weight. Twisting and churning, he fought to dislodge Lance.

The water, however, hampered Fuego's ability to move with any real agility or speed, and Lance remained on him, clinging tightly to his back. Frightened and fighting for his freedom, Fuego ran downstream, heading for some low-hanging branches in hopes of knocking the offending man loose. His head lowered, he charged toward the trees and raced beneath them.

Lance was knocked from his seat on Fuego's back and tumbled into the creek bed, where the water and the sandy bottom cushioned his fall. Sitting immobile in the swallow, slow-moving current, Lance took a moment to catch his breath and assess his injuries. Satisfied that nothing was broken, he got slowly to his feet. As he sloshed through the water to where several of the other warriors were holding Fuego, he was filled with even more respect for the rogue. He had always known that the golden one was smart and would use every trick available to fiercely guard his independence.

Walking around to face Fuego, Lance began speaking to him again in his low, comforting tones as he petted his neck and withers with easy, steady strokes. Lance drew a deep breath and then once more vaulted onto his back. Again the stallion went crazy, and again, to the amazement of the onlookers, who knew of his ability to break horses, Lance was unseated and thrown into the waiting stream.

Striking Snake had been observing Lance's attempts to ride the stallion, and he was smug as Fuego threw him for the second time. "Perhaps you should forget about riding the stallion and think only of riding women, Lance! *Old women!!*" he shouted, drawing guffaws from the other men.

Lance ignored Striking Snake as he headed downstream to where Wind Rider again had the stallion under control. Not giving Fuego time to rest, Lance mounted him once more.

Fuego could sense Lance's fierce determination to subdue him, and he grew equally determined not to surrender. He did not think of Lance's kindness since his capture. He could only think of the hated weight on his back trying to force him to do other than his own will.

Lance held on tightly as the stallion gave vent to his rage at being mounted. Yet all of his prowess did not prevent him from being thrown again, and he watched in aggravation as Fuego successfully eluded the warriors who would have caught him.

Trista had lain awake long after Night Lark had fallen sound asleep, for she had been tortured by images of Lance making love to the other woman. Unable to bear the Indian girl's presence even in repose, Trista had fled the confines of the lodge at first light and had wandered silently through the camp, feeling very lost and very alone. She longed to escape, but knew that on foot she would have little chance of success.

The sounds of distant laughter and jeering came to her then, and curious, she headed off in the direction of the noise. The sight of the crowd gathered on the banks of the creek drew her on. Just as she neared them, they parted in frantic excitement, and Fuego came racing up out of the stream heading straight in her direction. Her reaction was instinctive as she waved her hands before the blindly charging stallion. To her surprise, he halted his flight and stood quivering before her, his sides heaving in agitation. Trista approached him calmly and took up the hackamore that swung freely before him.

"Easy, Fuego . . ." Trista murmured as he stamped and sidled slightly away from her. She caught sight of Lance striding toward her, and continued to try to calm the jittery rogue. "Easy, big boy. Slow . . . slow, now . . ." Trista felt somewhat guilty as she eased the stallion's fears, for she shared his desire to be free of this place and this man.

Lance came running up from the creek then and came to a dead stop at the sight of Trista gentling Fuego. Irate indignation flared within him coupled with a reluctant admiration of her ability to handle the horse. The indignation won out, though, and he angrily moved forward to take the rein from her hands.

"You will return to my lodge and wait for me there," he ordered abruptly.

For just an instant upon seeing him, so tall and

171

virilely handsome, Trista had felt excitement surge through her, but she quickly quelled it as she remembered his betrayal with Night Lark. His coldness only hardened her heart against him, and she raised her chin defiantly at his command.

Lance read her expression and grew even more furious. "It would take little to encourage me to beat you this morning, woman. Do as I have commanded."

"It is no wonder Fuego will not let you ride him if you treat him as you treat me. Do you beat him for desiring the freedom you have stolen from him?" she countered. "Gentleness is a far better teacher than brutality."

"You will find no marks on the golden one or on yourself—yet!" He was amazed to find himself on the defensive.

"You have marked me, Lance! You have taken me against my will. . . . You have forced me to—"

"Wait at my lodge, woman!" He snarled, cutting her off.

Trista knew that she had pushed him as far as she could. Biting her lip to keep from crying, she hurried away.

The eyes of those gathered at the stream were upon Lance and Trista as they argued, and Striking Snake was the first to comment as Lance walked back toward them leading Fuego.

"It appears you are having trouble taming more than just the stallion!" he probed.

"She is but a woman and of little importance," he remarked, trying to keep his temper under control. "As for the golden one, he will be mine to ride within the week, but for today, he's had enough."

Wind Rider came up from the creek at his statement, and Lance thanked him for his help. The crowd began to disperse at his declaration, and only

Lone Elk remained to speak with him.

"Your captive is beautiful and obviously the envy of many, but it is not a good thing to allow any woman to speak to you so before the others," the chief chided.

Lance stiffened at his criticism, yet found himself defending Trista. "She is merely spirited, as the golden one."

"Then you must break her spirit."

"I will deal with her in my own way."

"Perhaps you should sell this one to Striking Snake."

"No!" His reply came much too quickly.

Lone Elk eyed him solemnly as he judged his reaction and then stated, "I would know all of it. Now."

"There is nothing to know."

"There is much you are not saying. No woman has ever held your heart. Why is this one special? Is it because of her white blood?"

Lance turned on his uncle viciously. "I keep her because it pleases me to do so."

"I do not understand. Many times before you could have taken white slaves, but you did not. Why this one?"

He did not want to reveal the complete truth, but having never lied to Lone Elk, Lance knew he could not start now. He met his uncle's gaze as he spoke. "I followed the golden one for many miles, uncle."

"Yes . . . so?" the chief urged.

"He led me south. . . ."

Lone Elk tensed, knowing that the Royal Diamond and all the beautiful memories of his childhood lay to their distant south. "Where did you find this woman?"

"I was on my father's land. She is the betrothed of my father's *other* son." His words were filled with hate.

"How do you know this?"

"She wears a ring of the Barrett brand, and claims

173

to be his fiancée. I have stolen my half brother's woman."

The chief nodded his understanding and approval of Lance's actions. He was pleased with his nephew's bold coup. "So you have finally taken your vengeance. Does Barrett know that it was you, his own son, who took her?"

"No, and I was careful to erase any hint of my trail."

"You have done well. Does the woman know of your connection to them?"

"I have told her nothing, and I would keep it that way. I am the son of Shining Star. I am Comanche," he said more forcefully than he had intended.

"It is good you know which path you walk," Lone Elk told him, wondering at the vehemence of his proclamation. "I will speak with you later."

When the chief had gone, Lance headed back to the pen where he kept his herd. After cooling the stallion down, he released him into the corral and started toward his tipi and Trista.

"Lance."

At the sound of someone calling his name, Lance looked up to find Striking Snake coming his way, leading two magnificent ponies.

"Striking Snake," he returned, eyeing him skeptically.

"I would speak to you about your white captive."

"What is it you want?"

"Though she is a troublesome woman, as we all could see at the creek, I am willing to give you two of my best ponies for her."

Lance knew the offer was a good one, for a captive seldom brought that much in trade. Still, for reasons he could not explain, he was not prepared to part with her.

"It is generous of you to offer so much for Trista, but she is mine. I am keeping her."

Striking Snake did not take his refusal well. He wanted that woman. He wanted to master her . . . to teach her her place . . . to make her his. "I will make it three ponies. You may choose the third yourself from my herd."

"Trista is not for sale, Striking Snake, at any price," he found himself refusing.

For the moment Striking Snake could do no more. "As you say," he agreed, but even as he walked away, he was plotting some other way to possess the yellow-haired, slender beauty.

Trista sat alone in Lance's lodge awaiting his return. She sat upon his bed, remembering what had happened between them there the day before and imagining what had taken place there in the hours before dawn between Night Lark and Lance. Her loathing for him was churning like a living thing within her.

At the sound of his approach, Trista went still. She remained seated where she was as he threw aside the door and entered the tipi. Though her heart leapt at the sight of him, she forced herself to ignore the sensation. She did not allow her thoughts to dwell on the tall leanness of his body or the piercing blueness of his eyes. Instead, she concentrated on keeping her composure as she met his stare unwaveringly. Though she was nervous and not sure what to expect, she was resolved not to betray her true feelings to him.

Lance paused motionlessly, just inside the entrance-way. He was furious with Trista because she had embarrassed him before the other members of his tribe. But as he stood there, gazing down at her

175

where she sat on his bed, he could only think of how gorgeous she looked and remember how passionate their lovemaking had been the day before. The pale silk of her hair tumbled in wild disarray about her shoulders. At the sight of it, he longed to tangle his hands in the heavy mass as he tilted her head back to receive his kiss. Her mouth was firm, almost grim, and he wanted to plunder her lips with his own and force them to sweet submission. Her blue eyes were locked upon him, and their expression was carefully inscrutable. The only clue he had to her state of disquiet was the way her breasts rose and fell rapidly with her breathing. He let his gaze linger on the soft flesh that was revealed by her torn blouse. Distractedly, he realized that he should get her different clothing so she would be protected from the lecherous looks of the other men . . . especially Striking Snake.

The thought that he wanted to protect her from Striking Snake troubled him. He scowled darkly as he wondered why he should care what happened to her. Why did it matter that he was to be the only one to touch her? If he truly wanted to seek his revenge against the Barretts, he would share her with the whole tribe. As quickly as the thought came to him, he dismissed it. He only wanted to keep her safe because she belonged to him—for now. She was his property, and he would take care of her just as he took care of all else that was his.

Trista grew slightly unnerved when he did not speak immediately. Flaunting her false bravado, she snapped, "Have you come to beat me?"

"You have much to learn, Trista," Lance stated stonily as he remained standing over her, "and the first lesson is that a Comanche woman is obedient above all else."

"I am not a Comanche woman," Trista shot back

angrily, "and I never will be!"

"It is time you recognized your fate and accepted it."

"I am just like Fuego, Lance," she told him steadily. "I will never accept your domination freely. Never!"

Her continued defiance sent his temper flaring, and in one step he reached her and pulled her forcefully up to him. His hold on her upper arms was viselike as he glared down at her, his blue-eyed gaze icy with contempt. "You will also learn to hold your tongue."

Trista felt the strength of his fury, but did not relent. "If I cause you such grief, why don't you just let me go? Let me return to my own people. Then you would no longer be burdened with me."

"No," he refused.

"Lance, let me go. I'm sure the Barretts would pay handsomely to have me back. Would you like a reward? Name your price. Horses . . . money . . . anything!"

The mention of the Barretts seared across the rawness of his fury. "I want no reward for you," he bit out.

"Why not?" Trista challenged, her eyes flashing fire. "What is the point in keeping me here when you know that I'll never surrender to you? I hate you, Lance!"

Her taunt severed what little restraint he had upon his wayward desires. "You always proclaim your hatred for me, Trista, but I can prove otherwise."

"No!!" She saw the flare of heat in his eyes and read his open intent. She tried to twist away from him, but his strength was overpowering.

Lance's anger was so great that there was no gentleness in him as he pressed her down upon his bed. She was going to pay for all the pain he had suffered. He did not bother with soothing caresses or soft words. His fury was so great that he was feeling little except the driving need to claim her completely. Despite her protests, he ripped her skirt from her and thrust deep within her.

Trista struggled to be free, yet knew that it was useless. Tears stained her cheeks as she lay still beneath his driving weight. To her horror, as Lance moved so rhythmically against her, a blossom of desire began to grow in the womanly heart of her. She fought it, tried to force the feeling from her, but it was like quicksilver flowing through her veins. How could this be happening to her? How could her body betray her this way? She despised this man, and yet he had but to touch her and she melted to his will. Trista groaned in tormented agony.

Her moan of protest affected Lance as no fighting or arguing would have. The hardness within his heart melted, and he immediately slowed his pace. Reaching down, he cupped her hips to draw her nearer. His mouth sought hers in a devouring exchange, and he was surprised by the abandon with which she responded.

"You are mine, Trista."

"No . . ." she protested weakly, but when he threatened to move away, she clasped him more tightly to her.

Together their passions spiraled to the peak of excitement. They soared to the heights and then drifted softly back, their limbs intertwined, their bodies still joined in intimacy.

Lance was smug as he moved away from Trista. *So she hated him, did she?* he thought with arrogant self-confidence. *She certainly had a strange way of showing it.* He stood up and straightened his clothing.

Trista was upset enough with herself for her weakness in giving in to Lance, but she grew outraged when she saw his expression. He might think he had conquered her, but he hadn't! Seething, she covered herself with her damaged skirt and faced him.

"You're bigger than I am, and you're stronger than I am, and you may be able to force my body to respond to you, but you'll never be able to touch my mind or my heart!"

His expression did not falter though her words struck him like a lash. He *had* overpowered her. He *had* forced her to respond. The satisfaction he was feeling at having brought her to passion's pleasure faded as he experienced a rush of unexplained guilt. Why was it that the truth as she saw it had the power to emasculate him? Angered, he needed to strike back at her.

"It is not your mind or your heart that I wanted to touch, woman. I have possessed all of you that I ever wanted. You are nothing more than a convenience for me, but you are becoming more and more trying to my patience," he sneered caustically, gauging the effect of his words upon her as she paled beneath their force. "Don't talk to me about ransom, either. I have no need of money or horses from the Barretts. Striking Snake has just offered me an outrageous sum for you, and I regret most deeply that I did not agree to the trade." He said no more, but let his gaze rake over her in disgust before stalking from the lodge.

Trista shivered beneath the impact of his words. She had hoped to cut him to the quick with her insult to his masculinity, but he had been impervious to her attempt. With shaking hands, she picked up her ruined garment and tugged it back on. Holding it together as best she could, she made her way from his lodge and hurried back toward She Who Speaks the Truth's tipi.

The old woman saw the condition of Trista's clothing as she approached and shook her head in disbelief. What transpired between the captive and her owner was none of her business, but she now understood why Lance had come to her moments before to ask her to provide new garments for her.

"Come." She Who Speaks the Truth directed her inside the lodge and moved to sort through a small bundle at the foot of the bed. She drew out a serviceable fringed buckskin skirt, top, and moccasins. "Here." She handed the Comanche apparel to Trista.

Trista had wondered what she was going to do, and she was struck by the woman's kindness. "Thank you, She Who Speaks the Truth. I will not forget your kindness in this matter."

"Lance asked that I give you some new clothing," she answered honestly, "and I can see now, why."

Trista flushed at her observation, and her spirits sagged to find out that Lance was behind her generous offer. Was there no escaping this man? "Do you always do what Lance tells you to do?" she asked, more out of curiosity than annoyance.

The Indian woman studied her for a moment before answering. "Lance is a fine, brave warrior. I have known him for many years and think highly of him. It is my pleasure to do his bidding, for someday he will be great chief. If you were smart, you would be proud to have such a man as your owner."

"No man will ever own me!" she declared.

"Ah, but Lance already does," she pointed out. "You are his, and you have been lucky so far."

"What do you mean, 'lucky'?"

"Not all captives fare as well as you have. The ones who resist our ways are generally put to death. You would be wise to obey him. Do as he says. Lance can be very kind, but in the ways of the warriors, he can also be very cruel."

180

"She Who Speaks the Truth?"

The older woman looked up questioningly.

"What do you know of Lance's background? I mean, it's obvious that he's part white —"

She bristled at Trista's query, and told her sharply, "To our way of thinking, Lance is all Comanche. His mother was the chief's sister. He denied his white past long ago. We do not speak of it."

Her answer did not satisfy Trista, yet she said no more. Stripping off her tattered clothing, she donned the Indian outfit.

Chapter Twelve

It was late. Darkness had long ago staked its hold on the hill country. In the lodge of She Who Speaks the Truth, both mother and daughter slept. Only Trista lay awake, recounting in her mind all that had transpired that day.

She had not seen Lance since their ugly encounter that morning, and the hours since they'd parted had passed with excruciating slowness. Judging from the way he'd acted when he'd left her, Trista had truly believed that he'd hurried off to find Striking Snake and take him up on his offer for her. Her fears had run rampant all day as she'd anxiously expected the savage brute to show up at any moment and claim her for his own. To her relief this hadn't happened, but still the long hours of constant worry had left her too tense to rest.

The sound of horses stirring restively outside drew her thoughts to Fuego. She wondered how the big stallion was holding up after his traumatic run-in with Lance that morning. Trista suddenly knew a great longing to see the golden rogue. The moccasins she wore permitted her to move soundlessly, and so, carrying the remnant of her skirt with her, she crept from the tipi and through the camp without detection.

The moon pointed out the way for Trista, and as she approached the corral she could see the magnificent rogue standing alone at the far side of the enclosure. He looked so aloof and so disdainfully regal that Trista could only stare at him in awe.

She called out to him in hushed tones, "Fuego . . . my golden one . . ."

Fuego lifted his head, and his ears came forward at the sound of her voice. Shifting his stance, he glanced in her direction and paused as he spotted her.

"Come, fiery one," Trista coaxed.

He took a hesitant step toward her, then stopped again, unsure of her and her intentions. His ears flattened, and he remained motionless, staring at her from across the distance.

Trista admired his perfect form and thought he looked much like a bronze statue she had once seen in a museum back home. "You are gorgeous, Fuego. Solid strength and masterful intelligence, it is no wonder that it took so long for a mere man to catch you."

Fuego, as if agreeing with her statement, snorted and moved slightly closer. His ears went up again as he picked up her scent and remembered her calm ministering that morning. His gaze remained fixed upon her.

She sensed that he was warming to her. Not wanting to make any sudden moves or do anything that would frighten him, Trista began to hum a lilting melody she remembered from her childhood. The soft refrains were a balm to the horse's jittery state, and he edged ever nearer.

"That's it, my golden beauty. Come, let me love you."

The gentle caress of Trista's voice broke down the stallion's last barrier of resistance, and Fuego loped straight to her. Thrilled by her success, she stroked the powerful lines of his neck as she continued to sing to him.

"You will come to know me, Fuego. We are alike, you and I . . . hostages of a cruel twist of fate. We have only each other."

Over and over she petted the sweeping curve of his body. As he grew more and more relaxed with her, she took up the cloth that had once been her skirt and began to rub him down with it. It was a trick she had learned from her father's master trainer, and she knew it worked well. The more familiar a horse became with your scent, the more easily he would be mounted when the time came.

The memory of Lance's futile attempt to ride Fuego occurred to her then. It had been difficult for him to admit defeat that morning, but what a blow it would be to his warrior's pride if she was the one who tamed the stallion! Her smile was tinged with cunning as she devised a plan. She would come to Fuego whenever she could and work with him. Then one day, before the entire tribe, she would mount and ride the golden rogue!

"We'll show him, Fuego. He cannot conquer us, no matter how hard he tries!" Trista stayed on with the stallion for a long time, gentling him with her crooning and rubbing, and talking with him of her plan.

Striking Snake's fury with Lance over his refusal to sell Trista kept him restless and awake all night. He wanted Trista with a passion that defied reason, and he meant to have her, one way or another. He did not know why he desired her so fiercely. He had had white women before and had always thought them lifeless and cold. Somehow this one, with her golden hair and lovely body, was different. He had wanted to possess Trista from the first moment he'd seen her riding double on the trail with Lance. She was brazen in her ways and needed a firm-handed man to control her, but Striking Snake knew he could be that man.

As he lay in his tipi, he thought of the way Trista had looked that morning when she'd caught the golden stallion. Her hair had been loose and flowing about her like liquid gold. She had still worn the torn blouse, and the creaminess of her flesh had been exposed for all to see. Striking Snake remembered the feel of her slender thigh beneath his hand the other day, and he felt himself grow hard with desire for her. He had to have her!

Getting up from his bed, he escaped the heat of his lodge and strode toward the tipi where the white woman was staying. It was as he was crossing the camp that he heard the unusual sound of someone singing. He did not immediately recognize the voice, but followed it anyway out of curiosity.

Striking Snake was completely surprised to find that it was Trista and that she was now wearing traditionally Comanche garb. He stood in the night shadows and watched her as she talked to the golden stallion and boldly rubbed him down. He had thought her desirable in her white woman's clothing, but the sight of her dressed as one of his own people only served to whet his appetite for her even more.

He waited in silence until she bid the horse good night and started to walk away before making his presence known. Stepping directly out to block her path, Striking Snake smiled down at her. He felt huge and powerful as he noted the fear in her expression.

"It would seem, white woman, that you have many talents."

"Striking Snake . . ." Trista gasped. Caught off guard, she was unable to hide her terror.

"I have come for you. I will make you mine."

"No! Lance—"

He cut her off as he grinned evilly. "What Lance does not know, does not matter." His hand closed around her upper arm, and he started to drag her off, away from the camp.

Trista's mind was racing as she hung back, trying to resist his lead. Had Lance sold her to this man? For some reason she didn't think so. Why would he feel the need to steal away with her into the night if he had bought and paid for her? And why would he say, *"What Lance does not know, does not matter"?* There was no doubt in her mind about what her fate would be at this man's hands, and in desperation, she screamed.

Her cry rent the air. At the sound of her distressed call, Fuego neighed and reared wildly. Racing about the enclosure, he stirred the other horses to action until they were all pacing and whinnying at the disturbance.

"Stupid woman!" Striking Snake snarled, clamping a hand over her mouth as he lifted her up to carry her.

Trista tried to break free, but he held her pinioned to his chest as he strode off into the darkness with her.

Lance had lain awake for a long time and had just managed to fall asleep when the sound of Fuego's scream woke him. In a flash he was out of his lodge, running toward the corral. He found the horses restive, but not endangered, and wondered at the cause of their upset. Poised for action, he waited in silent vigil, hoping to discover the reason for the disturbance.

Striking Snake didn't stop until he'd sought out a secluded spot among the trees near the creek. He knelt and, without removing his hand from Trista's mouth, lay her down on the rocky ground. She squirmed and fought to ward off the warrior, but there was no way her feeble efforts could thwart him.

Obsessed with the need to take her, he slipped a hand up her skirt and pawed at her tender flesh. Trista was sobbing hysterically beneath the oppressive weight of his hand over her mouth. She tried to claw at his eyes, but Striking Snake merely laughed low in his chest as he continued to roughly plunder her femininity. Pushing her blouse up, he bit at her breasts, and she cried in agony as he tortured the sensitive orbs.

Caught up in the excitement of finally having her within his power, Striking Snake made the mistake of releasing her for just an instant so that he could free himself from his breechclout. Trista could not believe that he had unhanded her, and knowing that this was her last chance for salvation, she screamed Lance's name with all her might.

The sound of her anguish echoed through the village, and Lance froze. Trista? Could it be Trista? He raced in the direction of the call, though he wasn't certain that he would be able to find her in time.

Striking Snake quickly covered her mouth again as he swore at her, and it was his own stupidity in speaking to her that revealed their hiding place to Lance.

"I will make you pay for your insolence, white woman," the warrior was declaring as he positioned himself to thrust into her.

"Striking Snake!" The moment Lance came upon them, his heart lurched painfully. A red haze of blood lust filled him. He launched himself at his rival, unmindful of anything save the need to kill the other warrior. He was touching Trista! No one took what was his and got away with it. And Trista *was* his!

Striking Snake had no time to prepare, and he was knocked forcefully from Trista by Lance's diving attack. They rolled through the brambles and bushes, each warrior struggling for dominance. Lance fought like a man possessed, landing blow after vicious blow upon the other man. Striking Snake was not about to give up, though. With savage intent, he used all of his considerable strength to throw Lance off of him and get to his feet.

Trista was shaken to the depths by what had almost happened to her. Lance had come! Thank God! Tears coursed down her cheeks as she scrambled to straighten her clothing. Her body was sore from Striking Snake's brutal fondling, but she ignored the discomfort. The sight of the two warriors circling each other, their expressions deadly, left her quaking with fright. Worry for Lance consumed her. She glanced around trying to find something she could use as a weapon to help him, but there was nothing. She was helpless and could only watch—and wait—and pray.

"Lance . . . please be careful. . . ."

Lance heard her plea and was moved to even greater anger. Striking Snake would die for what he'd dared! With the agility for which he was renowned, Lance jumped and kicked out at the bigger man. His feet made solid contact with the wide wall of the other man's chest and sent him tumbling backward. Lance fell himself, but recovered quickly and drew his knife. Just as Striking Snake made a weak attempt to right himself, Lance was upon him. His knees pinned the warrior's arms to the ground, and he held the blade poised at his throat.

"You dared to take my woman!" He was livid with rage.

"Your woman? Pah!" Striking Snake was contemptuous even facing death. "She is not your woman. She is only your slave."

"Trista is *mine!* No other will ever touch her!" He pressed the knife to his throat and let it draw blood.

Feeling the bite of death, the warrior lied, "Then you should tell her that. She offered herself to me. I was merely out walking through the camp, and she *approached* me. She begged me to take her."

Lance did not believe his story for a minute. "If that were so, Striking Snake, then why did she cry out in terror, and why was she trying to fight you off? I think, brave warrior, that you lie to save your skin. I shall put an end to your miserable ways . . . ."

Trista had not understood any of their words, but she knew what was about to happen as Lance raised his weapon. She was unable to stop her cry of horror that escaped her at the thought. Lance fully intended to drive it into the other man's neck, and only Lone Elk's sudden appearance stopped him.

"Lance! Stop!" the chief ordered harshly. He had heard the noise of the fight and was glad now that he had come to investigate.

Lance's blade was flashing in the moonlight as it began its downward arc, but at his uncle's command, he froze.

"What is going on here?" Lone Elk demanded as he looked from Trista to the two men.

"It is the woman! She is only a captive!" Striking Snake began, trying to weasel out of the seriousness of what he had tried to do. "Everyone knows how Lance feels about whites, so I thought it wouldn't matter if I had a taste of her, too."

"You took what was mine, Striking Snake. You knew that I would not sell her to you, so you attempted to steal her away!"

"Is this true?" Lone Elk's piercing, knowing gaze settled on the prone Comanche. He had known Striking Snake since he was born, and he was aware of just how devious and cunning he could be.

"She is untouched. I did not harm her!" Striking

189

Snake swore as he broke out in a nervous sweat.

"But you took her against Lance's wishes?"

He did not bother to answer, knowing that the evidence against him was overwhelming. Lone Elk took his silence as testimony to his own guilt.

"Lance, release him!" he ordered.

Lance was quick to comply with his wishes as his uncle continued to speak to the other warrior.

"You are banned from our village, Striking Snake. You know that it is against our ways to steal from your own people," the chief condemned. "Be gone from our camp before morning. I have no wish to see your face in the brightness of the sunlight." With that, he turned to Lance. "Come to my lodge as soon as you have taken care of the woman."

"I will come to you, Lone Elk," Lance promised, and he watched in silence as his uncle disappeared back toward the camp.

Striking Snake got jerkily to his feet, and his gaze filled with loathing as he regarded first Trista and then Lance. He spoke in English deliberately so she would know of his threats. "I will never forget this, Lance. Someday I will see you dead, and Trista will be my woman."

"I would have to be dead before I'd ever allow you to lay a hand on her," Lance declared as he watched the other warrior leave.

Trista was amazed by Lance's declaration, and she stared at him as if seeing him for the very first time. She was confused by the myriad of conflicting emotions she was feeling. She wanted to throw herself into Lance's arms and kiss him and hold him near. He had not sold her to Striking Snake! He had saved her! He had fought off her attacker and protected her! The last thought caused her to frown. Protected her? Lance was the man who had originally taken her against her will. She hated him . . . didn't she? He was the one who had possessed her as Striking Snake had only tried to do. Yet she was feeling as if he were her hero.

Lance's gaze met Trista's and despite her confusion, she rushed to him. A fierce gentleness filled him as he took her in her arms and held her close to his heart. He did not understand why he had reacted with such blind fury. He only knew that Trista had been in danger and that he'd had to save her from harm. Keeping her close, he smoothed her hair in a soothing motion as he spoke to her.

"Has he hurt you in any way?" Lance was startled to find that his voice was hoarse and gruff.

Trista shook her head as she nestled close in his protective embrace. "He was rough with me, but you saved me before he could . . . before he could . . ." Her voice broke as the harshness of what had almost happened began to take its toll on her. "Oh, Lance . . ." Her knees buckled as she thought of the ugliness of Striking Snake's touch and how close he had come to actually having his way with her.

Lance swept Trista up into his arms as she went limp against him. Cradling her to his chest, he strode to his own lodge. For a reason that he could not fathom, he knew he could not take her back to She Who Speaks the Truth's home. He needed to hold her close this night. . . . He wanted her with him, now and . . .

He needed to hold her close? He wanted her with him? A scowl marred his handsome features. He had never needed any woman since his mother had died. Why should it be this woman . . . this white woman . . . who could cause this rise of protective emotion within him?

Lance glanced down at her as she rested against his

shoulder. Her eyes were closed. Her features were wan and pinched. The sight of her so helpless tore at him. This was not his fiery Trista. This was not the woman who had defied him at every turn. This woman was soft and yielding, and the realization touched a chord deep within him. He had never known this side of her before, and it unsettled him.

Lance entered his tipi and lay Trista carefully upon the softness of his bed. He stroked the tangled curls back away from her face, then rocked back on his heels to study her quietly for a long moment. Knowing that his uncle awaited him, he stood up. As he did;, Trista opened her eyes and looked up at him, worriedly . . . questioningly.

"I must speak with Lone Elk. You are safe here. Rest. I will be back as quickly as I can." He did not understand why he'd felt the need to explain to her. He only knew that he wanted to wipe the hurt from her eyes and reassure her.

Trista nodded slightly, but didn't speak until he was about to step from the lodge. "Lance?"

Her call halted him and he turned back to her. "Yes?"

"Lance . . ." She paused, not quite sure how to phrase what she wanted to say. "Lance . . . thank you . . ."

He regarded her expressionlessly for a brief time before nodding curtly and striding from the tipi.

Lone Elk was waiting for Lance, and he called out for him to enter when he arrived. His stony face betrayed no emotion as he regarded his nephew across the small fire in the fire pit.

"The woman?"

"Trista will be all right," Lance answered tersely,

still tense over what had happened. He was puzzled by his uncle's request to see him, and he wondered what it was he had to say.

Lone Elk had always hated whites, and he voiced his feelings openly regarding the trouble her presence was causing. "This woman . . . this Trista is only a lowly captive, Lance."

"She is *my* captive," he bristled.

The chief was caustic as he spoke. "She is a white. She is the betrothed of the white man you call your half brother. You claim you hate her. You claim you took her captive and brought her back here because you wanted to punish her and those who hold her dear."

"That is so." Lance met his uncle's gaze steadily as he wondered what point he was going to make.

"Would not her punishment have been greater had you shared her with Striking Snake?"

The thought still had the power to send anger racing through him, but he betrayed none of his fury as he sat respectfully and listened to his elder.

"There would have been no need for the violence had you done so. No woman is worth such trouble, Lance, especially not a white one. Unless . . ." It troubled Lone Elk to even consider that Lance might be coming to care for the female. He had lost his sister to a hated white man; he did not intend to lose his beloved nephew to a white woman.

"Unless, what, my chief?" Lance asked coolly.

"Unless you are coming to care for this woman." Lone Elk's black eyes were riveted upon his face, trying to decipher some of what he was feeling, but Lance had learned long ago to keep his deepest feelings locked within him. His wooden expression revealed nothing to his uncle's probing gaze.

"Your question is ridiculous. I hate whites as much

as you do," he denied vehemently as he got to his feet. "Do not worry that I shall come to care for her, Lone Elk. I care only for the pain and suffering I can cause those who are associated with her." Yet even as he said it, he remembered Trista helpless in his arms, and he wondered if he truly meant it anymore.

For the moment, the chief seemed satisfied with Lance's answer. "Go then. We will speak of this no more."

"Good night, my uncle."

The chief lifted a hand in dismissal as Lance left his lodge.

When Lance returned to his own lodge and slipped silently inside, he was troubled. His conversation with Lone Elk forced him to face up to the special way he was treating Trista. Normally, if a friend admired something you owned, you gave it to him. Generosity was a very admired trait among his people, and since captives were considered possessions, it was not unusual for them to be used by the others. Still, he could not stand the thought of anyone else touching her, and the force of that emotion left him puzzled and confused.

He paused just inside of the tipi to watch Trista as she slept. His breath caught in his throat as he stared down at her, and he noticed for the first time how wonderful she looked in the Comanche clothing. As she lay on her side facing him, the soft buckskin of her V-necked shirt molded to her curves, hinting at the lush fullness beneath. The fringed skirt hugged the swell of her hip, and her long shapely legs were bare to his gaze.

When Lance looked at her face, though, the passion that had filled him faded. She looked childlike and innocent in her slumber, and he knew he would not slake his desire upon her tonight. His uncle's words returned to badger him. . . . *You claim you took her captive and brought her back here because you wanted to punish her . . . unless you are coming to care for her.*

Lance knew the jumble of feelings that he had for Trista made no sense. He hated her, yet could not bear the thought of her being hurt by anyone but himself. Annoyed by the seeming impossibility of his situation, he crossed the distance between them and lay down beside her, taking her in his arms.

Trista did not wake as he drew her close, but softly sighed his name in her sleep. "Lance . . ."

Without conscious thought, he tightened his hold on her. He loved the feel of her pressed so softly, so willingly, against him. Trista stirred, and her left arm shifted, her hand splaying out beside her on the bed. In the dimness of the night's light, Lance saw the ring. What had been a tender moment for him was transformed to one of bitterness as he stared at the gem-encrusted symbol of his father and his way of life. His hatred surged anew, and he moved away from her. Rolling to his other side, he put a little distance between them on the bed and then courted sleep, all the while trying to ignore the memory of her sweetly murmuring his name, and the inviting warmth of her still so nearby.

Chapter Thirteen

The new day dawned to find Michael already mounted up, waiting for the others in the search party to join him. Fatigue was deeply etched into his handsome features, and the effect aged him considerably. No longer was he carefree. His subdued manner reflected his seriousness and single-mindedness of purpose.

He scanned the horizon, his dark eyes clouded with worry. Trista was out there . . . but where? His heart was heavy with sorrow as he realized that they were about at the end of their rope. They had only enough supplies left for three more days, and he knew they would have to return to the ranch soon.

The trail had virtually disappeared several days before. They had been combing the area ever since in hopes of turning up some clue as to the direction the Indian had taken, but had met with no success. It was almost as if Trista had vanished off the face of the earth.

"Ready, son?" George rode up beside him and reined in to discuss their plan of action for the day.

Michael nodded and glanced back toward their camp. "What about the others?"

"They'll be along," he assured him. "I just came on ahead to talk with you for a minute.

"What about?" he challenged sharply. He knew that the time had come to decide whether or not to keep on with the search.

"Michael . . . there isn't much more we can do.

We've been over this entire area with a fine-tooth comb, and we haven't managed to turn up a thing."

"Don't you think I know that?" he agonized.

"We're going to have to call the search off soon."

"I'm not going to give up looking for her," Michael vowed.

"Michael . . . it's pointless. The Indian's probably a hundred miles away from here by now, and Trista—"

"You and the rest can head back any time you want, but I'm going to keep on until I find her or die trying."

George recognized some of his own obstinacy in his son's answer and knew there would be no deterring him. "Well, let's hope that we find something today."

"There's got to be some clue . . . some little thing that we've been overlooking. This Indian can't have been that good at covering his tracks . . ."

Trista came awake slowly. She had slept well and was feeling deeply contented. She felt so comfortable nestled where she was that she didn't immediately open her eyes, but lay perfectly still enjoying the peace of the moment. Only when Lance moved in his own slumber, tightening the arm that held her possessively about her waist, did the realization dawn Lance had returned and they had slept together in his lodge. Silently she cursed herself for abandoning herself and resting so completely with him near. He was her enemy! Yet in her sleep she had instinctively sought him out.

Her eyes flew open as he pulled her back against him so that they lay together intimately. Her back was to his bare chest, and her thighs were cupped by his thick, powerful ones. Awareness of him as a man shot through her along with the memory of the heat of his touch, and Trista knew she had to free herself. Trying not to disturb him, she inched slowly away.

For a moment she actually believed she was going to make her escape, but her movements woke Lance, and he clamped his arm more tautly about her, stopping her progress. The bitter feelings that had possessed him the night before disappeared as wisps of fog before the wind as he woke to find Trista warm and soft against him. Without conscious thought, his manhood responded to her nearness.

"Trista . . ." He groaned her name as he lifted a hand to caress the silken curls that lay tousled upon her shoulder. "Trista, love . . ."

She knew she should try to get away. Desperately she sought Michael's image, but the only face her mind could conjure up was Lance's . . . his dark hair and blue eyes dominating her very soul. She didn't want this! She couldn't! Yet his sensual assault, when it came, was so tender that she was defenseless against it. His lips were warm and gentle as they explored the sweetness of the back of her neck. Shivers of excitement raced down her spine, and she found herself arching backward against him. The heat of his desire pressed firmly against her bottom, and Trista could not prevent the little whimper of need that escaped her.

His hands were everywhere then, caressing her even as he pushed her skirt up higher. When he brought her full against him then and taught her a new way to accept him, she knew a surge of forbidden delight at the different position. Lance slipped his hands beneath her shirt to cup her breasts. He teased the peaks to hardness as he began to move within the womanly sheath of her.

Trista moved with him, glorying in the blossom of her passion. This felt right, so right. She covered his hands with hers . . . holding him, holding her. They reached the crest as one and strained together, wresting from the moment all the pleasure they could.

A physical peace engulfed them, but their thoughts, once the haze of ecstasy had faded, could not be ignored. In silence they lay, each caught up in their own agonies . . . their own guilts . . . their own regrets . . . .

Trista had fought it. She had not wanted it, but the truth could not be denied any longer. She responded physically to Lance as to no other. None of the few stolen embraces she'd shared with Michael had ever given her the rapture she experienced in Lance's arms.

Her guilt over betraying Michael was oppressive. She didn't want to want Lance. Yet even now as she kept her eyes tightly closed against the reality of the moment, his visage haunted her . . . .

Lance was stunned by the beauty of what had just occurred. Trista had not fought him . . . .There had been no denials of passion . . . no vows of hatred. She had surrendered to him, and they had shared love's greatest pleasure. He marveled at how responsive she was to his touch. No woman he had ever known before her had ever demonstrated such capacity for passion.

As he lay quietly with Trista in his arms, their bodies still linked in love's embrace, he thought of Michael's ring upon her finger and he smiled. There was no bitterness in him this morning. Today she had given herself to him without fighting, and that was a triumph for him. He had stolen Michael's woman in more ways than one.

Lance ignored the fact that he had wanted Trista as badly as she had wanted him. He told himself that every time she gave herself to him so willingly, he was making her pay for the sins of his father.

Trista stirred, and just that slight movement of her satiny hips against him sent a hot rush of fiery excitement through him. He strengthened within her. Trista had thought to move away, but the feel of him, hot and hard, filling her once again made her gasp.

Lance, too, was surprised by the power of his need. He wanted her again, but this time he wanted to see her face as he took her. He wanted to read the passion in her eyes and know that she was giving herself only to him. He moved away from her for just an instant.

Trista realized she should take this time to try to flee, but the sight of him kneeling over her, so proud and so very masculine, sent her pulses racing. She lay perfectly still beneath his hungry gaze.

Lance helped her strip off her clothes, and when she was naked before him, he paused to drink in the beauty of her slender, enticing body. When he moved over her, he spread her thighs and fit himself deeply within her. His mouth sought hers in a devouring kiss that promised much. Their hands roamed at will, Trista's exploring the sculpted muscles of his back and shoulders, and Lance's stroking the velvet curves and hollows of her breasts and hips.

They were so caught up in the splendor of their mating that they did not hear her coming or her call asking for admission. The entranceway to the lodge opened unexpectedly as Night Lark entered and the sunlight poured brightly within, scalding them with its brilliance.

"Lance . . . your captive has fled and . . ." Night Lark called out as she stepped inside, and what she saw there left her stunned. The sight of Lance and Trista making love was like a physical blow to her.

"By what right do you barge into my lodge, Night Lark?"

She recovered her composure quickly. "I'm sorry,

200

Lance. I called out to you, and I thought I heard you tell me to come in . . ." Her black eyes narrowed as she stared at Trista lying naked beneath an equally unclad Lance. There was no doubt about what they were doing, and she grew furious. Lance was hers! She had offered herself to him, and he had refused! Why had she been denied his passion, and yet this lowly white slave was not?

"What is it that was so important?" he ground out.

"I came to tell you that Trista had disappeared during the night. Now that I know where she is and why she is here, I can tell my mother and she can relax. My mother was very concerned, Lance. She thought your captive had run off."

"Tell She Who Speaks the Truth that there is no need to worry. Trista is with me."

"As I see. It is good to know that you are using her for something . . ." she sneered, giving Trista a hate-filled look. "She does not work very hard for us. Perhaps this is the best way she can serve her master."

"Leave us, Night Lark," Lance commanded as he felt Trista tense and begin to tremble beneath him.

"I'll go now," she replied, her light tone disguising her jealousy over the fact that it was Trista in his embrace.

Trista was destroyed. Never in her life had she suffered such degradation or been so humiliated. It had been bad enough to bear her shame privately, but to be actually seen glorying in Lance's possession . . . and seen by his future wife . . . All vestiges of desire drained from her. She went cold inside, and all emotion died within her.

As far as Lance was concerned, Night Lark could not leave quickly enough. His need for Trista had not abated, but had grown even stronger as he'd held himself embedded within her. As soon as the lodge's opening closed behind the other woman, he began to move again. His passion was so far gone that her lack of response did not touch him. He thrust avidly into her, unmindful of her quietude. Shudders wracked his body as he reached the pinnacle of release, and he collapsed heavily on top of her, his own desire sated.

When he raised up moments later to gaze down at Trista, he was shocked to see tears staining her cheeks. "Why do you cry, woman? Did you not enjoy our joining as much as I did?"

Trista lifted her gaze to meet his, and he was shocked to see the dullness in her expression. "I felt nothing, Lance. You know I hate your touch. Why do you take your pleasure with me when you know Night Lark would spread her thighs for you gladly? She will one day be your wife. Why don't you bed her?"

Her statement sent his temper flaring. He had thought that he had completely conquered her, but he had been wrong. He had touched only her body . . . nothing else. By her claim, she had been merely a vessel for his needs. He moved away from her, his tension obvious in every action as he straightened his clothing.

"Return to She Who Speaks the Truth," he ordered abruptly. "I have no more need of you . . . for now. . . ." He added the last ominously, and without so much as a backward glance, he strode from the lodge.

Night Lark was miserable as she raced away from Lance's tipi. She hated the white woman! She hated her with a driving passion! She didn't know just yet how she was going to do it, but she was determined to get rid of Trista. Night lark felt certain that that would be the only way she would ever be able to claim Lance as her husband.

The sun was high in the sky as Michael and George gathered with their men. Their morning search had yielded nothing, and their hopes were growing dimmer by the minute.

"I think we're going to have to give it up, Michael," George told him, his heart aching for his son's loss.

Michael flashed him a scalding look. "I told you this morning how I felt about quitting!"

"Mike—" One of the hands tried to reason with him, but Michael cut him off.

"I'll tell you what I told Pa. If you want to go on back to the ranch, go on. I'm not going to give up."

"It's not a point of wanting to go back to the ranch, it's a matter of having to go back. We've got a big spread to run, son. These men are needed on the Royal."

Michael softened. "I know that, Pa. I'm sorry. Look, do what you have to do. Just know that I'm not going back."

George looked to his men. "Whitey, you and Tom stay with us. The rest of you take what supplies you need and go on back to the ranch. Tell my wife that the four of us are going to continue the search."

"Yes, sir."

Half an hour later they had parted company, and the four remaining men were sharing a midday meal as they plotted their next move.

"Since we really don't know where they could have gone, we're going to have to guess. . . ." Whitey was saying.

"And there seems to be little doubt where they probably went," George remarked as he drank deeply from his canteen.

"Espada Canyon." Michael stated out loud what the other men were thinking.

"Yep. It's secluded, and the creek runs fresh all

year."

"Let's mount up and head out. We want to travel fast and light. We've wasted enough time already." Michael urged.

As they headed out, only George was troubled by the direction their search was taking.

It was dusk, and Black Water crouched low among the rocks as he watched the small group of white men setting up a cold camp below. They carried only the basic essentials with them, and the sparseness of their encampment clearly indicated that they were intent on traveling rapidly.

Knowing that Lone Elk would want to know of their uninvited presence in their territory as soon as possible, Black Water retreated from his hiding place and swung quickly up onto his pony's back. Racing through the night, he headed back toward his village to warn his chief of their approach.

With only a few stops for rest, he made it back to the Comanche camp by late afternoon of the following day. He charged through the village at a gallop and vaulted from his pony just as he halted before Chief Lone Elk's tipi. Rushing toward it, he called out for admittance. "Lone Elk! I must speak to you at once!"

At the chief's bidding, he hurried to find Lone Elk with his nephew, Lance.

"What is it, Black Water?" Lone Elk remained seated in his place of honor directly opposite the door, with Lance sitting at his right side.

"There are whites in our territory . . ." he related quickly, his breathing labored from his exertion.

"Where?" he demanded stormily.

"There are four of them, and they're riding in from the south."

"How close are they?" The chief grew solemn at the

news of their coming.

"Almost a day's ride. I watched them make camp last night and then came here to let you know. They are traveling light and are well armed."

Lone Elk cast a glance at Lance, who was sitting rigidly next to him. "Did you recognize any of them?"

"No. The distance was too great."

"You have done well, Black Water. Rest for now. We will talk again later," Lone Elk dismissed him.

When the other warrior had gone, Lance spoke for the first time. "I will ride with Black Water and see who trespasses on our land."

His uncle pinned him with a sharp, black-eyed glare. "It could be those who are trying to locate the white woman."

Lance nodded slowly as the tension began to build within him. The possibility that it might be his half brother and his father coming to claim Trista left his emotions in turmoil. "Since I am the one who brought Trista here, I'll take care of it."

"You will not go alone with just Black Water. . . ."

"No. I will take several of the other braves with me," he announced as he stood, suddenly needing to get away . . . to be alone for a time to deal with the violent emotions that were besieging him.

"Black Water is much in need of rest, so plan to leave at dawn."

"I'll be ready." Lance started from the lodge.

"Lance . . ." Lone Elk called him back. "If it is Barrett who crosses our land, remind him of the pledge we exchanged all those years ago."

"I will." Lance knew of the vow Lone Elk and his father had made at his mother's insistence. Lone Elk had sworn to Shining Star that he would not attack the Royal Diamond, and his father had promised, in turn, to stay away from the Comanche lands. Both men had held to that promise all this time . . . until now.

"Are you not concerned about this encounter? What if it is Barrett?" Lone Elk challenged, wanting to know more of his thoughts.

Lance's expression was hard and cold as he started again from his uncle's home. "Barrett will not know me." Yet even as he uttered the words, a part of him, long buried, carried the faint hope that maybe his father *would* recognize him.

"And what about you?"

"I know him, but to me George Barrett is just another white man." With that he was gone, leaving Lone Elk alone, staring after him.

Trista had not seen Lance since he had left her the morning before. She'd convinced herself that she was glad he'd stayed away from her, for whenever he was near, she found herself caught up in a complex twist of unfathomable emotions. Still, as much as she refused to admit that she longed to see him, she found herself watching for him and wondering where he was.

It was as she was working on one of the multitude of jobs Night Lark had given her that Trista spotted Lance for the first time. Her breath caught in her throat at the sight of him, so tall and muscular and handsome. A rush of excitement swept through her as she noticed that he was heading her way. His blue eyes were focused solely on her, and her hands went cold in nervous reaction to the intensity of his gaze. Though he wore no paint, his chiseled features were inscrutable, and Trista was at a loss to judge his reason for coming to her.

Her heart was pounding as Lance came straight toward her. She told herself that she was only reacting this way because she hated him so and because she was upset at seeing him again. But another part of her, perhaps a more honest part of her, chided her mercilessly, bringing to mind the utter joy she had experienced during their lovemaking. *If you hate him*, the inner voice taunted knowingly, *it was because of what he makes you feel*.

Trista clasped her hands together to still the trembling that had beset her, for she refused to display even the slightest weakness before him. Lifting her chin in a small, but open, gesture of continued defiance, she met his clear, blue-eyed stare without fear.

After his conversation with Lone Elk, Lance had spent long hours alone trying to come to grips with the situation. If indeed this was his father and half brother who dared to trespass upon their lands, then Trista was at the very center of his dilemma.

Lance felt that he had already gained a great amount of vengeance just by having taken her, but now he was driven to do more. He didn't know what the outcome would be if a showdown ensued with his father and the men he'd brought with him, but Lance did know that he would not give Trista up.

Trista was his now. He had taken her. He had fought for her. He had possessed her as only a man can possess a woman. Now, he resolved, he would claim her for his own before his people. He would make her his wife.

Lance saw the rebelliousness in her expression, and he prepared himself mentally to do battle with her again. He knew she was not going to like what he planned to do, but he was not going to give her a choice in the matter. Tonight she would be his.

"Come, Trista," he ordered brusquely as he stopped before the place where she knelt doing her woman's work.

Her eyes flashed in resentment at being ordered around, and she glared up at him as she got to her feet. "Where are you taking me?" she demanded in return, determined not to go along submissively.

"We go first to my tipi."

"No . . . I—" Trista didn't want to be alone with him again. She didn't want to face all the memories of what had happened between them in the privacy of his lodge.

"Do not cross me, woman! We go to my lodge!" He did not raise his voice, but his tone said it all.

Trista knew she could not keep on defying him so openly and continue to come out of it unscathed. In silent protest, she followed his lead across the camp.

Night Lark saw them go and hurried to her mother. "Did you know that Trista has gone with Lance?" she asked. She wondered why he had come for the other woman and felt great pangs of jealousy over the thought of her being alone with him.

"Lance does not confide his every move to me, daughter," She Who Speaks the Truth replied, adding teasingly, "But you may rest assured that she will not escape him."

The thought of Trista escaping from Lance greatly appealed to Night Lark and gave her food for thought as she drifted away from her mother's side. Trista might not escape while she was with Lance, but perhaps there was a way for her to get away when she returned to their tipi that night. For the first time since Night Lark had seen them together, she felt a ray of hope.

Lance entered his tipi ahead of Trista, and when she followed him inside, he pointed to a leather-

208

wrapped bundle lying on the bed. "You will wear those garments."

Trista stared down at the mysterious package. "What is it?"

"I will await you outside," he said, refusing to answer her question.

"But, Lance . . ." When she looked up again, he had disappeared. Puzzled, she knelt on the bed and untied the thong that bound the bundle. She opened it carefully.

Trista had not quite been sure what to expect, and she gasped in surprise at the dress within. White in color, the buckskin skirt and blouse were the most gorgeous Comanche garments she had ever seen. Decorated with beads and bits of silver, they had obviously been made with painstaking expert precision. Long fringe graced the sleeves and skirt, and there was a matching pair of moccasins with it. She held it almost reverently, stroking the soft material, as she wondered at the significance of Lance demanding that she put it on.

"Have you finished yet?" Lance asked from outside.

"No . . . I—"

"Would you rather I came in and helped you?" he threatened.

Trista, knowing full well that he would do it, hastily tore off the clothing she'd been wearing and slipped into the beautiful garb. The garment clung softly to her rounded curves, emphasizing the beauty of her femininity. It amazed her that it fit so perfectly. It was almost as if it had been made for her, and her alone.

Lance had had enough of waiting, and he impatiently stepped back inside the lodge. "If you are not dressed by now, I will—" He stopped speaking and went completely still. He couldn't take his eyes off of her, and he stared at her as if he was entranced. The dress that had been his mother's fit Trista faultlessly, and she looked like a goddess to him.

Trista glanced up as he entered and saw the blaze of emotion that reflected in his eyes. She shivered in instinctive recognition of his desire.

Lance turned away and opened a parfleche bag that hung on the wall to take out a comb. He handed it to her and then waited and watched as she struggled to work the tangles from her thick, golden mane. His offering her the comb puzzled her, but she did not argue as she drew it with some difficulty through the snarls.

"Come. It is time," he stated when she'd combed the silken tresses into order. He longed to drag his hands through the satiny length, but knew that that would have to wait until later.

"Time for what, Lance?" Trista asked, warily.

"Chief Lone Elk is waiting," he told her in way of explanation.

Trista wasn't satisfied with his oblique answer. "Waiting for what?"

"He is waiting in his lodge to marry us," Lance stated firmly.

Chapter Fourteen

For an instant, Trista stared at Lance if he were crazy, then she exploded in an outrage fueled by fear. She didn't want to be bound to this man. His control over her senses was far too devastating, and she couldn't risk losing her very soul to him. "Marry you?! I'm not going to marry you! Haven't you heard anything I've said? I hate you!"

"You have an interesting way of showing your hate, Trista. I need only to touch you and . . ." Lance's eyes were dark upon her, reminding her of her response to him. With an idle hand he reached out to caress her arm, and she trembled at his touch.

Trista jerked away from him. "I told you! I don't feel anything when you touch me! I wouldn't marry you if you were the last man on earth! Keep me as your captive. Use me as you will, but I will never want you, Lance! Never!"

"Don't say things you're going to regret, Trista."

"The only regret I have is that I was foolish enough to go out riding alone that morning! If I'd waited for Michael to ride with me, I would never have ended up here . . . with you . . ." Tears of angry frustration filled her eyes.

"Even if you had been with your Michael and I had decided that I wanted you, do you think you would still be free?"

His statement paralyzed her. She had always felt

safe with Michael. He seemed so strong and solid and dependable. But Lance . . . Lance was a fierce warrior. . . . Would he have been able to take her from Michael? In her heart, she knew the answer, and her knees threatened to buckle.

"Yes!" she denied. "Michael would have saved me."

Lance gave a derisive laugh. "You are wrong, Trista, and you know it. I took you, and I made you mine. After we are married, I will have all of you."

"No!"

"I will touch more than just your body when we are one. I will make you come to me and—"

"NO! I'll never go to you willingly! Michael Barrett is the only man I love. He's the man I want to marry!"

"Lone Elk waits." His declaration was stony. Tired of her foolish fight against the inevitable, Lance grabbed for her arm.

Trista danced nervously away, eluding his grasp. "He can wait forever as far as I'm concerned! You can't force me to marry you!"

His eyes glittered dangerously. "You don't think so?"

His threat was obvious as he moved closer, and she went pale. Trista felt cornered, trapped. She shook her head in vehement denial. "I don't want to marry you! I hate you! Why would you want a wife who hates the very sight of you?"

"I have my reasons," he answered enigmatically. His hand closer over her forearm like a band of steel.

"You're a fool to want a woman who doesn't want you!"

Lance had had enough of her tirade. "Shall I show you how false your words are?" Boldly, he lifted his hand to cup her breast through the soft material of the dress. He rubbed his thumb across the peak and watched in satisfaction as it hardened. "Why do you continue to fight against that which your body accepts?" he taunted. "You will marry me now, Trista."

She stood rigidly before him, trying to fight down the humiliation of her body's betrayal and wondering why Lance of all men had this power over her. "I do not want to marry you."

"The choice is yours. Come with me now or else . . ."

"Or else?" Trista gave a slightly hysterical laugh. "There could be no greater punishment for me."

A muscle flexed in his jaw. "You do not think that belonging to Striking Snake would be a worse fate?"

Trista blanched.

"The choice is yours. Which will it be?"

She trembled violently. Was there no way out of this? Was there no escape? Frantically, her mind raced, but in the end she faced her fate. She would become the wife of this warrior . . . this savage.

"I haven't heard your answer," Lance pushed her.

Only the thought that it was a Comanche ceremony and not binding by her standards gave her the strength to agree.

"I'll marry you." Trista spoke so softly that Lance wasn't sure that he'd heard her.

"I didn't hear you, Trista."

"I said I would marry you."

The interior of the chief's lodge was quiet, save for the sound of Lone Elk solemnly chanting the ritual that would join Lance and Trista in marriage. A small fire blazed brightly in the fire pit, casting dancing shadows on the tipi's walls and a golden glow on those gathered there before him.

The mood of the joining was subdued as Lance stood before his uncle, looking much the part of the magnificent warrior. Tall, broad-shouldered, his skin sun-bronzed, only his blue eyes betrayed his white heritage. His expression was inscrutable as not a flicker of emotion reflected on his features.

Trista was standing rigidly at Lance's side. She was dressed in the white buckskin skirt and blouse that had been Shining Star's, and Lone Elk had been stunned to see the white woman wearing his sister's most cherished garb. It troubled him that Lance had so honored this woman, and he worried that his nephew might truly be coming to care for her. Earlier he had argued this point with his nephew, criticizing his wisdom in marrying Trista. But, in the manner of his mother, Lance had proven impossible to convince of the error of his ways. No amount of persuasion had swayed him from his purpose. He was determined to marry the white woman before he went off to meet with the white intruders.

In one way, Lone Elk thought he could understand Lance's reasoning. By taking Trista as his wife, he had completely claimed that which had belonged his half brother. Yet still, the thought of his beloved nephew married to a white woman rankled, and he feared that Lance was making the same mistake his mother had. Perhaps in the future, Lone Elk prayed, he would marry a maiden, too, and then relegate Trista to the position of "chore wife."

Lone Elk sang the song of the ancient ones over them, seeking a blessing upon them. He took Trista's right hand in his to complete the joining, and he was surprised when she tried to pull away.

Trista had been holding herself aloof from the

ceremony, and she was startled by Lone Elk's unexpected contact. She resisted his touch for an instant. Looking up at the chief, who seemed so forbidding in his full-feathered headdress, bone breastplate, and painted face, Trista's eyes were wide and questioning.

Without meeting her gaze, the chief tightened his grip upon her, allowing her no last-minute escape. He took up the decorated leather thong that was used in the ceremony, and he tired it firmly about her wrist. She knew a moment of panic as she saw the symbolism in the tying of the thong and realized that she would be bound to Lance forever according to his custom. Lance stood unmoving as his uncle grasped his wrist and tied the other end of the thong to him.

"As you are one now, so you shall remain," he chanted in the Comanche tongue. "When your bodies join, so shall your souls join. You will be one in all ways."

Though she had no understanding of what he was saying, an unexpected shiver ran down her spine. She glanced quickly up at Lance, but he seemed totally impassive, as if the ceremony meant little to him. Only when the chief became silent did Lance turn to her. Her gaze met his, and she saw mirrored there in the blue depths a flare of emotion that she could not put a name to, but that singed the very essence of her being.

Her breath caught in her throat as she stared up at Lance, and she was helplessly entrapped by his piercing, heated regard. He seemed to move almost in slow motion as he bent to her, and she found herself wrapped in his arms and crushed to his chest as his lips sought hers. His mouth moved over hers with painful familiarity. His tongue delved into the dark sweetness of her mouth and evoked fires of excitement she was at a loss to deny. The rational part of her cried out *NO,* but deep within the heart of her, she melted before his scorching passion.

Lance felt her begin to respond and quickly released her, stepping back and away from her intoxicating nearness. He watched her for a moment in silence as she battled with the recognition, yet the denial, of her true response, and felt filled with satisfaction. Tonight he would teach Trista the complete truth of desire. Tonight he would have all of her.

Lance did not question why it was so important to him to conquer all of her resistance. He just knew that by dawn, he wanted her to be his in all ways.

Dawn Blossom was nearly dancing with delight as she made her way to the lodge of She Who Speaks the Truth. She was smiling widely as she approached. When she caught sight of Night Lark sitting outside by the cooking fire, she hurried forth to impart the news she had just learned.

"Good evening, Night Lark," she greeted her as she sat down close beside her.

Night Lark glanced at her and wondered at her jovial mood. "Hello, Dawn Blossom. You are happy tonight."

"I am always happy, Night Lark, but tonight I am especially so."

"Why? Has something happened?" she asked, but with little real interest.

"Oh, yes . . . but since Trista has been living with you, I felt certain that you would have known about it already. . . ." She let the statement hang teasingly.

"Known about what?" Night Lark's tone sharpened.

"Why, the marriage, of course."

"Marriage?"

"Lance has married his captive. They have only just now left Lone Elk's lodge."

Night Lark went completely still. "Lance has married the white woman?"

"Yes."

"But why would he marry her when she was already his captive?"

"I do not know, nor do I care. I just thought you might want to know about it."

"I'm sure you couldn't wait to tell me, Dawn Blossom," Night Lark snapped, controlling the urge to throttle the other gloating maiden.

Dawn Blossom was still smiling as she stood up and walked away without speaking. Night Lark was filled with rage as she watched her go. The ray of hope that had filled her earlier was extinguished. Lance had married his captive. . . . Why? The question tormented her, and she knew she was going to do all she could to find out exactly what was going on.

They were alone in the darkness of Lance's tipi facing each other across its width.

"Come here, Trista," Lance commanded in a tone that was both authoritative and gentle at the same time.

Trista balked. She knew what Lance wanted, yet she could not bring herself to go to him. She had married him only because he'd given her no alternative. Her vow not to go to him willingly had been heartfelt.

When she did not move, Lance decided to take matters into his own hands. He was going to destroy all the barriers she'd set between them. Like a stalking

217

jungle cat, he crossed the lodge and came to stand before her. With the lightest of touches, he reached out to caress the curve of her cheek.

"You are mine now completely, Trista." He spoke softly. "It is foolish for you to fight it anymore. Come to me, sweet one. Come to me willingly and let me show you the delights that can be yours."

At the touch of his hand, she shivered in expectancy. Was there any use in trying to deny that she physically responded to him? Trista didn't know, but she knew she had to try. She owed Michael and herself at least that much.

"I can't," she gasped as he trailed his hand lower and skimmed over the sensitive swell of her breast.

"I am your husband. You are my wife," he said fiercely as he pulled her against him and pressed a hot kiss to the arch of her neck.

"Only in your world . . ." she managed, trembling as his lips explored the silken cords of her throat.

"Oh, no, Trista . . . our vow is binding, as was my mother's to my father," Lance murmured as he sought her lips.

"No . . ." Her last protest was cut off as his mouth claimed hers.

Trista had expected him to be forceful, but Lance took his time. He teased her with quick, soft kisses that soon had her begging for a deeper, more heated exchange. She felt as if he was playing with her, much as a cat toys with a mouse, but she was helpless before his masterful ways. Every nerve in her body was crying out for him. Trista struggled to remember who she was and why she was there, but it all faded into complete oblivion as his mouth settled firmly over hers. Her lips parted automatically to accept the warm thrust of his tongue. As if they had a will of their own, her arms lifted to encircle his neck.

Lance knew a surge of triumph as he felt her opposition weaken. Lifting her into his arms, he knelt upon the bed. Together they stretched out upon the mat, and he continued his erotic assault. His every caress was designed to ignite fires within her as he fondled her sweet curves through the softness of the buckskin dress.

Trista was on fire with her desire. She wanted to feel his hands upon her bare flesh. She wanted to know the thrill of his driving possession again. Clinging to his broad shoulders, Trista fit herself fully against his hard, masculine frame and moved restlessly against him.

Lance slipped her garments from her, making the effort seem almost a caress. She was naked before him then, her perfect curves lush and pale in the darkness. His hunger for her was at a fever pitch as he stared down at her, but he fought against taking her too soon. Lance wanted more from this night than just the satisfaction he'd take from her body. Tonight they were man and wife. Tonight she would admit that she wanted him.

With the utmost of care, he began to stroke her quivering flesh, and wherever his hands touched, his lips followed. He sought out her most erogenous zones and teased her to the limits of pleasure until she was panting and alive with her need. His lips and tongue worked their magic upon the sweet swell of her breasts, tasting of those burgeoning orbs and pushing her desire to ecstasy's edge, but still he did not satisfy that passion that he had created within her. Over and over he aroused her to the peak, and over and over he left her hanging on that precipice.

Trista had never known such sensual torment.

Lance's every touch and every kiss added to the spiraling passion that was threatening to push her past the brink of sanity. She wanted only Lance. She needed only Lance . . . and yet he refused to give her the joy of joining with her.

"Tell me, Trista," came his voice, hoarse and rasping in her ear.

"Tell you what?" she whispered breathlessly as he trailed kisses down her shoulder and across the peaks and valleys of her breasts.

"I want to hear you say how you feel, Trista," he told her as he continued his erotic caresses. "Do you like it when I touch you here?"

"Oh, yes . . ."

"And here?"

"Yes . . . Oh, Lance!" she gasped in delight at his boldness.

"Can you tell me now that you feel nothing when I touch you? Tell me that you want me to stop. Tell me that you hate me, Trista."

Trista felt a slight chill sweep through her at his words, but it was not enough to lessen the heat of her passion. Noting mattered except being in his arms and sharing his embrace . . . nothing.

"I hate you, Lance. . . ." she managed.

Lance felt a surge of disappointment rocket through him at her words. If she could deny what she was feeling now, then he really believed that she truly did hate him. . . .

"I hate you for making me want you so!" Trista sobbed, finally saying aloud that which she'd kept locked deep within her for so long. She clutched at his shoulders in a fever of frantic need.

"Ah, Trista, love," he murmured softly as joy replaced the disappointment he was feeling. "You do want me. . . ." He went to her then in victory.

"I want you, Lance. . . . I want you. . . ." she repeated in a litany of desire as he found the center of her love and claimed it for his own.

As one, they rode to the stars. Streaking across the heavenly night in a blaze of fiery passion, they eclipsed all that had gone before. They were man and wife. They were together. They were one.

The peak was rapturous and heart-stopping in its breathless beauty. They plummeted back to reality, cocooned in the aftermath of ecstasy's heat. There was no past between them this night, and no future loomed threateningly before them. The only words spoken between them were love words that were understood in the heart and not the mind. There was only man and woman and an elemental need that swept all else from consideration.

All that Trista had vowed before was forgotten in the fiery web of ecstasy Lance had woven around her. Swept away by the ardor he could arouse, she went to him, willingly seeking his embrace and his kiss. Time and again, Lance nurtured her blossoming desires until they burst forth in perfect splendor and slaked both of their passions. They loved through the long night hours, sharing and giving the greatest of pleasures.

When at last they were sated, they slept. Trista lay curled against his side, her head resting on his shoulder, her hand resting possessively on his chest over his heart.

The lilting, muted strains of the morning bird's song stirred Trista to wakefulness. A sigh of utter contentment escaped her as she lay with her eyes closed savoring the peace of the moment. Stretching in sensual appreciation of her current rapturous state,

Trista was startled by the feel of the bed's softness against her naked flesh. Vividly heated memories of the night just past jolted through her consciousness, and her eyes flew open as she remembered all. She was surprised to find that she was alone in the lodge, and a coldness seized her heart as she wondered where Lance had gone. Trista barely had time to draw a blanket over her when the flap opened and Night Lark walked in.

"Get up, lazy white woman. There is much work to be done," the maiden ordered.

Trista was shocked at the other woman's unexpected appearance. What was Night Lark doing here? And where was Lance? "Where is Lance?" she managed, clutching the cover over her breasts.

"He has left the village. Did he not tell you of his plans?" Night Lark taunted as her gaze went scathingly over her. Her thoughts were filled with jealousy as she stared at Trista. Why had Lance married her? Surely her own figure was far superior to this white woman's, and she knew for a fact what a lazy complainer Trista was. Why had he done it?

"Lance is gone?" Trista's eyes widened at the unexpectedness of her announcement. Was it possible? Had Lance just taken what he'd wanted from her, proven that she was his completely just as he'd threatened to do, and then left without a word?

"He rode out of camp over an hour ago," she related smugly.

"When is he coming back?"

"Who knows?" Night Lark shrugged. "Word came that there were white men in our territory, and he has gone out after them."

"There are white men nearby?" Trista was jarred by the news. She was filled with expectant excitement and at the same time felt her heart grow cold and hard. Had Lance known all along that she might be rescued? Had last night only been a cruel game he'd been playing with her? The answer was obvious to her, and all vestiges of what she'd been feeling earlier were wiped away. She'd been a fool to surrender to him last night, but it would never happen again! A fierce determination settled over her. When Lance returned, he would find her gone. There were white people close to camp, and somehow, some way, she was going to make her escape and find them.

The thought of Michael searching endlessly for her through this rugged country filled her with agony. She longed to see him . . . to be held in his warm, cherishing embrace and know the safety of the haven of his arms—only then would she be whole again . . . only then would the horrible, cold emptiness she was now feeling be erased. Once she and Michael were reunited, she would marry him if he would have her, and she would make him a good wife. She loved Michael. Yet even as she grasped that thought and clung to it, the remembrance of Lance's gentle touch and passionate possession hovered disturbingly in her mind.

Night Lark had been watching the play of expression across Trista's face and was pleased with her reaction to the news. Perhaps, just perhaps, with the right encouragement, she could goad her into trying to escape. Then, once Trista was out of the way, Lance would be all hers. Her eyes narrowed as she considered her tactics.

"That's what Lance said. He came by to see me earlier this morning before he left," she related.

"He did?"

"Yes, and he also told me that he had taken you as

a wife and that he wants me to train you while he is gone."

"Train me?" Trista stared dumbly at Night Lark trying to understand what she was saying.

"Yes. Lance said that you warmed his bed well, but that there is much you need to know if you are to be a helpful wife to him. He asked me to teach you these things. If you are wise, you will pay attention and learn quickly. Then maybe, when Lance and I are married, we will keep you as a chore wife.

"A chore wife?"

Night Lark nodded, feeling particularly shrewd. "It is a better position than a slave, but not of the wifely status."

Trista could not believe what she was hearing. Last night she had thought . . . Almost violently she pushed all memory of the night before from her. She would not think of Lance and their endless hours of lovemaking. It had all been a painful sham. He had claimed he would make her come to him willingly, and to her humiliation, she had. Now that Lance had conquered her, she was no longer important to him. Bitterly, she wondered if she ever had been. Not that it mattered to her, Trista vowed silently. She hated Lance all the more for this, and as soon as she could get to Fuego and make her break, she would be gone. Trista knew she couldn't be sure that she would find the whites, but she knew she had to try.

"Hurry and dress, Trista. There is much to be done, and you linger there like the lazy one you are!" Night Lark snatched up the white garments and flung them at her. "I will be waiting outside. The first thing you must do is carry water from the stream."

Trista stared down at the beautiful outfit, rumpled now from Night Lark's carelessness, and a tear of misery traced down the curve of her cheek. Angry with herself, she dashed away the evidence of her pain. Searching the lodge, she found the regular Comanche clothing she had worn before the wedding and donned it. She had started from the tipi to join Night Lark when she suddenly hesitated and turned back. Almost reverently, she took up the white garments and folded them neatly upon the bed. Then, without a backward look, she left Lance's lodge, hoping she would never have to return to it again.

Chapter Fifteen

At its zenith now, the sun beat down mercilessly on the small group of riders heading toward Espada Canyon. Among the rocky outcroppings on a hillside some distance away, a small band of Comanche kept track of their every move.

"It is as I told Lone Elk. They are traveling light. Few provisions . . . many guns. For some reason, they are in a hurry to reach the canyon," Black Water remarked.

"That they are," Lance agreed, intently studying the men who rode before him. He couldn't be completely certain until they were closer, but something deep within him told him that this was his father and Michael who were trespassing on their lands.

"I am tired of just watching," Black Water complained. "Let's go after them. They do not know we are here. We can surprise them. . . ."

"Not yet." Lance, the undisputed leader of the party, was firm. "They will rest once they reach the cutoff, and that's where we'll be waiting."

"Their horses are good stock. I will enjoy taking them into my herd." Little Buck was eager at the thought of ambushing the whites.

"We will not be raiding," Lance told them. "Lone Elk wants no bloodshed. I will handle it."

Little Buck and Black Water looked outraged by the news. "Lone Elk has forbidden us to attack them?"

Lance nodded. "I will speak with them. They will turn back."

The other two warriors wanted to argue but knew better than to defy Lance. He was the bravest warrior in the camp and, as such, due all their respect.

"And if they shoot at us?"

"Then we will attack."

His answer satisfied them for the moment, and they wheeled their horses about and moved off at an angle out of sight of the whites. Racing away cross-country, they arrived at the scheduled rendezvous spot in advance of their prey.

Michael once again was setting the pace as he tirelessly led the way across the rugged Texas terrain. He was a driven man, a man obsessed with the need to find the woman he loved. Though he knew they would have to stop soon to rest their mounts, he still pushed them to the limit. Time was of the essence, for they had wasted far too much time already. Espada Canyon was so close, and it was their last and only remaining hope.

"Michael . . ." George's call slowed him.

Reining in, Michael waited for his father and the other two men to catch up to him.

"The horses have to rest. There's a cutoff up ahead, and just beyond it is a small watering hole. Let's take about an hour and cool off there."

"All right." His agreement was less than enthusiastic, but he knew the horses came first. He would be of little help in rescuing Trista if he ran his horse into the ground before he found her.

At a more measured pace, they traversed the final few miles to the cutoff, then headed to the watering hole. Situated at the base of a low rise, the small pond was naturally camouflaged by brush and rock. The riders from the Royal Diamond approached it cautiously. They knew they were crossing Indian land and were alert to the possibility of an ambush.

Lance and the others waited until the whites had reached the watering hole and had dismounted. Still mounted, they urged their ponies to the crest of the hill overlooking the pond.

Whitey had dealt with Indians many times in his life, and he had been hunkering down to refill his canteen when he felt a sudden chill shoot unexpectedly down his spine. "They're around here somewhere close . . ." he advised the others in low tones as he pivoted around to survey the area. It was then that he caught sight of the three Comanche warriors on top of the hill, their fierce silhouettes black against the brightness of the noonday sky. Automatically he reached for his gun.

"No, Whitey." George's harsh command stopped him. "If they'd have wanted us dead, they would have killed us by now."

"Pa . . ." Michael argued, his hand resting on the butt of his sidearm. He was ready to shoot to kill, but his father put him off, too.

"Let's see what they want. Maybe they just came to talk. . . ."

"But they're the ones who have Trista!"

"We don't know that, Michael. Even if they are, killing them won't help her. You have to keep your head. Get your hand away from your gun. I'll handle this." His order brooked no comment.

Michael relented to his father's wishes and fell silent, though it annoyed him greatly to do so. These were probably the bastards who'd stolen Trista and done God knows what to her! He wanted to kill them all!

"White man! Why do you trespass upon our land?" Lance's tone was stern as his voice boomed across the

228

barren land. Though he sounded fierce, deep within he was troubled as he recognized his father and Michael.

A shaft of vicious emotion he did not want to identify shot through him at the sight of his half brother standing so proudly erect beside their father. Why did this son find favor with his father, while he was forsaken? Was he not the firstborn? Was he not worthy to stand at his father's side? The faint memory of his father's drunken ramblings all those years ago answered his questions. . . . It was his Comanche blood that had turned his father from him.

Lance stiffened as he regarded them. He was not ashamed of his mother's heritage. He was proud of his Indian blood.

George stared up at the three warriors in silence for a long moment, his attention riveted on the fine figure of a brave who sat so proudly on his horse. George's vitals lurched at the thought that this might be Lance, but try though he might, looking into the sun as he was, he could not readily identify him. It was just that something about him seemed so familiar. . . . "We are looking for a white woman," he finally replied.

"Chief Lone Elk sends word that you should honor your agreement of many years standing with him and turn back," Lance shot back.

"Pa . . . I didn't know you had any kind of agreement with the Comanche. Who is this Lone Elk?" Michael asked under his breath, stunned by the knowledge that his father had had previous dealings with these people.

George ignored his younger son as he answered, "I am causing no harm to Lone Elk's land. In truth, I had come to seek his help in finding the woman."

"There is no white woman here." Lance did not lie.

Trista was in the village. "You are not welcome. Leave our land now, while you can." Lance and the others lifted their rifles to show the men from the Royal Diamond that they were equally well armed and just as prepared to use their weapons.

Stymied, George knew he had no alternative. A fight would accomplish nothing. "We will go as Lone Elk has bid."

"But, Pa!!" Michael was furious. They couldn't back down! They couldn't give up! They were close . . . so close . . . he could feel it!

"It is good that you leave. Do not return. We will not be so welcoming next time." Lance's reply filled the air, and when the white men looked up again, the warriors had disappeared from sight.

"I can't believe you agreed to go!! Trista's somewhere close by! I know it!"

"There's no other way, Michael," George told him. He was just as frustrated as his son, but more realistic.

"There were only three of them! We could have fought!"

"Son, we could have tried to fight them, but we wouldn't have stood a chance. We might have seen only three of them, but there could have been a dozen others just waiting for the chance to swoop down on us. They had position and surprise on their side. We're lucky they gave us that much of a chance to parlay."

"Mike . . . your Pa's right. We're real lucky to still be breathing and have our hair." Whitey fully concurred with George's decision.

Michael was crestfallen. The taste of defeat was bitter, and his failure weighed heavily upon him. "I won't stop . . . I can't . . ."

"Michael, you have to. There's nothing more you

can do. If you tried to go on, you'd only end up getting yourself killed," Tom added.

"Somehow, right now I'd rather be dead . . ." Michael agonized as he accepted the truth of Trista's loss.

George put an arm around his slumped shoulders. "You've done everything you could, son. None of this was your fault. . . ."

Slowly they started back the way they'd come, their hearts heavy with grief and sadness, their minds filled with thoughts of Trista, believing that she was now lost to them forever.

Lance was angry as he watched their retreat. He did not understand the fury he felt toward them; he only knew that he was filled with bitter resentment as he watched his half brother ride off at his father's side.

It had seemed as if a sharp blade had pierced him when he realized that his father did not know him. They were of the same flesh and blood, yet even separated by such a small distance, George Barrett had shown no evidence of recognition. Lance knew he shouldn't care, for he had given up that life long ago. He knew he shouldn't want the bond that had once been theirs to still exist, but the illogical part of him that hurt so badly right now gave testimony to the fact that, for some reason, he still did.

As she headed back toward the camp, Trista staggered under the weight of the water she was carrying. Exhausted, she paused for an instant to catch her breath.

"Hurry, woman! There is no time for you to rest. There is still much work that must be done before the sun sets," Night Lark snapped as she strode angrily toward Trista, intending to prod her along.

For the better part of two days now, Trista had been

suffering the sharp bite of Night Lark's sarcastic criticism as she'd labored from dawn to dusk on the most demanding of tasks, and she had about had enough. Only the thought that tonight was the night she'd finally be able to escape restrained her from physically attacking the gloating female. Keeping her expression carefully blank, Trista picked up the water and started off again.

"Lance will never be pleased with you," the Indian maiden scoffed as she trailed along beside her. "Just look at you! You are too scrawny to do the work an Indian wife is supposed to do. If you do not try harder, I will see to it that you are sold as a slave when Lance and I marry."

At this point, Trista thought that the life of a slave would be infinitely preferable to the life she was now leading. Certainly it couldn't be much worse. She was the sensual plaything of a man who cared nothing for her, and she had been relegated to the lowly position of chore wife. Trista couldn't stop herself from glaring at Night Lark as she kept on walking. Night Lark saw the venom in her expression and reacted quickly at her show of defiance, shoving her with all her might and sending her sprawling into the dust.

"You are useless, white woman!" Night Lark ridiculed as she stood over Trista. "See how clumsy this new wife of Lance's is?" she pointed out to the other women in the village, and they all laughed in derisive delight.

This was the final straw! Trista reached without thought as she surged to her feet in a frenzy of fury. Grabbing one bucket with both hands, she threw the last dregs of the chilling contents on the unsuspecting Night Lark, drenching her.

The women of the camp erupted into hysterical laughter. "You cannot push that one too far, Night

Lark! She is as untamed as the golden stallion. . . . Lance must like his women fiery!" they teased, and even some of the children gathered round to see the sight of the haughty Night Lark soaked to the skin.

In dripping outrage, Night Lark responded savagely. Snatching up one of the sticks the children had been playing with, she attacked Trista. Trista threw her arms up to ward off the blows and quickly turned her body away from the brunt of the angry woman's assault.

As soon as she'd thrown the water, she'd regretted it. She had not meant to show defiance; she had meant to be submissive and quiet so no one would suspect that she was going to attempt her escape. She longed to grab the rod from Night Lark and use it on her, but she knew she couldn't. She had to take this abuse just one last time. . . . there were only a few hours left. . . .

Blow after stingling blow landed on her back and buttocks as Night Lark meted out her unrelenting punishment. Only the arrival of She Who Speaks the Truth, who'd come to see what all the laughter was about, stopped her from injuring Trista seriously.

"Night Lark!" Her mother's voice cut through the titters of conversation. "Stop this at once!"

"She did this to me!!" Night Lark indicated her sodden state and raised her arm to swing at the white woman again.

She Who Speaks the Truth looked from her daughter to Trista, who was glancing nervously in her direction. When she spoke again, it was in Comanche tongue. "You are letting your jealousy run away with you, girl. What do you think Lance will say when he returns and finds this one bruised and beaten?"

"I do not care. She is lazy and—"

"I said stop! I do not want to see you raise your

233

hand to her again."

Night Lark threw the stick aside as she glared at Trista. "Get moving, lazy! Now that you've spilled all the water, you must go for more. I will wait for you by the lodge." She stomped away, her head held high despite the muffled sounds of laughter that followed her.

Near exhaustion and aching from the beating she'd received, Trista slowly gathered up the buckets and headed back toward the stream to refill them. In the two days since Lance had left, her life had become a living hell. She had suffered more abuse at Night Lark's hands than she'd ever known in her life, and she only prayed that night would come quickly so she could leave this place behind forever.

As Trista lugged the water back toward the lodge, she let her thoughts drift to the night before and how she had managed to slip from the tipi undetected after everyone had been asleep. She had sought out Fuego in the corral and had been cheered by the fact that the stallion had actually seemed to be waiting for her. His manner, surprisingly, had been calm and almost trusting, and she had spent long hours rubbing him down and talking with him.

Trista hoped that Fuego's sweeter nature was a sign of his complete acceptance of her, for tonight he would be put to the test. With the whites so near, she could not let the opportunity pass without at least trying to escape. Tonight she would take the chance, for the thought of spending another day at Night Lark's beck and call left her shaking with barely controlled rage.

Trista reached the tipi where Night Lark sat waiting, clad now in a dry set of clothing. She only had time to place the water before her when the other woman began to bark out a series of different orders for her. Without a word, Trista went off to do her bidding, all the while biding her time until night claimed the land.

It was late, and day had long ago surrendered the earth to the night's hungry grasp. Huddled on the hard mat that served as her bed, pretending to be asleep, Trista waited in tense silence. Her anticipation of making her break to freedom filled her with excitement, and she was hard put to lie still. Soon she would be away from here! Soon she would be free of Lance!

At the thought of Lance, the memory of his kiss and caress threatened to destroy her will, but she fought it down. It was true that he had been able to arouse her as no other, but, she reasoned, she had been his slave and helpless to do anything except respond. She would put this time behind her and never think of him again. Tauntingly, her mind conjured up a vision of the wedding pledge the chief had pronounced over them, but Trista quickly, logically denied it. It was a heathen ceremony. He was but a savage . . . a barbarian. Michael would be her husband.

Thinking of Michael and the safety of the Royal Diamond made her eagerness to flee almost unbearable, and she quietly shifted position to look around. Given the lateness of the hour and the fact that neither of the other two women had stirred for some time, Trista felt certain that Night Lark and She Who Speaks the Truth were asleep. Silently rising, she fled into the night.

It was warm, and a heavy cloud cover screened the moon from view, leaving the night inky in its blackness. The darkness was a balm to Trista's tautly strung nerves, for without the moon's revealing light, her escape might be undetected until morning. She hurried on to where Lance's horses were penned. Even in the enveloping darkness, she could still make out Fuego's brilliant golden form, and she was relieved to see that Fuego was waiting there in all his powerful magnificence, watching her approach.

"Ah, my golden one . . . I missed you today." She rubbed his neck affectionately, and he whickered softly as if in understanding. "We can wait no longer, you and I," Trista told him. "Tonight we must seek our escape from the man who would break us . . . tonight we must help each other. . . ."

Fuego did not understand her words, but he recognized her intent as she entered the pen and came to his side. Swiftly Trista climbed onto his back, and he hesitated, not quite sure whether to accept the foreignness of her weight upon him or not. His every muscle was quivering as Trista leaned forward low over his neck and spoke to him in a soft, muted voice.

"Easy, my big fella . . . easy, Fuego. We're one, you and I. . . . We both want the same thing. . . . We both want to be free of the warrior who sought to claim us and tame us. . . ."

A shiver passed through Fuego's tense body as he shifted nervously, but Trista only continued her crooning and slowly gained his confidence. When Trista gathered up a handful of this mane and tugged lightly, he responded, moving as she bid.

Trista knew a surge of joy unlike anything she'd ever experienced before. Fuego had responded willingly to her touch! Staying low over his neck, she used her knees to guide him as she edged him as quietly as possible to the gate. She leaned over, opened it, and urged Fuego out of the corral. Once freed from the enclosure, Trista manuevered him so she could pull the gate closed behind them.

At a slow, measured pace, Trista guided the rogue

away from the camp. Her breathing was strained and her hands were shaking as she expected at any moment to be discovered and possibly killed. Only when they had topped the hill and moved out of sight of the village did she breath a deep sigh of relief. With one last glance back over her shoulder to be sure that no one had seen them escape, she put her heels lightly to the stallion's sides and hung on as he took off at a full gallop in the direction of the Royal Diamond.

As if in cooperation, the clouds broke apart, and moonlight fell unheeded across the land. A vision of moonstruck gold, the wild rogue and beautiful maiden raced across the countryside and disappeared into the night.

Night Lark smiled from where she stood hidden in the concealing shadows of the night. She had hoped that Trista would run away when she had left the tipi on the previous night, but to her disappointment, she hadn't. Tonight, however, her hopes had come true. The white woman had fled, and Lance would now belong only to her.

Feeling quite satisfied with herself, she returned to her tipi and settled in for the night. Night Lark did now know how soon Lance would be returning, but she hoped it would not be too soon. The longer the white woman was gone, the less chance he would have of finding her — not that he was going to. When he got back, Night Lark was going to prove to him that she was the only woman he would ever need.

Lightning flashed on the night-shrouded horizon, and the low rumble of thunder echoed distantly across the land as the three warriors rode for their village. Lance was lost deep in thought as he led the way across the darkened landscape. He had expected to come away from the encounter with his father and half brother feeling heady with victory at having exacted his long-overdue vengeance against them. Instead, the incident had left him feeling ungratified, as if he had lost more than he'd won. The sensation disquieted him. He hadn't lost anything. He had Trista. He had made her his wife. She belonged to him now, in all ways. . . .

Trista. . . . She filled his thoughts now, and Lance found himself spurring his pinto to an even greater speed in his desire to see her again. How great was her golden beauty . . . how silken her limbs as they wrapped around him in passion's embrace. The wedding night of love they had shared had been the most memorable night of his life, and he couldn't wait to be with her again.

Lance regretted that he'd been forced to leave her while she was still asleep that morning, but she had been resting so peacefully that he hadn't wanted to disturb her. He hoped she was waiting for him and that she would be welcoming when he returned, for the idea of another sensual night in her embrace filled him with excitement.

They crossed into the valley where the camp lay just as the sun made its dingy appearance behind the blanket of threatening thunderheads that filled the sky as far as the eye could see. Putting their heels to their mounts, the three charged at top speed toward the village. Lance longed to do nothing more than seek out his wife, but he knew that first he had to stop at Lone Elk's lodge to tell him of their trip.

The chief heard the disturbance as they raced into camp, and he came outside to greet his returning braves.

"Was your trip successful?" the chief asked as the three reined in before him.

"We did as you asked." Lance supplied curtly.

"Then you have done well. Lance, come. Little Buck and Black Water, I will speak with you later." When the other two men had gone, Lone Elk led the way into the privacy of his tipi so he and Lance could speak without interruption.

"We found the whites," Lance said, offering little real information as they sat down cross-legged facing each other.

Lone Elk eyed him skeptically for a minute before pressing for more details. "And what was their reason for being on our land?"

"It was Barrett," Lance supplied curtly. "He's gone now."

"You are sure?" Lone Elk's expression was filled with loathing as he remembered the man who had taken his sister from him and hurt Lance so badly.

Lance nodded, but did not speak.

"Did he know you?"

His uncle's question astutely delved into the heart of what had been troubling Lance. "No."

"Perhaps that is best."

"It was not my concern," Lance asserted aggressively. "I am Comanche, the son of Shining Star."

Lone Elk's obsidian gaze rested on him for an unsettlingly long moment before he spoke. "You have done well."

"I only did what you asked." He stood up, uncomfortable with the direction of his uncle's probing questions.

"We will speak more later," the chief was saying when they were interrupted by the sound of someone shouting Lance's name. Lance and Lone Elk exchanged curious glances as they stepped from the tipi.

"Lance!" It was Wind Rider who was racing toward them.

"I had never expected such a warm welcome from you, my friend," Lance quipped, but his lightness of spirit soon faded as he read the anxious expression on his faithful companion's usually controlled features. He knew something was terribly wrong, and for one desperate moment he feared that something had happened to Trista in his absence. "Wind Rider . . ." He sobered. "What is it? What's happened?"

"The stallion!"

"Fuego? Is he hurt?"

"No . . . he's not hurt. . . ."

For an instant Lance was relieved, but what Wind Rider said next left him speechless with fury.

"He's not hurt . . . he's gone!"

"What?" Lance stared at him in disbelief.

"I had just gone out to check on my own ponies and noticed —"

"The rest of my herd . . . ?

"Is still there. Only the golden one is missing," Wind Rider informed him.

"I must see this for myself. How could he have escaped? Unless . . ."

"Unless maybe Striking Snake returned during the night and took him. . . ." 'his friend offered as a solution to the disappearance.

"Surely if Striking Snake had tried to touch the stallion, all would have heard it. Few could get near the rogue without a fight. Only myself and . . ." Lance went suddenly still as his gaze focused on his own lodge. Trista could handle the stallion —, she'd proven that the other day with the entire village watching. Would she have dared? Could she have dared? Without another word, he broke into a dead run, heading straight for his own lodge.

Chapter Sixteen

Lance threw open the flap to his tipi and stepped inside. A strange, sickening feeling assailed him as he stared about the deserted interior. Trista was not there. . . . She was gone.

"Surely you don't think Trista took the golden stallion?" Wind River asked derisively as he joined him inside.

"She's gone. . . ." Lance stated the obvious tersely.

"She is probably just staying with She Who Speaks the Truth," Wind Rider dismissed. "No mere woman could handle such a powerful, wild mount."

At his remark, Lance realized how little his friend really knew about Trista. Trista was a resourceful, intelligent woman, and he had learned long ago not to underestimate her. Still, a part of him hoped that Wind Rider was right. Saying nothing, he turned and brushed passed him on his way to the older woman's abode.

Wind Rider was puzzled by his friend's behavior and hurried after him. "I am sure she is with my aunt and Night Lark," he assured Lance. "She has been with them most of the time since you were gone."

As they both moved in the direction of She Who Speaks the Truth's tipi, they saw Night Lark emerge. As they approached, she smiled brightly in welcome.

"Lance!" Night Lark called out in greeting, her delight in seeing him clearly visible on her lovely features. "It is good that you are back," she purred. "I have missed you."

Lance ignored her insinuations. "It is good to be back," he replied distractedly. He had no interest in Night Lark. Trista was the only woman in his thoughts. "Where is Trista?" he demanded impatiently.

Night Lark wanted to scream her frustration at the direction of his attention. How could Lance be so blind to her own love for him? Didn't he know that she would make him a much better wife than his weak white captive?

"I have just awakened, Lance, and I do not know for sure." She shrugged indifferently as she lied.

"Did she spend the night here?"

"Yes. She was already asleep when I went to bed."

"See, I told you," Wind Rider put in.

"Where is she now?"

"She has probably just gone down to the stream for water. . . ."

Before Night Lark could say any more, Lance was striding off toward the creek. Seeing how eager Lance was to be reunited with Trista left Night Lark fuming. Hands on her hips, she glared at his back as he walked away with Wind Rider close by his side. It annoyed her that Lance had returned so quickly. She had hoped that it would be some time before anyone discovered Trista's absence. Now that she only had a few hours headstart, there was a very good chance that he would find her. The only happy thoughts Night Lark had about the situation were that Lance might beat the white woman for her escape attempt or, better yet, hate her for defying him so and sell her to another tribe. Those possibilities almost brought a smile to her pouting lips as she went back inside to await their return from their futile trip to the creek.

"There is no sign of her," Lance remarked to Wind River as he found no evidence of Trista's presence on the bank of the stream.

Wind Rider found himself beginning to doubt his own initial judgment. "Do you really think she was capable of riding the rogue out of camp without being seen?"

Lance turned on him, his stony expression revealing none of the anger that was churning deep within him. "I learned long ago not to minimize Trista's abilities."

The low, muted rumble of thunder came to them, and they both looked up at the threatening sky.

"I'd better check the horses before the rain start. . . ." Lance headed off toward the place where his herd was kept penned.

"I will look in camp for her and meet you there," Wind Rider offered, starting back the way they came.

Lance was livid as he stalked across the clearing. Trista was gone. He was certain of it. Earlier he had let himself hope that Wind Rider had been right and that she was with She Who Speaks the Truth, but he knew now how foolish that had been. He should have remembered how deceitful and lying the whites were, and that Trista was one of them.

The memory of their wedding night . . . their last night together . . . scorched his thoughts, and he was hard put to control his outrage. Trista's willingness had no doubt been a ruse designed to put him off guard. He had thought that he'd won her total surrender, but he'd been wrong. He had not conquered her. He had only managed to subdue her for a time.

As Lance reached the corral, his decision was made. He was going after her. Trista may have escaped the camp, but she would not escape him. As the thought occurred, a bolt of lightning split the heavens, and the roar of its thunderous force soon followed.

Lance glanced up at the black, roiling clouds and cursed the storm he knew would soon burst upon the land. If he was to find Trista, he knew he had to act quickly. Circling out away from the enclosure, he searched the hard-packed ground for some sign of Fuego's trail and found the hoofprints of the stallion heading in the direction he'd suspected . . . due south.

"She's not in the village, Lance. Did you find anything?" Wind Rider asked as he found him studying the ground.

"It is as I thought. The stallion headed off this way." Lance stood up and gestured toward the Royal Diamond.

"How long ago?"

"Many hours . . . probably near midnight when the village was asleep." As he spoke, the wind picked up, whipping dust and grit about them. Lance studied the ominous black sky. "I will have to set out right away or the tracks will be lost. . . ."

"Do you want me to ride with?" his friend offered.

"No." Lance was somber as he moved into the pen and captured a pony to ride. "I found Fuego on my own once, and I will do it again," he vowed. He slipped a hackamore over the horse's head and swung up on its back in a lithe, masculine motion. "Tell my uncle that I have gone after the golden one. I do not know when I will return."

Lance wheeled his mount around and rode toward his own lodge. He stopped there only long enough to get the weapons and the few supplies he would need and then raced from the Comanche camp without looking back.

Lone Elk regarded Wind Rider silently for a long moment. "He has gone after the golden one. . . ."

"Yes," the warrior replied, wondering at the chief's pensive mood.

"I just wonder which 'golden one' he really wants. . . ." The Comanche chief stared off across the hill country, his inner voice telling him that he had lost his nephew that day.

"Surely the stallion means the most to him," Wind Rider said. "He will return soon. You will see."

But Lone Elk, remembering Lance's golden vision during his quest all those years ago and the way the white woman's hair had shone like spun gold in the firelight the night he had joined them, was not so sure. "Yes," he replied, his tone holding more than a hint of sorrow. "Yes, I will see."

Lance tracked the powerful stallion's trail through the rugged countryside for almost a full hour before the cloudburst that had been threatening actually unleashed its full fury. Frustrated, but knowing there was no other way, he sought shelter beneath a rocky overhand to wait out its soaking wrath.

Turbulent emotions seethed within Lance as he realized that the drenching downpour was washing all traces of Trista's passage from the land. He was furious with Trista for fleeing, and yet, perversely, he found himself worrying about her. She was at the mercy of this storm, and she was riding Fuego, a horse known for his wild ways. A vision of her thrown and hurt tormented him, and his hands clinched into fists as he realized just how helpless he was to go to her aid.

As Lance realized the direction of his thoughts, he

swore bitterly under his breath. He did not really care about Trista, he told himself. The only reason he was so determined to find her was because she was his property. He had struggled to capture her, he had fought to keep her, and he would not let her go . . . ever.

The lightning subsided, and the torrential rain slowly began to ease. Refusing to be delayed any longer, Lance urged his mount from their dry haven. The track of Fuego's hoofprints had been scoured away by the gully-washing rain just as Lance had known it would be. Aware that it would be useless to try to find Trista's trail again, he headed directly for the Royal Diamond.

Trista came upon the water hole quite by accident and stopped there to let Fuego rest and drink. Though she was bone-tired from the exhausting hours of riding, her spirits were soaring. She had made it! She was free! She had been watching carefully ever since she'd left the village, and there was no sign of anyone following.

The distant sound of thunder interrupted her thoughts, and Trista glanced back the way she'd just come to see vicious-looking thunderheads crowding the sky. She knew she had been lucky to have escaped when she did, for the storm looked bad, and she had no idea how manageable Fuego would be under such circumstances.

The thought of the stallion brought her attention back to the present. With a caressing, thankful hand, she stroked the rogue's strong shoulders as he drank his fill. So far he had been magnificent. She had given him his head, and he had responded beautifully, carrying her with enduring power across the rugged terrain.

Trista knew the trip back to the Royal Diamond was going to be difficult, but somehow she felt confident that they would make it. The big rogue's complete acceptance of her made her feel safe, and she trusted him as fully as he did her. He finished drinking, then gave a nervous toss of his head, eager to be on his way.

"All right, big guy," she crooned, grabbing a handful of mane and swinging up on his broad back again. "If you're ready, I'm ready."

With slight pressure from her knees, she turned him toward the south and continued her journey back to civilization.

Only when his pony was lathered and exhausted did Lance stop for the night. He had ridden at a steady ground-eating pace since the rain had let up, and though he was pleased with the distance he had covered, he was still impatient over the need to rest. He longed for his sturdy pinto but knew that, after the trek to meet with his father, the little horse had been in no shape for another cross-country venture.

Camped in a small, desolate ravine, Lance passed the long, dark hours of the night sleeplessly. With only his troubled thoughts and conflicting emotions for company, he sat alone beneath the star-dusted heavens lost deep in thought. It occurred to him that he might not find Trista right away, and he was surprised to discover that that worried him. He found himself wondering where she was and how she was and remembering the night not so long before when they had shared pure sensual bliss.

The memory of their mutual lovemaking sent a shaft of pure desire through Lance, and he swore

247

between gritted teeth as he fought to bring it under control. Lance knew this was not the time to be concentrating on Trista's ability to please him in bed. Wife or not, she had defied him at every turn. She had stolen Fuego, his most prized possession, and fled his home. When he finally found her, he was going to teach her her place as a captive wife.

The thought came to him then that she might prove more resourceful than ever and somehow locate the men from the Royal Diamond who were looking for her. The prospect of Trista being reunited with Michael filled him with an illogical fury, and though he tried to dismiss the possibility as ridiculous, it would not be so easily banned from his thoughts. She had told him over and over again that she loved only Michael—that Michael was the one she wanted, not him. Some rational part of Lance tried to point out that he didn't care about Trista, so it shouldn't matter to him what her feelings were about anything, but he found that the thought of her with any other man left him furious. She was his wife. She would not belong to anyone else.

Unable to sit still any longer, Lance got up and climbed from his secluded camp to a precipice where he could overlook the countryside. He stood there, poised like some granite statue, staring out across the darkened land and praying that dawn would come soon so he could be on his way.

Trista could ride no farther. The long, torturous hours on Fuego's back had taken their toll. Tugging at the lock of mane she'd been clinging to, she murmured a few words of encouragement to the stallion, urging him to stop. With the last of her strength, she slipped from his back and leaned heavily against his side as she tried to get her bearings. Fuego was puzzled by her actions and turned to nudge her questioningly with his nose.

"I'm sorry," she told him softly as she petted him. "I've just got to get some sleep."

He whickered low in response as Trista made her way wearily to the protection of a rocky formation nearby. Dropping down, she curled back against a boulder, seeking what little comfort she could. Hunger pains assaulted her, but she had little strength to worry about it. She knew a moment of concern over the thought that she might awaken to find Fuego gone, but pushed the thought away. He understood. He would stay. Trista wrapped her arms about herself to ward off the night's chill and closed her eyes. The last thing she saw in her mind's eye before she fell asleep was a vision of Lance, so tall and handsome, his blue eyes focused piercingly upon her.

Cupping a half-full tin mug of coffee in his hands, Michael sat alone before the campfire as the others slept, his grief showing plainly on his drawn, tired features. A great sense of failure filled him. Trista was lost to him forever, and somehow he felt responsible. Logically, he knew it wasn't his fault. He knew he had done everything humanly possible to get her back, but the realization did little to ease the ache of loneliness that besieged him. He had loved her, and now she was dead.

At that moment, Michael would have given anything just to see Trista once again. He remembered the night of the party and how wonderful it had felt to hold her in his arms as they had danced. He remembered the sweet taste of her as they had shared those stolen kisses on the porch, and he remembered the joy he had felt at the thought that she would soon be his wife.

His eyes burned as tears threatened, and he was forced to choke back a sob of anguish. Getting jerkily to his feet, he tossed the remnants of his coffee aside and wandered away from the fire's protection. Needing time alone . . . time to work out his sorrow, he moved off into the enveloping darkness. When Michael returned to the camp a long time later, the bright warmth of the fire was only a memory. Only ashes remained. As Michael lay down upon his bedroll, he found the cold, gray ugliness fitting, for he felt as dead and lifeless inside as the burned-out blackened coals. Stretching out, he closed his eyes to try to sleep.

The following day passed in a blur of strenuous, continuous travel for Trista. She had awakened at dawn to find Fuego nearby, refreshed and eager to be off again. Though every muscle in her body ached, she had maintained her determination to make it back to the Royal Diamond. Clinging tightly to Fuego through the long hours of riding, she had directed him ever southward.

The sun was setting in the west when Trista brought the stallion to a halt at the top of a low rise. It was a secluded location, bounded on three sides by a jumble of rocks. She felt certain that it would give her the protection she needed not only from the elements, but also from the chance of being spotted. Her hunger gnawed at her as she sought some comfort on the ground's unwelcoming hardness. The few berries she'd found near a creek earlier in the day had done little to satisfy her. Curling on her side, she sought sleep, hoping that slumber would ease the pain of her hunger and agony of her sore limbs.

The men of the Royal Diamond made camp slowly. They were all exhausted from their many days of useless pursuit and were looking forward to returning to the ranch. Michael and George worked side by side in silence as they rubbed down their horses while the other two men took care of building the campfire and fixing what little food they had left for the evening meal. No one thought much of it when Whitey wandered off for a moment, but when the shot rang out, slicing through the quiet of the early evening, they all went for their guns. Only when Whitey's laughing call came to them did they holster their weapons.

"Easy there," Whitey called out as he came back into the clearing where their camp was located. "I was just a little hungry tonight and thought I'd go out and see what I could find."

The others looked up and smiled at the sight of him carrying a good-sized rabbit.

The sound of the gunshot echoed across the land. Trista, who had been almost asleep, sat up quickly and looked around, confused. Her heart was pounding wildly within her breast as she imagined that Lance was closing in on her. Fuego was nervous and moved restlessly about. Trista, sharing his agitation, went to him to try to calm him.

"Easy, love. Easy, Fuego," she told him softly, afraid to speak too loudly for fear that Lance was near. As she petted him, Trista let her gaze sweep out across the valley before her, and she paused in mid-motion, stunned to see a campfire flickering some distance away.

Joy swept through her at the thought that rescue

might be at hand, but it was immediately replaced by fear. She realized that she did not know whose fire it was — she only knew that there was someone out there who had made camp for the night and that they weren't worried about their whereabouts being discovered.

Alternating between excitement at the thought of possible salvation and terror over the danger involved, Trista finally decided that she had only one choice. As quietly as possible, she had to work her way down nearer to the fire so she could find out just who was camped there. She realized that there was the risk of discovery, but as long as she was riding Fuego, she knew she would be able to make a fast break if the situation called for it. All thoughts of hunger and weariness were forgotten as she mounted the stallion again. Slowly, picking their trail with care in the darkness, they began their descent into the valley.

Whitey's unexpected main course, though tough and stringy, had been a welcome addition to their sparse fare, yet Michael ate solemnly, hardly tasting his portion. When the meal was over and the others retired for the night, he remained sitting before the glowing embers, his mood black. Nothing seemed to help dispel the feelings of failure and depression that had settled over him like a mantle of despair. He was as lost and alone in his misery as the coyote that howled in eerie solitude in the shadows of the night.

An inexplicable restlessness filled Michael. Though it was a dark night, the moon's light being shuttered by a high blanket of clouds, he hoped a walk would help ease his agitation. Standing up, he strode from the small camp. Michael hadn't gone far when the sound of a tumbling rock halted him in mid-step. Though not a particularly threatening noise, it put him on alert, and he slowly drew his gun as his gaze searched the area for some sign of intrusion.

Whatever Michael had been expecting, it was not the sight that greeted him as the moon slid out from behind the cloud cover. He blinked, believing himself to be dreaming, as he stared in wonder at the rider who sat on a low rise overlooking the camp. Silvered by the moon, shadowed by the night, the motionless horse and rider were a golden image that seared his very being, and he truly believed that he was imagining them.

Fuego . . . Trista? Their names shot through his consciousness, and he felt an aching tightness in his chest. As much as he wanted to think that it was Trista seated on the golden stallion, he logically could not accept it. It was only his mind and the night playing tricks on him.

Closing his eyes, he paused, then looked up again. The woman was still there, silhouetted before the moon. He studied her in silent awe, taking in the Indian clothing she wore and the graceful way she sat on the bare back of the horse, her hand tangled in the pale, lustrous mane to control the stallion's movements. It was the golden cascade of hair, though, that struck him an almost forceful blow, and Michael could not stop himself from speaking Trista's name.

"Trista?" It was a question; it was a heart-wrenching prayer.

Trista had ridden as close as she could to the strange camp. She had brought Fuego to a halt at the crest of a small hill overlooking the area and was trying to make out just who was camped there when the moon emerged from its place of hiding. Though the light helped her to some degree, she realized that it also revealed her place of observation all too well. Prepared to flee, she hesitated, studying the encampment before her.

Trista was not conscious of Michael standing slightly off to the side until the faint, indistinct sound of his voice came to her. Fuego moved nervously in tense excitement at the discovery that someone was near. Frightened now that she knew she'd been spotted, Trista urged the stallion to turn and was about to dash madly off into the night when he called out to her more loudly.

"Trista! Wait . . . Trista! Is that you!?" Michael's heart plummeted as he saw the woman turn the horse and start to ride off. It had to be Trista—it had to be!

The sound of his voice, so well remembered, sent a shiver of recognition up her spine. Michael? Confused, she hesitated in her flight, her gaze combing the land. Could it really be Michael? Her pulse was pounding erratically as unbelievable joy shot through her. "Michael?"

"Here, Trista! I'm here!" Michael charged forward through the brambly brush.

"Stay . . ." Trista whispered to Fuego as she slipped from his back. It seemed to her that she was moving almost in slow motion as she started down the incline. Trista did not know how she had come to be so blessed as to have found him, and she did not question her good fortune. All she could think of was that at last she was safe.

Michael made it to the bottom of the hill and looked up toward Trista as she descended. Watching her approach dressed in the Comanche fashion sent a shock of reality through him, and that shock registered in his eyes. *Dear God, what had they done to her? She actually looked like one of them save for the golden hair!*

Trista had been filled with ecstasy at the thought of being reunited with Michael, but as she was rushing to him, she saw the sudden change in his expression and knew a moment of heartbreak. She knew how much the whites hated the Comanche, and she realized how naive it had been of her to think that just by returning, everything would be the same. She paused in her descent, unsure of his real welcome.

"Michael . . ." Trista breathed his name, her uncertainty of his feelings for her reflected in her unsteady tone.

The sound of her voice, so tremulously fragile, shattered his calm. Going to her, he took her in his arms. "Ah, Trista . . . darling . . . I can't believe it. . . . I can't believe I've really found you. . . ."

Trista settled against him, trembling. "Michael, oh, Michael . . ."

"God, Trista, are you all right? Trista, I . . ." The questions that had haunted him could not be held back as Michael drew slightly away to look down at her. He was still not convinced that she was really there in his arms. Staring down at her, he finally accepted that she was truly with him. A sense of overwhelming serenity possessed him, but it was peace marred by the fear that she had somehow been hurt during her captivity. With the utmost care, he lowered his head to gently claim her lips for a tentative kiss. "Trista . . ."

Trista accepted his kiss, expecting to be swept off her feet by his passion. His hesitancy left her troubled. Hadn't he missed her? Didn't he love her?

"Michael . . . oh, Michael . . ." She cried his name softly. Wrapping her arms about him, she clung to him in desperation, needing to know that he still wanted her.

Her reaction startled Michael, and thinking that she was near hysteria, he broke off the embrace instead of deepening it. "Let me take you back to the camp. . . ." he said hoarsely as he swept her up into his arms. "You must be exhausted. . . . You've been through so much. . . ."

"Michael . . . I missed you so," Trista told him. Yet even as she said the words she felt strangely distanced from him, and she feared that maybe too much had happened for them to ever bridge the gap again.

"Pa!!"

Michael's shout woke George and the others. Not quite sure what was happening or where Michael had gone, they scrambled from their bedrolls and grabbed up their weapons.

"Michael!? Where are you?" George shouted into the night as Whitey threw dirt on the last glowing embers of the fire to afford them the shielding protection of the darkness.

"Here, Pa . . . it's all right," he called back. "I've found Trista!"

"What?" The men exchanged bewildered looks as Michael moved into the clearing carrying Trista.

George was momentarily stunned at the sight of Trista wearing the Comanche garb. A surge of pain jolted through him as he remembered another time and another beautiful woman dressed in such clothing.

"You found her . . . where? How?" George demanded as he rushed to his son's side. "Trista, are you all right?"

She met his worried gaze. "Yes, now."

"But where were you? How did you manage to get away?"

"I escaped from the Comanche," Trista told them, and the men immediately tensed, ready for a possible attack.

"Were you followed?" George needed to know if they were in danger.

"No. I fled the village two nights ago. No one saw me go, and no one has followed. I've been watching."

Michael carried her to the fire that Whitey had hastily rebuilt and sat down with her before its blazing warmth. "I just thank God you're here and you're fine. . . ."

For just an instant, the memory of Lance and his touch crossed her thoughts, and her expression clearly reflected her moment of disconcertion. Michael saw the change in her, and immediately regretted his choice of words. She wasn't fine. . . . She never would be again. A rage swept through him, and he wanted to kill the filthy redskins who'd dared to hurt her.

"What happens, Trista?" he asked in a low voice, his nerves taut as he awaited her answer. "Who captured you?"

Trista glanced nervously about, wanting to avoid his question, but knowing she had to answer. "I saw the golden stallion that you'd been talking about, and I went after him. . . ." Trista paused, remembering vividly the first time she'd seen Lance as he, too, had been giving chase. "He was chasing Fuego, too."

"Yes . . ."

"My horse lost its footing and fell. I was stunned for a moment, and when I looked up, he was there."

"Who was he, Trista?" Michael's tone demanded honesty.

"He was a half-breed, but he lived with Lone Elk's tribe. . . ."

George and Michael went perfectly still at the news.

"His name was Lance."

Chapter Seventeen

George and Michael were caught completely off guard by Trista's answer. Michael looked up, his dark eyes troubled as they met and held his father's tormented gaze in silent, shocked acknowledgment. *Lance* . . . Could it possibly be? The name alone struck a painful chord within Michael. Could this be the older half brother he'd never known . . . the older half brother who'd denied his father and his white heritage and had gone to live with the Comanche?

Long ago when he was small, his father had told him of his marriage to the Indian woman, Shining Star, and of Lance, the son he'd had by that marriage. Michael could still remember the pain in his parent's voice as he'd related the story of how Lance, a young boy then, had chosen to live with the Comanche and how he'd never heard from him again.

Michael had often wondered why his older brother had shunned them. Sometimes he'd even wondered if death had claimed Lance, but Michael knew now almost with a certainty that his half brother was alive. He doubted that there could be two half-breeds in Lone Elk's village named Lance.

At the thought of the Comanche camp and the suffering Trista must have endured there, Michael put an arm protectively about her.

"Did he hurt you?" It was painful for Michael to ask—in fact, he was dreading her response—but he

258

needed to know the full truth.

"Does it really matter now?" Trista countered shakily, not wanting to dredge up any of the memories of her time with Lance. It was all best forgotten.

Her evasive reply told Michael as much as a direct answer would have.

"Don't worry, Trista," he vowed in solemn, earnest tones, his eyes glittering dangerously. "He's going to pay for every minute you were held captive. I'm going to find this Lance, and when I do, I'm going to kill him. . . ." Michael was determined to avenge her. Grimly, he started to rise.

"No! you can't!" Trista frantically grabbed Michael's hand to stop him. Confusion reigned supreme within her as she wondered why she should care what happened to Lance. She tried to convince herself that she didn't, that it was Michael's well-being she was really worried about, but somehow the argument didn't ring true.

Michael was jarred by her protest, and his gaze narrowed as he regarded her stricken, pale features. "Why not?" he demanded heatedly. "I would think you, of all people, would be the one who'd want him dead for what he's done to you. . . ."

"No, please, no bloodshed. . . . Don't you understand? I just want to go back home with you and forget this ever happened! Please, Michael . . . just take me home. . . ." Traumatized by her feelings, Trista buried her face in her hands and began to sob.

Michael stared at her helplessly, lost in the storm of emotions that were battering him.

"We'll talk more later," George said quietly to Michael as he and the other men moved off to allow them privacy.

Michael nodded curtly, then took Trista in his arms. He wanted to reassure her, but his own feelings were in such an uproar that there was nothing he could say. Glancing down, he noticed with some surprise that she still wore his ring. The sight of the glittering keepsake still on her finger left him disconcerted. She was his fiancée. She was the woman who was to become his wife and bear his children, yet his half-breed brother had taken her innocence and now stood as an invisible barrier between them. Filled with anger over the horror of their situation, Michael only hoped that he was man enough to put the knowledge of all that had happened to Trista behind him and make a good life with her anyway.

"If all you want is to go home, Trista, then we'll go home," he finally promised.

Trista pulled slightly away to look up at him. "Yes, Michael. That's all that I want . . . to go home and to forget that this ever happened."

The sight of her tear-streaked face was heartbreaking to him. "We'll leave at first light."

George stood off in the darkness alone. He was overcome with emotion as he thought of all that had just been revealed to him. Lance, his beloved firstborn son, was still alive. He was positive that it could be no other, and yet with that surety came agonizing pain. If this was Lance, then why hadn't he come back to the ranch . . . to his home? Why hadn't he answered the messages he'd sent?

Guilt settled over George like a heavy burden as he realized how wrong he had been all those years ago. He should never have let Lance go with Lone Elk that day, but he had been so filled with his own sorrow and grief that he'd believed it to be for the best. What tortured him even more now, though, was the knowledge that Lance had come back to the ranch that one time while he'd been gone to town, but had disappeared before he'd returned from his trip. George had been tempted to drop everything and go after him, but at Eleanor's insistence, he had stayed on the Diamond. Instead, he had sent a message to his son asking him to return.

There had been no response to that message or to any of the many others he'd sent afterward. It was as if Lance had vanished. George had known then that he should have broken his agreement with Lone Elk about trespassing on the Indian lands and gone after his son personally, but the demands of the ranch and his new wife and baby had restrained him. He deeply regretted their separation and longed to know why Lance hated him so much that he'd never come back.

George glanced toward the encampment feeling overwhelming to blame for the situation in which they now found themselves. For some reason Lance had been intent on vengeance against them, and innocent Trista had been the one to pay the price for his hatred. With a heavy heart, he started back.

"Pa . . ." Michael's quiet call stopped him and he paused, waiting for his younger son to come to him.

"How's Trista?" he asked, concerned.

"Better, I think. I gave her a drink of the whiskey I brought along. She ate a little bit, and I've got her bedded down now for the night."

Though George couldn't make out Michael's features clearly in the darkness, the distress his son was feeling was discernible in his voice.

"That's good. Rest is probably the best thing for her," he remarked. "That and your support. She needs you more now, Michael, than she ever did before."

"I know." His answer was gruff with emotion as he struggled to bring his chaotic feelings under control. "I know."

Though Lance was in both their thoughts, neither brought him up. It was an ordeal that was best put from them—for Trista's sake and for their own.

Michael had placed his bedroll in a semisecluded spot slightly away from the other men's to allow Trista some privacy, and she lay trembling in its protective warmth. It was over. She was safely with Michael and would soon be back at the Royal Diamond.

Trista knew her joy at being rescued should have been great, but oddly, she found herself more miserable than ever. She had thought returning would solve everything, but now she worried that nothing would ever be the same again.

Staring off into the darkness in the direction Michael had gone in search of his father, Trista realized that her ordeal had affected not only her, but Michael, too. He had seemed so thrilled to see her in the first moments of their reunion, but as he'd found out all that had happened, she could sense that he was growing apart from her.

Fearfully, she wondered if they would ever be able to recapture what they'd had before. She wanted that. She wanted to be a good wife to him, but she also knew how women freed from Indian captivity were regarded by society. No matter what she and Michael did, it was not going to be easy.

Michael and George returned to the campsite then, and Michael approached her, his expression shuttered. As George made his way to his own blanket to settle in for the night, Michael went to speak with Trista.

"Are you all right?" he asked, going down on one knee before her.

"Yes," she told him softly.

"Well, just get some sleep. We'll be heading out early." He stood up, intending to sleep on the far side of the camp with the other men.

"Michael . . .?"

He glanced down at her questioningly.

"Michael . . . could you just hold me for a while?" Trista wanted to reestablish their closeness, to let him know that she needed him.

Michael was stunned by her request and said nothing for a moment. A short time before, he knew she would never have dared suggest such an intimacy between them, but now . . . Where once the idea of lying with Trista and holding her through the night might have thrilled him, now it left him strangely disquieted. He went to her uneasily. Taking great care to keep the blanket securely between them, he gathered her close.

Trista had thought that she would be happy in his embrace, yet as she lay in his arms, she felt anything but contented. Not only did she sense a definite remoteness about Michael, but she was also feeling oddly uncomfortable in his arms. His very nearness felt almost foreign to her, and she realized with a start that she was subconsciously remembering Lance and the sweet forbidden heat of his touch.

A shudder wracked her as she mentally berated herself for her folly in thinking of him. He had taken her captive against her will. . . . He had taken her virginity. . . . He had made her his wife . . . .

The last thought jolted through her, leaving her bewildered and more confused than ever. She was not Lance's wife! She wasn't! It had been an Indian ceremony, and it had meant nothing! She was going to marry Michael! It was Michael she loved. He was the one she wanted, not the blue-eyed warrior!

Even as she denied Lance, he was there, the memory of his kisses and arousing caresses filling her with shameful desire. Desperate to wipe him from her mind, she turned to Michael.

"Kiss me, Michael. . . . Please, kiss me. . . ." she pleaded in a hushed whisper, wanting his embrace to erase Lance from her mind and body forever.

Michael was shocked by her boldness, but reasoned that she just needed to feel wanted. His lips sought hers in a gentle, caring kiss, but that was not enough for Trista. She wrapped her arms about him and clung to him, deepening the embrace herself. Though his thoughts and feelings were in tumult, Michael's desire for her had not waned, and he responded to her sensual invitation. His arms tightened about her and crushed her to his chest as his mouth moved hungrily over hers.

For an instant Trista was thrilled, but as his body pressed tautly to hers, letting her know of his need, she suddenly knew it was all wrong. Wrenching herself free, she stared at him in horror as she realized what she'd just done.

"I'm sorry, Michael. . . ."

Bewildered by her sudden resistance, Michael went still and then slowly withdrew from their embrace. "No, Trista, I'm the one who's sorry."

Trista blanched at his words as he moved rigidly away from her and got to his feet. The silence between them was awkward.

"I'll be with the others if you need anything. . . ." he told her stiffly.

Trista could only nod in response. Her heart lay heavy in her breast and tears traced damply down her cheeks as she watched Michael walk away.

The dream was vivid, a swirling vortex of color and

264

light that twisted into patterns and memories Lance wanted to forget. Trista . . . She was there in his mind looking as she had on their last night together . . . pale, golden, and far lovelier than any woman he'd ever seen. As her vision moved through his slumber, he could feel the heaven of her touch and the heated silk of her body against him.

Fuego charged through the imagery then, his flashing golden beauty complementing Trista's. Perfectly matched in coloring and temperament, the two exquisite creatures elusively evaded him at every turn, and in doing so, made his all-consuming need for them even greater. In the dream, Lance reached for them, but they fled his grasp, disappearing into a cloaking gray mist and leaving him alone and cold in the sudden darkness that followed.

The lone, shrill howl of the coyote rent the night, and Lance came abruptly awake. His heart was pounding as he lay still, and sweat beaded his brow as he thought of how much he missed the golden one. . . . Slowly reality returned, and with it came the anger that fueled his actions.

Gauging the hour by the position of the moon, he got up and talked to his pony. They had rested enough. He would push himself and his mount to the limit if necessary, but he was going to find Trista and Fuego and claim them again. Putting his heels to the horse's sides, he headed to the south . . . to the Diamond.

Fuego shifted nervously as Trista spoke to him in a gentle, cajoling voice the next morning. Though the presence of the men rendered him more than a little frightened, he remained close to Trista, trusting her promise of safety.

Trista had slept deeply after her tense encounter with Michael, and she had been so caught up in her emotional turmoil that she hadn't even thought of Fuego until she'd awakened a little before dawn. She had been thrilled to discover that he had not left her, and had rewarded the big stallion with encouraging praise and some of the grain the men had brought for their own horses.

"You're planning on riding him," Michael said in complete astonishment as he stared at Trista and the rogue.

Trista nodded firmly. "Fuego has brought me safely this far."

"I can't believe this," Michael went on. "I knew you were quite a horsewoman, but to have tamed the rogue . . ."

She managed a smile as she thought of their joint captivity. "He's my friend. He knows me, and he knows that I'd never do anything to hurt him."

"That's quite an accomplishment," George complimented her. "Are you sure?"

"I'm sure," she cut him off, "and I'm ready to leave whenever you are." For some reason Trista felt compelled to ride back to the ranch on Fuego.

The rest of the men looked on in admiration as she mounted the golden stallion and urged him forward, but Michael found himself feeling resentful of her easy handling of him.

Mary Lou Harris's expression was sympathetic. "Darling, I'm just so sorry all this had to happen. Have you heard anything?"

"No, Mary Lou, not a word. Most of the men who'd ridden out with Michael and George returned several days ago. They reported back that they had found nothing, but that Michael had refused to give up." Eleanor explained the situation to her friend.

"This is all so terrible," Sukie put in, her heart aching over the trauma poor Michael must be going through. "I know how much Michael cared for Trista and how awful this must be for him. Do you think there's any hope of them finding her?"

"I don't know, Sukie," Eleanor admitted. "You know how the Comanche are. . . ." She shivered at the thought of Trista in captivity.

"Sometimes it's almost better if the captives are killed outright." Mary Lou bluntly stated what the other women had been thinking. "I've heard about the condition of some of these women when they're finally located and freed, and it isn't pretty."

"Mary Lou!" Eleanor protested.

"Now, Eleanor, you know I'm just speaking the plain truth. We all know what happens to those women, and think of poor Michael's dilemma if he does find Trista," Mary Lou stated.

"I pray to God that he does find her," she insisted, heartsick over the entire situation.

"Mrs. Barrett," Sukie spoke up as she slanted her mother a reproachful look, "if there's anything we can do, please call on us."

"Sukie, you're a dear." Eleanor smiled at her sadly. "I'll let you know the minute I hear something. When Michael returns, I'll tell him that you came by and that you were concerned about him and Trista."

"Yes, well, we'd better be going." Mary Lou stood up a bit huffily and started from the room. "Be sure to let us know, Eleanor."

"I will," she promised as she walked them to the door.

As Mary Lou took up the reins of their buggy and slapped them against the horse's back to start them on their way back home, she gave her daughter a pensive look. She knew how heartbroken Sukie had been ever since Michael had announced his engagement, and though she regretted what had happened, she could also see a promising outcome to the whole situation. "You know, I feel terrible about what's happened, but . . ."

Sukie had been lost in thought, imagining Michael's pain and empathizing with him over his loss, when her mother's comment interrupted her. "But what?" She gave her a curious look.

"But this might work out for the best in the end," Mary Lou concluded with a shrewd certainty.

"I don't understand, Mother. What are you talking about?" Sukie was truly confused by her statement.

"I'm talking about Trista's disappearance."

"It's just horrible, isn't it?" she remarked sincerely. "I feel really bad for Michael. . . . And can you just imagine what poor Trista is going through?"

"Let's don't talk about Trista. Think about Michael and how you're going to comfort him when he returns without his fiancée."

"Mother!" Sukie was both embarrassed and outraged by her suggestion.

"If Trista doesn't return, Sukie, then Michael will be a free man again."

While her spirits lifted at the thought, she could not bring herself to celebrate the other woman's misfortune. She struggled inwardly with her conflicting emotions as her mother continued.

"There may still be hope for a union between our two families."

"There's always the chance that they'll find her, Mother," Sukie pointed out.

"Sukie, dear, do you think for one moment that Eleanor is going to stand by and let her only son marry a girl who's been held captive by some filthy Comanche?"

"But Michael loves her." Sukie found herself in the odd position of defending Trista.

"Maybe he does, but things change. Mark my words." Mary Lou's tone was final, and Sukie said no more as they continued on their way home.

Eleanor stood at the window of her bedroom staring out across the vast acreage of the Royal Diamond. Her thoughts were on her son and her husband, and she wondered how much longer it would be before they gave up the search for Trista and came home. Eleanor shook her head slowly in weary denial of all that had happened. Just a short time before everything had been so perfect in Michael's life. He had found the woman he loved and had been ecstatically happy. Regretfully, she realized that Mary Lou had probably been right, for things would probably never be the same if they found Trista alive now. It was a fact that the Comanche were unspeakably cruel, and Eleanor deliberately avoided dwelling on what poor Trista might be suffering at their hands.

A deep, sorrowful sigh escaped her at the thought of Trista's father. She had notified him of his daughter's disappearance shortly after it had happened, and he had sent a message back stating that he would be there as soon as possible. She did not know when he would be arriving, but she was dreading it. Still, she knew there could be no help for it. One way or the other, he would have to be informed of his daughter's fate.

As Eleanor was about to turn away from the window, she saw a rider racing toward the house from the north. She gripped the windowsill anxiously as she tried to make out who it was, but her efforts were to no avail. Gathering up her skirts, she hurried from the room and rushed downstairs. She had just stepped out onto the porch when Poker reined in in a cloud of dust before her.

"Poker . . . what is it?" she asked worriedly.

"It's them, Mrs. Barrett. . . ." He was so excited that he was having trouble getting out the news.

"Who, Poker? My husband and Michael?"

"Yes, ma'am, and Miss Trista, too. They found her."

"She's alive. . . ." Eleanor breathed.

"Yes, ma'am, and she looks to be pretty well 'ceptin' for the Indian clothes she's wearin'. They're headin' this way right now," Poker related.

"Dear God . . . thank heavens. How soon will they be here?"

"They been ridin' pretty hard all day, so I imagine it's gonna take 'em another half hour or so. Mr. Barrett asked me to ride ahead and let you know."

"Thank you, Poker. Thank you so much . . ." Trembling, Eleanor stared off to the north, waiting for some sign of her men returning and wondering how Trista had fared at the hands of the Comanche.

Chapter Eighteen

When Rosalie had departed Trista's bedroom, leaving her alone at last, Trista quickly discarded her Comanche garb and lowered herself into the hot bathwater. Sighing, she leaned back against the side of the tub and closed her eyes. She tried to relax, but every nerve in her body was still tense and on edge despite the fact that she was once more safely with Michael on the Royal Diamond.

The soothing warmth of the bath helped to ease the weary soreness from Trista's aching muscles as she lay there, but it did little to relieve the complex jumble of emotions that were trapped within her heart. Instead of calming her, it had the opposite effect, reminding her of the bath she'd taken that night in the pool . . . and how it had ended.

Lance! Would he never leave her thoughts? Trista despaired as guilt surged through her. She felt deeply ashamed of all that had happened with Lance, and she was finding it difficult living with the knowledge that she'd submitted to the handsome half-breed.

She was grateful that Michael had only questioned her about her situation one time and then, tactfully, had never brought it up again. He was being so kind, so considerate and so attentive, and she was feeling so guilty. . . .

How could she have betrayed Michael as she had? How could she have gone so willingly to Lance that last night? Regrettably, though she didn't understand it, she knew the answer. The dangerous warrior had only to touch her to set her senses reeling and strike all reason from her mind.

Trista bit back a sob as Lance took possession of her thoughts again, and she couldn't stop herself from wondering where he was and what he was doing. Had he returned to the village yet and discovered her absence, or was he still off on his raid, knowing nothing of her successful flight to freedom?

Angrily, she fought to banish all thoughts of Lance as she stared down at Michael's ring on her finger. She was Michael's fiancée. She wanted her future to be with him. Certainly, once she was Michael's wife, she would forget all about Lance.

Agitation gripped her, and Trista picked up the scented soap Rosalie had provided and began to wash her hair. Wanting to cleanse herself of all that had happened, she scrubbed every inch of her body. Her skin was glowing when she finished, the peachy tint that living in the outdoors had given her adding a blossom of color to her otherwise pale complexion. Her bath completed and feeling a bit more like her normal self, she rose from the tub and toweled herself dry.

As she moved to the wardrobe to get her wrapper, Trista caught sight of her reflection in the mirror above her dressing table and gasped in dismay, shocked to discover that her back was covered with bruises. She had known that Night Lark's blows the other day had been painful, but she'd had no idea that they had left such vivid marks upon her. Her heart hardened as she thought of Lance directing the other woman to "train" her so she could become a chore wife, and she smiled thinly in pleasure at the thought of his anger when he returned to find her gone.

Determined that Michael would never see any outward sign of her mistreatment, Trista donned her wrapper and belted it securely about her waist. She moved to sit at the vanity table and carefully studied her face in the mirror as she worked the comb through the heavy mane of her hair. Trista was worried that there might be some outward change in her that might reveal the chaos of her feelings, but to her immense relief there was no telltale sign revealing her inner torment. It was bad enough that she had to deal secretly with her shame, but she certainly didn't want Michael to discover the full extent of her betrayal. No matter what, Trista vowed, she was going to put it all behind her. She was going to try to act as if nothing had happened, and maybe, with time, she could convince herself that it was true.

"Michael, what are you going to do?" Eleanor asked, her concern obvious in her worried expression as she glanced from her husband to her son.

Michael took a deep drink from the tumbler of whiskey he was holding and then looked up, meeting her gaze steadily. "Trista has suffered enough, Mother. I love her, and I see no reason to alter our plans."

"Are you sure about this?"

"Very," he replied unwaveringly, his expression stony.

"George?" Eleanor turned to her husband for further counsel.

"It's Michael's decision, Eleanor, but I am in total agreement with him."

With an effort, Eleanor put her concern about appearances aside. If this was what Michael really wanted, then she would support him fully. No one would dare question or cross a Barrett about this matter once it was made clear that Trista would indeed still be marrying Michael. Certainly the girl had been easy enough to guide before this incident, but now Eleanor was sure she would be even more easily intimidated. She found the prospect pleasing.

"Very well," she agreed without further objection. "Shall we move up the wedding date then? Since her father is on his way here now, there's really no reason to delay the ceremony once he arrives."

"That's fine with me, if it's all right with Trista," Michael consented, understanding the possible need for an earlier wedding date.

"I'm sure she'll agree. It seems the only logical course. . . ." Eleanor told her son as she went to him and lay a comforting hand upon his arm. "Trista's very, very lucky to have you, darling. I hope you'll both be happy."

"We will be, Mother. I love her, and she loves me. Now that I've got her back, I'll never let anything or anyone separate us ever again," Michael stated fiercely as he drained the last of his whiskey, stood up, and went to the liquor cabinet to refill his glass.

George and Eleanor exchanged a short, troubled, glance. Michael was not a heavy drinker.

"I'd better get cleaned up now before dinner," Michael told them, starting from the room with a full tumbler of liquor in hand.

"Of course, dear." They watched him go in silence and were both relieved and worried at the same time.

"George, is Michael all right?"

"He will be, given time," George responded sagely.

"And Trista? She seemed rather withdrawn when you arrived Lance and she looked so terrible dressed that way. . . ." Eleanor clutched at her husband's arm as she remembered the sight of her future daughter-in-law looking so much like a wild Comanche squaw.

Thinking of Trista and her time in captivity, George paused before he answered, "She's been through a lot, darling, but she's a strong-willed young woman. With Michael's love and our continued support, she should be just fine."

"Good . . ." she breathed in relief.

When Eleanor left him a few minutes later and at last he was alone, George let his mask of deception drop. His expression was heartbreakingly sad, and his movements were almost jerky as he strode to the liquor cabinet to pour himself a stiff drink. George stared about the study with unseeing eyes, thinking of the past and his son, his firstborn.

Lance . . . It had been Lance . . . his son. Excitement mingled with fear at the thought. He'd wanted to question Trista more about the half-breed who'd captured her, but knew it was impossible. She had escaped her captor, and she was safe. From now on they would endeavor never to mention him or this time again. But even as George knew he could never speak to her of the savage half-breed who'd taken her prisoner, his heart longed to know more of his long-lost son . . . the boy he had loved and yet forfeited during the darkest days of his life.

The late afternoon breeze shifted, and Fuego, safely penned in the Royal Diamond's main corral, tensed and raised his head. He was suddenly alert . . . suddenly threatened, and he moved agitatedly about the enclosure as he studied the surrounding terrain.

Hidden among the rocks at the top of the hill overlooking the ranchhouse, Lance remained motionless, his blue-eyed gaze locked on the golden stallion dancing nervously about the corral. *Fuego.* A tightness gripped his chest as he watched the golden one. If the stallion was here, then Trista was also. Lance refused to acknowledge the relief that flooded through him with that hoped-for discovery.

Glancing toward the west, Lance judged the lateness of the hour and knew that there was only a short time left until sundown. A fierce smile curved the grim line of his mouth as he plotted his plan of action. Though he longed to sweep down upon the unsuspecting ranch and forcefully take what was his, Lance, knew it was not yet time. He would wait until the darkness provided him with sheltering cover and then claim his stallion and his wife. Moving carefully away to avoid detection, Lance sought a secluded hiding place to pass the next few hours.

Trista was starting from her bedroom, intending to join Michael and his parents for dinner, when she heard the sound of Fuego whinnying nervously. She hurried to the window, wondering at what could be causing his upset, but the cloaking darkness of the night prevented her from seeing as far as the stables. Trista paused to listen, and as Fuego grew quiet again, she realized that he was probably just having some difficulty adjusting to his restricted freedom. She had not seen him since they'd arrived. Wanting to make sure that he really was all right, Trista made a mental note to be sure to check on him after they'd eaten.

Turning away from the window, she took one last glance in the mirror to make certain that she looked her best. She wanted to appear as normal as possible tonight to convince Michael that she was fine and that everything could be the same again. She'd combed her hair into an upswept style that she knew Michael

liked, and her choice of dress had been deliberate . . .
a demure, high-necked, pale blue gown that fit her
perfectly. Though not revealing, it hugged her slender
form, giving testimony to the feminine curves beneath, before flaring out softly in gentle emphasis of
the swell of her hips. Trista felt much better since
she'd bathed and changed back into her own clothing,
and she was sure that she was calm enough now to
carry on normally. Without further hesitation, she left
her room and descended to join the family in the
dining room.

Lance had been cautiously making his way toward
the house when Fuego had picked up his scent and
begun to stir restively in the corral. Fearful that
someone would emerge from the bunkhouse to check
on the stallion, Lance had faded back into the
shadows and waited in tense silence to see what would
happen. As minutes passed and no one come out to
check on the jittery horse, he moved from his place of
refuge and started once again toward the building that
had long ago been his home.

It was then that Lance saw Trista silhouetted in the
window of her room. Just the sight of her sent a shaft
of pure desire through him that left him slightly
shaken and more than a little angry at its power. Still,
he could not tear his gaze away as he remained
motionless in the darkness watching her. He remembered that her hair had been arranged in much the
same fashion the first time he'd seen her there at the
ranch, and he decided immediately that he preferred
her hair down, loose and flowing about her shoulders.
He knew a sudden impatience to be with her again.
He wanted to release the cascade of her hair from its
bonds and run his hands through the silken strands
while he . . .

Lance grew irritated by the direction of his

277

thoughts, and he forced all memories of their love-making from him. He was in far too dangerous a situation to let his attention be diverted even for a moment. On silent tread, he moved through the shadows of the night, skirting the outbuildings and heading for the ranchhouse.

"Trista, you look lovely tonight." Michael was waiting at the foot of the stairs for her, his dark eyes upon her as she descended.

"Thank you, Michael." Trista graced him with a bright smile as she came to him.

"You're more than welcome, darling," Michael responded, tucking her arm protectively under his as he led her to the dining room, where his parents were waiting. "Your timing is perfect. Dinner is just about ready to be served."

"I'm glad I didn't keep you waiting," she offered to him and his parents as they joined them.

"Even if you had, you would have been worth the wait." He smiled down at her. His gaze was warm upon her as the whiskey he'd consumed helped to anesthetize the pain from the trauma of the past few weeks. Trista looked so lovely to him . . . so sweet and so beautiful that he vowed silently to himself to make it up to her for all the agony she'd suffered.

For the first time since her rescue the day before, Trista was actually beginning to feel comfortable.

"Indeed, Trista," George agreed, thinking he had never seen her looking prettier as he led the way to the table.

"Thank you," she replied demurely as she took the seat Michael held out for her.

As soon as they were seated, Rosalie served the meal. As they ate the succulent fare, Eleanor brought up the subject she knew had to be discussed.

"Trista, darling, you know I mentioned to you when

you first arrived this afternoon that your father was on his way here now. . . ."

"Yes." She looked up at her questioningly.

"Well, we've discussed it, and we thought it might be appropriate to move up the wedding date. Since your father will be here soon, I can think of no reason to delay the ceremony any longer than necessary. Can you?"

Anger flared within Trista. She knew Eleanor was suggesting the change in dates to still possible gossip and protect her reputation, but it annoyed Trista to no end. It hadn't been her fault she'd been captured! Insidiously, the other reason for moving up the wedding date struck her and a flush stained her cheeks. There was always the chance that she could be pregnant with the half-breed's child, and Michael was gallantly offering her the protection of his name. She glanced to Michael, wondering what he was truly feeling.

Michael quickly lay a warm, caring hand over hers. "Everything will be fine. Don't worry."

"Oh, Michael . . ." She bit at her lip. Michael was so kind. . . . Her feelings for him were in turmoil.

"The wedding will take place as soon as her father arrives from Philadelphia." Michael displayed no regret over the decision.

"There will be no wedding."

The china cup Trista had been holding dropped from her numb fingers and clattered noisily to the tabletop at the sound of Lance's voice. She was stunned, and her pulse quickened as she turned to look toward the doorway; the sight of him leaning almost negligently against the wall caused her heart to pound wildly in her breast. *Lance was here.* . . . She couldn't help but think of how handsome he looked . . . his chest—so broad and firmly muscled; his

279

eyes — so piercingly blue and vivid in the sun-bronzed darkness of his face; and his hair — so raven-black, and just long enough to brush the nape of his neck. *He had come for her.* . . .

"Lance . . ." His name was a hushed whisper on her lips.

Only an instant had passed, but it seemed an eternity to Trista as her gaze met his across the width of the room. Time stood still. The universe narrowed to just the two of them.

Though he was unarmed, Michael reacted first to the sight of the Comanche. Charging to his feet, he meant to physically attack the warrior, but Lance was too quick for him.

"Lance . . . NO!" Trista cried desperately, afraid that Michael might be injured.

Her protest was too late as Lance drew his knife with lightning speed and threw it. As the blade sliced through the air, Eleanor let out a bloodcurdling shriek of terror, fearing for her son's life. Michael dove quickly to the floor as the weapon buried itself deep in the far wall of the dining room several feet above his head.

George stood up, violently overturning his chair in the process. His expression clearly reflected his stunned disbelief in all that was happening. "What the hell?" He was poised, ready to do battle with this intruder, when Trista's words finally penetrated his fury-fogged consciousness. "Lance?"

Lance stepped farther into the room. His manner was tense and threatening, but controlled as his gaze swept away from Trista to his father and Michael, who was slowly getting to his feet. A sneer curled his lips as he openly studied the men who had been the cause of so much pain in his life.

"I have not come to kill, but I will if you push me,"

Lance stated coldly.

"What do you want?" Michael demanded belliger-
ently, his hands clinched into fists at his sides as he
glared at him.

"I have come to claim what is rightfully mine,"
Lance stated coldly, looking pointedly over at Trista.

George stared at him, his gaze feasting on the sight
of him. This was Lance . . . his son . . . Shining
Star's son. George could see so much of Shining Star
in him that it left him speechless for a moment. Lance
had returned. . . . He had come home. He was
almost ready to welcome him with open arms when
Michael's question revealed the awful truth.

"What do you mean?" Michael asked, his dark eyes
narrowing as he regarded him suspiciously.

"I have come to claim my wife."

"Wife?" Michael and George both echoed the same
sentiment as Eleanor only looked on in distress.

"Trista is my wife," he insisted. "She belongs to me."

"NO!" Trista retorted defiantly.

"It is bound." Lance's tone was deadly earnest as he
met his father's gaze. "Lone Elk has decreed it."

George paled at the news. Lance had married
Trista in a Comanche ceremony. Memories of his own
marriage to Shining Star assailed him . . . memories
of a happier time, a loving time. Michael could only
look on in confusion as Trista faced Lance.

"Trista is engaged to me," Michael challenged, taking a menacing step toward Lance.

Lance went still as he turned on his brother. His
expression was fierce, his manner barely restrained.
"You may have laid claim to everything else, but
Trista is mine," he spoke in low tones.

"Lance . . . Michael . ." George finally started
toward him, wanting to break the tension between his
sons as they faced each other, prepared to do battle.

"You know Lance?" Trista broke in, bewildered by George's reaction to him.

George answered Trista in a grave tone. "Yes, Trista, I know Lance." His gaze swung back to the tall, magnificent figure of a man who stood before him. "Lance is my son. . . ."

"Oh, dear God . . ." Eleanor murmured faintly.

Trista's eyes widened, revealing her shock as she stared at the three men in profound confusion. "Son? Lance is your son? I don't understand. . . ."

"Do not claim me now, Barrett," Lance mocked bitterly. "You have denied me for years. Why acknowledge me now?"

"Lance . . . I've never denied you!" George protested, startled by his revelation and wondering why Lance thought that.

"Years ago, when I needed you the most, you couldn't wait to be rid of me. . . ."

"That's not true!" Again he refuted him. "Lone Elk said you could return at any time, but you never came back. . . ."

"I came back once, but it was clear you did not want me, white man," Lance told him resentfully.

"But you didn't stay. . . . Why didn't you wait for me to return? I sent message after message to Lone Elk, but I never heard from you."

"Save your lies, Barrett. They do not change anything," Lance snarled. "Do you think I didn't know that you couldn't stand the sight of me?"

Trista could see the misery mirrored plainly on George's face as Lance's words struck him like a physical blow, and she wondered at the cause for so much hatred between them. Was it true? Had George denied him? Trying to grasp some clue as to what had happened, Trista glanced at Lance. His words sounded indifferently sarcastic, but in the depths of his blue eyes—eyes so like his father's, as she realized now—she could see reflected a deep, abiding pain that testified to a bitter disillusionment.

"Lance . . . I—" George wanted to tell him everything, to explain the pain of that miserable night all those years ago, but Lance would hear none of it.

"I have come for Trista." He rebuffed his effort at conversation. "She is mine."

"Trista's not going anywhere with you," Michael challenged, pulling himself together with an effort. He was torn between the desire to kill the man who stood so arrogantly before them telling them of his claim on Trista, and wanting to embrace him and welcome him into the family. This was his brother . . . this was Lance . . . yet this was also the fierce Comanche who'd stolen the woman he loved and . . .

Lance turned a glacial glare on Michael. "She is my wife. She belongs to me, and she will come with me."

"I will not! I don't belong to you or to anyone! I'm Michael's fiancée and I—"

"You are my wife!" he said sharply, infuriated by the thought of her belonging to anyone else.

As Michael took a step forward, George quickly moved between his sons, his hands outstretched in supplication. "Lance . . . we must talk. . . ."

"I have nothing to say to you, Barrett, or to the white son who pleases you so well." Lance gave Michael a cold, disparing look.

"I am your father, Lance," George agonized, thinking that Lance would leave again and that he would never get the chance to tell him that he loved him. "Give me this much."

"I give you nothing, white man"—he stiffened—"just as you gave me nothing."

"Lance . . . please . . ." George put aside all manly pride as he pleaded with his son, but he did not feel

283

less a man for it. If anything, he knew that for the first time in years he was being honest about what he was truly feeling.

Lance wanted to take Trista and leave, but his father's desperation touched something deep within him. A faint thought skimmed through his mind that maybe, just maybe he'd been wrong all this time. Yet the facts spoke for themselves. He had never received any messages from his father. He had had no contact at all after his one attempt to return home. Still, there was the chance. Without waiting for George to lead the way, Lance left the dining room and walked into the study—the study he remembered so well.

Shocked into silence, Eleanor had remained quiet during the exchange, but the instant Lance moved out of the room, she turned on her husband. "George . . . I don't understand. . . . How can this be Lance? I thought he was dead."

"It's Lance, Eleanor," George assured her as he disappeared out into the hall after him.

Eleanor cast Michael a troubled look as he started to follow them from the room. "Michael?"

"When Trista told us that first night that her captor's name was Lance, Father and I both suspected, but—" he began to explain.

"Michael . . ." Trista was distraught over all that had transpired. *Lance was George's son and therefore Michael's half-brother. Yet for some reason he had been cast away from his family.* "How can Lance be your father's son?"

"Pa was married to a Comanche woman before he married my mother," Michael answered. "When she died, evidently Lance left the ranch and went to live with his mother's brother and his tribe."

"Lone Elk . . ." she said his name softly.

"I don't know exactly what happened," Eleanor put in. "Lance had been gone for some time when George and I married, thank God. Why, just the thought of that filthy half-breed being related to Michael is almost more than I can bear." She covered her heart with her hand in a melodramatic gesture.

Though Trista hated Lance, she found herself bristling at Eleanor's insulting remarks. Even if Lance was half-Comanche, he was also half-Barrett. He was part of their family. That thought gave her pause, and she grew outraged with Michael and George. Why had they kept Lance's identity a secret when they had known who her captor was and hadn't told her?

"Michael . . ."

Michael heard the seriousness in Trista's voice. Thinking that she was concerned for her safety, he hurried to assure her, "Don't worry, darling. I won't let him hurt you again. I'll protect you from him. . . ."

"Just like you protected me from the truth about him? How could you have known that Lance was your brother and not told me?!" The more she thought, the more angry she became.

"We were never positive it was him." He defended their actions. "But even if we had been, it would have made no difference."

"Made no difference?! I intended to become part of your family, but if you think for one minute that I'll marry you when you keep such secrets from me, you're wrong," she accused heatedly.

Michael did not understand why she was so angry. He had only been trying to keep her safe. "Trista," he began in coaxing tones, thinking that she was just upset by Lance's unexpected appearance.

"Don't Trista me, Michael Barrett! I'm not some delicate little miss who can't handle the truth. Considering the situation, I should have been told everything! How many more things have you kept from me

285

to protect me?"

"I'm not the only one who's kept secrets, Trista!" he charged defensively, angered that she would accuse him of being secretive when Lance was the one who had surprised them all by declaring that Trista was his wife.

"I don't know what you mean. . . ." She regarded him suspiciously, the strength of his hostile retort surprising her.

"You didn't tell me that your captor had married you," he told her bitterly.

"It was a Comanche ceremony, Michael. Besides, do you really think that I had a choice in the matter?" Trista returned just as furiously. "Do you think that I would have married a man I didn't know willingly? I was his captive. I was his slave. I did not choose to marry him! I was forced!"

Michael's jaw was rigid as he strode from the room to join his father and Lance in the study.

Eleanor turned to Trista when he had gone. "I'm sorry this had to happen, Trista. I know how difficult and upsetting this must be for you."

Trista felt some of her anger ease at her soothing words, yet oddly, it resurged as the older woman continued.

"I know how much you must hate the half-breed, and I pray to God that George and Michael get rid of him, and fast! Why, you know for yourself that he's no more than a vicious savage." Eleanor shivered as she thought of the way Lance had looked standing there in the doorway of her dining room. He'd been almost naked and had seemed so brutal and uncivilized.

Trista knew Lance could be vicious; she had seen him fight with Striking Snake. Yet she had also seen him at other times . . . times when he'd been gentle and tender and . . . Her traitorous thoughts disturbed her greatly.

"Eleanor, if you will excuse me . . ." Trista stood suddenly, needing to get away . . . to get her wayward thoughts under control.

"Of course, dear." She was understanding. "Don't worry about a thing. You're safe here. I'm sure they'll never let him bother you again."

Eleanor's words . . . *they'll never let him bother you again* . . . followed Trista from the dining room as she hurried to seek out the sanctity of her own room, unshed tears stinging her eyes.

Chapter Nineteen

When Trista had gone, Eleanor nervously began to pace the dining room. She longed to know what was transpiring in the study, but realized that her presence would not be welcomed by the three men. Deeply troubled, she wandered out into the hall and paused before the study door, hoping to be able to hear some of the conversation. To her disappointment, she could distinguish nothing of what was being said. Frustrated, she moved into the parlor to await George's coming to her.

What had taken place that evening troubled her deeply. The half-breed's unexpected arrival at the Royal Diamond had infuriated her. How dare Lance return to the ranch after all these years?! And how dare he claim that Trista was his wife!? The possibility was just too ridiculous to consider. Trista was engaged to Michael, and now that she was safely home, they could be married as soon as her father arrived from Philadelphia.

A deep fear possessed Eleanor that Lance would now be staying permanently at the ranch. The thought provoked a grim determination within her. In a silent promise to herself, Eleanor vowed she would do everything in her power to keep the half-breed from coming there to live. The Barretts had a name and a reputation to uphold. She had no intention of allowing George to sully it with Lance's presence or allowing Lance to share in Michael's inheritance. The Royal Diamond was to be Michael's, and Michael's alone. She would not allow him to share it with anyone, least of all a half-breed brother.

Eleanor hoped and prayed with all her heart that George would quickly dispatch his half-breed offspring back from where he'd come. He had no business there on the ranch. He was nothing but a filthy savage, and he deserved to be treated that way. His kidnapping of Trista proved what a brutal red devil he really was.

Eleanor thought of Trista then and was amazed that she had held up so well under the strain of a confrontation with the Comanche who'd taken her captive. She was certain it must have been a terrible ordeal, and she admired the fact that Trista had been so controlled when she'd seen him. Only Trista's sudden display of temper in her argument with Michael and her threat to call off the wedding had bothered Eleanor. She had approved of Michael's choice for a wife because she had truly believed that Trista could be easily handled. Now, however, the opposite appeared to be true. Trista seemed headstrong and most opinionated, and it concerned Eleanor. She definitely didn't want Michael marrying a strong-willed woman. She didn't want to risk his coming under the influence of a wife who might steer him away from her own guiding, maternal love.

Lance entered the study and, for just the briefest of moments, was transported back to the last time he'd stood there . . . the last time he'd faced his father. The memory left him feeling young and confused and torn, and he fought it down with all his might. No longer was he a small boy begging for love from a distant, dismissing parent. He was a man now.

As he heard his father enter the room behind him, Lance purposefully kept his expression remote and more than a little disdainful. It would never do to let Barrett know how deeply he had been hurt or how long that hurt had remained with him in the guise of bitter hatred.

"What is it you want to speak of, Barrett?" Lance demanded as he turned to face him.

George stared at the haughty warrior before him, recognizing the son he had once known, yet also seeing Lone Elk in him. "With Lone Elk's help you have become a fine man," he said in an attempt to bridge the gap between them.

"Lone Elk has been a good father to me as well as an uncle."

Again Lance's words cut George to the quick, and he was hard put to remain in control of his emotions. This was Lance . . . the son he'd longed for . . . the son he'd loved and lost in a time of his life that was filled with great sorrow and grief. He wanted him back with him on the ranch at any cost.

"He loves you as I do," he agreed hoarsely.

"I have come for Trista, not to speak of unpleasant things." Lance cut his father off, not wanting to hear any declarations of love from the man who had abandoned him years ago.

"Trista won't be going anywhere with you," Michael stated aggressively as he entered the study and closed the door behind him. "She's engaged to me. We're going to be married."

Lance studied Michael coolly. "I have already made her mine. She is my wife."

A surge of jealousy consumed Michael at the thought of him possessing Trista. "Only by your custom!"

"It is enough."

"Not by our civilized standards! Your wedding ceremony carries no significance here!"

George broke in, speaking his younger son's name threateningly. "Michael . . ."

Though his temper was on edge and he longed to throttle Lance, Michael backed off.

"I asked you in here not to discuss Trista, Lance, but to deal with something far more important."

Lance merely arched a dark brow in response to the urgency in his tone.

"Now that you are here, with me . . . with us . . ." George glanced to Michael and saw that he was listening with interest. "I want you to stay."

His statement took Lance by surprise. Lance had not expected this kind of welcome from the man who had made no effort to contact him in all this time. Yet here his father was, offering him the very things that he had longed for . . . his home and his namesake and his inheritance.

"You would bribe me with such an offer just to keep Trista for your white son?" he sneered hatefully.

"Bribe you? I'm not bribing you. I want you to come home. Your place should be here with me." George was serious. "With us."

"Why now, Barrett?" Lance scoffed.

"You obviously don't believe that I've tried to contact you, but the truth is that I did. When you didn't respond, I thought that you didn't want to come back to me. Lone Elk and I had agreed long ago that the choice would be yours, and yours alone."

"You thought right. I came back once, and that one trip was enough. How quickly you had forgotten us . . . my mother and me! How quickly you started a new life without us!"

"Is that what you think? Is that why you left?"

"It doesn't matter now." Lance refused to say any more. He felt he'd already revealed far too much about the inner feelings he'd kept hidden for so long.

"It does matter. You're my son . . . my firstborn. I loved your mother and I love you. I'm sorry for all the misunderstandings that have occurred between us. Stay and let me make up the past to you. Stay and be part of our family. This is where you belong—here, on the Royal Diamond, with me."

Lance knew he should refuse. He knew he should return to his village and forget that he'd ever spoken with his father, but Trista stole into his thoughts. *She was his*, he thought fiercely. He would not leave until he could take her with him.

"Lance . . . you don't have to decide this minute." George didn't want to rush him and risk a refusal. "Stay with us for a few days. Then make your decision. Just know that I want you here. I want you beside me, helping Michael and me to make the Diamond the finest spread in Texas."

Lance glanced to the brother he could now claim and wondered at his thoughts, but Michael's impassive features revealed neither the raging hatred Lance had expected nor a welcome he would not have believed. Through the turmoil of his coming to a decision, Trista remained, her blond beauty beckoning him elusively onward in much the same way that Fuego's mystique had once drawn him. He was a captive of her golden allure.

"I will stay," came his grudging answer.

His positive response was unexpected. George felt as if his heart would burst with joy, but his excitement was tempered by the reality they had to confront.

"I'm glad," he told him with heartfelt emotion, "but there is one thing we must decide. The matter of Trista captivity . . ."

Lance looked at him coldly. "She's my wife," he stated flatly.

"Not by our custom, Lance. The marriage is not valid."

Lance stiffened at his father's statement, but said nothing.

"It's hard for me to believe that you would have taken a white captive after all your years on the ranch as my son. I would have hoped that more of your past would have stayed with you." He eyed his older son with more than a little disappointment reflected in his gaze. "But this is not the time or place. We need a reasonable story to explain your sudden appearance here and Trista's return. We must protect her reputation if at all possible. I think I have the perfect story that our neighbors should believe if you both agree to go along with it. . . ." George offered, glancing between his sons.

"What?" Michael asked curtly, disliking deception, but willing to do anything to help Trista.

"We'll tell everyone that Lance rescued Trista from the Comanche warrior who originally took her captive, and once he'd discovered who she was, he brought her directly here to us."

Lance was angry at the thought that her reputation needed to be protected from him. He was her husband. They were married. He longed to defy them all, but he wanted Trista more. Grudgingly, he nodded his agreement to go along with the tale.

Michael also consented.

"Good." George breathed a sign of relief, for he knew that the first hurdle in bringing Lance back had been conquered. As long as the neighbors accepted their story, everything would turn out all right.

Fully clothed, Trista lay upon her bed struggling to come to grips with the emotions that were besieging her. So much had happened in such a short time that she was still trying to sort it all out. She hated Lance—she knew that for a certainty. He had taken her captive, he had stolen her innocence, he had forced her into a marriage she hadn't wanted, and then he had disappeared, leaving her at Night Lark's mercy. Still, it haunted her that he had but to touch her to make her completely forget herself. Trista didn't understand why he had that sensual power over her, and it distressed her that she was so vulnerable to him. Why, just seeing him downstairs and knowing that he had come after her had set her pulse racing. His embrace was her hell . . . and her heaven.

Trista hoped Lance would leave the Royal Diamond and return to his home with the Comanche. She didn't want him here. All she wanted was to forget him. She was to marry Michael. She would be happy with Michael, and they would have a good life together.

As Trista fought to put Lance from her mind, she remembered their first encounter and vaguely recalled some of the things he had said to her at the time he'd taken her captive. She frowned as his words took on a deeper meaning. When she had threatened him by telling him that Michael would kill him if he hurt her in any way, Lance had stated that the Barretts would have to track him down first, and they wouldn't want to do that. Knowing what she did now, Trista realized that Lance had truly believed his father had hated him.

Now, too, Trista sensed that Lance really did love the Royal Diamond, for despite all his Comanche ways, hadn't he told her that she and Michael were the trespassers on the Royal Diamond, and not him?

She'd thought that he'd meant they were on what had once been Comanche lands, but now it was all very clear to her. The estrangement between Lance and his father was the result of some terrible misunderstanding when he was a child.

Trista didn't know what it was that had happened between them, but she felt almost driven to find out. She knew she shouldn't care about Lance and his past, but somehow this vulnerability she sensed in him touched her deeply. First thing in the morning, she resolved, she was going to talk with Rosalie. Trista knew that the servant had been with the family for a long time and that she might be able to provide her with the insights she needed to understand all that had happened.

"Your room . . ." George began hesitantly, and Lance glanced at him, his eyes coldly questioning. "Your room is much as you left it. . . ."

The news surprised Lance, but he betrayed none of the emotion to his father.

"Do you remember where—"

Lance interrupted him, "I remember where it is." He started toward the study door.

"Will you need anything?"

"No. Nothing." His answer was curt as he opened the door.

"Well then, I'll see you in the morning?" George was nervous as he followed his older son into the hallway. He wanted to hug Lance, to touch him and convince himself that this was really happening, but as he reached out to put his hand on his arm, Lance flinched away. The action hurt George deeply, yet there was little he could do. He realized that Lance's trust in him had been destroyed by long years of separation, and it would take a long time to rebuild it. As much as he was hurting, George knew their relationship could only get better.

"I will be here in the morning," Lance stated without emotion as he started up the steps, his father watching him with a tear-filled gaze.

Eleanor had heard Lance and George leave the study and had quickly taken up a place near the parlor doorway to the hall so she could eavesdrop on what was being said. Lance's declaration that he would be there the following day sent her anger soaring. Her most dreaded fear had come true! The half-breed was staying! She waited until Lance had disappeared down the upstairs hall before coming forth to confront her husband.

"George—is it true? Is he really staying?" she could not keep her disgust from her voice.

George, however, was so elated over Lance's decision to remain that he missed the snideness of her tone. "Yes, Eleanor, he's agreed to come home. . . ."

Eleanor saw the happiness in his expression and felt her heart sink. George *was* welcoming him back with open arms! Was he a total idiot?! Why, this Lance might murder them all in their beds!

"George, you can't be serious about this?! He's nothing but a filthy savage, and you're welcoming him back. . . ." she exclaimed, distraught.

"He is my son, Eleanor!" George countered quickly in defense of Lance.

"He is also the Comanche warrior who kidnapped Trista! Have you forgotten that?"

"We haven't forgotten, Mother." Michael spoke from where he stood behind her in the study doorway. "We never will. . . ."

"How can you say that so calmly?" she challenged.

"Lance is my brother," he said flatly, the feelings

296

that were churning inside of him too perplexing to understand completely just yet.

"You're claiming that hideous half-breed as your kin?!" Eleanor asked in a strangled voice.

Michael was quiet for a moment before replying. "I am."

"But what about Trista and her ordeal?"

"Trista will never have to deal with Lance again. I'll see to that," he told her determinedly. "Trista and I will be married as we discussed at dinner."

"But Trista said—" Eleanor started to point out Trista's declaration that she wouldn't marry a man who kept secrets from her.

"I know what she said, Mother, but she was just upset. It doesn't change anything."

"I don't believe you two! You're inviting the same man who caused us such terrible grief and heartache into our midst?!"

"If we had known of his existence sooner, maybe none of this would have happened," George put in. "But I promise you, darling, everything is going to work out fine. You'll see."

Eleanor shot him an icy glare and stalked rigidly away from them.

Lance entered the room slowly, cautiously, wondering if what his father had told him was the truth. At first, because his eyes were unaccustomed to the darkness, he had trouble seeing, and the furnishings seemed foreign and strangely threatening to him. After a moment he managed to pick out the lamp on the dresser across the room, and he moved to light it.

As the warm glow filled the room, so did a tide of memories fill Lance. His father had been serious. Everything looked much as it had when he'd last walked out the door to leave with Lone Elk. With a sense of awe, he looked about. Each piece of furniture that had seemed so dark and ominous moments before now seemed familiar and right in this setting. It was his room, and he realized with a start that it had never ceased to be his room. It was almost as if his father had expected him to return at any moment. The truth jarred him deeply, easing some, but not all, of the mistrust he felt toward George.

Lance saw the daguerreotype on the small night table and moved mechanically across the room to pick it up. His heart constricted as he stared down at the picture of himself and his mother taken over twenty years ago. He had been so filled with sorrow when he'd gone with Lone Elk that he had deliberately left it behind. Now it touched his soul as nothing else could, and he wrestled with the surge of tender emotions that tore through him.

"Lance?" Rosalie spoke his name hesitantly as she stood in the hall, her arms full of clothing.

He turned, the sound of her voice penetrating the last dark corners of his heart. "Rosalie . . ."

Rosalie stared in amazement at the fierce-looking Comanche warrior who stood before her, but as his features softened into his first real smile of the day, she recognized him. "Dear God, my prayers have been answered! It is you! Little Lance . . . oh, Lance . . ."

There was no hesitation or reserve in the old woman as she dropped the clothing heedlessly and hurried to Lance. She wrapped him in a warm embrace. The long-forgotten, now-remembered, sweet scent of her wove about him, engulfing him once more in the past, and he was again, for an instant, a child. Without thought, he returned her embrace.

"Rosalie . . ."

Stepping away from him after a long, gentle hug, she dabbed at her eyes with a corner of her apron. "We waited so long. . . . We had given up all hope, you know," she told him confidingly. "Your father was so afraid that you were dead. Why did you stay away so long?"

Lance's composure was severely strained at he stared down at her. When he'd left, her hair had been dark and her complexion smooth and unlined, but now her hair had gone silver and wrinkles marred her once lovely features. Still, she was Rosalie to him, and through these long years he had always remembered her with kindness.

"I was not wanted here," he explained simply.

"That's not true!" Rosalie replied without pause. The scathing look he gave her stopped her from saying more.

"It is long passed and of no importance." Lance shrugged it off, not wanting to hear more protestations of his father's concern for him. While some of it might be true, it still remained that at any time he could have come after him, and he did not.

"You're absolutely right," she agreed, surprising him. "What matters is that you're here now and intend to stay. This is a joyous day for all of us. I don't think I've seen your father this happy in years. . . ."

Bitterly, Lance wondered when the last time was . . . his marriage to the white woman or the birth of his white son.

"Señor George told me that you were here, and Michael asked that I bring these to you," Rosalie said as she picked up the pile of clothes she'd dropped earlier in her excitement. She regarded him critically for a moment. "They should fit you. . . . You and

Michael look to be almost the same height and weight."

The last thing Lance had wanted to do was to dress as a white man, but since he'd decided to remain — for at least a little while — he realized that he would have to conform. He took the clothing from her with obvious reluctance. "Thank you."

Rosalie had always been attuned to his feelings, and her gaze met his in loving understanding. "I know this will be awkward for you for a while. You've been away so long. . . ." She paused, wanting him to open up to her, but when he didn't, she merely rested a gentle hand on his forearm. "I'm glad you're back, Lance, and don't worry. Everything will be fine."

He watched in silence as she left the room.

Eleanor lay in her bed, her fury unabated. She had been waiting for hours for George to join her. She had heard Michael retire long before, yet George still had not come upstairs to retire. Needing to talk with him, wanting to convince him of the terrible mistake he was making with Lance, she finally rose, drew on her wrapper, and went downstairs in search of him.

The hall was deserted, and Eleanor moved quietly down its length to the staircase. As she started down the steps she noticed that the study door was open and that a soft light shone from within. She continued on down and was about to enter when she heard the sound of his voice. Eleanor wondered if Lance had come back down to speak with him, but realized, when there was no answering voice, that George was alone and he was talking to himself.

She moved nearer and saw that he was sitting at his desk, an open, half-empty bottle of whiskey before him. His shoulders were slumped, his elbows were braced on the desktop, and his head was resting in his hands. He seemed to be staring down at something on the desk before him, and he looked altogether despairing. Eleanor was about to go in and make her presence known when he spoke again, his voice low and sad.

"Shining Star . . . at last he's come home to me. . . ." George's tone was hoarse with emotion. "I waited so long, my darling . . . and I was so afraid. . . ."

Eleanor stiffened in outrage. How dare he! He was thinking of that Comanche bitch he'd been married to before her and no doubt staring at the daguerreotype he had of her!

"You'll never know how much I miss you, love. There were days when I didn't think I could go on. But now that Lance is here . . . everything will be all right. . . ."

Eleanor was livid as she backed away from the door. His words were daggers to her heart, killing all of her love for him. She had given him the best years of her life. . . . She had given him a son! A WHITE SON! Yet George was more concerned with the damned breed!

She was furious as she raced silently back to her room. George might think that everything was going to be all right, but he was wrong. The Royal Diamond belonged to her son, Michael. No half-breed was going to come between Michael and his inheritance. She didn't know how she was going to do it yet, but somehow, someway she was going to get rid of Lance once and for all.

It was late as Lance lay restlessly on the comfort of his bed staring at the ceiling. His encounter with

Rosalie had awakened many feelings he'd long thought dead and had filled him with even greater confusion. He didn't want to believe everything that he'd been hearing . . . that his father had missed him and had tried to get him back. Yet Rosalie had confirmed that all his father had told him was the truth.

The possibility was painful for him. For years Lance had thought that George hated him. That firm belief had fueled his need to prove himself among the warriors of the tribe. Being only half-Comanche, he had been looked down upon in his early years there. He had managed to best the others through cunning and strength and, in doing so, had won their respect and been accepted as an equal among them. His father's hurried remarriage had compounded his desire to prove to himself that he could best the Barretts. It had taken many years, but he had finally accomplished it with his taking of Trista.

Trista swept into his thoughts then, and he smiled wolfishly to himself. Michael would never have her now. Yet as he thought of his brother and of how he had stolen the woman who was to be his wife, he wondered why he felt no surge of final triumphant satisfaction. Instead of feeling as if he'd won a great battle that he'd been fighting for a long time, he felt empty, as if the victory had been a hollow one.

Trista . . . The thought of her pale loveliness filled Lance with desire, and he was hard pressed not to seek her out in her room just down the hall. He remembered the first time he'd seen her from a distance out on the porch the night of the party. He had wanted her then, even before he'd found out that she was Michael's fiancée, and discovering that she belonged to his brother had just been an added bonus. The fact remained that she was his wife. He had claimed her and made her his, and he intended to keep her.

Restless now that he was lost in thoughts of Trista, Lance got up from the soft bed and strode to the window. The sky was black velvet studded with a golden moon and a myriad of twinkling stars. The endless acres of the Diamond stretched out before him, and Lance suddenly knew a sense of peace. Perhaps, he thought strangely, he really had come home. . . .

Chapter Twenty

The first pink-gold streaks of dawn in the fading night sky found Lance already up and getting dressed. Lance shifted uncomfortably as he pulled on a pair of his brother's pants and fastened the waist. He had lived as a Comanche for so long that he found the tight fit of the trousers restraining and uncomfortable. He shrugged into one of the shirts Rosalie had brought him and noted the way it fit him almost perfectly across the shoulders. She had been right. . . . He and Michael were about the same size. Lance sat back down on the bed to pull on the socks and boots, and then, snatching up the Stetson that had been included in the bundle, he started from the room. He was anxious to get outdoors, for he felt as if he had been inside far too long already.

The house was quiet as Lance made his way downstairs and outside. The morning breeze was fresh and cool, and he gloried in the sweet scent of it as he stepped off the porch and headed in the direction of the stable to see Fuego.

The golden rogue trotted briskly about his enclosure as he watched Lance's approach. Though he did not recognize him, he sensed that there was something familiar about him . . . and something dangerous. His ears flattened at some instinctively remembered threat, and he paused in his movements to regard him cautiously.

Lance understood the horse's reaction to his nearness, and as he climbed the fence to enter the corral, he began talking to him in his crooning, seductive tone. "Easy, golden one . . . easy." He spoke calmly, wanting to renew the bond he had created while they were in the village. Moving with slow, deliberate motions, he crossed the pen toward the stallion.

The rogue backed skittishly away from his encroachment, and Lance thought of how like Fuego Trista was. He had made them both his, yet they still struggled to escape him. A look of resolve hardened his features. They might try to get away, but he would never let them go. They belonged to him.

Trista did not sleep well. Unbidden dreams of her time in captivity had disturbed her rest. Threatening visions of Striking Snake and Night Lark loomed in her consciousness, and several times during the night she had come awake with a start. Trista had known from the beginning that it was going to be difficult for her to forget the time she'd spent in the Comanche village, but Lance's presence here was making it next to impossible.

When at last Trista awoke and it was light, she felt more drained and more exhausted than she had when she'd first retired. She would have lain in bed longer except that the sound of Fuego's distressed whinny disturbed her. Without bothering to put on her wrapper, she rushed to the window to see why he was sounding so restless.

The sight of a tall ranchhand she didn't recognize trying to approach the stallion in the corral frightened her. Fuego could be deadly dangerous! She realized that there was no time for her to reach the pen and warn the stranger, so mindless of her lack of proper dress, she leaned farther out the window to call out her warning.

"Don't trust the stallion!" Trista shouted, wanting to get his attention before Fuego panicked and tried to trample him. "He's not as tame as he looks!"

As the man paused in his pursuit of the horse and turned slowly toward the house, Trista gasped in stunned amazement. The stranger who stood in the corral with Fuego was Lance! She stared at him in mute surprise, noting how completely different he looked in denim pants that fit his strong, muscular thighs to perfection, and the dark-colored shirt that emphasized the broad, firm width of his chest and shoulders. The brim of the black Stetson he wore shaded his features from her, but she could imagine the mocking, derisive look that would be mirrored in his blue eyes because she'd warned him away from Fuego. Frozen, she stood unmoving, looking down at him.

Lance had heard Trista's call and realized with amusement that she did not recognize him in Michael's clothing. Turning to confront her, he stopped. The sight of her framed in the bedroom window with her hair unbound, and clad only in white nightdress, left him entranced, and he could only stare up at her in silence. A heat filled his loins as he remembered the last time he'd seen her with her hair down around her shoulders, and he was just about to start back inside to claim his husbandly rights when he saw Michael come out of the house and head in his direction.

In a cocky and boldly deliberate gesture, he nodded slightly in Trista's direction as he said, "You are most beautiful in the morning, Trista. I regret that I was

306

not there to awaken you the morning after our wedding night, wife. . . ."

A flash of fury seared Trista at his confident, arrogant reminder of her time with him . . . a time, she told herself, that she would rather forget. The moment of enchantment that had held her mesmerized exploded into shards of angry outrage. She started to retort angrily, then Michael appeared below.

Michael was on his way to the stable to saddle up his horse for his morning ride when he discovered that Lance was already at the corral with the golden rogue. He was curious to see if Lance could handle the stallion. Just as he was starting toward the enclosure to watch, he heard the sound of Trista's voice and saw Lance turn toward the house, his gaze focused on an upstairs window.

"You are most beautiful in the morning, Trista. I regret that I was not there to awaken you the morning after our wedding night. . . ."

Lance's words sent a shaft of pain through Michael, and he looked up to see Trista, clad only in her nightdress, at the window of her bedroom. Jealousy pounded through him, and he wondered angrily just what she was doing standing in the window so scantily dressed talking to Lance. The night before she'd been adamant that she wanted nothing to do with him, and yet here she was speaking to him of their "wedding night" while she was wearing only a nightgown. The thought that she might actually feel something for Lance occurred to him then, and Michael looked up at her suspiciously.

Trista was shocked to discover that Michael had overheard Lance's remark. Her worried gaze met Michael's dark, anger-filled one, and she flushed guiltily. Suddenly aware of her state of undress, she quickly withdrew from the window.

Michael faced Lance across the corral. Their eyes locked in silent combat as they regarded each other warily. Trista was the prize they both sought, yet she was a treasure that right now eluded them both.

"Trista is *my* wife, Michael." Lance's tone was flat as he spoke what he believed to be the truth.

"Not in my book, Lance. Trista's going to marry me. She will be *mine,* and," he added angrily, "she won't have to be forced!"

"Is that what Trista told you?" he asked derisively, his taunting tone adding more doubt to Michael's growing misgivings.

Michael glared at him. "She ran away from you, Lance. She came back to me."

Lance only smiled. "That does not change the fact that she is married to me."

Infuriated, Michael stalked off into the stable, leaving Lance to return to his work with Fuego.

Rosalie was in the parlor when she saw Trista coming down the stairs. "Good morning, Trista."

"Good morning, Rosalie," she greeted her warmly.

"Would you like your breakfast now, or would you prefer to wait for the others? The señora and Señor George are still sleeping, and Lance and Michael have left the house."

"I'll have mine now if you don't mind," Trista responded, pleased that she would have the chance to dine alone. She had not relished the possibility of sharing breakfast with Lance. She wanted to stay as far away from him as she could.

"I'll bring it right out to you," she promised as she started toward the back of the house, but Trista's question stopped her.

"Rosalie . . . you worked for the Barretts when

Lance lived here before, didn't you?"

Rosalie regarded her solemnly. "Yes, Trista. I worked for Señor George when he was married to Lance's mother."

"And you know all about the time when Lance left to live with the Comanches?"

The servant nodded, her expression growing sadder at the memory. "It was not a happy time," she said slowly.

"What happened? Why did Lance believe his father hated him all this time, and why did he stay with the Comanche when he had such a wonderful home here?"

Rosalie studied the younger woman, and seeing no guile in her expression, she decided to tell her. Trista was, after all, caught up in the middle of this. She sighed deeply as she began to relate her tale of the past. "It was not always such a wonderful home. After Shining Star died of the fever, Señor George was beside himself with grief." She went on to explain how he had locked himself in his study and had tried to drink himself into oblivion. "It was so tragic. . . . He loved her so much. It seemed as if his life had no meaning without her. He has been a different man ever since that time. It's almost as if a vital part of him died when Shining Star did. . . . He loved her that much."

"Was she beautiful?"

"Oh, yes. She was lovely, and you can see how handsome her only son has become. Señor George's love for her was boundless. . . . He cherished her." At Trista's understanding nod, she continued, "After her death it was as if the sight of Lance was just too painful for Señor George. When Lone Elk heard of his sister's death and came for the boy, he did not even try to stop him from leaving."

"But why would Lance have gone?"

Rosalie shrugged. "He was but a little boy who had lost his mother. He was desperately lonely, and Lone Elk offered him what his father at that time could not . . . love."

"Why did he stay away so long? Didn't Lance ever want to come back?"

"There was one time . . ." Her voice faded as she remembered Lance's return and the heartbreak he'd suffered when he'd found out that his father had already remarried and fathered another son.

"What happened?" Somehow Trista sensed that this was the real tragedy.

"It was not long after Lance had gone with Lone Elk. Señor George had already remarried, though, and the señora had had Michael."

"George remarried that quickly?" She found the news disturbing as well as surprising considering the obvious strength of George's feelings for Shining Star.

"Oh yes. He was so lonely without Shining Star. He loved her so much. . . ." She paused. "Anyway, they had all gone to town when Lance came. Once Lance learned of the marriage, he disappeared, and he never came back."

"Oh, no . . ."

Rosalie shook her head slowly. "Señor George tried to contact him when he got home, but there was never any answer to the messages he sent. According to the agreement he had reached with Lone Elk, Lance had to make the decision whether to come home or not. After a while the rejection of Lance's silence became too much for Señor George, and he did not try to contact him anymore."

Eleanor was still bristling with anger about George's weakness for Lance and the half-breed's presence there. She had left her husband to sleep off his overindulgence and was on her way downstairs for breakfast when she heard Rosalie and Trista talking about the past. Each mention of George and his undying love for Shining Star increased her fury tenfold. For years she had fought the ghost of the Comanche woman in her marriage. She had thought that the Indian woman had finally been exorcised from George's heart, but now, with the return of Lance, all the old wounds were being reopened. It had been bad enough hearing George talking to her picture last night, but it was even worse to think that even after all this time the servants still held Lance's mother in such high esteem. Schooling her indignant features into a bland expression, Eleanor swept into the dining room to greet Trista.

"Good morning, Trista, dear." She smiled at the younger woman. "We'll have breakfast now, Rosalie." Eleanor dismissed the servant with cool efficiency, putting an abrupt end to their revealing conversation.

"Yes, señora," Rosalie replied, tactfully leaving the room.

"Did you sleep well, Trista? Since it was your first night back, I thought you might have needed your rest," she inquired with interest. She was determined to be nice to Trista despite her show of anger the day before, for she wanted to enlist her help in getting rid of Lance. Certainly, if Trista asked George to send him away, he would do it.

"I was exhausted, Eleanor, but I was too upset to get much sleep."

"Indeed, I can understand why. It must be terrible for you with that heathen here in the same house! I just can't believe that he's going to stay!"

"It is difficult. . . ." Trista understated.

"Well, dear, you're lucky to have Michael. Not every girl who's gone through what you have is so fortunate." Her pointed meaning was clear, though cleverly disguised in gracious language. "I'm looking forward to your father's arrival so we can proceed with our plans."

Trista controlled her temper with some difficulty. "I told Michael last night that I couldn't marry someone who didn't tell me the truth, and I meant it, Eleanor."

"Trista, darling." Eleanor's smile was pained as she scolded her gently. "It's not as if Michael deliberately lied to you. Michael loves you very much. Certainly you must see that. You mustn't let such a little thing as a misunderstanding come between you." She was Michael's advocate as she continued, "I'm sure his decision not to mention a possible relationship to Lance at that time was based on sound judgment. As Rosalie was telling you when I came in, there had been no contact between Lance and his father in nearly twenty years. How were we to know for sure that he was the one who took you captive or that he would show up here as he did?"

Trista fell silent. The entire situation had become too complicated. She hated Lance for his arrogance. He had almost destroyed her life. She despised him, and if she'd had her way, she would never have seen him again.

"It's still so hard to believe that he is George's son and Michael's brother," she sighed, frustrated by her situation.

"I feel the same way, Trista." Eleanor's eyes were steely and indignant as they met Trista's. "I can barely stand the thought of him staying in my home. I don't see how George can allow him to remain, knowing that what happened to you was his doing. I want him gone as soon as possible. He's got to send him away."

Trista knew she would have no rest until Lance was gone from her life. He haunted her every moment of the day and night. "Maybe I should be the one to leave," she offered, beginning to believe that there was no solution to the problem.

"Heavens no! You're Michael's fiancée. The Royal Diamond is your home now, too. Surely George wouldn't sacrifice Michael's happiness for Lance!" His name was a curse on her lips.

Rosalie returned with their meal then, and both women fell silent as they contemplated Lance's disrupting presence on the ranch. Trista was torn between the desire to get away from Lance as quickly as she could and her desire to stay and marry Michael and make a life with him. Eleanor was caught up in her hatred of Shining Star's offspring and her need to save the Royal Diamond for Michael, and Michael alone.

"This will all be yours one day," George said to his two sons as they looked out across the distant hills of the Royal Diamond from their vantage point atop a bluff later that afternoon. "I've worked all my life to preserve the ranch for you . . . to make it prosper. I want you to continue my dream of a Barrett dynasty right here in the heart of Texas."

Lance stared at the beauty of the land as he considered his father's words. In the beginning he had believed that his stay here would be temporary . . . that he would remain only long enough to claim Trista and then would leave. But his determination to go had eased since learning from Rosalie of his father's attempts to find him. His father seemed so earnest in his desire for him to stay that he found himself actually thinking about it. His heart, so long denied, told him that this was his home. Through all of his thoughts the image of Trista danced in seductive temptation. . . . Trista, his reason for coming here in the first place . . . Trista, his wife.

When neither Lance nor Michael spoke, George went on, "I know this is difficult for you, but you are brothers, and you should always remember that."

At his words Lance and Michael eyed each other distrustfully. As long as Trista stood between them, they would find no peace nor have any common ground to build on.

George had hoped that a day alone together out on the range would help to create a bond of friendship between the two. Now as he watched them together, he felt he had failed miserably.

"I guess we'd better be heading back."

"I'd like to work with Fuego when we get back," Lance told him as they rode toward the house.

George looked at him with something akin to surprise. "Work with him?"

"I had been trying to break him before Trista left. He's not completely tamed yet, but he will be. I intend to ride him."

"Trista told us that you tracked him down all by yourself," George ventured.

"It took many weeks of hard riding, but I finally captured him," Lance answered proudly.

"I almost had him once myself." Michael spoke up spontaneously. "Got close enough to get a rope on him, but he still managed to break free."

"Fuego's one powerful horse. . . ." George remarked. "I still find it hard to believe that Trista rode him here."

"She always had a way with him." Lance thought of that day by the creek when she'd controlled the rogue no one else could touch.

"We can put him to breeding as soon as you want, Lance," his father told him. "My stables are among some of the finest in the state."

"If I stay, we will see." He retreated from making any promises about staying permanently.

His coolness to George's suggestion ruined the rapport that had been developing among them, and they were silent during the rest of the ride back to the ranch. They reached the house and, after stabling their horses, went out to the corral to see the stallion.

Lance had been preparing himself for the encounter with the wild rogue, and he entered the pen filled with the resolve to break him.

"Lance . . ." Michael spoke as he watched his brother move toward the horse.

"What?"

"I'd like a shot at him, too."

They stared at each other for a moment.

Lance, feeling confident that Michael would meet with little success, agreed. "All right."

With the help of several ranchhands, the nervous mount was readied for breaking. As Michael and George held Fuego's head, Lance swung up into the saddle and braced himself for the explosion of fury that was sure to come. Releasing the indignant rogue, father and brother raced away to the safety beyond the corral fence, leaving Lance to bear the full brunt of the horse's rage.

Fuego felt desperate as he stood quivering in the middle of the enclosure. He had accepted Trista's domination, but felt threatened by the man who now sat on his back. Strong thighs gripped him and firm hands held the reins that took away his freedom. Quivering, he spun viciously in a circle wanting to rid himself of the unwelcome burden of the man's weight. He would be free! He would not submit to this!

His unexpected cyclonic move surprised Lance. His Stetson flew from his head, but he managed to hang on tightly enough to keep his seat. Each bone-jarring motion of the rampaging horse wracked his body, yet he would not quit. It was only when Fuego ran toward the fence and threatened to crush him against the boards that Lance jumped from his back and landed heavily in the dust of the corral.

Trista was in her room, trying to think things through, when she heard the disturbance down at the stables. A quick glance told her what was happening, and though she was reluctant to face Lance again, she felt she needed to be there for Fuego.

George and Michael quickly brought Fuego under control again and waited for Lance to mount up for another try. Several ranchhands who'd been working in the stable came out and crowded around the pen to watch the excitement. Trista reached the group and managed to work her way through them to the fence. Stepping up on the lowest rail, she braced herself on the top and watched as Lance stalked toward the stallion.

Fuego was following Lance's approach closely. His ears flattened and his eyes went wild with fear as he sensed his renewed determination. He stood, tense and waiting, as Lance prepared to climb on his back.

Again Lance mounted. Again Fuego rebelled against his attempt to ride him. It was a battle of their wills . . . one determined to dominate, the other determined not to be dominated. In a superior display of strength, the stallion bucked straight up, unseating Lance completely and leaving him sprawled in the dirt, gasping for breath.

"Lance, look out!" Trista could not prevent the cry of alarm that escaped her as the rogue's hooves landed heavily close beside his head.

Michael pivoted. His expression was thunderous as he regarded her. Was that fear and concern he saw written on her perfect features? Was she worried about Lance, a man she said she hated? He tore his gaze away from her as he cornered the stallion and grabbed up the reins.

Lance heard Trista's cry and looked up to find her staring at him wide-eyed with worry. George had come to his aid, but he ignored his outstretched hand as he got nimbly to his feet and strode across the pen to where Trista stood. As he came toward her, she stepped back from the corral, poised to flee.

"It is good to see that my wife is concerned about my health," he told her, chuckling softly.

"You!" Trista choked, all her loathing for him reflected in that single word. Before she could say any more, Lance had turned his back on her and was walking back to where Michael and George stood with the stallion.

"I'll try this time," Michael stated firmly. His dark eyes appeared stormy as he glared ominously at his brother.

Lance only shrugged and took up his position at Fuego's head, holding tightly to the bridle to keep the rogue quiet until Michael was on his back. Fuego noticed little difference between them, and he treated Michael to the same disdainful, painful treatment as he had Lance. With sheer brute force, he spun in wild circles about the corral, twisting and bucking until Michael's tenacious grip was torn loose. His wind was knocked completely from him as he landed awkwardly, and he lay stunned and still.

Trista's reaction to Michael's fall was not nearly as spontaneous as it had been to Lance's. Expecting that he was fine, she waited for him to get up. When he didn't move after a instant, she climbed the fence and raced toward him.

"Michael! Oh, Michael . . ." She was on her knees

beside him, touching him tentatively, her expression frantic.

George, too, had expected Michael to get up right away. When he remained unmoving in the dirt, he knew a moment of panic. Hurrying to where Trista knelt beside him, he vowed silently to put a bullet in the damned rogue's brain if his son was hurt.

Lance stood slightly apart watching them. He felt alone, alienated and very jealous. Trista had made no move to rush to his side when he'd been thrown, yet she could hardly wait to rush to Michael. As Michael sat up, Lance turned away with something akin to disgust.

"Maybe you'd better come back to the house. . . ." Trista was saying, but Michael shook off her hand where she clung to his arm.

"I'm not going anywhere until the stallion is broken," he snarled.

Lance was surprised at his words, and as he turned to look at Michael, his gaze reflected a new measure of respect for him for not quitting. When he saw Trista staring up at his brother, her love for him clearly mirrored in her worried expression, he moved away, quickly shuttering all of his own emotions from view.

Snatching up Fuego's reins, Lance glanced back only to make sure they were all out of the way and then swung up onto his back. Gritting his teeth, he challenged the stallion to try to conquer him. Fuego did not hesitate to respond as he reared violently and then raced madly about the corral in desperation. He was going to be free of the man! Yet even as Fuego fought to escape subjugation, Lance became deadly determined to win. He would conquer this horse or he would die trying! In an exhausting, maddening clash, they each tried to best the other as the rest of those gathered there looked on in speechless amazement.

It was inevitable. Empowered by the same deep-seated need that had driven him to track down and capture the horse in the first place, Lance refused to give up. His hold on Fuego was relentless, and despite the stallion's own fierce resolve not to be conquered, fatigue was his final master.

Lathered and straining for breath, his muscles twitching in exhaustion, he finally stood in the center of the corral and allowed the man to stay upon him. As Lance nudged him firmly with his knees, Fuego moved in the direction he'd indicated. At this show of submissiveness, Lance lightened his hold on the reins, allowing the rogue a little freedom, and the stallion's gait became smoother. The praising stroke of Lance's hand on his foam-flecked neck sent a shiver through him. He did not react skittishly, though, but whickered softly and unsteadily as he continued to trot about the enclosure, controlled completely by Lance's desire.

Michael looked on in amazement. He had known it would take a lot to bring the golden rogue under control, but he had never expected to witness a display of horsemanship as outstanding as what he'd just seen Lance perform. George, too, had been totally delighted by his older son's ability with the rogue, and he gazed upon the horse and his rider with pride.

Lance's victory over Fuego left Trista stricken. In her heart she had identified with the freedom-loving rogue. To see him vanquished and reduced to doing Lance's bidding rendered her frightened and unsure. If an animal as strong-willed as Fuego could be brought under his firm control, then what chance did she have if he set his mind to conquering her resistance, too? Frightened, but refusing to give in to her fear, Trista stiffened as she met Lance's knowing, blue-eyed gaze as he sat triumphantly upon the stallion's back. Lance saw her chin lift in defiance of him, and he urged Fuego forward, coming to stand still right before her.

"Fuego is mine, Trista, just as you are. It will do you no good to fight me." His statement was arrogant and confident.

Trista was overcome with rage. She wanted to shout at him that she would never submit herself to his will, but he put his knees to the horse's sides and rode away from her. Glaring at his back, she heaped hateful thoughts upon him. Yet even as she did, she couldn't help but admire how right Lance looked seated upon the now-yielding rogue.

It was a short time later that Poker faced George across the width of his desk in the privacy of the study.

"I'm tellin' you I won't stay on here if that filthy Comanche stays. . . ." Poker snarled.

George glared at him icily. "I'm sorry that we've had to come to a parting of our ways, Poker."

Poker could not believe that he was actually going to let him leave. He had worked for the Royal Diamond for over ten years. Outraged, he stormed, "I've worked for you for years, and you're choosing that damned savage over me!"

"That 'damned savage,' as you call him, is *my son!*" George thundered, charging to his feet. "You can tell the other men that if they have any objections about working for me *and* my sons, they can collect their pay first thing tomorrow."

Poker stared at him bitterly. He regretted losing his job, but most of all he was filled with hatred for the half-breed who dared to enter the white man's world.

"I'll tell 'em," he muttered resentfully and he strode quickly from the room, anxious to be gone from the ranch as soon as possible.

Chapter Twenty-one

Though everyone tried to act normally at dinner that night, undercurrents of emotion charged the atmosphere. Eleanor gave the appearance of calm acceptance of Lance's presence, conducting herself with her usual grace, but her manner was a devious cover for the ulterior motive that lurked in the dark corners of her heart.

"George, I was thinking today that we should give a party in honor of Lance's return. Many of our neighbors are your longtime friends, and they knew Lance before he left. No doubt they would enjoy seeing him again."

George was surprised by her offer. Her earlier objections to Lance's presence had hurt him deeply, and his heart warmed toward his wife for her more tolerant attitude.

"Darling, that's a wonderful idea," he answered enthusiastically.

"Good, I'm glad you agree." Eleanor had known that he would. "I think next weekend would be fine. That gives me plenty of time to plan."

Michael wondered at his mother's wisdom in arranging this celebration. Feelings ran high against the Comanche, and despite Lance's blood connection to the Barretts, many would still consider him a savage animal worthy only of being killed. He wanted to advise her that it did not seem the wise thing to do, but his father's excitement was such that he held his tongue.

George was elated over Eleanor's willingness to finally consider Lance family. The thought that his friends might object to Lance's Indian blood never occurred to him.

"Next weekend will work out well," he told her. "That will give Lance more time to become accustomed to our ways and to living here again." George looked proudly at his older son, who was remaining silent through the entire discussion. "It will also give us time to get to town and buy him some clothes of his own."

"These are fine," Lance put in, not relishing the idea of mingling with so many whites.

"True, they do fit you, but you should have your own things," his father insisted. "We'll ride into San Antonio tomorrow. Eleanor can let me know what she needs for the party, and we can take care of all of that while we're in town."

"Why, thank you, dear," Eleanor replied, thrilled that Lance would be out of the house for a few days.

Trista was amazed by Eleanor's suggestion to have a party for Lance, considering what her attitude had been that morning. She felt betrayed by the other woman's apparent approval of the man she'd claimed earlier to despise.

Michael was filled with misgivings about the whole thing, but voiced no objections as he turned to Trista. "Darling, shall we go outside for a little while?"

"I'd like that, Michael," she quickly assented, eager to flee Lance's disturbing nearness.

Trista didn't relax until they were safely outside away from the others. Darkness had settled like a black velvet blanket across the land, and a sense of peace filled her. She breathed deeply of the sweet, flower-scented air and felt some of the tension ebb from her.

"It's going to be all right, you know," Michael wanted to reassure her. "As soon as we're married—"

"Michael . . ." Trista turned to face him. "I told you how I felt about the way you kept the truth from me."

Michael smiled tenderly as he took her hand and brought it to his lips. In an erotic, yet innocent gesture, he pressed a kiss to her palm. "I understand why you were upset with me, Trista. I promise you it will never happen again."

Trista felt the warm gentleness of his kiss on her hand, yet no shiver of desire followed. It puzzled her that she felt such little reaction to his caress. "But can I truly count on the promise?"

"I give you my word, darling," Michael vowed solemnly, his dark eyes catching and holding hers.

Trista didn't try to resist as he took her in his arms and drew her close. His mouth sought hers, and she surrendered to his embrace. Trista wanted to feel the excitement she knew was possible from such lovemaking, but to her dismay no thrill of passion possessed her as Michael kissed her. His touch was nice . . . it was tender and caring, but there was no violent eruption of desire deep within her as she'd experienced in Lance's arms.

Michael was surprised when Trista withdrew from him. This was their first time alone together since the other night in camp, and he had expected a far more inviting response to his advances.

"Trista . . . is something wrong?" he pressed as he watched her edge away from him to stand by the porch railing. Her gaze was averted from him, and she stared out across the night-shrouded landscape.

"No, Michael, nothing's wrong. I suppose I'm just tired, that's all. . . ." she hedged, not understanding herself why she felt strangely guilty in his embrace. "I think I'll go on up to bed."

"I'll walk you up," he offered.

Though her first instinct was to refuse his offer, she agreed to his company. They noted as they passed through the house that it was quiet; everyone else seemed to have retired already. Trista paused to say good night as she opened her bedroom door. Michael took her action to be an invitation of sorts, so he boldly swept her into another embrace and kissed her soundly. The heated ardency of his kiss should have stirred a fire in her soul, but Trista felt only relief when Michael released her.

"Good night, Michael," she said quickly. Before he could try to kiss her again, she hurried into the privacy of her room and locked the door behind her.

Trista remained poised in the darkness until she heard him walk away. Only then did she realize that she'd been anxiously holding her breath. She turned to light the lamp on her dresser, meaning only to undress and go to bed, but suddenly found herself trapped by a pair of steely arms.

Before she could even shriek her outrage, Lance brought his lips down brutally on hers. He had had enough. Her treatment of Michael when he'd fallen from Fuego had fanned the smoldering fire of his jealousy, but when she'd disappeared out onto the porch with his brother after dinner, he'd become a man possessed. She was his, and she was going to admit it! With angry precision Lance raped her mouth, taking what she would not give him freely, openly. His tongue was bold and arousing as it speared within the sweetness of her mouth, dueling with her own.

Molten desire flowed through Trista, but she refused to give in to its burning pleasure. Struggling against Lance, she tried desperately to escape his sensual assault. Bound to him by his relentless embrace, she fought to ignore the heat that had blossomed deep within her, but to no avail. As he pressed himself fully against her, Trista became aware of the muscular sleekness of his bared chest and the power of his need thrusting hungrily against her softness. Her resistance dissolved as her excitement became a blazing inferno of desire. Defeated, yet marvelously so, Trista gave in to the glory of his touch.

As quickly as she surrendered, Lance coldly released her and pushed her away.

"Is that how you responded to Michael, wife?" Lance asked in a furious tone.

Trista was shaking. She felt ravaged and hopelessly confused as she groped her way to the dresser and finally managed to light the lamp. Pulling herself together, she whirled about to face him, her hands on her hips.

"How I kiss my fiancé is none of your concern," she said haughtily, her false bravado concealing the conflicting emotions that were raging within her.

Pushed to the edge of violence, Lance grabbed her by her upper arms and gave her a rough shake. "You are my wife, Trista. You belong to me, and me alone. No other man shall ever have you!"

Tears filled her eyes at his treatment of her, yet she knew a driving desire to hurt him as he was hurting her. "How do you know Michael hasn't already?" she challenged.

Lance went still for a moment, then sneered, "Believe me, Trista, if he had had you already, he wouldn't have been satisfied with that little intimate scene I just witnessed at the door. I'm the only man who's touched you so far." He was arrogantly self-assured. "And I'm the only man who ever will."

"Why you . . ."

Lance shook her again, his hands biting into the soft flesh of her upper arms. "We are married."

"No! I am no man's wife until I marry by white man's law!"

He snorted in derision. "You are my wife, Trista."

"Never! I hate you! I despise you! I loathe you! I'm engaged to Michael!" She pounded on his chest to punctuate her avowals, refusing to accept his words, denying any connection between them.

Her words sent his temper spiraling out of control. Viciously, he crushed her to his chest, needing desperately to drive all the hatred she felt for him from her. His mouth covered hers fiercely at first, but he lessened the pressure when she whimpered with pain. His lips turned from punishing to teasing, and the thrust of his tongue became seductive rather than vanquishing.

Trista's whimper turned to a low moan of denial. She didn't want to feel this way with Lance. Why was he the only one who could arouse her so? Why couldn't Michael's touch bring her such ecstasy?

Trista held herself rigid, wanting to refuse the passion that threatened to leave her weak and pliant in Lance's arms. But all of her opposition to him melted away when he unbuttoned the bodice of high-necked gown and slipped a questing hand within to fondle the soft swell of her breast. The tender orb tautened, responding fully to his knowing touch.

Her body betraying her so, Trista could no longer deny it or fight it. It was useless to resist. She wanted this man as she'd never wanted another. It made no sense; she could find no logic or understanding in it. All Trista knew was that she desired Lance with every fiber of her being.

Any thoughts of keeping herself from him were swept away in a tide of frenzied abandon. Hungrily, she returned his kiss. Lance sensed the changed in her, and he loosened the restraining hold he had upon her. Trista looped her arms about his neck, pressing herself more completely against his hard, manly frame.

Lance's response as she yielded to him was immediate. He picked her up in his arms and strode purposely to the bed. Gently laying her upon the softness, he quickly stripped her of the confining white woman's garments. Trista did not protest his actions; rather she exulted in them. Her every sense was attuned to Lance, and Lance alone. She wanted him . . . she wanted him . . . she wanted him . . . .

Her arms lifted to accept him after he'd shed his own breeches and returned to her. He came down upon her, the heat of his big body searing hers, branding her forever. His hands trailed fire over her quivering alabaster flesh, molding her to his length. He moved sensually against her nest of womanly pleasure, tempting, offering, yet not claiming.

Lance was compelled to please her, to renew the passion that existed between them. Yet as he strove to increase her need, he found himself lost in a maelstrom of emotion that eclipsed anything he'd ever experienced in his life. He knew what existed between them was perfection. He wanted to touch her and give her the purest ecstasy. He wanted to create within her a need for him that could only be matched by his own need for her, and one that she could never deny again.

His caresses became demanding as he sensually forced her to that higher plane of feeling. Trista did not resist his lead, but became his apt student in the art of love. Avidly, she matched him kiss for kiss, touch for touch. With eager intent she explored the taut, powerful ridges of his chest and shoulders. Her hands skimmed over him provocatively, teasing him to even greater heights.

At the brink of rapture, Lance positioned himself and then moved with piercing sweetness into the heart of her womanly sheath. They shuddered as thrilling emotions surged through them. Lance began to move, and Trista could not remain still beneath his driving hips. Delirious in her need to be close to him, she clutched at his shoulders, holding on to him with all her might. When Lance reached down to cup her buttocks and pressed more deeply within her hot velvet depths, excitement shot through her. Trista's ecstasy peaked in an inferno of blazing splendor. Never before had she been so transported. She went rigid in his arms as the pulsing, pounding rapture played out is course.

Lance knew he'd pleased her, and that realization pushed him beyond control. As she attained total bliss, he followed. They soared to the heavens, desire's delight binding them together. They were one.

Exhausted, they plummeted from the heights. Lance drew Trista above him, and she lay spent against his chest. It was then, in the dim glow of the lamplight, that he saw the marks upon her back. He went rigid in fury as he wondered who would have dared to beat her that way.

"Trista," He spoke sharply. "Who beat you?"

His question destroyed the mellowness of the moment, and she was suddenly angry that he hadn't guessed. "You need to ask?" she retorted bitterly, trying to pull free of his grip, but Lance refused to let her go.

His hands tightened on her arms, and his eyes glowed with an inner light. "Tell me, woman! Did Michael do this to you?!" Lance was ready to kill his brother at the thought.

Trista gave a harsh, derisive laugh. "Michael? Michael would never touch me in anger."

"Then who?"

"It was *your* fiancée, Lance. Your darling Night Lark. She told me how you'd left her in charge of me and how she was to teach me to be a chore wife for when you married. When I didn't learn the Comanche ways quick enough to suit her, she thought it most entertaining to discipline me!"

"Night Lark?" Lance could not believe what Trista had just told him. He had never told Night Lark to take care of Trista.

"Yes, Night Lark!"

Lance realized then that the other woman must have taken the opportunity to take out her jealousy on Trista. It hurt him that she had suffered while he was gone, and he understood far more clearly her reason for running away from the village. Wanting to make it up to her, wanting to try to erase the misery of that time, he eased his hold on her and pulled her near.

Trista resisted for a moment, but when his lips claimed hers again, she surrendered to the undeniable magic of his touch. Much later they lay wrapped in each other's arms, neither speaking nor thinking for fear of ruining the beauty of what had just occurred. Sensual peace flowed through Trista, carrying her to blissful contentment. She slept, unaware of Lance studying her in the darkness, pondering the hold she had on his heart.

Disturbed, Lance left the bed and strode to the window, raking a hand nervously through the thickness of his hair. Brushing aside the curtains, he stood quietly, staring out across the land that he loved. The wafting night breeze cooled his love-heated body, and as his senses calmed, rationality returned. He would not love Trista. She was but a pawn in his game to best Michael. He would not allow her to mean anything to him. Yet even as he vowed to himself that he would not let her into his heart, he feared that it might be too late.

Lance turned from the window then. He considered spending the night there in her room. He was, after all, her husband and entitled to her bed, but he decided against it. He had proven a point to her tonight, and it was one she would not soon forget. Quickly pulling on his pants, he paused only long enough to stare down at her for a moment and then silently left the room.

When Trista awoke late the following morning, she was filled with an extraordinary sense of well-being. Unconcerned with the time, she stretched in luxurious leisure. Only as she felt a slight soreness in her limbs did the remembrance of Lance's possession return.

Trista sat bolt upright in bed, her expression one of horror-filled outrage. How dare he!?! She suddenly realized her state of undress and quickly clutched the covers over her breasts. Memory after exciting memory tumbled through her thoughts, leaving her trembling and uncertain and finally furious.

While Trista was angry with Lance, she was far more angry with herself. For all her protestations of loving Michael and planning to marry him, she had been unable to resist Lance's touch. She had given to him exactly what he'd demanded. How could she ever face Michael again knowing that she had responded so fully to Lance?

Guilt filled her, and she dreaded the thought of seeing either man that day. The knock on her bedroom door startled her, and she grabbed desperately for her wrapper at the foot of the bed.

"Yes? Who is it?" she called out nervously.

"It's Rosalie, Trista. The señora sent me to see if you were all right."

Her heartbeat quickened as she wondered ashamedly if everyone knew about the night before. "Of course I'm all right," she answered quickly. "Why wouldn't I be?"

"Well, it is almost noon. . . ." Rosalie told her.

"Noon?!" Trista was truly shocked by the news. "I'm sorry. I had no idea. I guess I was more exhausted than I thought. Tell Eleanor that I'll get dressed and be down soon."

"I will tell her," the servant replied as she moved off down the hall.

Trista put a trembling hand to her lips as she took a deep, steadying breath. She knew that she had to act as normal as possible, but she wondered if she would be able to if she came face-to-face with Lance. Lost in her riotous thoughts, she dressed, and then, girding herself for the worst, she started downstairs.

Eleanor was in the dining room just starting her lunch when she caught sight of Trista on the stairs. "Trista . . . join me for lunch," she called out in invitation.

Gritting her teeth, but knowing that there was no way to avoid it, she ventured in to join her. At any

332

moment Trista was expecting to run into Michael or, worse yet, Lance, and her manner was anything but relaxed as she sat down at the table across from Eleanor.

"You look a little pale this morning," Eleanor noted. "You aren't sick, are you?" There was an edge of tension to her voice that Trista had never heard before, and she suddenly realized what the other woman was implying.

"No . . . no, it's nothing like that, Eleanor," she protested quickly. "I'm just not used to sleeping so long, that's all."

"Oh, well. I'm glad that's all there is to it," she answered. Still, she was a bit skeptical of Trista's manner. She seemed a bit nervous or rather tense this morning. "Are you hungry? Would you like something to eat?"

"Coffee would be good," Trista answered distract-edly as she glanced toward the hall.

Rosalie had been serving Eleanor, and when she finished she hurried to bring Trista the hot, reviving drink. Trista took a deep drink. It strengthened her somehow, and she finally got up enough nerve to ask in a casual tone, "Is Michael in the house?"

"No, dear, I'm sorry, he isn't. I suppose he didn't want to waken you to tell you, but they all rode into San Antonio earlier this morning."

"They?" she questioned, hoping and praying that Lance had gone with them.

"Michael, George, and Lance," she supplied, and was surprised at the relief that showed for a moment on Trista's pale features.

"Oh . . ." Trista could have shouted for joy. "Will they be back soon?"

"I suppose in about three days or so. That should

give you plenty of time to relax and catch up on your rest."

"Yes," she replied almost happily, "it certainly will."

All eyes turned to watch George and Michael Barrett as they rode into town. It was not their presence that created such a stir, but the presence of the stranger with them who was riding the most magnificent stallion they'd ever seen. As they reined in in front of the Plaza House Hotel, E.R. Smith, the short, rotund proprietor, hurried outside to welcome them.

"George, it's good to see you and Michael," he smiled widely, always pleased that the Barretts frequented his establishment. "Same rooms as usual?"

"Yes, but we'll be needing one more, E.R. I've brought my older son, Lance, along this time," he told him proudly.

"I didn't know you had an older boy. . . ." E.R. frowned. As he swung about to meet the man George was talking about, his mouth fell open in shocked dismay. The man Barrett was introducing as his son was a breed!

"E.R., this is Lance. Lance, this is E. R. Smith, owner of the best hotel in San Antonio."

E.R. was nervous and more than a little upset. Neither Indians nor breeds were accepted in town. He had always refused them service of any kind before, but now . . .

George read his misgivings and responded tersely, "Lance is my son, E.R. If you find you don't have room for him, we'll just have to go elsewhere from now on."

The threat of a loss in business straightened out his

thinking in a hurry. "No, no," he protested quickly, not about to lose the Barretts as customers, "you know Barretts are always welcome here."

"It's good to know that," he told him, giving Lance a barely discernible nod of confidence. On the trip to town, they had discussed Lance's worry that he would not be easily accepted into the white society. George had reassured him at the time that the Barrett name would give him entrance anywhere in San Antonio. He was pleased that he had been proven right.

E.R. bobbed an introductory nod in Lance's direction and then stared admiringly at Fuego. "Your mount is the best piece of horseflesh I've ever seen."

"Thanks." Lance's reply was curt. He felt little respect for a man who based his judgment of people on money.

E.R. took a step toward the golden rogue, but when Fuego snorted nervously, the little man moved away. "Still kinda wild, is he?"

"He's tame now, E.R. You should have seen him when Lance first started working with him."

"Interested in selling him, George?"

"You'll have to ask my son. Fuego's his."

"This is Fuego? The rogue everyone's talked about for years?"

George nodded proudly. "Sure is. Lance caught him and broke him himself."

"What about it?" E.R. turned to Lance, his eyes greedy at the thought of the quick profit he might make on the stallion.

"Sorry. The stallion's not for sale. He's mine, and what's mine . . . I keep."

For some reason, Michael looked up at his brother just as Lance spoke. Their eyes locked, and Michael knew that Lance was talking about more than just the stallion. A muscle flexed in his jaw. He turned abruptly away, snatched up his rifle and saddlebags, and stalked off inside the hotel.

"Let's get settled in, shall we?" George suggested, wondering at Michael's abrupt departure.

"Sure," Lance agreed easily as he followed his father indoors.

Word spread like wildfire through town that George Barrett had a half-breed son and that he was back living with his father on the Royal Diamond. Where generally Lance would have been treated with outright hatred because of his Comanche blood, at George's side he was guaranteed full acceptance in all the better establishments in town. No one ever dared to cross a Barrett, for they wielded too much money and power.

It was much later that night, after they'd eaten in the hotel dining room, that the three Barretts ventured into the White Elephant saloon for a drink and a friendly game of cards to pass the evening.

Hank Rodgers, the barkeep at the White Elephant, had heard the rumors earlier in the day about the half-breed Barrett son. He smiled a friendly greeting to George and Michael as they sidled up to the bar, but he eyed the tall, dark-haired stranger suspiciously, noting his slightly longer hair and the sidearm he wore low and easy on his hip. When their gazes met, Hank immediately saw his resemblance to Barrett and decided that all that was being said must be true.

"We'll have three beers, Hank," George ordered nonchalantly. "I suppose you heard the news about my son Lance being back home?"

"Yep," Hank answered. "I got word this afternoon. You know how news travels here in town."

"I know." He smiled.

Two tall, unshaven, tough-looking drifters were standing at the far end of the bar swilling whiskey. They stiffened perceptibly when they saw Lance. The idea of an Indian in the same saloon with them outraged their drunken sensibilities, and they called out loudly to the barkeep as he served the Barretts their beers.

"Yo! Barkeep! What the hell you doin' servin' a damned Indian?" the more hostile of the two demanded viciously.

"Yeah. We don't like breeds drinkin' where we're drinkin'! Throw the bastard out!"

Lance tensed but didn't acknowledge their presence or remarks as Hank set his beer before him.

"I said, you don't serve half-breeds!" The men moved threateningly closer.

"He serves who he wants to serve," George put in without looking at the two directly.

"Well, he don't want to serve him, do ya, Hank?" They edged closer to Lance, their hands hovering over their guns as the crowd in the saloon backed nervously away.

In a single, fluid motion, Lance drew his pistol and turned on the stunned troublemakers. "I think Hank can decide who he wants to serve, and I think you're the ones who are finished in here. Not me."

Furious in their helplessness before him, they swore violently under their breath as they backed quickly away from a losing confrontation. "You'll pay for this, you filthy redskin. We'll see you dead. . . ."

Lance didn't holster his gun until they had disappeared through the swinging doors and out into the street. He visibly relaxed then and slid the sidearm back into his holster as he turned back to the bar. Only then did he notice his father and Michael staring at him in obvious disbelief.

"Where did you learn to draw like that?" George asked, in awe of his lightning reflexes.

Lance looked at him steadily as he replied, "You taught me some when I was little. Later, I practiced when I was alone."

George clapped him firmly on the shoulder as Michael spoke up. "From now on, watch your back. I don't like the looks of those two."

"Neither do I," Lance answered grimly.

"Glad you handled that so easy," Hank complimented Lance, showing him the double-barreled shotgun he'd been holding just beneath the counter. "Hey, Sal! C'mere and give this gent a welcome!" he called out, glad that his saloon had been saved from destruction at the hands of the drunken louts.

Sal, the buxom, red-haired bargirl whose popularity was legendary among the frequenters of the White Elephant, hurried to do her boss's bidding . . . this time a chore she did not find repulsive at all. Even if he was part Indian, this Barrett was as good-looking as the rest of them. With catlike sinuousness, she rubbed up against Lance as she moved between him and George at the bar.

"How about it, big guy?" Sal batted her long, darkened lashes at the handsome stranger as she ran a hand boldly up his shirtfront.

"Give the lady a drink, Hank," Lance ordered, less than enthusiastically. All he could think of as he stared down at her painted features was how lovely and fresh Trista was in comparison.

"I wasn't wantin' just a drink," she teased, winking at him audaciously.

"Well, that's all I was after, ma'am," he told her bluntly.

338

Sal took his rebuff easily, for her charms were too much in demand elsewhere to be concerned with one cowboy. Still, she couldn't help but wonder at his lack of interest as she wandered away.

The few days the men were gone passed far too quickly for Trista. Whenever she thought of her night of abandon with Lance, she found herself growing more and more uncomfortable with her own introspection. Her situation was a total dilemma. She hated Lance, and still she found herself thinking of him while he was gone and wondering what he was doing.

Trista was dreading their return, and when she did see them riding in, she hastily disappeared upstairs to her room. Hidden behind the fall of her curtains, she watched Lance ride up proudly on Fuego. He looked somehow different after this trip to town, and she stared at him in wonder, as if seeing him for the first time. Her pulse quickened in remembrance of his embrace. Her hands grew cold and clammy and she swallowed convulsively as she nervously wiped them on her riding skirt. It troubled her that she should have such a reaction to the sight of him. How was it that he could affect her so? It seemed to her that there was something changed about his appearance, and it took her a moment to realize that the difference was his hair. It had been cropped shorter. Not that it had been overly long to begin with, but now that it was cut in a civilized fashion, he looked more like George's son and less like the savage she knew him to be. He moved like a white man . . . in his clothing . . . in his manner . . . in his movements.

Lance seemed to sense her presence, and he lifted

his gaze to her window. To Trista it was as though he could see her standing there behind the protective shield of the gauzy curtains, and she knew a moment of panic as she wondered if she would ever be able to escape him. Only when he led Fuego off toward the stables did Trista breathe a sigh of relief and promise herself that from now on she would avoid him at all costs.

With Lance away at the stables, Trista felt that it was as safe as it was going to get, and she left her room to greet Michael. As she started down the stairs she wondered in confusion why her heart did not beat faster at the prospect of seeing her fiancé again even after all these days apart.

Chapter Twenty-two

"I don't believe any of this!" Sukie Harris stared at her mother, the pain she was feeling plainly revealed in her tormented gaze. By some strange act of fate, Trista had returned, and despite her time with the Comanche, Michael was still continuing with his plan to marry her.

"I know it's hard to believe, but I spoke with George while I was in town. He told me the whole story," Mary Lou explained, hoping to soften the blow to her daughter.

"That Trista was rescued by George's long-lost son and returned to them unharmed?" Sukie was incredulous.

"And it's obviously the truth, for, according to George, the wedding's on."

Sukie's spirits flagged. She had not wished bad things on Trista, but she had held out hope that, with her disappearance, she might be able to win Michael back. Now it looked as if things would never work out for her.

"George explained that Trista was indeed kidnapped by a Comanche warrior. Evidently George's half-breed son, Lance, who's been estranged from his father for I don't know how long, rescued her from that terrible

341

fate before anything untoward could happen to her. Apparently he recognized the ring she wore bearing the Barrett crest and, upon discovering who she was, brought her home."

"George's other son is a half-breed?" This news did surprise her. "I didn't even know that he'd been married before Eleanor, and especially not to an Indian."

"It's not something that we talk about, Shining Star having been a Comanche and all," her mother remarked caustically.

"How many years ago did all this happen?"

"It's been at least twenty years. She died of the fever, if I remember rightly. After that George allowed the boy, who was about six or seven at the time, to go live with his mother's relatives." Mary Lou suppressed a shudder at the thought. "I have no idea why. Everyone wondered, but no one ever dared to question him. It was just something that wasn't spoken of again, and as the years passed, it was forgotten . . . until now."

Sukie was amazed by it all. "His return is the reason they're giving the party tomorrow night?"

Mary Lou nodded. "It seems the half-breed has decided to stay on at the Royal Diamond and live with his father now. I have no idea how he's going to fit in. You know how filthy and savage the Comanche are, and if this Lance has spent all these years living wit them . . . why, he's probably little more than an animal himself."

"Did you see him while you were in town?"

She hedged, "Well, yes . . ."

"What did he look like?"

"What do you mean?"

342

"I mean, was he dressed like an Indian?"

"No, of course not," she snapped, "but the fact remains he is half-Comanche. I'm sure there are plenty of neighbors who aren't going to be pleased to have a half-breed living here."

"That's probably true, Mother, but since he did rescue Trista and bring her back home, there must be some good in him."

"Sometimes, daughter, you are just too nice." Mary Lou shook her head. Only Sukie would have looked for the good in him. She felt certain that there were quite a few others who wouldn't bother. "I suppose we'll know more after we see how he fits in at the party tomorrow night."

As her mother rattled on about how Trista was going to be greeted at the party the following night and about how Lance was going to be accepted, Sukie was lost in her own thoughts. Trista was back, and Michael was going to marry her. Nothing had changed despite her mother's earlier predictions. The chance of a future for herself with Michael was at an end. The new dress she'd painstakingly sewn for herself patterned after Trista's trendy gown at the engagement party would have no impact on Michael at all. With a heavy heart she realized that he was lost to her forever.

Lance entered his father's study, needing to ask the question that had been burning within him ever since he'd returned. "I was wondering if I could talk to you for a few minutes."

George had been busily sorting through some business papers, but he immediately set them aside to give

Lance his full attention. He longed to be as close to Lance as he was to Michael, and he knew that it would be a long, slow process to achieve that goal, a process that would include a lot of discussions and a lot of patience.

"Sit down. I was just checking some contracts. It's nothing that can't wait." He gestured toward the chair in front of his desk as he leaned back comfortably in his own.

Lance dropped down into the chair and faced his father across the massive desktop. "There's something I've been meaning to ask you. . . ."

When he hesitated, George encouraged him. "What is it? I want you to feel free to talk to me about anything."

"I want to know where my mother is buried." The request was a difficult one for him to make.

George was stunned by his question and by his own negligence in not having thought to take him there sooner. "We'll go together. It's not far. . . ."

As he stood and strode from the room, Lance followed. They were quiet as they crossed the backyard and made their way down a path that was slightly overgrown. The narrow, winding trail led to a large shade tree, and beneath it, in the midst of all the underbrush, was a small, well-kept area that was bordered by a white picket fence. Within the protected confines was the single headstone of Shining Star.

"I know she never could stand being closed in, but I had to put the fence up to protect her grave. It was all I *could* do for her. . . ." His words became choked, and his eyes misted as he remembered the terrible day when he'd had to put her into that cold, dark grave, never to see her again.

"You didn't bring me here." Lance's accusation pierced him painfully.

"I did a lot of things then that I regret now, son." George raised anguished eyes to Lance that pleaded for belated understanding.

"None of it made sense. . . . I tried to reach you, but Rosalie wouldn't let me talk to you. . . ."

"I was drunk and out of my mind with grief. I told her to keep you away."

"But why?"

"Why?" George shook his head at the memory of his pain. "I couldn't bear to see you or to hear your voice. You were so much like her. . . ." His gaze drifted to the grave. "Your mother was the only woman I've ever truly loved. I loved her more than anything in this entire world. . . . She was my world! Then, when I lost her . . ." His shoulders slumped. "I wanted to die. I wished that it had been me who'd died instead. Sometimes, even now, it all comes back to haunt me. I had to let you go. I knew I couldn't be what you needed, and Lone Elk was so fierce in wanting you." His expression was beseeching. "After you'd gone, it took me a while to get myself together . . . months, in fact. I wanted to come and get you, but Lone Elk and I had agreed that it would have to be your decision to return. I held out hope in the beginning, but then I never heard from you. I take it Lone Elk was good to you?"

"Lone Elk took me into his lodge and raised me as his own," Lance replied, struggling to come to grips with all he'd just been told. A question still remained in his thoughts about the most important cause for their lengthy separation. "If my mother meant so very

345

much to you—" he began almost insolently, and George interrupted him viciously.

"There is no 'if' about it, Lance." His tone was hard, and his gaze had gone icy.

Lance went on, undaunted. "Why did you marry Eleanor so soon? I came back that one time, and you had already married and had another son. . . ."

"So you felt as if you'd been replaced?" George was amazed at Lance's logic.

Lance did not answer, but his eyes met his father's in silent accusation.

"I married Eleanor because I couldn't bear the loneliness. I felt dead inside. Without you and your mother, it seemed my life had ended. I was in a self-imposed hell. Beginning a new family with Eleanor seemed the only way out." George studied him closely, hoping that he believed the truth when he heard it.

"So you *were* looking for replacements. . . ." he charged, his fierce belief in all his father's cruelties difficult to put completely aside.

"There is no way what your mother and I shared could be replaced. What I feel for Eleanor is nothing compared to the love I had for your mother. She's never taken your mother's place, just as Michael hasn't taken yours. You are both my sons. I love you equally. You will both someday own the Royal Diamond."

Standing downwind, Eleanor could barely keep herself from raising her fists to the sky and shrieking her hatred. Whatever anger she'd harbored toward George burst to full-fledged loathing as she eavesdropped on their conversation. She had seen them leaving the house and had carefully trailed them at a distance to keep her presence a secret. Now she was glad that she had.

Wrath-filled, Eleanor turned away and fled back to the house. She had hoped that merely having the party and watching Lance embarrass himself would be enough to drive him away, but now she feared more drastic action would be necessary to preserve Michael's birthright.

So Michael was supposed to share the ranch equally with Lance, was he? The thought left her livid. For twenty years she had slaved, worked the Royal to make it successful for her own son, and now George planned to give half of it to that stinking half-breed?!? Never! She would not—no, could not—allow that to happen. The ranch was Michael's and Michael's alone!

Seeking out the safe haven of her bedroom, she began to make her deadly plans. No one would be allowed to rob Michael and her of their security. Wracking her mind for the thought of someone who could help her, she finally remembered the confrontation between George and Poker that first day Lance was back. Poker had been a faithful employee up until that time, but she also knew that he now hated George and Lance. He would be the one, for his loathing for the Comanche had been obvious. All she had to do now was locate him. She was certain that he would be willing to do anything she asked, for a fee, especially if it had to do with killing Indians. . . .

Leaving her room, she went down to the stables to find out if any of the ranchhands knew where he'd gone, telling them that she needed to contact him about some back wages he'd forgotten to collect. It was a perfect ruse, for one of the younger cowhands volunteered to take a letter into town and give it to him. As she returned to the ranchhouse, Eleanor was

347

more than pleased with the way things were turning out.

Lance and George made their way slowly back toward the house. Their mood was calm and reflective, and neither spoke for some time. Finally, it was George who broke the quiet.

"Lance . . ." He stopped walking and put a lightly restraining hand on Lance's arm.

Lance paused and glanced at him questioningly.

"You've never said, but I need to know . . . you will be staying on permanently, won't you?"

He knew the answer his father wanted to hear, but thoughts of Trista prevented him from responding too quickly. Trista was his wife by his own standards, yet she refused to admit it. He realized that the day of her marriage to Michael was fast approaching and that he had to do something quickly or risk losing her.

It suddenly occurred to him that he didn't want to lose her, and the realization came to him as a bit of a shock. All along he had led himself to believe that he had desired her only because she was Michael's, but now he knew that was no longer true. In the beginning that had been his motivation in taking her, but somehow during their time together, she had come to own his heart.

Lance loved Trista. He would not be able to stand idly by and watch her marry his brother. His dilemma was very real, and Trista was the only one who could solve it. Somehow he had to win her away from Michael, but if for some reason he failed . . . would he be able to remain on the ranch with her married to Michael?

A fierce surge of the Comanche in him taunted him to kidnap Trista again and run off with her. She was his wife. . . . She should be with him. Yet he now realized that Trista's happiness had somehow become important to him, too. That recognition confused him even more. Not only had George been a civilizing influence on him, but his love for Trista had been, too.

Knowing that his father was waiting expectantly for his answer, he replied somewhat evasively, "I will stay . . . for now."

George wanted to press him for a firmer commitment, but said nothing. He sensed that Trista was somehow the key to the entire situation, for she was certainly the reason Lance was here. After their first confrontation that night in his study, George had deliberately avoided the issue, trying to act as if the lie they'd made up was the truth. He feared that there might be a showdown between his sons if Lance truly believed she was his wife. It was something he wanted to avoid at all costs.

"I'm glad," he told him solemnly.

"Trista, darling," Eleanor said in a slightly condescending tone later that afternoon as they sat in the parlor, "we really should start making the final preparations for the wedding as soon as the party for Lance is over. I expect your father to arrive sometime early next week, and as soon as he's settled in, the ceremony can take place."

Trista found herself hesitant to agree to rush things along. She was far too confused over her chaotic feelings for Lance to begin planning her wedding to

Michael. When she'd first returned, she had thought a quick marriage to Michael would solve all her problems, but now she wasn't so sure. "I want to wait until my father gets here before I make any definite changes in the plans."

"But, Trista," Eleanor argued, "this is what Michael wants. . . ."

"I don't care what Michael wants!" Trista snapped uncharacteristically, and her future mother-in-law stared at her aghast.

"I don't understand," she responded icily. "It was decided to move up the wedding date to protect *your* reputation."

"It is my wedding, and I think I should be the one to say when it will take place." Trista stood and started from the room. "If you'll excuse me . . ."

In a huff, she mounted the stairs, seeking desperately to escape any thoughts of her imminent wedding to Michael. As she charged down the hall, her head down in concentration, she wondered why she felt such a growing reluctance to go through with the ceremony. A vision of a tall, black-haired man with vivid blue eyes came to her then, and though she wanted to deny it, she couldn't. It was Lance who had her so confused and so filled with guilt and . . .

Trista ran directly into the solid wall that was Lance's chest. She gasped in surprise and outrage as his arms closed around her, and she glared up at him to find him smiling mockingly down at her.

"Let go of me, you big lout!" she snapped, trying to push free.

"Why, Trista," Lance taunted, "that's not what you were saying the other night."

"You . . . !" Trista was seething. It had been bad

enough having words with Eleanor, but to physically run into Lance upstairs when there was no one around left her nervous and unsure. He was so bold with her . . . so brazen . . . she never knew what he might do next.

"Easy, love," he coaxed, rubbing her shoulder with a gentle hand. "You're far too tense. . . ."

"I'm tense because you won't let me go!"

"Of course I'm not going to let you go. You're my wife, Trista. We're going to be together."

"Oh, no we're not!" she choked. "I've already told you that I'm going to marry Michael."

Lance laughed with seeming delight at her continued defiance, leaving her completely baffled.

"Are you so sure that your first baby won't be mine?" he taunted.

"I won't have your bastards, Lance Barrett!"

His grip on her suddenly tightened as he scowled blackly. "Any baby of mine you carry won't be a bastard, Trista. We are married."

His mouth swooped down to take hers in a flaming, demanding kiss with. Passionate precision he demanded and got an answering response from her. This time Trista did not even bother to deny the hot flush of excitement that thundered through her. She knew there was no point in fighting it, for Lance would only overpower her with his sensuality again and prove to her the futility of her resistance. She wanted him . . . damn him! Despite everything he'd done to her, she still wanted him desperately!

When she looped her arms tightly about his neck, he responded instantly by crushing her to him. Her breasts tautened at the hard, sensual contact with his firm chest, and the hard peaks pressed invitingly through her clothing to tease Lance to even greater heights of mindlessness. Trista found herself moving restlessly against the strength of his hips as if encouraging him to give her the pleasure she knew could be hers in his most potent embrace.

Lance groaned low in his throat at her subtle urging. He traced his hands lower to cup her hips and draw her fully against the heat of his arousal. Trista gasped in delight at the feeling of his need pressed so erotically to her. She tangled her fingers in his hair and kissed him passionately, letting him know with her lips and tongue just what it was she wanted.

Trista was almost mindless with the ecstasy that was throbbing through her, but the sound of someone mounting the staircase came distantly to her. With the sound came a vague awareness of where she was and who she was. Taking Lance completely by surprise, she broke off the embrace and moved quickly away, flattening herself against the wall just as Michael appeared at the top of the stairs.

Michael's gaze swept quickly from Trista's flushed look to Lance's stony expression. "Trista," he ventured, looking at Lance accusingly, "are you all right?"

Trista forced a bright smile on her face as she slashed Lance a vicious look and then turned toward Michael. "I'm fine, Michael."

"I was just coming up to see you. Mother said you had some concerns about the wedding. . . ." Michael didn't realise it, but his words shored up Lance's fading hopes.

Trista knew Lance would pick up on his remark, and she quickly denied it. "Just prewedding jitters, that's all. . . ."

"Oh . . ." Again he glanced at Lance questioningly.

"I really came upstairs because I needed to rest. I'll see you later. . . ." Turning her back on the both of them, she hurried down the hall and disappeared into her room.

Both men watched her go. When they were certain she was safely out of earshot, they regarded each other in silent assessment.

"I want you to stay away from Trista," Michael told him in a lethal tone of voice.

"No one tells me when I can speak to *my wife*, Michael," Lance returned arrogantly.

"I've had about all I can stand of you. . . ."

When Lance gave him a mocking, smug look, Michael lost control. Diving at Lance in the narrowness of the hallway, he knocked the other man off his feet. They rolled wildly about, landing blow after punishing blow on each other, as they fought for superiority . . . and the right to Trista.

Trista heard the commotion at the same time that George did in his study below. Charging from her room, she stood in stunned disbelief watching the two pummel each other.

"Stop! Stop it, both of you!" She was outraged by their behavior.

George rushed from his study and took the steps two at a time. He reached the top to find his sons in violent combat.

"Michael! Lance! What the hell is going on here? You should be ashamed of yourselves!"

It took all of George's considerable strength to haul Lance off of Michael. Wiping blood from the corner of his mouth, Michael got quickly to his feet and stood glaring at his disheveled brother.

"Nuthin'," Michael answered sullenly, regretting

353

that he hadn't been able to land a more vicious punch to Lance.

"Lance?" George turned to his other offspring.

"Nothing," Lance replied, too, knowing that this was private business between Michael and him.

Without another word, not caring that Trista was there, Michael stalked away and disappeared downstairs. George gave Lance a strained look before he followed after his younger son. Alone in the hallway, Lance faced Trista.

"It seems he doesn't like the thought of our marriage, love," he sneered. "I think you'd better convince him of the fact, because I'm never going to let you go." Then he, too, headed downstairs and out of the house.

Chapter Twenty-three

Sukie knew she shouldn't be out riding alone after what had happened to Trista, but at this point, she didn't care. She'd needed to get away from the house and prepare herself for seeing Michael again the following night at the Barrett party. She realized it wasn't going to be easy to face him, knowing that there was absolutely no hope that she would ever become his wife. She wanted to take the time to gird her tender emotions against the battering they were going to suffer in the final realization that he'd chosen another over her.

Reining in by the small, clear-flowing stream, she dismounted and led her horse to drink. She often came here to think in this quiet, shady spot between the boundary of the Barrett spread and her own. As a child she had frequently played here, and sometimes Michael had joined her. The fact that he had intruded on her thoughts annoyed her, but as deeply as he was imbedded in her heart, she knew he couldn't be exorcized in just one day. It would be a long, painful process, but she had to do it if she was to get on with her life.

The sparkling waters were restful to watch as they rushed by, and her spirit needed soothing today. The sun had been hot on her ride to the creek, and after tying up her mount, she sought out the cooling shade beneath an oak. There was little relief to be found beneath the spreading limbs as sweat trickled miserably down her neck and between her breasts. Wearily, she unbuttoned several of the buttons of her blouse to try to cool off. The idea came with sudden, devilish delight, and she eyed the splashing water for only an instant before divesting herself of her boots and socks. Hiking up her riding skirt, Sukie waded joyfully out into the surprisingly icy brook. Forgetting for a moment the sadness in her life that had brought her here, she splashed playfully in the calf-deep stream with the exuberance of a child, completely unaware of the man who sat his horse a short distance away watching her.

Michael had needed to get away from the ranch for a while to sort out all that was going on in his life. He was angry, but he wasn't sure with whom. Certainly some of it was directed at Lance, who seemed to be the root of all his trouble, but then again, he had been less than completely comfortable with Trista since her return. Her erratic behavior toward him left him slightly bewildered. When they had first rescued her, she had been passionate and willing, but lately he'd sensed a reluctance in her that he couldn't understand. The scene in the hall had heightened his suspicions that the hatred she claimed to have for Lance was actually something else, but he didn't even want to consider that. He loved her, and he wanted her for his wife. . . .

He had headed toward the stream instinctively, as if drawn there by some unseen force. It had been one of his favorite places to play when he was a child, and just now he needed a place that was undemanding and quiet.

As he'd topped the low rise, he'd been caught completely by surprise to see Sukie wading in the water. They had often played there as innocents. She had been his close friend and confidante. He enjoyed the sight of her obvious pleasure in her actions, and he remembered many times when they'd cavorted in just the same way together. It occurred to him after several moments that he shouldn't sit and watch her so secretively, so he urged his mount down the slight embankment to join her.

"Sukie . . ." he called out, wanting to alert her to his presence.

Sukie almost thought she was dreaming as she looked up to see Michael riding toward her. She blinked in confusion. Could it really be him sitting so tall and darkly handsome on the mount? Her eyes widened as she stared at him hungrily. He had to be a fantasy; life couldn't possibly be so cruel as to bring him to her now . . . just as she was trying to forget him. Sukie closed her eyes, hoping he'd disappear. However, when he didn't, there was no stopping her bright, warm, welcoming smile.

"Michael! Hi!" She fought not to reveal her joy at seeing him. "What are you doing—" She had meant to make an innocent attempt at chitchat, but stopped short when she noticed his swelling lip. "What happened to you?"

Self-consciously, Michael touched his lip. His smile was wry as he hurriedly tried to manufacture a good line. "Just a little friendly misunderstanding with someone who packs a good left." He dismounted easily and tied his horse near hers.

As he walked down the bank to stand before her, Sukie tried not to look at the way his pants hugged his muscular thighs or the way his shirt was partially unbuttoned, revealing a hint of the furred chest beneath. "Listen, I'm really glad that everything worked out so well for you and Trista. My mother told me all about it. I'm happy for you." Sukie hoped she sounded sincere.

A strange look clouded his handsome features as he responded, "Thanks . . ."

Sukie wondered at the change in his expression. "I'm sure you're going to be very happy. . . ."

"Yes, I'm sure we will be." Michael's answer seemed almost terse, puzzling her even more. "How come you're out here all alone?" He quickly changed the topic, not wanting to discuss Trista right then.

"I know I shouldn't be, after what happened to Trista and all, but I just had to get away from the house for a while. What about you? I didn't know you still came here."

"I guess I was feeling the same way," he replied honestly enough as he sat down on the bank. "I've always liked it here. It's so calm . . . so peaceful . . ."

Sukie was trying not to let her love for him show, but the sight of him sitting so casually with her, talking to her as they used to talk, demolished all the progress she had made in barring him from her affections. She did love him . . . she did! And she would probably go on loving him until the day she died! Her green-eyed gaze memorized every beloved line of his lean frame and every expression that flitted across his face. Michael Barrett was the only man for her; she knew it.

Then she realized she had a choice. She could let this moment pass as a friendly visit, or she could take destiny into her own hands and grab a bit of happiness for herself before it was too late. She wanted him. She always had. Almost immediately she made the decision to try to seduce him. Sukie knew she was risking everything, for if he refused her, she would be completely, totally devastated. Still, she knew she had to try.

Sukie understood that he loved Trista. She realized

that he was going to marry Trista, but she believed she wouldn't be hurting anyone since they weren't married yet. If they made love today, she would at least have that memory to last her the rest of her life.

The thought of her own future didn't bother her at all, for there was no other man she wanted to marry. She would have Michael just this once, and she would live with the remembrance of having had his love for that short time.

Deliberately, she bent forward in a pretended effort to pick something up from the creek bed, offering Michael an unobstructed view of her bosom where she'd unbuttoned the buttons for relief from the heat. There was a different heat building within her now . . . a heat that could only be relieved by Michael.

"Michael . . . look!" As she'd hoped, when she glanced up, his dark eyes were riveted on her cleavage.

Michael felt a sudden shock of desire surge through him as he accidentally found himself staring at the sweetness of her partially bared breasts. A slight breeze stirred just then, and the scent of her perfume came to him, enveloping him in a warm flush of unbidden need. Sunshine was burning her hair to a molten red-gold, and she looked wild and slightly pagan as she stood poised artfully before him.

With an effort Michael fought to bring his sudden, unexpected desire for her under control. Bewilderment filled him. This was Sukie. . . . How was it that just now he was discovering how truly lovely she was?

"Sukie . . . what is it?"

Deciding to be brazen, she told him the truth. "Nothing really."

"What?" Michael was puzzled and still unable to look away from the pale-hued flesh that threatened to spill enticingly from her blouse. He was torn between being a gentleman or lewdly ogling those tempting orbs. He knew a driving need to see the pert darker tips that even now pressed tautly against the soft white fabric of her shirt.

"I really didn't want anything, Michael." Her tone was sultry.

His gentlemanly instincts finally won out after a desperate encounter with his baser yearnings. "Uh, Sukie . . . you really ought to button your blouse." Now Michael was trying to look everywhere but at her.

A slow smile curved her lips as her tongue darted out to wet them. "Why, Michael? Don't you like what you see?" she asked huskily as she moved toward him.

"Sukie!" Michael was startled.

"Yes, Michael?"

"When did you become so . . . so . . ." He groped for wards as his gaze fastened on her sensuous display again.

"So bold? So brazen?" she supplied teasingly with a slight smile. "So in love with you?"

"In love with me?" he gulped, totally bemused.

Michael was unable to take his eyes off of her as she moved up the bank toward him with the stalking sinuousness of a female jungle cat. With lithe grace her delicate fingers worked slowly to unbutton her blouse the rest of the way. He found himself holding his breath as he watched the sides of the blouse drop down and away, but still the glorious fullness was elusively hidden from his avid gaze.

"Yes, Michael. I'm in love with you. . . . I have been for years. You just never noticed before." Her voice was a soft, velvet caress, and Michael felt enthralled as he stared up at her.

Sukie came to stand directly before him. Her emerald eyes were luminous and openly inviting. Knowing that she had his full attention, she boldly slipped the lightweight garment from her shoulders, revealing to him for the first time the lush, full beauty of her breasts.

She had never done this before, but somehow she did not feel self-conscious about being unclad before Michael. She loved him, and to her this was as natural as living and breathing. With a calm she didn't know herself capable of, she held out her hand to him.

"Michael, I'm yours. . . . I always have been."

Her words were spinning a web of sensuality about him, and he was caught. He swallowed nervously as he lifted his gaze from the perfection of her bosom to her lovely features. Had he been acting on instinct, he would have taken her in his arms then and there, but an inkling of honor still remained.

"Sukie . . ." Her name was almost a moan as Michael got to his feet in jerky, awkward movements. She was Sukie, his dear companion and friend. For all of her profession of love, he could not rob her of her virtue, and it would be robbery, he told himself, for he was going to marry Trista. "Put your blouse back on. You really should be getting back."

She sensed that he was leaving her, and she knew she couldn't let him get away. It must be now or never.

"Michael, please . . . don't go," she pleaded desperately. "I need you so."

"Sukie . . ." he agonized, wanting her, but caring about her, too.

"I know you love Trista, but we could have this afternoon . . . I won't put any ties on you. You'll owe me nothing, but I'll have this memory to last me forever after you're her husband." Sukie knew she was risking his rejection, but she had to try. Moving boldly forward, she let her eyes meet his as she linked her arms behind his neck. "You know, you aren't married yet, Michael . . ." And with that, she drew his head down to her and kissed him full and flaming upon the lips.

At the touch of her mouth, he could no longer fight. There was something so achingly familiar, but riotously exciting about her embrace that he felt he was drowning in it.

Sukie put everything she had into that single kiss, fearful that it would be her only chance. She had expected him to pull away, considering how he'd been acting, but when he responded, her heart sang with joy. When she pressed herself completely against him in enticing invitation, Michael locked his arms about her. Unconsciously, he found himself marveling at her full curves and amazed that he'd forgotten the wonder of her kiss.

In that moment Trista no longer existed for Michael. He was caught up in the splendor of Sukie's love and could think of nothing else. He wanted this firebrand of a woman who was stirring flames of passion deep within him. He wanted her with an intensity that was breathtaking. Sweeping her up in his arms, he carried her to the shelter of the spreading tree and lay her on the carpet of soft grass beneath.

Sukie was lost in a haze of romantic excitement. Though logically she knew that tomorrow it would be over, for now she was happy to pretend that she was the one Michael wanted . . . she was the one Michael loved, and in truth, at that moment, she was.

With eager hands, she helped him to undress her and then helped him shed his own clothing. Naked, they came together in a surge of blazing desire. Their bodies intertwined before the initial joining, tasting and caressing, until their bliss took them soaring beyond reality.

Michael was most careful as he moved to take her, and when he met with that virginal resistance and would have withdrawn, Sukie refused to let him. Surging upward, she impaled herself upon his strength. She bit her lip at the unexpected pain and tasted blood in her mouth.

"I am yours, Michael . . . now and forever. . . ." she told him as her hands continued their maddening play over the hard contours of his male frame.

"Ah . . . Sukie . . ." he groaned, and she gloried in the thrill of knowing that he was aware of her and loving her and needing her.

Michael began to move then, and though innocent, Sukie soon understood what was required to fulfill love's greatest pleasure. At his lead, she followed, matching and moving, giving and taking, until a sunburst of ecstasy filled her, and she cried out his name in passionate abandon. Sukie lay beneath his driving weight in total awestruck wonder. It had been so perfect . . . so beautiful. She became aware of his own pinnacle of release then and clasped him tightly to her as he shuddered in satisfaction.

They lay still. The sights and sounds of the fading day slowly became more and more penetrating as the haze of abandon that had engulfed them dissolved before reality's painful presence.

Sukie did not want to let go of the moment. It had been so wonderful that she never wanted it to end. Still, she kept her promise to Michael and said nothing as he moved away.

Michael had been like a man possessed as he'd claimed Sukie's virginity and made her his own. But now as his rationality returned, guilt filled him. Inwardly, he berated himself for his loss of control in taking her. He had always liked and admired Sukie. She'd been his friend, for God's sake, and now he had taken her most precious gift. It did not occur to him that she had given it freely. He thought only of his selfishness in satisfying his own needs.

"Sukie . . . I can never tell you how sorry I am—" he began, but she cut him off sharply.

"Don't you dare tell me you're sorry, Michael Barrett! It was perfect. . . . We were perfect! Don't ever say that you regretted our making love together! Ever!" Tears were burning her eyes as she forced herself from her mellow mood and began snatching up her clothes.

Michael somehow was feeling her pain. He wanted to hold her and comfort her, but restrained himself. He had to get away from her nearness. Why, even now as he watched her buttoning her blouse over those tender, sensitive breasts he'd so avidly laved with kisses only a short time before, he felt his need for her arise again, full and powerful.

"It was wonderful, Sukie. . . ." he managed lamely as he pulled on his pants and then shrugged into his shirt. "It's just that nothing more—"

Sukie gave him an agonized look. "I know that there was nothing more to this than a moment of mutual satisfaction for the both of us. I told you before that I expected nothing from you, and I meant it. Don't worry, Michael. I'll never make a claim on you." She had finished dressing as she'd spoken those words. Moving away from him, she mounted her horse. Before he could say anything more, she put her heels to her mount and rode rapidly away from him without a backward glance.

Michael stood in silent helplessness watching her go. He felt disoriented and deeply troubled. He loved Trista; he was to marry Trista. Yet while Sukie claimed to make no demand upon him, somehow, by her openness, she had exacted a far greater toll.

Later that night Sukie lay in her bed sobbing out her unhappiness. She had thought that she would be able to bear being separated from Michael if she only once had the chance to love him to the fullest. But now that she'd tasted of passion's greatest delight with him, she knew she'd been wrong. It was only going to be worse now . . . now that she'd known the intimacy that would be Trista's every night after they were married.

Jealousy seared her soul. She didn't want to hate Trista, and in fact, she didn't really. She just envied the other woman her position in Michael's heart and wished with all her might that it had been her fate to hold his love instead.

As misery gave way to weariness, Sukie curled on her side and hugged her pillow to her bosom. The night seemed unending to her. The rest of her life loomed emptily before her as her tears gave way to dry-eyed contemplation of endless days and weeks without the man she loved. She thought of the party and wondered if there was any way she could keep from going. Knowing that her mother would be instantly suspicious if she tried to stay home, she didn't even bother to try to invent an excuse. No, she decided, she would go and she would have a good time. No matter what, she would stand by her word. She would not let Michael know that she was dying inside without him.

Miles away in his own solitary bed, Michael lay wide awake and restlessly unable to sleep. He had returned to the house to find that Trista had already made her excuses and retired for the night. In a way,

365

he'd been glad. His own emotions were in such turmoil that the last thing he wanted was to see her.

Images of Sukie imposed themselves over his mental vision of Trista. He shook his head as if to clear the red-haired vixen from his thoughts, but she would not be banished. The warm gift of her freely given love had etched itself upon his soul. He had known her before in so many other ways . . . as a childhood friend . . . as a close companion . . . and now he knew her as a lover. Every facet of Sukie had touched his life. Yet today she had professed to love him, and her profession had taken him completely by surprise. As well as he'd known her, he had never suspected that she harbored any deeper feelings for him.

The more Michael considered it, the more baffled he became. His heart, once set on Trista as his bride, wavered in its loyalty. With that doubt came heavy guilt. Trista needed him. Trista loved him. No matter what his newly discovered feelings for Sukie were, he could not abandon Trista.

Michael realized painfully that he would have to put any thought of Sukie from his mind, not that she would take him now anyway after the way he'd treated her that afternoon. His future was with Trista.

Yet when sleep finally took him, his dreams were of a slender woman with fiery hair and eyes the color of the richest emeralds.

Chapter Twenty-four

The night of Lance's party was clear and warm. A sliver of a moon hung low in the sky, and the dark heavens were dusted with a myriad of twinkling stars.

The lighthearted sound of music emanated from the house, but there was nothing lighthearted about Michael's mood as he retreated to the study to get a glass of bourbon. He splashed a considerable amount into the tumbler and then downed it in one drink.

As the potent, fiery liquor hit his stomach, it brought with it a deceptive calm, and he drew a deep, ragged breath. Sukie had just arrived with her parents. He had planned to greet them casually in his usual manner, but the sight of her had sent a completely unexpected shaft of desire coursing through his loins. It had taken all of his considerable willpower to control the feelings that surged through him. He had been tense in their company and had been almost delighted when they'd taken their leave of him to join the other guests.

Michael hadn't expected to have this kind of reaction to seeing Sukie again, and he knew he had to keep his wayward desires under tight rein. He couldn't allow himself to be alone with her again. He was to marry Trista, and his loyalties lay with her.

Still, as Michael stood there, he envisioned Sukie as she'd looked coming into the front hall, and his blood heated. She'd been absolutely gorgeous. Her emerald gown had been the latest fashion and had enhanced the beauty of her red-gold hair and the fairness of her complexion. Its bodice, though modestly cut, had still offered him a teasing view that hinted at the fullness beneath. It was there that his gaze had lingered, and it was there, even now, that he wanted to press short, devouring kisses upon her responsive flesh.

Annoyed with the direction of his thoughts, he refilled his tumbler again and took another deep swig. He told himself firmly that he had to forget her. Straightening his shoulders in an unconscious gesture, he started from the study much like a warrior preparing to do battle.

Sukie had been nervous and unsure as she'd entered the Barrett home. Her heart had been pounding wildly, and her hands had been cold and damp in frightened anticipation of seeing Michael again. She wondered what his reaction would be to seeing her. In her dreams, she had fantasized that he would sweep her into his arms and declare that it was her he loved, but in reality Sukie knew that wouldn't happen. The best she could hope for, she reasoned logically, was for him to keep their relationship on the same level as it had been previously—they would still be friends.

Sukie had not expected to come face-to-face with Michael as soon as she came into the house, and the sight of him standing there in the hall filled her with a thrill unlike anything she'd ever known. She wanted to throw herself into his arms and kiss him, but the cold, angry look that glinted in his eyes killed any hope she had that he might, indeed, have realized a great love for her. Michael looked furious to her, and she held herself under strict restraint. Forcing a gentle smile, she greeted him as usual. She took extra care not to let any of her love for him reflect in her manner, and it was the most difficult thing she'd ever done in her life.

Yet despite Sukie's calm outward appearance, she had sensed that Michael was tense in her company and seemed almost eager for her and her parents to go on in to the party and join the others. Keeping her head held high, she led the way into the parlor, and though her heart was breaking into a thousand brittle fragments, she did not give in to her need to weep. Determinedly, she found Emily Warren and several other of her friends and let herself be caught up in their gaiety. No matter what, she would not let Michael know how miserable she was. It had been her decision, and now she had to live with the consequences.

Clad in an eye-catching square-necked gown of pale yellow faille, her hair styled up to please Michael, Trista stood momentarily alone near the refreshment table enjoying a cup of punch. The evening was progressing far better than she'd hoped. Few questions had been posed about her time with the Indians. More often than not, the topic had been discreetly avoided. However, some of the women had met Lance and had obviously been charmed by him. They had told her how "lucky" she was to have been rescued by him and what a blessing it was for George to have his long-lost son back home once again.

Gritting her teeth behind a polite smile, Trista had agreed with them. But in truth, she longed to reveal the entire sordid truth behind his "rescue" of her. He was no hero! Though she had to admit as she stared at him now across the width of the room that he did look the part. Lance was tall and devastatingly handsome in his form-fitting dark pants and white shirt, and there was a certain aura of danger about him that was apparently attracting the women like moths to a flame. All evening long she had watched as the ladies had practically swooned before him, and it had angered her. They were such ninnies! Couldn't they tell that his manners were just a civilized veneer? Couldn't they see that he was still a savage Comanche beneath all the white man's trappings?

A shiver raced down her spine as she remembered her first sight of him in his breechclout and paint, and she found it hard to believe that this was the same man. Outwardly he looked so very different, and yet she knew he was the same within. His appearance might be altered, but he had not changed that much. He would take what he wanted, when he wanted. Wasn't she living proof of that?

Trista wanted to look away, but it was almost as if her gaze was held magnetically to him. From beneath lowered lashes she studied him as he conversed with George and several neighboring ranchers, and she realized that he was mesmerizing. Damningly so! For a moment, caught up in the mood of the party, she almost allowed herself to forget the trauma of their earlier time together.

Michael reentered the parlor. Seeing Trista by the refreshments, he started toward her, eager to be in her company and distracted from his guilty thoughts of Sukie.

"It looks as if Lance is being accepted well enough." Michael gave a slight nod in his brother's direction as he joined her. He took a drink of his bourbon as he positioned himself so he wouldn't have to see Sukie standing a short distance away with some of her friends.

Trista kept her voice cool as she faced Michael. She

was glad that he had not noticed how deeply Lance had disturbed her. "The party does seem to be going quite well," she agreed.

"I'm just glad everything is working out for us. It's hard to believe that in just a short time you'll be my wife," he told her as he slipped a possessive arm about her waist. He was going to devote himself to being extra attentive to Trista tonight to assuage his guilt over Sukie. As the music began again with a waltz, he asked, "Shall we dance?"

"Yes, I'd like that," she assented eagerly, glad to do anything that would help keep Lance out of her thoughts.

Taking her in his arms, he danced her gracefully about the room, unaware that Sukie and Lance were both watching them surreptitiously.

Lance was pleased, as was his father, that the party was succeeding so well. The fact that Lance had met with none of the carefully veiled hostility he'd expected had surprised him, and his bigoted opinion of whites in general was slowly beginning to change.

It occurred to Lance as he talked stock and horse breeding with his father and several of his friends that he might really be able to live here permanently and be accepted as an equal. Never before had he given serious thought to remaining indefinitely. Somehow, in the back of his mind, he had always believed that he would return to Lone Elk and his tribe. But now, knowing that he could find happiness here with his father working the Diamond, he knew he truly wanted to stay. This was his home—the one he'd longed for all these years. Only Trista stood in the way of his complete reconciliation. Yet only Trista really mattered to him.

Lance looked up then, searching for her among the crowd, and felt a searing pang of jealousy when he saw her dancing with Michael. He had never wanted to dance as the whites did. In fact, he had thought their actions ridiculous. But the sight of her in Michael's arms, moving in rhythm with his body, made him want to hold her the same way. He kept his gaze shuttered as he followed their progress about the dance floor.

"They certainly look great together, don't they?" Sam Frederickson commented as he, too, watched the engaged couple.

"Yes. Trista is a lovely woman."

"She was sure lucky that you came along when you did. Why, I hate to think how Michael would have held up if he'd lost her. She means everything to him. You should've seen them at the engagement party a while back. Real lovebirds, that pair." He chuckled good-naturedly.

Lance winced inwardly at his declarations. He had come to respect Michael during his time here, and it troubled him greatly to think that their mutual love for Trista would keep them apart.

He glanced at Trista again as they danced past him, and by accident his eyes locked with hers. Heated recognition shot through him as he saw the same desire that flowed through his veins mirrored in the blue depths of her gaze. His jaw tensed, and only with great self-restraint was he able to keep himself from following her across the dance floor.

George spoke to him then, and he turned his attention back to the conversation at hand. Still, even as he spoke openly and animatedly with the ranchers, he was aware of Trista's every move. He knew the exact moment she left the parlor with Michael to go out into the hallway. Shifting his position somewhat, he had an unobstructed view of the front door, and he was relieved when he saw Trista disappear outside alone. Quickly making his excuses to the others, Lance moved away without drawing attention to himself. Determinedly, he followed her from the house.

Ace Page and Dan Walker had been drinking heavily. Longtime friends of the recently massacred Lawson family, they were outraged by Barrett's open acceptance of his half-breed son and by the unquestioning support of all his neighbors. Didn't they know that the Comanche were all no damn good? The drunken pair thought it was infuriating that an Indian, even if he was a breed, could be brought into their community so easily.

They had stayed on the sidelines throughout the evening's festivities, grumbling their discontent between themselves. Despite their state of inebriation, they did not have enough nerve to voice their protest openly, for Barrett was rich, and everyone knew it could be foolhardy to cross him.

They had been watching Lance closely, making sneering, derogatory remarks about him all night. Ace was particularly angered by the way the white women present were so openly taken with him, and both men wondered how any good woman could even consider being in the same room with him, let alone speaking to him.

A hate-filled, alcoholic haze enveloped them as the hour grew late. When they saw Lance leave the house, they decided it was time for a little retribution for the Lawsons. It didn't matter to them that Lance had not taken part in the raid. All that mattered was that he had Comanche blood in his veins, and he deserved to die.

Ace and Dan stalked him cautiously. They knew that he was probably a fierce fighter and that surprise would have to be a major part of their confrontation with him. Ace led the way, emboldened by the liquor and by his own sense of righteousness.

Lance had stepped outside expecting to find Trista there, catching a breath of fresh air. It surprised him to discover that she was not on the porch, and he paused as he waited for his eyes to adjust to the darkness before moving off in search of her. He found her alongside the house in an area that was Eleanor's flower garden. Watching her for a moment in silence, it seemed to him that her mood was pensive and almost sad, and he wondered what it was that could be causing her such upset.

"Trista . . ." He called her name just loud enough for her to hear him as he approached.

She had needed a moment alone, and she gasped in surprise at having been found. "Lance . . . what are you doing out here?"

"I was looking for you, love," he told her easily. "I saw you come outside and thought I'd keep you company."

"I don't need your company, Lance. Go on back inside," Trista snapped irritably. She didn't want him to come near her. She didn't want to risk that he might touch her, and all would be lost. She had left the house because no matter where she turned, Lance had been there, looking marvelously attractive and oh, so virile. He was haunting her, driving her slowly out of her mind. She couldn't allow him to destroy her this way. Why, when she'd been dancing with Michael, all she could think of was Lance. She needed to be free of him again. Free to resume her life and live it the way she saw fit.

"I don't think so, wife," Lance answered confidently as he strode forward and boldly took her in his arms. "A husband's place is at his wife's side."

"Don't . . . Lance; please, just let me go. . . ." Rather than sounding angry with him as he'd expected, she sounded terribly, terribly weary.

"I've told you before, Trista," Lance vowed solemnly, "you are mine, and I'll never let you go. . . ."

Sensing the strangeness of her mood, Lance kept his touch gentle and caressing. Even so, Trista fought to keep herself stiff in his arms. She couldn't let him see how easily he conquered her. She couldn't let him see that all she wanted to do was to surrender to his demanding embrace. She had to maintain her dignity. She was engaged to Michael and was to marry him. . . .

All of her arguments against surrendering to Lance's will were lost as soon as he kissed her. He was soft rather than forceful. He was persuasive rather than overpowering, and the results were even more devastating to Trista's battered senses.

Trista wanted to fight the need that his nearness was arousing within her, but it was useless as his lips moved hungrily over hers. She found herself clinging to the broad width of his shoulders for support as her knees threatened to buckle. "Oh, Lance . . ."

In the study, which overlooked the garden, Michael was hurrying to refill his tumbler with bourbon so he could join Trista outside. She had told him that she would wait for him there while he went to freshen his drink. Refilled glass in hand, he paused briefly as he was leaving the room to glance out the window to see if she was there yet.

The scene that greeted him left him momentarily stunned, and he could only stand and watch in complete confusion. Trista was in Lance's arms, and for all intents and purposes, she did not appear to be fighting him off. Baffled, he frowned. He had noticed a change in Trista's attitude toward him, and he wondered if, in spite of everything that had happened, Lance was the cause of that change. Determined to find out, Michael set his drink aside and left the room, intending to confront them.

Trista was almost completely lost in the glory of Lance's embrace. It was heaven being in his arms and knowing his kiss, and yet, it was her hell, too. Tears of frustration dampened her lashes as she wondered why it had to be this way. Why was Lance the one man who could set her soul on fire with desire for him? She wanted to return his kiss. She wanted all that he was offering her and more. . . . Yet even as she admitted it, Trista realized that there was something more important at stake here than just her own desires. Her honor, and Michael, stood in the way of her willing surrender. With what little resistance she could muster, Trista pushed weakly at his chest trying to free herself from an embrace she never wanted to leave.

Ace and Dan had been pleased when Lance had moved off the porch and out into the concealing darkness. They had expected to corner him easily. They had not expected to find him attacking a white woman in the garden. Ace was completely furious, and at that moment he wished he had his sidearm with him.

"All right, you red devil, get your filthy hands off that white woman!" Ace snarled as he and Dan appeared unexpectedly on the scene just as Trista began to struggle to be free.

"What the . . ." Lance was taken completely by surprise, and he looked up to see the two white men closing in on him.

"Just step aside, little lady. We'll take care of this for you," they told her, gesturing her away from Lance.

"Lance?" Trista looked up at him questioningly and

tried to grasp his arm, but he shook off her touch as his gaze locked on the two approaching strangers.

"Get in the house, Trista. Now." Lance spoke tersely as he stood his ground, poised and ready to fight.

"You've got this all wrong—" she began, wanting to explain to the men what they'd just witnessed, but Lance stopped her.

"Just shut up and get out of here." His tone was more savage than she'd ever heard before.

Trista backed nervously away, her eyes round with worry and fear for his safety. Though she knew Lance was a fierce fighter, these two white men looked equally as dangerous.

With no further warning, Ace and Dan jumped Lance. Driven by the memory of the mutilated bodies of their friends and filled with their own brand of righteous fury, they had only blood lust on their minds as they attacked.

Trista watched in spellbound horror as Lance managed to throw one man off, but just as soon as he was freed of one, the other came at him. Lance was battling bravely and seemed to be about to beat him when his companion recovered and came up from behind him. Trista screamed a warning, but it was too late, and his well-aimed blow laid Lance low, knocking him to his knees. Dan scrambled to help and kneed Lance viciously in the face before he could regain his senses. Ace grabbed Lance's arms and held them pinned behind his back as Dan continued to pummel him.

The sight of Lance being helplessly beaten by the two thugs snapped Trista out of her shock and into action. As the two men continued to beat him, she raced forward to defend Lance and try to fight them off.

"Leave him alone! Stop! What do you think you're

doing?" she screamed, battering Ace with her fists in an effort to make him stop.

"Easy there." Ace brushed her aside. "We're just protectin' you, that's all."

"I don't need your kind of protection!" Trista choked in fury as she came back at them again.

Michael had just left the house when he heard Trista scream, and he reacted instantly, racing toward the garden at full speed. His first thought was that the scene he'd witnessed had not been willing, but as he came upon Dan and Ace assaulting Lance, he knew the cause.

"Get out of the way, Trista," Michael ordered as he grasped Dan by the shoulder and spun him around.

Dan was surprised by Michael's interference and even more surprised when Michael hit him with a hard right. He fell heavily and was slow to recover. At Michael's interference, Ace released Lance and watched in satisfaction as he fell nearly unconscious to his hands and knees before them.

"What the hell are you doing, Michael?" Ace demanded. "This here breed you're claiming as a brother was attackin' your woman. We just saved her from him. He was kissin' on her and she was fightin' and—"

"Shut up, Ace." Michael spoke through clenched teeth.

"It's the truth! We were—" Before he could go any further, Michael hit him, too, knocking him to the ground.

Trista had dropped to her knees in the dirt beside Lance as Michael had dispatched the assailants. "Lance . . . let me help you up. . . . Come on, we'll go in the house and . . ."

Lance was furious. This was what he'd expected from the whites. This was the way he had always known he'd be treated. The fact that he'd been unable to defend himself and Trista left him shamed and angry. That it was Michael who'd had to come to his rescue only made the humiliation worse.

Lance violently shoved her hand off his arm as he staggered to his feet. "Leave me alone, Trista. Go back to your fiancé," he managed bitterly as he clutched at his injured side. With one burning look, he glanced from Trista to Michael and then lurched off into the darkness to be alone.

"Let him go, Trista," Michael ordered, understanding what his brother was feeling just then.

Thinking that Michael believed what the men had just told him, she wanted to set everything straight. "But, Michael, it isn't what you think—" Trista wanted to tell him everything, to tell him that it was more her fault than Lance's that this had happened, but he silenced her quickly.

"Leave it." His statement was sharp.

Trista became quiet, miserably aware of the terrible thing that had just happened and of her own inability to deal with any of it. No doubt Michael now believed that Lance had been trying to harm her when, in fact, the opposite had been true.

"I don't think these two will be rejoining the party." Michael moved around the sprawled bodies of the slowly recovering men to take her arm. "If I ever see either of you two on Diamond property again, I'll do more than knock you down. Do you understand me, Ace?" Michael waited until he'd nodded his reply before he turned to Dan. "Dan?"

"Yeah," Dan mumbled in reply through swelling lips.

Without another look in their direction, Michael led Trista back toward the front of the house. As they were about to start up the steps, she pulled back reluctantly.

"Michael . . . wait . . ."

"What is it?"

"I don't want to go back in. It's late and the party's nearly over. Walk me around to the back of the house, and I'll just go up to my room by way of the kitchen stairs."

Michael wanted to talk to her about what had happened, but he knew this was not the time. "All right. I'll make your excuses for you."

"Just tell them I wasn't feeling well or something. . . ." Trista replied vaguely.

"I will."

A few minutes later Trista started up the back staircase, relieved that she was going to be able to escape the disaster the evening had become. Feeling completely drained, she locked herself in her room and quickly undressed. She donned her nightgown and, stretching out on the bed, pondered the deep, burning ache that was locked within her heart.

Chapter Twenty-five

Eleanor's original idea had been to have this party in order to embarrass Lance. Now, however, she realized that her plan had been a complete failure. To her utter dismay Lance had conducted himself quite well, and to her disgust, the women had found him most attractive. There had been no community outpouring of outrage over his acceptance into society, as she'd expected.

It frustrated her that things hadn't turned out the way she'd planned. Still, she was buoyed by the hope that, if everything went the way she and Poker had planned in their private meeting earlier that day, Lance and George would soon be out of the picture entirely, and Michael would have everything he'd ever wanted . . . the Diamond and Trista.

As Mary Lou came to join her, she pushed aside all thoughts of her vicious plans to chat amiably with her friend.

"Well, Eleanor, darling, you still haven't told me what you really think of Lance turning up so unexpectedly after all these years," Mary Lou began cattily, sensing that there was something hidden behind the mask of pleasantry that had been pasted on her features all evening.

"Why, it's just wonderful, Mary Lou," Eleanor replied, not wanting her to guess the hatred that filled her.

"Did George tell you that I ran into him in town this week?"

"No, as a matter of fact, he didn't."

"He told me all about Lance's dramatic rescue of Trista and how he saved her from those savages. I must say he is a handsome man," Mary Lou remarked appreciatively, "even if he is a half-breed. If you didn't know, he could almost pass—"

"Mary Lou!" Eleanor faked outrage at her statement, wanting her to believe that she backed her husband's sentiments entirely in this matter. It wouldn't do for anyone to be suspicious of her true feelings for him. "Lance is a Barrett, first and foremost."

"Of course, dear, of course." Mary Lou was happy now that she sensed she'd hit a nerve. "I just never knew that you were particularly fond of Comanches, that's all. I mean, with what George went through after Shining Star's death . . ."

Eleanor stiffened. Mary Lou remembered far too much for her comfort. "It was a difficult time for him, I'm sure." She gritted her teeth as she made the remark. "As for Comanches . . . well, we all know what they're like, but let me assure you Lance is family. He is George's son, and they are now happily reunited. I doubt that anything will ever come between them again." Regrettably, Eleanor knew that was the truth, and it was the main reason behind the drastic measures she was taking.

"I understand Michael and Trista haven't changed their plans. . . ." The other woman led the conversation.

"No, they haven't," Eleanor answered bluntly. "Is

there a reason why they should have?"

"I know all this about Lance rescuing her, but it still stands that she was traveling with him unchaperoned for several days. Her reputation, you know." She said it confidingly.

"Her reputation is intact," she huffed defensively, not liking the thought that Michael's fiancée might be the source of tasteless gossip. She had to protect Trista at all costs if she was to be Michael's wife. "However, since I notified her father of her disappearance and he will be arriving sooner than originally anticipated, they are considering marrying as soon as he gets to town."

"Certainly a wise idea, I would think," Mary Lou agreed, tongue in cheek. At Eleanor's hostile glare, she quickly changed her tone. "I mean, it's obvious how deeply they care for one another. Did you see how beautifully they danced together? Why delay any longer than necessary?"

"Indeed. Michael loves Trista very much." She noticed that Michael had just reentered the room alone. "Excuse me, Mary Lou. There's Michael now, and I do have something I have to tell him."

"Of course, dear. I'll see you later."

Eleanor made her way to her son's side. "There you are," she said casually. "Where's Trista? I thought you two left together. . . ."

"We did, Mother, but she wasn't feeling too well, so I told her you wouldn't mind if she went ahead and retired for the night."

"No, of course not. It's Lance who's the celebrity tonight anyway. Have you seen him?"

"He was outside earlier, but I'm not sure where he is now." His answer was evasive, yet truthful at the same time.

Eleanor was puzzled by Lance's absence, but she

really didn't mind. The less time she spent in his company, the better.

Michael was tense as he fended off his mother's inquiries. The last thing he wanted to do was to reveal everything that had just happened outside here at the party. He would tell his father everything later in private. He had been surprised at the time that no one else had heard Trista's scream. But as he stood inside now with the din of conversation and loudness of the music flowing around him, he realized how it had been missed, and he was glad. He felt the need to protect Lance and Trista both, and he wondered at it.

Excusing himself, Michael moved off to the study to get his tumbler of bourbon. For some reason, he felt deeply in need of a few minutes alone to try to understand all that had happened tonight in the garden. Michael was relieved to find the study deserted. He took up the glass he'd abandoned earlier and drained its contents. The potent liquid seared its way to his stomach, and he found some relief in its burning comfort.

He thought of the embrace he'd witnessed between Trista and Lance, and then he considered what Ace and Dan had tried to make him believe. He knew, without a doubt, that Trista had not been fighting Lance off when he'd seen her. He felt reasonably certain that the two men who'd attacked Lance had done so out of their hatred for his Indian blood and not because of any attack on Trista.

Theirs had been a good lie, and had Michael not seen Lance and Trista embracing before he left the house, he might have been inclined to believe it. But he knew the truth now. Trista wanted Lance, and Michael knew for a fact that Lance wanted Trista. He'd already married her, and despite all her protests to the contrary, he now knew that she was bound to his brother.

The realization filled him with a relief he found puzzling. He should have been angry, he supposed, but he wasn't. Instead he found that Sukie was the center of his thoughts . . . responsive, loving Sukie. She had said that she'd loved him for years, but she hadn't let him know the extent of her feelings for him until yesterday when it had been almost too late. Michael smiled slightly to himself as he realized that things just might be working out better than he'd ever hoped.

"Michael . . ."

The sound of Sukie's voice tentatively calling his name seemed almost a part of his imaginings, and he turned slowly to see her standing framed in the study door. "Sukie . . ." He set his glass aside and walked toward her.

Sukie nervously watched him approaching her and tried to read his mood. He did not seem as cold and angry as he had earlier when he'd greeted her, and she felt a bit of her nervousness drain away. She hoped that they could talk for a moment, for she'd been feeling quite guilty about what had transpired between them, and she wanted the opportunity to apologize.

"I was just wondering if we could talk for a little while," she ventured softly.

"I'd like that," Michael replied, surprising her by drawing her into the room and closing the door behind her. "I'd like that very much. . . ."

Before Sukie could say another word, Michael took her in his arms and kissed her with all the pent-up passion he'd felt for her since seeing her arrive at the start of the party. His kiss was potent and excited, and he in that moment needed her more than he'd ever needed anyone.

Sukie responded wildly for an instant, but then suddenly yanked herself free of his arms. Her thoughts were racing as she faced him angrily. She believed by his behavior that Michael thought she was now his for the taking whenever and wherever he pleased, and it infuriated her. He had spent the entire evening with his fiancée. Now that she was out of the picture, even for a few minutes, he was coming after her. How dare he think that she was that kind of woman! She had told him the truth of her feelings for him, and he dared to take advantage of her this way!

"Sukie . . ." Michael was bewildered by her withdrawal from him. He had thought that she would be as anxious as he to share a heated embrace, but now he knew he'd been wrong.

"Don't you say a word, Michael Barrett!" she stormed, her temper as fiery as her hair. "I came in here to apologize for yesterday with the hopes that we could continue our friendship, but I realize now that it's impossible. You obviously think that I'll be willing to come to you whenever you want me, but I've got news for you; you're wrong! I place a higher value on myself than to carry on with you without the benefit of marriage."

"Sukie . . . it's not—"

"It most certainly is! I heard your mother discussing your wedding to Trista. It's coming up real soon. Well, let me tell you something. What happened yesterday was a terrible mistake. Not only did I lose my virginity, but I've lost your friendship as well, and it was the one I valued most in the world. I'm sorry I made love to you yesterday, Michael," she told him as tears coursed down her cheeks. "I wish it had never happened! I wish I could take it all back!"

Without a backward look, she fled the room and the house, leaving Michael standing in the middle of the study more confused than ever. Silently he thought . . . *Would it matter if I told you that it was you I loved and not Trista?* Upset by what had just happened, but knowing that he could say nothing to reassure Sukie until he'd talked with Trista, he took another drink of his liquor and dropped down into a chair. Tomorrow he would have to face Trista with all he had learned tonight and see what she said. If everything went as he expected it to, he could probably be at the Harris ranch by afternoon.

Long hours later Trista was still unable to sleep. Haunted by the memory of the trauma in the garden, she wondered where Lance had gone. All the guests had departed, and she thought the rest of the family had gone to bed long ago, but she had not heard him retire to his room. A cold knot of fear formed in her heart as she worried that he might have left the ranch. Hadn't he pushed her away and told her to go to Michael?

Desperate to know how he was, Trista quickly pulled on her dressing gown and quietly left her room. She did not question the true reason for her actions as she approached his bedroom door cautiously. Frightened of possible discovery, Trista did not bother to knock, but carefully tried the knob. To her surprise, it was unlocked. Hurriedly, soundlessly, she moved inside.

Trista had expected the room to be empty, and she was not disappointed. It was obvious that Lance hadn't been there all night. Despairing, she moved around the room touching his belongings and coming to know more about him. The picture on the table drew her interest. Picking it up, she went to the window to try to see it better in the dimness of the light of the fading moon.

The images on the daguerreotype touched her deeply . . . loving mother and adoring child. For the first time Trista realized the pain Lance must have gone through in losing his mother at such a young and tender age. With infinite care she placed the picture back on the table. He was a complicated man, and yet he was the man she *loved*. . . .

The realization was not as shocking as she would have expected it to be. She loved Lance. She did not know exactly how it had come about, she only knew that he was the only man she wanted. He was the only man she needed. Acknowledging it openly to herself finally freed her emotions, and she knew a surging thrill of joy.

But even as happiness filled her, thoughts of Michael crept into her mind, dampening her mood. Though she loved Lance, her loyalty and her honor were pledged to Michael. She was promised to him, and he was the one she would have to wed. The wedding was already planned, and soon after her father arrived, it would take place. Her spirits heavy, Trista resigned herself to her fate.

Trista knew she should leave, that it would be terrible if she were discovered in Lance's bedroom, but somehow she couldn't. She needed to see him again, to reassure herself that he was all right. Testing the softness of his bed, she lay down on the comfortable mattress and curled up to await his return. He had to come back . . . he had to . . . and when he did, she would be there waiting for him.

Lance patted Fuego's sweaty neck and turned the weary mount back toward the ranch. After leaving the garden, he'd gone to the stables and taken the golden stallion. At first he had intended to leave, to return home to Lone Elk and his people, but as he'd ridden with the night wind, the humiliation and hatred that had clouded his thoughts had cleared.

Leaving was exactly what those two drunken thugs wanted him to do. While it would be the easiest way to handle things, he wouldn't do it. The Royal Diamond was his home. He belonged there. His father had convinced him of that. Lance rubbed his aching side as he guided the stallion back toward the house.

Trista entered his thoughts then, and he knew that she was the main reason for his return. When he'd considered going home, he had tried to decide if he really could live without her. The answer was painfully clear to him. He loved her, and he would not give her up. She wanted him. He could feel it in her kiss.

All he had to do, Lance realized, was convince her that they could be happy together. He knew it would be a major undertaking considering the fact that he had told her to go to Michael when he'd left tonight, but he was not a man who gave up easily.

By the time they reached the stables, Lance and Fuego had both cooled down. He stabled the horse and then made his way slowly back to the house. Every inch of his body was aching as he moved silently into the house and down the hall toward the staircase. He didn't want to disturb anyone and hoped to make it to his room without any kind of confrontation.

George, however, had stayed up waiting for him and, at the sound of the door closing, quickly emerged from his study.

"Lance . . ." He sounded tremendously relieved as he came forward to greet him. "Are you all right?"

"I'll be fine," he managed, keeping his voice low.

"You came back. . . ."

Lance read the anxiety in his father's expression

and understood the cause. "I just went for a ride."

They regarded each other for a long moment.

"You're staying. . . . You're not going to let this drive us apart again?" George asked, no longer fearful of expressing himself openly with his son.

"No. I'm staying." His answer was firm.

"Thank God. I was so afraid after what Michael told me. . . ."

"It'll take more than a couple of drunken fools to drive me away. The Diamond's my home. I don't intend to leave it ever again."

George was filled with poignant emotion. "I'm glad . . . so glad. This is where you belong."

Lance remained silent in agreement. "I think I'll go on up now."

"Good night, son. I'll see you in the morning." George watched him as he slowly climbed the steps. He knew Lance had to be in pain, but he also knew that if he'd needed anything, he would have told him. Feeling truly content for the first time in years, he went back into his study to turn out the light before going up to bed himself.

Lance entered his room and locked the door behind him. He didn't bother to light a lamp because he had no desire to see his own battered reflection in the mirror that hung over his dresser. Because of the pain, his movements were edged with caution as he undressed. When he'd finally stripped down, he took the pitcher from the stand near the dresser and splashed some cold water in the washbowl to wash the dust and grit from his sore body. He had just finished washing and was toweling himself dry when he returned toward the bed and saw her.

Lance went completely still. Trista lay sleeping on his bed clothed in only a nightgown and wrapper. His breath caught in his throat, and his heartbeat quick-

390

ened. She was here . . . waiting for him. He'd been right. . . . She did want him!

He moved to the side of the bed and stood looking down at her, studying the sweetness of her features in sleep. She looked delicately feminine as she lay there, yet Lance knew it was all illusion. There was nothing delicate and helpless about her. Trista was a fighter . . . a survivor.

Without conscious effort, Lance reached out to caress the pale, silken length of her hair where it tumbled in disarray about her shoulder. Trista felt the warmth of his touch and stirred, her eyes opening to stare up at him dreamily.

"Lance . . ." Trista breathed his name in a sensual, verbal caress. She lifted a hand to cover his and drew him down on the bed beside her. "I've been waiting for you. . . ."

Lance was almost afraid to speak for fear that he would spoil the moment. "Why, Trista?" He forced himself to keep all emotion out of his voice as he asked.

"Because I needed to know that you were all right," she answered simply.

"I'm fine, Trista. . . ." he began, not wanting her sympathy.

Trista let her gaze wander over him, and she saw the dark, ugly bruise forming on his side. "No, you're not. . . ." she returned as she ran a caressing hand over his injured ribs. "I want. . . ." She hesitated, not quite sure in her sleep-fogged mind what she was going to say.

"What do you want, Trista? Tell me. . . ." Lance suddenly needed to know.

"I want to stop your hurting, Lance."

Their eyes met, and there was no further need for words. It seemed to Lance as if he were moving in slow motion as he bent to press a soft, cherishing kiss upon her lips.

"Stop my hurting, Trista. Only you have the power to do it. . . ." he confided before taking her in his arms and deepening the exchange.

Excitement exploded in her as he lay down beside her and brought her full-length against him. Already she could feel his need for her, and it filled her wit a deep sense of womanly power. Ecstatically, she returned his kisses, arching toward him as he began to caress her through the soft material of her gown. Straining closer, she sought to be nearer to him. Trista wanted oneness with Lance. She ached to hold him within her, but tonight he would not be rushed.

Seeking out the sweetness of her throat, Lance trailed a burning path of heated kisses down her neck and even lower to the full, burgeoning curve of her bosom. Cupping her breasts, he pressed kisses upon them through the gown, and the sensation was so different that Trista murmured in enchanted surprise. She longed for him to strip away her garments so she could feel his flesh upon hers, but Lance was in no mood to hurry. He wanted to savor every moment of her willingness.

Rising above her, he stared down at her, enthralled by the look of heavy-lidded desire on her face. "I want you, Trista, more than I've ever wanted another."

"Oh, Lance . . ." Trista gasped as he moved his hips suggestively against her. "I want you, too. . . ."

Trista couldn't control the urge to move, and she began to rotate her own hips hungrily against his, letting him know that her passion matched his. Lance lowered his head slowly, his mouth taking hers in a devouring exchange. His hands continued their practiced pursuit, caressing her from breast to thigh, coming near, but never satisfying the building ecstasy within her. Impatiently, Trista stroked his back and hips, tracing patterns of fiery excitement that nearly took Lance over the brink. He felt nearly ready to explode with his desire for her, and he drew away, meaning to strip away the offending gown and wrapper.

"Lance . . . please . . ." she begged, thinking that he meant to leave her for some reason.

"Easy, love . . ." he hurried to reassure her as he lifted the hems of the garments and drew them over her head. Tossing them carelessly aside, he turned his heated regard back to the slim beauty of her body. The sight of her so open and willing sent his passions soaring, and he could not postpone the inevitable any longer when she lifted her arms in welcome to him.

"Love me, Lance . . . love me now. . . ."

With a muffled groan, he went to her, burying himself between her thighs and exulting in the rapture that threatened to overwhelm him with that intimate contact. His rhythm was steady and driving, and Trista moved in concert with him, wanting to savor his possession completely, glorying in having him joined with her.

Lance paused in his movements and levered himself up on his forearms to stare down at her. His blue eyes darkened as he studied the pale silk of her hair and the slight flush of passion staining her cheeks.

Trista, too, was caught up in the heart-stopping moment, and she stared up at Lance with all the emotion she felt for him mirrored in the depths of her own blue-eyed gaze. She was transported as she studied the harsh, yet handsome angles of his manly features and the vivid blueness of his eyes against the darkness of his skin. She thought him beautiful, if it was possible for a man to be considered beautiful. Lovingly she lifted her hands to frame his face, and she raised up a bit to kiss him softly on the mouth. There was something so enthralling . . . so perfect about this, their blending, that Trista could no longer deny what she was feeling, and the words were out before she could stop herself.

"I love you, Lance. . . ."

Her confession created a wildfire of desire within Lance. He had wanted to hear those words for so long, and now, at last, she'd admitted the truth of her feelings. Crushing her to him, he kissed her deeply and passionately.

"I love you, too, Trista. . . ." he told her in a voice hoarse with emotion just before he claimed her lips in another devastatingly erotic exchange.

Lance began to move again, needing to please her, needing to show her just how fully he did love her. Their mating was indeed lovemaking this time as each touch became a cherishing caress and each kiss a sealed vow. They loved.

Trista reached the pinnacle of passion in unison with Lance, and in hushed cries of adoration they called each other's name. Still joined as one, they drifted in the serenity of satiation, at peace with each other.

"Lance . . . I have to go. . . ." she murmured softly as she pushed at the weight of his shoulders in an unsuccessful effort to dislodge him from atop her.

Lance had been lost in the beauty of being still imbedded within the hot, silken confines of her body and did not immediately understand her protest. "What?"

"I have to go." Trista's tone was more firm this time, and there was a quiet desperation in her as she tried to wriggle free of his intoxicating, dominating nearness.

Lance sensed the change in her and lifted his body

from hers. "What's wrong, darling?"

"I have to get back to my room. It's so late and—" Trista had already left the bed and was reaching for her gown when Lance's hand snaked out and grabbed her by the forearm.

"And what?" he demanded icily as his grip tightened menacingly on her arm.

She swallowed nervously as she met his gaze. "Someone might discover that I was here . . . with you. . . ." she admitted guiltily.

"Would that be so bad, Trista?" Lance managed smoothly in spite of his barely concealed fury that was about to erupt.

"Well . . . Michael—"

"Michael?!" he snarled in anger. "What has Michael got to do with any of this?"

"I'm engaged to Michael," Trista said simply. "He's the man I'm going to marry. I feel so guilty. . . . I just can't do this to him. . . ."

Her last words set Lance off. She had just professed to love him, and yet she was planning on going through with her wedding to Michael? He was beyond control as he jerked her back down on the bed.

"You just said that you loved *me*, Trista," Lance pointed out viciously. "You just made passionate love to *me!*"

"I know . . . but I can't do this to him! I just can't!"

"You're telling me that you still are determined to go through with this farce of a wedding with my brother even though I'm the one you love?"

His questions were coming too quickly and too angrily, and she was confused and consumed with her own inner turmoil.

"Don't you see? I have to?"

"You don't have to do anything you don't want to, Trista! You are my wife! There is no shame in sharing a marriage bed!"

"We aren't married . . . not really. . . ."

"We are married by my ways, and they are just as binding as yours!" A sudden stricken thought took him, and he pinned her body to the bed with his own as he held her arms pinioned above her head. "Maybe that's the real cause. . . ." he said in a tone filled with loathing as he stared contemptuously down at her.

"What?" Trista gasped, frightened by his intensity.

"I'm good enough for you to sleep with, but not good enough for you to marry," Lance snapped. "Is that it, Trista? Is Michael's white blood the only Barrett blood that's good enough for you to marry? A few minutes ago, you weren't concerned with my Indian blood. . . ." He rubbed himself against her in a degrading motion. "Has all that changed now, Trista? Has it?!"

Trista stared up at him in horror, her eyes wide with misery over his misunderstanding of her motives. It wasn't because he was part Comanche—it was because she had promised to marry Michael. It was her honor that stood in her way. She couldn't hurt him like this by betraying him with his own brother, even if it meant denying herself her heart's desire.

"Lance, let me explain. . . ." Trista wanted to explain to Lance, but he would hear none of it.

Lance had never been violent with women, but he knew the urge to strangle her at that moment. To keep himself from hurting her, he moved quickly away from her. Stalking to the window, he stood there staring out at the slowly brightening predawn sky.

"Get out, Trista."

"Lance . . ."

"I said get out!"

In tortured agony, she drew on her gown and wrapper and started for the door. She paused once to glance back at him, wanting to tell him of her confusion, but he was still standing ramrod straight with his back to her, his entire aura one of un- approachability. Her heart breaking, she stumbled from his room and returned to the safety of her own.

Chapter Twenty-six

The flickering brilliance of the campfire cast harsh shadows on the faces of the six renegade warriors crouched about it, rendering them even more fierce-looking than they already were. Outcasts from their various tribes, they had banded together to raid and pillage the Texas countryside under their new leader, the murderous Striking Snake.

"Why do you want to do this, Striking Snake?" Big Bull asked, skeptical of his daring plan to attack the ranch of the rich white man, Barrett.

"Yes, Striking Snake," agreed Many Robes. "It is far too dangerous."

"If you are women, then leave me now," Striking Snake insulted them. "I want only brave warriors with courage to ride with me, not weak, helpless females who are afraid to fight."

Big Bull stiffened at his slight. "I am not afraid. I am cautious. I do not see the reason for so bold a raid. It would be suicide, and for what?"

Many Robes nodded. He was familiar with the layout of the Diamond's ranchhouse and knew it would be difficult to attack openly. "The whites there cannot be taken by surprise. It would be a stupid thing to do. I will not go."

Striking Snake had remained silent as they criticized his plan, but he grew tired of their cowardly complaints. In a slick, quick move, he drew his knife and threw it at Many Robes. Slicing through the air with lethal force, the knife buried itself in the warrior's throat and he died instantly. Before the full realization of what had happened could penetrate the others, Striking Snake dove across the campfire at Big Bull, attacking him with the same cold deliberateness at his namesake.

Big Bull had no time to prepare himself for the assault. With overpowering strength, Striking Snake beat him to unconsciousness. He rose savagely above the prone warrior, intending to finish him off, but a word from one of the others stopped him.

"He is a fine, strong warrior, not a woman like Many Robes. He will go along with us now or he will leave us, Striking Snake. There is no reason to kill him." His defender was Two Mules, Striking Snake's most ardent supporter among the group. For that reason, he listened to his advice.

"You are right," he answered, slowly bringing himself back under control. "I will let him live."

When they had disposed of the dead warrior's body, they returned to their camp to find that Big Bull was waiting for them.

"You have decided to stay and make the raid with us?" Striking Snake questioned him openly before the others.

"I will stay."

The leader nodded and sat down cross-legged before the fire to explain his strategy. "We will attack the house tomorrow night after sundown."

"What is the prize you so desire at this place?"

"I go to kill Lance, half-breed nephew to Chief Lone Elk, and to take the woman who should be mine."

"You do this strictly for vengeance?"

"Is there a better reason?" he challenged. There were no more comments. "If we are successful, there will be many horses for us."

"We will be ready whenever you are."

"Good. There will be much cause for celebrating tomorrow after the raid. You will see."

In the once-deserted cabin out in the middle of the wild Texas countryside, Poker Bradley stood before the six men he'd chosen to help him with his task. "I have to have your word that no one, and I mean no one, will ever reveal anything about what we're going to do."

Les Crocker, sober now for the first time in weeks, rubbed his chin and looked suspiciously at Poker. "I ain't promisin' nuthin' till I know what it is we're gonna be doin'."

"I'm not telling anyone anything until I have your word. I've already told you everything I can. It's going to be dangerous, but it's a job that will pay real good. Now, I need to know who's in and who's out."

Five of the six agreed readily, with only Les remaining doubtful. "How do we know you're gonna pay off when we're done?"

"I'll pay off, Les. You don't have to worry about that. All you gotta worry about is shooting straight and keeping your mouth shut. Are you in or not?"

"All right," he agreed, thinking of the fast money he was going to earn. "I'm in."

"Good. Now, here's the plan. . . ." He related the details of the treacherous plan Eleanor had devised.

"So the blame gets put on the Comanche?" One of the men remarked, slightly amazed at the cleverness of the deadly plot.

"Yep, and we're off scot-free with our pockets well lined. All we gotta do is move in fast, make the kill, and get out outta there."

"Sounds simple enough once we make it into the house. What about the payoff?"

"We'll have the money once we make the raid. The rendezvous is all set. We take care of our end of the deal, and we'll get paid."

"What time do we ride out?"

"We'll leave here a little before sunset. That should put us at the ranchhouse after it's fully dark. With any luck, we can be in and out of there in no time," Poker said, remembering how Eleanor had told him the perfect time for the attack and exactly which doors would be open for them.

"We're ready." Les spoke eagerly for the whole group.

"Well, all we gotta do is wait for sundown."

Randolph Sinclair surveyed the surrounding landscape with less than complete enthusiasm. What he'd seen of Texas so far had all been jaded by his worry over his daughter's safety. The land looked godforsaken to him, and he wondered how Trista or anybody could ever have agreed to come live in such a barbaric place.

"How much farther is it to the Barrett ranch?" he demanded grumpily of his driver.

The hired driver chuckled at the easterner's question. "Why, Mr. Sinclair, you've been riding on the Diamond for the last hour and a half."

Randolph sat back on the uncomfortable seat of the buggy and stared out at the low, rolling hills with a new respect. "How much longer until we reach the house?"

"We should arrive in about another half hour," he answered, and then they both fell silent as they continued on their journey.

Since receiving word of Trista's disappearance, Randolph had been desperate with worry. Trista was all he had left in life, and he had always wanted only what was best for her. Had he known that her venture into Texas was to end in such terrible tragedy, he would have forbidden her engagement to young Barrett. He only hoped that by the time he arrived she would be back safely on the ranch. He knew the odds on that having happened were slim, but he had to hold on to that thread of hope, for he loved his only child dearly.

It was near noon, and Michael had passed the morning in growing frustration. More than anything, he had wanted to find time to speak with Trista alone, but she had remained secluded in her room, telling them all that she didn't feel well. He had doubted the truth of her excuse until Rosalie had assured him that she was a bit under the weather. Worried that she might be really ill, Michael had pressured her for more details. Reluctantly, she had confided to him that Trista was suffering from a feminine complaint brought on by her monthly flux. Though he'd greeted Rosalie's explanation with outward calm, actually Michael had been thrilled by the news. The fear that she might have gotten pregnant during the time of her captivity had weighed heavily upon him, and he was relieved to know that she'd been spared that trauma. Feeling considerably lighter of spirit, he left the house and headed out to the stables to get to work knowing that there would be plenty of time to speak with Trista later about what they both really wanted out of life.

Trista lay in her bed, curled on her side, hugging her pillow to her stomach. She was heartsick as well as miserable as she lay there. A short time ago, she would have welcomed this womanly pause in her life. It would have severed all connection to the past and to Lance. But now she found herself achingly disappointed that she had not been carrying Lance's child.

That perverse thought had come as a shock to her, but she understood more clearly than she ever had before what it was she really wanted. Trista could deny it no longer. Lance was the only man she wanted. Lance was the only man she loved.

She knew that she would have to be honest with Michael even though she would hurt him in the process. This troubled Trista, for she really did care for Michael. She was more than fond of him and respected him greatly. But, she acknowledged now, she did not love him, and it would be a terrible mistake if she were to marry him under these pretenses. As soon as she was feeling better, she would have to be honest with him. In the long run, it would be a far more honorable thing to do than to enter into a loveless marriage in which they both might eventually suffer.

Lance had not slept after Trista had left him at dawn. Instead he had dressed and gone down to the stable to spend time with Fuego. Somehow he found comfort in the company of the still-proud, yet manageable rogue. He had always hoped that Trista would come to respond to him as Fuego had, but he knew now that it was not to be. Her claims of loving him had been false-hearted lies.

Last night, before his encounter with Trista, he had been determined never to leave the Diamond. Now, however, he was beginning to believe that perhaps he could find more happiness with his tribe. At least, with his people, the truth was spoken. He had dwelled on the issue all morning and had decided that leaving was the only way he would find peace. He still felt the intruder here, though they had tried to make him welcome. In all, he reasoned, it would be better if he left.

Not wanting to see anyone until he'd reached his decision on what to do, Lance had purposefully avoided the house all morning. He had been glad that no one had come looking for him. Now, as he started back, he was discomfited to find Michael coming in his direction. If there was one person he did not want to see right now, it was him.

"How are you feeling?" Michael was concerned, for he hadn't spoken with him since that time in the garden the night before.

"My side's a little sore, but I'll live," Lance answered with studied indifference.

"I'm sorry I didn't get there sooner. . . ." he began earnestly.

"It wouldn't have mattered. It was bound to happen eventually." He shrugged off his concern.

Michael bristled, puzzled by his attitude. "It wasn't 'bound to happen.' The majority of our friends are your friends now, too. You're a Barrett, Lance."

Lance wanted to sneer that he was only half-Barrett and that half wasn't enough for Trista, but he had no desire to get into any of it. He would leave the ranch,

Trista would marry Michael, and everyone would be happy . . . including himself.

"Right. I've got to go up to the house for a while. I'll talk with you later." He started to walk away when he noticed the rise of dust on the horizon and paused. "It looks like somebody's coming. You expecting company?"

Michael turned to follow the direction of his gaze. "Just Trista's father . . . He's due in at any time." As the buggy drew near he recognized it as one that hired out from the stable in town. "It looks like it's him. I'd better get up to the house and let Trista know. She wasn't feeling well this morning and was still resting in her room."

Michael hurried off to spread the word of Randolph Sinclair's imminent arrival. Lance watched him go and grew even more despairing than he had been. Upon her father's arrival Trista and Michael's wedding was to take place. It looked like the time had definitely come for him to leave.

"Yes? What is it?" Trista asked in a strained voice as a knock came at her bedroom door.

"It's Michael, Trista. I think you're father's on his way in."

"Papa's here?" She wasn't sure how to react. She was overjoyed with the thought of seeing her father again after such a long separation. But according to Eleanor's plans, the wedding was to take place as soon as he arrived, and that made her situation even more difficult. She had definitely decided that she could not marry Michael, but at least she had thought she had time to break the news to him delicately. Now that her father was here, she felt as if she'd been pushed into a corner.

"Looks like he's coming up the drive right now."

"All right," she finally managed. "I'll get dressed and be down as soon as I can."

Though her body still ached with the feminine complaint, she tried to push it from her mind as she pulled on her clothing. In a few short minutes, she was dressed. Once she was decently clad, she brushed aside her curtains to see the buggy winding its way up the last stretch of the Diamond's drive. Even from this distance, she recognized her parent. Trista did not realize just how much she'd missed him until she saw him again, and she rushed from her room excitedly to greet him.

Randolph had just begun to step down from the carriage to greet Michael and his folks and ask about any progress in finding Trista when she came running out of the house.

"Papa . . . oh, Papa . . . you finally got here!" Trista launched herself into her stunned father's embrace.

It took Randolph only a moment to recover from the shock of seeing her. He had been expecting nothing but bad news, and he was thrilled to find that she was here and alive and apparently quite well.

"Trista, darling, thank God you're alive! I was so worried!" He clasped her tightly to him as tears fell unheeded.

Trista, too, found herself crying as she clung to the broad, supportive width of his chest. "Oh, Papa. I'm so glad you're here. . . ."

"Why don't you come inside? I'm sure you must be just exhausted from your ride out from town," Eleanor invited as she stood with George on the porch.

With his arm still around Trista's slim waist, he

looked up. "Eleanor . . . it's good to see you again, and under such happy circumstances." His mood was lighthearted now that he was assured of Trista's safety and good health.

"Randolph, this is George, my husband." Eleanor made the introduction easily.

"My brother Lance is down at the stables, but I'm sure he'll be along soon," Michael added as the parents exchanged warm greetings.

"I didn't know you had a brother, Michael," Randolph remarked casually as they made their way inside.

"It's a long story, but one I'm sure you'll want to hear." Michael smiled as he followed his mother's lead into the parlor.

Eleanor was mentally rubbing her hands together, for her plans were going more smoothly than she could ever have imagined. With Sinclair here, the wedding could take place at any time, and as far as she was concerned, the sooner the better. Trista was the woman Michael wanted, and Trista was the woman Michael would have.

As they settled into the comfort of the parlor, Eleanor was quick to make Randolph feel welcome. Rosalie was directed to bring refreshments, and they sat about filling him in on all that had happened since she'd contacted him about Trista's disappearance all those weeks ago.

Trista explained everything to her father, holding to the story that George had devised regarding her return home. Randolph was impressed with this tale of George's brave older son and, though told of his Comanche blood, was not in the least bit put off by it. Rather than reacting as a native westerner might to the fact that Lance was a half-breed, Randolph found the idea intriguing. He grew anxious to meet him and thank him for saving his daughter from almost certain death.

Though Eleanor took no notice of Lance's absence, Trista began to wonder where he was. She hadn't seen him since they'd parted in his room last night, and she wanted desperately to set things straight between them. She wanted to tell him that she did love him and that she had decided not to go through with her marriage to Michael.

Trista knew she owed it to Michael to break the news to him first that she wanted to call off the wedding. Yet with the excitement of her father's arrival, she feared that she wouldn't get the opportunity to speak with Michael alone until the following day. That troubled her. She didn't want to have Lance believing her to be as ugly a person as she had seemed last night any longer than necessary.

Trista also feared that at any moment Eleanor might bring up the subject of the wedding. She knew that the older woman was quite excited about the whole thing and would no doubt want the ceremony performed just as quickly as possible. Her anxiety over the situation kept her tense and on edge all afternoon as they passed the hours in friendly conversation, her father taking the time to get to know George and to learn all about his operation of the ranch.

"Well, now that you've arrived, Randolph" — Eleanor finally broached the subject Trista had been dreading — "we can proceed with the wedding plans."

"By all means," he replied heartily. During the hours of visiting, he'd come to admire and respect the Barretts, and he had grown even more fond of Michael.

Michael had been dreading discussing the subject of the wedding and had been mentally preparing himself to skirt the issue when it came up in any way that he could. He was anxious to speak with Trista about all that he'd witnessed last night, but he could foresee no moment in the near future when they would have the privacy needed.

"Listen," Michael cut in boldly, addressing Randolph alone, "why don't we discuss that later, after you've had a chance to settle in? I'm sure you'd probably like to rest up before we begin to fill you in on all the details."

Trista had never been so relieved in her life. She fervently hoped her delight at Michael's changing the subject didn't reflect too openly in her expression.

"That's a good idea," she put in hastily. "It's almost dinnertime anyway."

"Perhaps you're both right," Eleanor agreed sweetly, unaware of the undercurrents of the situation. "Michael can show you to your room, and then we can talk more about it over dinner."

"That'll be fine," Randolph responded as he stood and followed Michael and Trista from the room.

Striking Snake looked at the warrior who'd just returned from scouting out the way to the ranch and frowned. "There are white men dressed as warriors ahead?"

He nodded in reply as he pointed out the direction. "Just over the rise. I do not know why, but they are disguising themselves to look like some of our people."

Striking Snake smiled venomously as he quickly understood the white men's devious ways . . . dress like Indians and allow them to take the blame for their actions. "Come, we will find out the reason and then teach them of real Comanche ways."

The small band of murderous braves headed directly for Poker's unsuspecting camp. Without any warning except for the whooping of their war cries, they attacked. With Striking Snake in the lead, they rode straight into the whites' hiding place.

Diving for cover, Poker and his companions tried to escape the surprise attack by the savages, but they were cut off from their horses and unable to flee to safety. The area was slightly hilly, but afforded little in the way of real protection.

The renegade Comanche enjoyed riding down the panicked white men and killing them on the spot. Only Striking Snake wanted to take a man alive. He wanted to find out the true reason for their disguises.

On foot, the hapless Poker could not elude the fierce warrior on horseback, and he was quickly subdued and taken captive. Striking Snake tied his arms brutally behind his back and threw him to the ground. Calling out to his men to join him, he turned toward his captive, the glint in his eyes clearly revealing his deadly intent.

Poker watched helplessly as the barbarous-looking brave came toward him. He felt naked and vulnerable, dressed as he was like an Indian, and he fervently prayed for rescue. Knowing that he faced certain death, he began to shake, and he cowered before the powerful warrior.

Striking Snake stalked menacingly toward the white man and stopped before him. Hands on hips, he stood with his legs braced apart staring down at the shivering Poker.

"Why are you dressed as one of us?" Striking Snake demanded as he pulled his wicked-looking knife from its sheath in his waistband. The blade glinted in the fading sunlight.

Poker swallowed nervously as his gaze followed the path of the knife, and he found he was unable to speak.

"You are unwilling to speak?" Striking Snake questioned in a cold voice as he pressed the weapon to Poker's chest, allowing the point to draw blood. "I have many ways to convince you to tell me all you know."

"What do you want to know?" Poker stammered, feeling the bite of the knife.

"Where are you going in such a disguise?"

"The ranch . . ." he managed.

"What ranch?" Striking Snake pressed the blade more firmly against him. Poker wriggled desperately, trying to get away, but the gathered warriors only laughed at he feeble efforts.

"The Barrett spread. We were hired to kill the breed. . . ."

At the mention of the breed, he stopped his torture. "Who is this 'breed' of whom you speak, white man?"

"His name is Lance . . . Lance Barrett."

Striking Snake found it amusing that someone else hated Lance as much as he did. "You have done well." He nonchalantly wiped the blood from the blade of his knife and put it back in his waistband.

"I can go now?" Poker was incredulous.

Striking Snake turned his back on the weak-willed man. He had little respect for anyone who surrendered so easily. In Comanche tongue, he told his companions, "He is yours. I will wait for you beyond the hill. From there we can see the ranch."

"Wait . . . wait . . . am I free?" A horrified scream followed Poker's last words as he was set upon by the

411

bloodthirsty Comanche.

Striking Snake paid no attention as the man was put to a grisly death. Mounting up, he rode in the direction of the ranch. He crested the nearby rise and sat there in the growing darkness staring out in the direction of the Diamond. When the raid was through tonight, Lance would be dead, and he would have the woman he'd long desired.

Trista obsessed him, and he knew he could not rest until he'd had her. Tonight would be the night; he was sure of it. As his companions joined him, they put their heels to their mounts and headed toward the ranchhouse still some miles away.

Chapter Twenty-seven

Trista has just left her father and had started down the hall toward her own bedroom to freshen up when Michael appeared at the top of the stairs.

"Trista?" His mood was somber and his manner subdued. "I was wondering if we could talk."

Puzzled by the unexpected seriousness of his request, she quickly assented. "Of course. Is something wrong? You look worried. . . ." she went to him.

Michael avoided her questions as he led her downstairs. "I think we can be alone if we go outside in the garden."

"All right." She'd noticed his hesitancy in answering her and knew that something had to be troubling him deeply for him to be so solemn.

They passed through the house without notice and walked side by side to the privacy of the garden. The memories of the fight there the night before came back to haunt her. She had not seen Lance all day, and she wondered distractedly where he was as she waited for Michael to speak.

"There's something I've been meaning to talk with you about for some time now. I've been waiting for the right moment, and yet it seems the right moment never comes. . . ." He sounded distressed.

"I don't understand," Trista ventured slowly, suddenly fearing that he knew all about the nights she'd spent making love with Lance. "What is it that's bothering you?"

"Trista . . . about last night . . ."

"Yes?"

"Trista," he began again, growing more and more nervous at the thought of bringing up what he'd seen. Last night he'd believed that she'd fallen in love with Lance, but now that he had the opportunity to face her, he wondered if indeed that was true. A doubt filled him. What if he faced her with this, and she denied feeling anything for Lance? What would he do about Sukie then? He cleared his throat to start once more. "Last night, before I heard you scream for help, I was in the study refilling my drink. . . ."

"Yes, I know. We had agreed to meet in the garden afterward. . . ." she supplied, wondering at the direction of his thoughts.

"Well, while I was in the study I happened to see you with Lance." There, he thought, it's out.

Trista paled for a moment, and then a deep flush stained her cheeks.

"I saw the two of you kissing. It didn't appear to me that you were fighting him or that he was attacking you as Ace and Dan would have me believe."

"I see," she said softly. Trista wasn't sure if now was the time for total truth or if she should try to lie to save Michael's feelings. Before she had to make the decision, Michael went on.

"Trista, I need to know the truth before we go any further with our plans. Is Lance the one you love? I know he considers you his wife. Tell me, Trista. How do you feel about him? How do you feel about me?"

Trista searched his earnest gaze for anger or despair, but saw none. His expression seemed guarded, but not condemning. All day she'd hoped for the opportunity to speak with him about her feelings for Lance, and she knew that now the time had come.

"I'm sorry, Michael. I'm sorry about all of this. . . ."

"What are you sorry for?"

"I care about you. I really do, but Lance . . ." She faltered, still timid about openly admitting her love for him.

"But Lance is the man you love?" Michael finished for her.

Trista nodded. "Yes. I do love him, Michael. I knew I would have to speak with you about this sooner or later. I knew I couldn't go through with our marriage feeling the way I did about him, but I cared for you so deeply that I didn't want to hurt you. . . ." When Michael smiled wryly, her expression reflected her puzzlement. "You're smiling! I don't understand. . . ."

"I've been wanting to talk with you, too."

"You have?"

"Yes, you see I care for you deeply, too, but there's someone else I've come to love. . . ."

"There is?" Trista brightened at this surprising news. "Michael, that's wonderful! Who is it?"

"It's Sukie Harris," he confided.

"She's a lovely girl. . . ." Trista remembered her well from their introduction at the engagement party. "How does she feel about you?"

"Well, it's really strange." Michael wanted to explain everything to Trista. "Sukie and I have known each other since childhood, and I never knew she harbored any love for me until just recently. It came as a complete surprise, but I was already engaged to you. Then with the kidnapping and all . . . I figured you needed me more than ever. I love you, Trista, and if you think we should marry, I know we could make a go of it. . . ."

Trista was touched by his offer. "Michael, the reason I came to love you as I do is because you are a

415

very special man." She smiled tenderly as she spoke. "But we both have found the true loves of our lives, and I think we owe it to ourselves to grab that happiness and hold on to it with all our might."

Michael lifted a hand to touch her cheek. "You are a very special woman, Trista Sinclair. Lance is a lucky man to have your love."

Her happy expression faltered as she thought of the terrible way they'd parted the night before. "I don't know if he still loves me, though."

"Why? What do you mean?"

"We had an argument last night. . . ."

"It's none of my business what you argued about, but there's one thing you should know. My father loved Lance when he was a child, but he let him go live with the Comanche anyway. It was a mistake he's regretted all his life. If you love Lance, then you go get him, Trista. He's a good man, and I think he loves you deeply."

"You do?"

"Why else would he have risked his life to come here after you? He's had many years to return to the Diamond, if that was what he wanted. He didn't come back here to claim his heritage. He came back here to claim his wife. I don't think Lance exchanged those vows with you lightly, Trista. You have to go to him and tell him what you just told me."

"And you . . . what will you do?"

Michael grinned wickedly. "Well, we can break the news to my mother tonight before she sets our wedding up for tomorrow at daybreak, and then first thing in the morning I'm going to ride over to the Harris place and see if Sukie will have me."

"You are so wonderful. I was so afraid when we had this conversation that I would be hurting you."

Michael took her in his arms. "You could never

hurt me, sweetheart," he told her as he clasped her warmly to his chest. "I want only your happiness, Trista."

Drawing back slightly, he claimed her lips in one last kiss, unaware that Lance had just started toward the house from the stables and could see them. Lance stopped dead in his tracks for a moment and then continued on his way into the house.

Lance was filled with a mixture of regret, anger, and jealousy as he mounted the stairs to go to his room. Tonight would be his last meal with his father. He knew he had no future here on the Diamond. He would tell his father after dinner tonight that he was leaving the ranch and returning to his life with Lone Elk. He had tried his best to win Trista's love, but he knew now it was impossible. She would only be happy with Michael.

It was the dark period of night between sunset and moonrise that afforded them the greatest protection, and Striking Snake knew it was time for the raid to begin. From their observation point, he could see that there was little remaining activity at the ranchhouse. Two lookouts had been posted about the main group of buildings, but Striking Snake knew they posed no problem. As long as surprise was on their side, the guards could be easily killed without drawing any attention.

The lack of preparedness pleased him. It seemed that Lance had forgotten much during his time with the whites, especially how to be constantly on guard against the unexpected, and their attack would certainly be unexpected. He smiled into the darkness at the thought of finally besting Lance.

Giving the hand signal to the men he'd positioned

near the guards, Striking Snake motioned them on. Soundlessly, within moments both unsuspecting white men were dead. Onward the Comanche crept, ready to do battle.

Eleanor was a bit nervous about what was going to take place that night. Her plan was proceeding perfectly, and she hoped within a matter of hours all her problems would be solved. Despite her edginess, she presided over dinner as usual, engaging Randolph in inconsequential conversation. She'd noted a new ease in Michael and Trista's relationship and believed it to be the result of knowing that their wedding would soon take place. Eleanor felt almost lighthearted in spite of Lance's brooding presence at the far end of the table.

Michael was overjoyed with his newfound discovery of Trista's love for Lance. He was particularly pleased that they had discussed their feelings before the marriage so that no one was hurt in the long run. He could hardly wait for the appropriate time to break the news to his mother so he could begin his active pursuit of Sukie. Time seemed to be passing much too slowly to him, and he ardently wished the meal would end so he could take his mother aside and tell her what had happened.

But while Michael was delighted with the way things had turned out, Trista still had her doubts about his claim that Lance truly loved her. She was relieved that everything had worked out so well with Michael, but as she sat at the table secretly observing Lance, it seemed to her that they would never be close again. He didn't look her way during the meal, and his mood was almost surly as he responded to her father's polite inquiries and thanks.

Still, there could be no denying that her heartbeat had quickened when he'd entered the room. Even

418

though he seemed so coldly remote, she longed to go into his arms right now and proclaim her love to him. Caught up in her own daydreams, Trista wondered vaguely just how everyone would react if she did. She fought down a smile at the thought of Eleanor's, no doubt, hysterical reaction. Restraining herself, she knew she had to bide her time until Michael could speak with his parents alone.

The attack, when it came, was so unexpected and so vicious, no one had time to respond to the deadly threat. Led by Striking Snake, the band of warriors rushed into the dining room, catching everyone completely by surprise.

"Striking Snake!" Lance came to his feet first as he recognized his enemy, but unarmed, he was no match for the raiding Indian.

Without pause, the evil warrior lifted his gun and fired. Lance was struck a glancing blow in the head by the bullet. Knocked backward by the force, he fell and lay lifelessly on the dining room floor.

"Lance!" Trista screamed in horror as she saw him struck in the head by the bullet.

She thought him dying and tried to race to his side, but Striking Snake was too quick for her. With bruising force, he grabbed her up around the waist and started to drag her from the room.

"NO! I have to go to Lance! He's hurt! Let me go!!!" she cried, fighting tooth and nail to be freed from the savage's punishing hold.

But Striking Snake only laughed viciously in her ear. "I told you that you would one day be mine. Now he is dead, and you will know *my* touch!"

Striking Snake's shot set the others into motion. As Michael and Randolph attempted to give chase, a hail of bullets filled the room, and the two men dove for cover. But neither George nor Eleanor had a chance as both were hit.

The Comanche knew they had to act, and act quickly, for the gunfire had no doubt alerted others on the ranch to their presence. Racing from the house, they opened the gate to the corral just as several hands came running from the bunkhouse. They fired at the whites, driving them back inside, as they made off with the horses in the enclosure.

Striking Snake threw Trista roughly over his shoulder and then ran toward his own mount. In one easy motion, he vaulted onto his horse's back and was off. Following the rest of his men, who'd already made their escape, he disappeared into the night quite pleased with himself and the bounty he'd taken.

Randolph and Michael got to their feet slowly, gazing in shocked disbelief at the destruction around them. Rosalie rushed into the room to help and screamed when she saw the carnage wreaked by the raiding party. Her presence stirred Michael into action, and he dropped on his knees beside his mother's still form.

"Mother . . ." he murmured as he turned her over in his arms. He could barely fathom that she was dead, shot through the heart, and he stared down at her in mute confusion.

"Lance!" Rosalie had hurried to his side as Randolph had gone to see if George had survived the attack. With the utmost care, Rosalie knelt beside Lance and lifted his head onto her lap. From the amount of blood that covered him, she feared he, too, was dead, but when he groaned, she cried out her happiness. "Michael! Lance is alive. . . ."

"So is George," Randolph added. "Where can we take them? Is there a doctor nearby?"

Michael hurried to Randolph's side and examined the wound in his father's shoulder. Two inches more to the center and Michael knew his father would have been killed, just like his mother. Snatching up some napkins off the table, he wadded them up and pressed them firmly to the wound.

"We have to get them upstairs. Then I'll send someone to town to get the doctor. . . ." Michael managed. "How bad is Lance?"

"It looks terrible. . . ." Rosalie dabbed nervously at Lance's head wound, thinking him near death.

Michael instructed Trista's father to keep pressure on George's injury as he raced to Rosalie's side to see to Lance. Just as he knelt beside her to take a close look at the bullet wound, Lance opened his eyes. Lance had trouble focusing for a moment, but eventually the double vision cleared, and he saw Michael and Rosalie hovering over him.

"Trista . . ." he croaked painfully. "Where's Trista?"

"Don't worry now. Just lie still. . . ." Michael tried to calm him, but Lance would have none of it.

Angrily, Lance grabbed hold of his forearm as he jockeyed himself to a sitting position. "Where is she? Did Striking Snake kill her?"

"No . . . she's not dead. . . ." Michael did not think he was in any condition to handle the truth.

"Tell me, Michael! I want to know the truth! Where is she? Trista!" he called out her name, his desperation obvious in his strangled tone.

"Easy, Lance . . . easy . . ." Again he tried to restrain him. "He took her."

"Striking Snake took her. . . ." he repeated dumbly as he lifted a shaking hand to his forehead. "And Father?"

"He's been shot, and it looks bad. My mother—" His voice broke as he was about to relate what had happened to her.

Lance struggled to his feet, fighting dizziness and nausea, and saw that Eleanor was dead and beyond any help they could give her. Staggering, he made his way to George's side. "We've got to do something for him. . . ." He looked to Michael.

"Randolph and I are going to get him upstairs into bed and—"

As he was speaking, Whitey and Tommy came charging through the front door, guns in hand.

"Are you all right?" The sight of Lance standing there covered with blood, and George unconscious on the floor stopped them. Then they saw Eleanor where she lay, unmoving. "I'll send a man for the doctor. . . ."

"Tell them it's an emergency. It's too late for my mother, but Pa's still alive. It looks pretty bad, though. . . ." Michael told them as he helped Randolph lift George and carry him from the room.

Lance started to follow, but Rosalie took his arm. "You can be of no help to them now. Come with me. . . ."

He offered no protest as she led him out into the kitchen and told him to sit at the table there. With practiced care, she cleansed the wound. When the bleeding finally stopped, she bound it tightly.

"Thank God he didn't shoot any straighter. . . ." Rosalie breathed as she put the finishing touches on the bandage.

"It's not like Striking Snake to miss. . . ." Lance replied distractedly, trying to ignore the pounding in his head.

"You knew those savages?" Rosalie was taken aback.

"Yes," he replied grimly, guilt sweeping through him. "I know the leader."

"Why did he attack us?"

422

"Vengeance, Rosalie," Lance explained as simply as he could. "He hated me, and he wanted Trista for himself."

She nodded as she remarked slowly, "He probably believes you are dead. . . ."

A determined look crossed his strained features. "That's good. Now the element of surprise will be on my side. . . ." He got to his feet.

"You can't mean you're going after them alone?"

He shot her a fierce look. "I'm going after them, all right, and when I find Striking Snake, I'm going to kill him. . . ." Without another word, he walked steadily from the room.

Upstairs, Michael and Randolph fought to bring his father's bleeding under control. When Lance entered, followed slowly by Rosalie, Michael looked up.

"You're all right?" he asked.

"I'm fine." Lance dismissed his worry. "How is he?"

"I think he'll make it if I can get this bleeding stopped. Whitey's already sent for the doctor. He should be here early tomorrow if he's in town when they get there."

Lance stared down at his father's pale features for a long moment before declaring, "I'm going after them."

"Now?"

"Now," he answered firmly.

"But I want to go with you. . . ." Michael was torn. He wanted desperately to help rescue Trista, but the knowledge that his father might die if he left him held him bound to the house.

"No. You stay here and take care of him," Lance told him solemnly. "I know how Striking Snake thinks, and I'll be better able to track him alone."

"Alone? You can't possibly go alone. Take all the men you need, and all the guns, too. . . ."

"No." He was firm. "I'll travel faster alone. This is

something I have to do by myself."

"Let me go with you," Randolph offered, fearing for his daughter's safety.

"No, sir." Lance turned to address him. "I can't afford to let anyone slow me down. Stay here, where it's safe. They won't be back. Striking Snake was only after two things, and right now he believes he's gotten them both."

"He's right, Randolph." Michael defended Lance's position when Trista's father would have argued the point further.

"But my daughter—"

"Your daughter couldn't have a better man go after her," Michael said earnestly, his eyes on Lance. "He is, after all, her husband."

"What? I thought you and Trista . . ." Randolph was shocked by this revelation as he looked from brother to brother.

"I'll explain it all to you later once Lance has gone," he told him. "Lance, she loves you. Go get her."

Lance was just about as shocked as Randolph had been by his brother's earlier statement. "What are you talking about?"

"Trista and I had a long talk before dinner, and she admitted that she loves you. I've sensed it ever since you returned. . . ."

"She does?" He still found that hard to believe after what she'd done the night before.

Michael nodded his confirmation. "She was going to tell you that the wedding was off later tonight after I'd spoken with my mother. . . ." The realization of Eleanor's death hit him full-force then, and he couldn't go on.

Lance went to him, and for the first time, they embraced as brothers. "I'm sorry about your mother, Michael. . . ."

Emotion choked him, and he couldn't respond just then.

"But what about you and Trista, Michael?" Lance asked.

"I care deeply about her, Lance," he told him when he'd pulled himself together, "but Sukie Harris is the woman I love. You and Trista were meant to be together. Go find her, Lance."

Their gazes met in silent understanding, and their hands clasped in a bond of friendship and mutual respect. Then Lance turned to Trista's father, who was still totally bewildered by all that had been said.

"I'll find her, and I'll bring her back," he pledged. To his brother he said, "Take care of Father, Michael. . . ."

"I will."

With that Lance was gone, heading back to his own room to get ready to leave.

Trista fought against Striking Snake's overpowering strength until she became totally exhausted. Riding before him on his horse, crushed against his chest, seemed a nightmare revisited. She could do nothing but hang there in his hated grasp.

Lance was dead! The thought pounded through her mind and, with each passing mile, drove her deeper and deeper into a black vortex of mindless depression. Her will to survive faded with her strength. Trista knew what her fate would be in Striking Snake's hands, and she wished that death would claim her first.

They rode for hours through the black gloom of the night. One by one the other warriors drifted off in different directions so that anyone trying to follow would have multiple trails to confuse them. It was an old Comanche trick, but an effective one.

Striking Snake was immensely satisfied with the way things had turned out. He headed back toward Comanche land knowing that few white men would dare follow him onto Lone Elk's land. On through the darkness he raced, putting as much distance between himself and the Diamond as he could. He didn't feel threatened by the thought of a posse from the ranch, for everyone knew what poor trackers most of the whites were. Had Lance been alive, he might have been more cautious, but Striking Snake felt certain that he'd killed him with a single, clean shot to the head.

The sky was beginning to brighten in the east when he finally slowed his pace to give his horse a rest. Heading to the northwest, he made his way toward a secluded box canyon that was seldom frequented by his people. He knew he could set up camp there and be alone with Trista for as long as he liked.

Thinking of Trista, he wondered why all the fight had gone out of her so easily. He had found her feistiness perversely appealing and resented that she was now lifeless in his arms. Determined to get a response out of her, he deliberately covered one round breast with his hand and brutally squeezed its plumpness.

Trista had only been halfway conscious of what was happening, having long ago lost interest in her situation. She did not want to react to anything that Striking Snake did, for she knew that he reveled in getting a response out of her. Gritting her teeth, she fought against the pain of his tormenting hand.

When she merely stiffened against him, Striking Snake grew irritated. Resolved to force her to fight him, he slipped his marauding hand lower to cover the softness of her stomach, his fingers resting tanta-

426

lizingly near the juncture of her thighs.

Trista longed to pull herself free of him, to kill him as he'd killed Lance, but she had no weapon to use and little force to deal with him otherwise. All she could do to stop him was to throw in his face the fact that she was having her monthly flux. She remembered in the village that the women were considered untouchable during that time and that men were forbidden contact with them. Though she didn't care about living without Lance, she certainly didn't want to suffer at Striking Snake's hands any more than necessary.

"You would be wise to keep your hands off of me," she told him in a low voice.

Striking Snake laughed haughtily at what he thought was her attempt to dissuade him from taking what he had long desired from her. "Do not tell me what to do, woman. You will be mine soon . . . very soon."

"I think not, Striking Snake," she returned, and she gasped as he clutched at her viciously.

"We will see," he said pompously.

"It is my time," she said evenly. "Is it not true that even the bravest of Comanche warriors is in danger of losing his power if he touches a woman during her monthly flow?"

At her statement, he quickly withdrew his hands from her, cursing her soundly in his native tongue. If what she said was true, it might be days before he could take his full pleasure of her. Still, knowing that Lance was dead and that there was no one who posed much of a threat coming after her, he was not greatly disturbed by the news.

"If this is so, then I will just have to wait to make you mine, Trista. All that really matters is that I have killed Lance and taken you. The rest will come with

427

time."

Trista realized that she had gained a reprieve, but only a minor one. Her fate was sealed. She was doomed to Striking Snake's domination. All she could hope was that somehow, some way she might be able to escape, not that she believed she might make it back to safety, but any kind of death would be preferable to suffering the evil warrior's endless torture.

Chapter Twenty-eight

"What!?" Sukie cried, aghast.

"There was a Comanche raid at the Barretts' last night, Miss Sukie," Rusty Taggert, the foreman of her ranch, informed her. The news had traveled quickly, and most of the neighbors had already been alerted to the possible danger.

"Was anyone hurt?" Mary Lou demanded as she came to stand beside her daughter on the porch of the Harris homestead.

"I only know for a fact that Mrs. Barrett was killed—"

"Oh, dear God! No, not Eleanor . . ." Mary Lou looked stricken and faint, and Sukie quickly put a supporting arm about her waist.

"But Michael . . . what about Michael?" Sukie demanded fiercely, needing desperately to know how he was. Her heart constricted at the thought that he, too, might have been killed.

"I don't know any more than what I've already told you, Miss Sukie," he apologized.

Sukie gave her mother a determined look. "We have to go there, Mother. We have to help them. I have to know. . . ."

Mary Lou recovered enough from the shocking news to agree with her daughter. "We'll leave as soon as we've gathered up some supplies. If things are as bad as I think they are, they'll be needing them," she told her daughter before turning back to the foreman. "Have the buggy brought around. We're going to the Diamond."

"Yes, ma'am," he agreed. "I'll also get a couple of men to ride along with you. It might not be safe for you to ride unescorted."

"Thank you, Rusty. We'll be ready when your men are."

Within the hour they were on their way to the Barrett spread ladened with supplies they thought might be needed. With every passing mile, Sukie grew more and more nervous. All she could think about was Eleanor's death and the possibility that Michael had been killed, too.

Sukie cursed herself soundly for having turned Michael away the other night at the party. She had wanted him so badly, and yet she had denied both him and herself in a fit of pride. Silently Sukie swore that if Michael was alive, she would never refuse him again.

Michael paced the upstairs hall as he anxiously awaited the doctor's findings. Dr. Spalding had arrived shortly after daybreak and had immediately rushed to George's side. Once he'd seen the extent of the gunshot wound and witnessed Michael's upset, he had banished him from the room so he and Rosalie could tend the unconscious George without interruption. That had been almost an hour ago, and Michael was still in emotional limbo as he waited to learn his father's fate.

Though Michael heard someone pull up in front of the house, he thought it was just some of the hired hands and paid little real attention. All his energy was focused on his father's survival.

Mary Lou and Sukie exchanged worried looks as they noted the carriage tied up in front of the house.

"That's Doc Spalding's buggy, isn't it, Mother?" Sukie asked, growing more tense by the minute.

"It looks like it. . . ."

Sukie couldn't wait any longer. As soon as her mother reined in, she jumped down in a most unlady-like manner and rushed up the steps to the door. She knocked loudly—frightened, yet needing to know the truth of all that had happened.

Whitey had come up to the house to wait for news of his boss's condition, and he quickly answered the door. "Why, Miss Sukie . . . Mrs. Harris . . ."

"How is he, Whitey?" Sukie demanded, moving on inside without waiting for an invitation.

"It's serious, Miss Sukie," he answered, thinking she was asking about George. "We don't know yet if he's gonna make it or not."

"Oh, no . . ." She swayed on her feet, and Mary Lou led her into the parlor to sit down.

"Then it's worse than what we had heard. . . ." Mary Lou glanced at the foreman as she helped Sukie to a chair. "How soon will you know anything?"

"I wish I knew, ma'am," he replied, shaking his head defeatedly. "The doc's with him now, and he's been up there over an hour."

"And Eleanor?"

"I'm sorry, Mrs. Harris." He hung his head in sorrow. "I know you were close friends. . . ."

Mary Lou was so stricken with grief that she could only nod in acknowledgement of his expression of regret.

"And the others . . . Where's Trista?" Sukie managed.

Whitey looked puzzled for a moment and then realized that they probably didn't know what had happened. "The Comanche took her with them. Lance went after them to try to bring her back. He left last night."

This news stunned them even more deeply. It seemed almost impossible to believe that any of this had taken place. The raid was hideous enough, but to think that Trista had been taken again . . .

Michael had been so worried about his father that he didn't notice those who'd entered the house below. Only when he heard Sukie's voice did he hurry to the top of the stairs.

"How's George taking it?" Mary Lou ventured, wondering at his absence.

Whitey frowned at their obvious misunderstanding of what was going on, and he was about to explain when Michael came down the steps and stopped at the parlor door.

"Sukie?" He could hardly believe that she was here, in his home.

"Michael!?" Sukie was on her feet in an instant and ran to him without hesitation. Throwing her arms about his wide shoulders, she held him tight as she pressed slightly hysterical kisses all over his throat. "Michael . . . you're all right . . . you weren't shot. . . you're here. . . ." She was crying in happiness.

Michael was confused by her actions, but he tightened his arms about her, not wanting to waste the opportunity to hold her close. "Of course I'm all right. Why did you think otherwise?" He glanced over to Whitey, who looked as befuddled as he was.

"Whitey said that you were in serious condition. . . ." Sukie explained, drawing slightly away to look up at him. Her eyes were wide and luminous, and were brimming with tears of joy.

"No, Miss Sukie. George is the one the doc is with,"

Whitey corrected.

"And it seems as if he's been in there forever. . . ." Michael added as he looked back up the steps toward the ominously closed bedroom door.

"Michael, we just thank heaven you're fine." Mary Lou came to him, too. "What really happened last night? Everything we've heard is so confusing. . . ."

Michael briefed them on the terrible trauma of the past evening. "Pa was so bad, I couldn't leave him," he concluded, "so Lance went after Trista alone."

"If anyone can find her, he will," Whitey put in.

"I hope so," Michael began, intending to tell Sukie all about Lance's love for Trista. He could hardly wait to tell her that he and Trista had called their wedding off and that he was now free to marry her. But just as he began, the door to George's bedroom opened and Dr. Spalding came out.

"Michael?"

The solemnity of his tone caused Michael to stiffen perceptibly as he moved away from Sukie. "Down here, Doc . . ."

Dr. Spalding, a tall, distinguished, gray-haired man, looked exhausted as he came downstairs to speak with him. His sleeves were rolled up past his forearms, and bloodstains marred the front of his shirt.

Michael met him at the bottom of the staircase. "How is he, Doc?" His eyes were dark with concern, and his manner was uncertain as he tried to read the physician's expression.

"It looked bad there for a while, Michael, but your quick thinking last night no doubt saved his life."

"Oh, Michael." Sukie breathed a sigh of relief as she came forth to take his arm in a cherishing, supportive gesture.

"He's going to be all right?"

"It'll be slow going for a while, but he should make it as long as infection doesn't set in."

"Thank God," Michael murmured, struggling to control his runaway emotions. He had barely been able to contain his grief over his mother's death, and he had been horribly afraid that he was going to lose his father, too. The realization that his father was going to live swept through him in a wave of relief. He turned to Sukie and embraced her tearfully. "Can I see him now?" he asked when he'd released her.

"Yes. He's awake, but he's very weak. I haven't told him anything. I thought it would be better if I left that up to you."

Michael tensed at the thought that he would have to be the one to tell his father of his mother's death, but he knew it was his duty. "I'll go on up." He looked down at Sukie and lifted a hand to caress the softness of her cheek. "Don't leave. Wait for me, darling. . . ."

Misty-eyed, she nodded. "I'll stay as long as you want me to, Michael."

Unmindful of the others, he bent to her and kissed her sweetly before hurrying up the steps to see to his father. Sukie turned back to her mother, her expression mirroring her love for Michael and her confusion over his openly loving actions.

"Let's go back in the parlor. I'm sure Michael will come down and fill us in on George's condition just as soon as he can," Mary Lou encouraged.

Just as Michael started down the hall to the room, Rosalie emerged. "Michael, good . . . He's anxious to see you now."

"How is he, Rosalie?" he asked worriedly. In all his years, Michael had never seen his father laid low by anything, and he found the thought of him wounded and near death slightly unnerving.

"He's weak, but I think he'll be all right. He knows

nothing about your mother, and he keeps asking about Lance. I avoided all his questions as best I could, but you're going to have to tell him. . . ."

"I know." As she patted him comfortingly on the shoulder, he moved past her into the bedroom.

His fight for life having drained much of his vitality from him, George looked pale and very old as he lay on the big double bed. For a moment Michael thought he'd fallen back asleep, but at the sound of the bedroom door closing, his eyes opened and he focused on his son.

"Michael . . ." His tone was barely above a whisper. "You're all right?"

Michael went quickly to his bedside. "I'm fine, Pa. I wasn't injured at all. Neither was Randolph."

George only nodded slightly, but the effort cost him much. "Lance . . . is he . . . ?" He was obsessed with the need to find out if his oldest son had been murdered by the raiders. He had seen the shot hit him, and he was filled with anger and guilt at having been unable to protect him.

Michael knew that the last thing his father had seen before he was shot was Lance being wounded. He hastened to assure him that Lance had come to no lasting harm. "Lance is just fine. The bullet only grazed him. He didn't even need to see the doctor."

At that news, George drew a deep, steadying breath and closed his eyes as if in relief. "Good."

"Pa . . ." Michael knew he had to tell him of his mother's death, but he wasn't sure how to break it to him.

At the tentative sound of his voice, George sensed that there was something else . . . something terrible that Michael had to tell him. "Michael . . . what is it? What's happened?" Suddenly realizing that Eleanor hadn't been in, he knew. "It's your mother, isn't it?

435

Something's happened to her?"

The pain that he had held in check and denied all night long exploded within him. "She's dead, Pa, and I couldn't do anything to save her. . . ." he choked as he finally gave vent to his feelings. Burying his face in his hands, Michael wept.

"Your mother is dead?" George repeated dully as he watched Michael nod in response.

Tears of regret and sorrow filled George's eyes, and his heart grew heavy with the loss. He had loved Eleanor in his own way. It hadn't been the all-consuming passion he'd known with Shining Star, but she had been a good wife and a good mother to Michael. She had helped him to pull his life together after Shining Star's death, and though he had often thought that she had only married him for his money, it had never mattered. They had found a measure of happiness together, and they had been content.

Even in his weakened state, George felt a driving need to see both his sons together, and he reached out to grasp Michael's hand.

"What is it, Pa?"

"Get Lance. I want to talk with you both. . . ."

Michael had not wanted to tell him about the kidnapping, but his request left him no alternative. "Lance isn't here, Pa."

"What? Where did he go?"

He explained quickly about Trista's being taken and how Lance had known the warrior who'd come to steal her away.

"You must go after him. . . . You have to help him, Michael," he insisted. "Lance is your own flesh and blood. He's your brother."

"But I can't leave you."

"I'm going to be all right," George said in as stern a tone as he could manage. "Go . . . and bring them both safely back to me."

"I'll go as soon as I get everything ready."

Comforted, George closed his eyes, and the tension that had gripped him faded. "Good . . . good . . . I'll be waiting for you." He seemed to drift off to sleep then.

Michael remained in the room awhile longer to pull himself together before going downstairs to face Sukie and the others. At the sound of his approach, Sukie raced into the hall.

"Michael . . . how is he?" she asked as she noticed the signs of strain reflected on his handsome features.

"He's going to recover," he told her, glancing up at Mary Lou and Whitey as they came out of the parlor to join them.

"That's wonderful." Mary Lou was relieved.

"Whitey, as soon as I've made arrangements for my mother's burial, I'll be riding out after Lance. Get my horse ready and pack extra ammunition."

"Right away, Michael," he responded, hurrying off to do his bidding.

"Michael! You can't go! You're needed here." Sukie protested, still fearful of losing him.

Michael gave her a sweet/sad smile. "Sukie, I have to go. Lance is my brother. He might need me."

His response troubled her, and she looked at him questioningly. "I don't understand. . . . You're going because Lance needs you? What about Trista?"

"I think we need to have a long talk, love."

"Love?" Surprise registered on her lovely face, and he smiled tenderly.

"Yes, Sukie," he told her ardently right in front of her mother, "I love you."

"Michael! You can't know what you're saying. Trista—"

"Trista is in love with Lance, and he with her.

437

Luckily, we discovered the truth of our feelings before we went through with the wedding ceremony."

Sukie was completely dumbstruck by this revelation, and she could only stare up at him, her emerald eyes sparkling with happiness. "Oh, Michael," she finally breathed before she lost herself in his embrace. Hungrily, she lifted her lips to meet his in a pledge of undying love.

In the midst of all his pain, this one moment of beauty struck Michael deeply, its meaning bittersweet. He had just found his love, and now he had to leave her. He clasped her tightly to his chest. He felt jaded and weary, and she was so innocent and beautiful.

"I love you, Michael. I always have, and I always will."

"Wait for me, love. I've got to go help Lance find Trista, but I'll be back."

"I'll be here, Michael," Sukie promised, tears of happiness filling her eyes even as her heart ached for all the tragedy that surrounded them. "You go and help your brother. Find Trista and bring her home. I'll wait forever for you."

Michael stood over his mother's grave several hours later. He knew that Whitey was waiting nearby with his mount and pack horse, yet he found it difficult to leave. He knew he was needed here desperately, but he also knew that Lance could be in great danger. It had been foolhardy of his brother to go after the raiding party single-handedly, and Michael realized he could afford to waste no more time in following after him. He had to go.

"Sukie . . ." He turned to her as she stood by his side, supportively. "I'll return just as soon as I can."

"You just be careful," she ordered. "I've waited too

long to have you, to lose you now."

"Don't worry. I'll be back."

"Mother and I are going to stay here for a while. We thought Rosalie could use our help in nursing your father since he's so badly wounded."

"I'd really appreciate that."

"My darling, there is no appreciation involved in this. I love you. That's all that matters."

It occurred to him that he had never proposed to Sukie. Michael knew he could not leave without letting her know just how deep his feelings were for her. "Sukie . . ."

His tone was so serious, she glanced at him nervously. "What is it, Michael?"

"I know I've been taking this for granted, but . . . will you marry me? We can have the ceremony just as soon as I get back."

Sukie felt a rush of joy unlike anything she'd ever experienced before. "Oh, Michael! I love you so! Of course I will!"

They embraced then with tenderness and devotion before breaking apart.

"You'll tell Pa everything when he's better?" Michael implored, regretting that he wouldn't have the opportunity to tell him himself.

"As soon as he's strong enough I'll explain it all," Sukie promised.

Michael gave her a quick kiss, and then, after saying a quick farewell to Mary Lou, Randolph, and the doctor, he walked away from the grave, a solitary, but determined man.

"You be careful, Michael," Whitey instructed as he handed him the reins to his mount.

"I will, I'll—" He looked on down the trail and saw four men, mounted up and waiting for him. "What's this all about?"

439

"It's Tommy and some of the other men who are good at trackin'. They want to see them Comanche caught, too. They're goin' with you."

Michael was appreciative of the extra help. "All right. We'll get back as soon as we can . . . with Trista and Lance."

"I'll keep things runnin' here till your pa's on his feet again. You take care."

"I will," Michael said with grim resolve. Putting his heels to his horse's sides, he rode forth to speak with the other men. Then, together, they headed out in search of Lance.

Chapter Twenty-nine

In moon-bronzed splendor, horse and rider sat unmoving on the precipice of the hill. They were a magnificent pair — the bare-chested warrior and the golden stallion. Framed by the night as they were, they looked almost otherworldly. Only the telltale twitch of the horse's ears as he grew restless gave testimony to their true existence.

"Easy, Fuego." Lance spoke in low, calming tones to the powerful rogue. "She's out there. We just have to be certain that we know exactly where before we go charging in after her."

When the stallion snorted in annoyance, it was almost as if he'd understood his master's words. Lance bent low over his neck to stroke him reassuringly. Then, aggravated himself because there was no sign of a campfire in the distance, he turned Fuego around and guided him down to the tree-sheltered watering hole at the base of the hill, where he intended to make camp for the night.

Lance tethered Fuego near the water after he'd allowed the stallion to drink his fill, and then spread his blanket on a smooth bed of grass. He settled in, needing a few hours rest, but he lay staring up at the sky. Sleep was elusive again, as his worry over Trista's well-being grew unbounded.

Lance had stayed tight on their trail, but it was the end of his second day of tracking, and he felt that he was no closer to them than he had been in the beginning. Since Striking Snake thought him dead, he had expected the braggart warrior to grow careless during his flight, but that had not happened. Lance wasn't sure if the other man was aware that he was being followed, but he knew that Striking Snake certainly wasn't taking any chances on being discovered.

Frustrated, Lance closed his eyes and tried to blank all thought from his mind. Realizing that he would be of little use to Trista if he was totally exhausted when he finally found her, Lance forced himself to relax and to sleep. His last thought as he drifted off into a restless slumber was that there was nothing more he could do to help her until daylight, anyway.

Long miles away in Striking Snake's camp in the box canyon, Trista lay huddled in a blanket, bound hand and foot. When her captor had discovered the truth of her claim regarding the state of her monthly flux, he had picked up the pace of their flight and had hurried without stopping to the place where they were now camped. Since then, he had essentially left her alone. He'd bound her so she couldn't flee and then had remained a good distance away from her, never speaking to her and only negligently throwing her bites of food as a seeming afterthought.

Trista had been numb through the whole ordeal. She hated Striking Snake with every breath she took, and she wished there was some way she could get her hands on a weapon so she could kill him. Over and over in her mind, she witnessed Lance's death. Alone in the night, she cried endless tears for her lost love. Trista thought it tragic that she had never had the opportunity to tell him the truth of her love for him. She had come so close to true happiness, but it was lost to her forever now.

As she passed another sleepless night, Trista wondered how much longer she would be safe from Striking Snake. His patience wouldn't last forever, and she realized she would probably have the protection of her womanly condition for no more than another day or so.

The terror of being taken by the cruel brute sent shivers of dread through her. Trista knew from what she'd gone through in the beginning with Lance that she could be strong, but Lance had been so different from Striking Snake. In Lance there had been a chord of goodness, yet in this savage warrior she sensed only evil. He would physically force her into submission. He would slake his lecherous desires upon her whether she was willing or not. If she dared to defy him as she had Lance, Trista didn't doubt for a moment that he would beat her and possibly even kill her.

Shifting position, she rolled uncomfortably to her side and closed her eyes. It would be a long night and an even longer day tomorrow.

Lance guided Fuego carefully through the rocky terrain as he followed Striking Snake's trail through the badlands. He was familiar with this area, though he hadn't been here in some time, and he felt reasonably certain that he knew where Striking Snake had taken Trista. The box canyon that lay not far ahead was known by his people, but seldom used because of its isolated location. Lance reasoned it would be the perfect place to hide out, and it seemed logical to him, now that he had followed him this far, that Striking Snake was heading there.

Despite the ruggedness of the countryside, the thought of Trista helpless in the other warrior's savage captivity spurred Lance on to even greater speeds. Onward he rode, unmindful of the heat or the constant throbbing in his head from his wound. All that mattered was Trista. A man obsessed, Lance wanted only to save her from Striking Snake's savage possession.

It was late afternoon when he reached the canyon. Taking every precaution, he dismounted and went ahead on foot, leading Fuego behind him.

Striking Snake was irritated with his plight. Though he knew he had won in killing Lance and claiming Trista, he was restless over not having been able to enjoy the spoils of his triumph. He realized that he could not take her for at least another day, yet the knowledge that she was there in his camp and totally helpless filled him with the restless need to prove his domination over her.

He glanced toward where Trista sat on the far side of his camp. The golden beauty of her hair hung in wild disarray about her slender shoulders, and Striking Snake longed to run his hands though it. He had taken white women before, but never had one aroused him as Trista did. She was fire and spirit and totally woman, and he was aflame with desire for her. Only the fear that he would lose his powers if he touched her now held him back. Cursing under his breath at the weakness he had for her, he stood up and stalked off into the wilderness.

Lance had followed the stream that fed the canyon

444

and had come upon their camp a short time later. He had tied Fuego some distance away and had approached on foot. The sight of Trista tied and alone on the far side of the camp gave him hope that the rescue itself would not be too difficult. Only the confrontation with Striking Snake would be dangerous.

Tense and ready to do battle, he studied the layout of the encampment, wanting to make sure that Striking Snake was the only renegade there. He had found no sign that the other warriors had met up with him yet, but he knew he couldn't be too cautious. It was a matter of survival. It was a matter of life or death.

Steadily he took aim with his rifle, but when the brave suddenly left the camp for no apparent reason, his plan was thwarted. Frustrated, Lance waited and watched, trying figure out where Striking Snake had gone. As long moments passed and he didn't return, Lance knew he had to make a move anyway. With any luck, he calculated that he could get in and out of the camp with Trista in a matter of minutes.

Moving quickly, Lance made his way through the brush toward Trista, taking care to keep out of sight. He didn't know where Striking Snake was, and he did not want to risk a confrontation with Trista caught in the middle. He skirted the small clearing and didn't reveal himself to her until he was right behind her.

All day Trista had been aware of Striking Snake's growing restlessness. He had spent most of the morning simply glaring at her threateningly from his own place across the campsite, and she feared that her time of safety was nearing an end. In spite of her outward calm, her mood was almost hysterical, for no matter how hard she tried to insulate herself from the thought of his taking her against her will, she knew it would be horribly traumatic.

The last person Trista had expected to see was Lance. She believed him dead. She believed she would never again know the tender wonder of his embrace or be able to tell him of her love for him. Then he emerged from the brush, looking much as he had the first time she'd encountered him while chasing Fuego. Her eyes rounded in complete shock and she gasped his name in disbelief.

"Lance . . ."

Lance was thrilled to see her, but he firmly controlled his desire to sweep her into his arms and kiss her. He motioned for her to be quiet as he set about releasing her.

Trista's gaze clung to him, devouring the sight of him clad as the fierce warrior — the broad, muscular width of his chest and the powerful strength of his thighs. She had never, ever thought that she would rejoice at seeing a Comanche brave, but her heart and spirits soared. She had thought him dead. She had seen him shot, and yet . . . She lifted her gaze to stare at the bandage about his head and slowly grasped what had really happened.

"You're all right. . . ." Trista whispered faintly, lifting one hand toward his head after he'd freed her arms. But he ducked to avoid her touch as he moved to free her legs.

"Don't talk," he ordered tersely in low tones. Lance knew that Striking Snake had probably not gone very far, and he meant to be ready to face him when he returned. "Fuego is tied up a short ways down the creek. As soon as I've got these ropes off of you, I want you to move, and move fast."

446

"But why? Didn't anyone else come with you?" She glanced past him, looking for men from the ranch . . . for Michael.

"No. I came alone." At her worried expression, Lance doubted all that Michael had told him. "Don't worry, Michael is safe. Father was shot, and he stayed behind to take care of him. Now, if you'll just do what I say, we'll both get out of here alive."

"Why do you want me to go on alone? Why aren't you coming with me?"

"I have unfinished business to settle with Striking Snake. You go on. I'll follow later."

"I can't leave you! I won't!" she declared, fiercely and protectively.

"Trista . . ." he ground out as he glanced about the area for some sign of Striking Snake's imminent return, "you'll end up getting us both killed if you don't go . . . now."

Striking Snake had gone some distance before he realized the danger of leaving Trista so completely alone. He knew how resourceful she could be and was not prepared to lose her. Circling the camp, wanting to frighten her by reentering their camp from an unexpected direction, he headed back.

Striking Snake paused at the sight of the golden stallion tethered to a tree near the creek. As he studied Fuego, he realized, much to his disgust, that Lance must have survived the raid at the ranch. The only pleasure he got from the discovery was the knowledge that now he would be the one surprising Lance, and not the other way around. Edging closer to the stallion, Striking Snake released the tether and waved his arms in the horse's face, sending him racing away out of sight. He was satisfied that he had cut off Lance's only means of escape, and he drew his knife

447

as he started back toward the camp, vowing that this time he would cut out the other man's heart just to make sure he was dead.

Though Lance had been vigilant in watching for Striking Snake, his moment of inattention as he'd finished removing Trista's bonds had given the ferocious warrior the time he'd needed to work his way behind him. Knife in hand, he crept through the bushes intending to pounce on Lance, but Trista saw him and screamed. Her warning gave Lance just enough time to dodge the fatal blow that Striking Snake had aimed at his back. Both men tumbled in the dirt and came to their feet facing each other. Lance drew his own knife and circled his deadly opponent warily.

"So you have more than one life, Lance. . . ." Striking Snake sneered. "This time I will aim for your heart instead of your head."

"You have already shown that your aim is bad," Lance insulted him, moving backward away from Trista, wanting her to run for freedom. "I know little fear at your threats, Striking Snake."

At his remark, Striking Snake was filled with fury. Up until now Lance had beaten him in every one of their encounters, but this time he was determined to be the victor. He felt certain that Lance's head wound had to have weakened him, and he believed that just unceasing brute force would defeat him. Lunging, he sought to bury his knife in his chest, but Lance sidestepped him. Striking Snake recovered quickly from his missed assault, and he turned, ready to attack again.

Lance was outraged to see that Trista had not moved. "Get out of here, now!" he snarled, never taking his eyes off the aggressively closing Striking

Snake.

The evil warrior laughed. "Why do you tell her to run, Lance? Are you so sure that I will win?"

"You'll never beat me, Striking Snake. You are a coward. You have never won a fair fight in your life. Why do you think you will start now?"

Again he laughed. "I will win this time, Lance. You are wounded and weak. Your strength is like a woman's. I will win."

Lance lashed out at him, the wicked blade of his knife catching him in the upper arm. "Think again," Lance challenged. "I am not the only one wounded."

Though he had been startled by the quickness of Lance's movement, the wound was actually minor. It bled heavily and looked worse than what it really was. Striking Snake deliberately favored the injured arm to give the impression that it was a bad wound in hopes that his strength would take Lance by surprise.

"Today I will see you dead," he bragged.

Trista was unable to leave. She feared for Lance's safety against the brutal savage. Even now, with Striking Snake wounded, she would not run off and leave Lance alone. She held her breath as the two men thrust and parried, ever circling, always attempting to find a weakness.

Lance eluded his every assault. He knew he should be concentrating completely on Striking Snake and any possible devious moves he might make, but he couldn't take his mind off of Trista. He wished she would leave. He wanted to know that she was safely away.

"The woman is your weakness, Lance," Striking Snake taunted as he noticed the direction of his glance. "Why do you worry about her? Do you fear what I have done to her?"

"No!" Trista cried, not wanting Lance to think that he had touched her in any way.

Striking Snake chuckled evilly. "She is only a woman, Lance. They are all alike when they spread their thighs."

"Trista is my wife," Lance claimed ferociously as he charged at his foe.

"Soon, Lance, she will be your widow!" he scoffed, stepping away from his assault.

But this time Lance followed through on his attack, and they hit the ground hard, locked together in mortal combat. As the sun beat down upon them, they grappled fiercely. Their sun-bronzed, sweat-streaked bodies strained together in a dance of death as they rolled about, each trying to gain the advantage over the other. Blood from Striking Snake's wound stained them both, and their breathing grew labored. The blades of their knives flashed harshly in the sunlight. Muscles strained as they twisted and bucked, each seeking to dislodge the other and gain dominance.

Trista watched the brutal battle in horrified fascination. Fearful of distracting Lance, she said nothing. She remained tense and unmoving as the two men struggled before her.

Lance was more than holding his own with Striking Snake, and he managed to lever his weight so he came up fully on top of the other warrior. Striking Snake was humiliated to find that Lance was besting him again. His outrage at the possibility of suffering another defeat at his hands knew no bounds. Using all his strength in one last, desperate effort, he managed to throw Lance off of him momentarily.

Knowing that his strength was fading, Striking Snake looked around, seeking another way to win.

His gaze fell on Lance's rifle where it lay near Trista, and he rushed in her direction before Lance had time to come after him. Trista's scream of terror rent the air as Striking Snake snatched her cruelly into his arms and crushed her to his chest with brutal force. Facing Lance, he smiled as he pressed the blade of his knife to the delicate arch of her throat.

"Will you watch me kill her?" he challenged, his obsidian eyes never wavering from Lance. He enjoyed the desperation and frustration he saw reflected there.

"Let her go, Striking Snake."

"I may . . . after I tire of her," he leered, moving his hand to fondle her breast as Lance looked on.

Trista tried to jerk free, but Striking Snake forced the blade more tightly against her throat to still her objections to his touch.

"Striking Snake . . . you fight like a woman," Lance derided, hoping to draw him back into their own fight.

"It does not matter how I win this fight with you, Lance. It only matters that I win," he returned. "Throw your weapon aside now or I will kill her right here while you watch."

Lance was filled with torment as he looked from Trista's pale features to Striking Snake's flushed face. He realized with fury that his enemy was enjoying this.

"Don't do it, Lance. . . ." Trista cried, but her captor silenced her as he tightened his grip on her.

"Now, Lance," he threatened. It thrilled him to see Lance squirming as he obeyed his command.

"What are you going to do, Striking Snake?" Lance asked as he held his knife out away from his body and dropped it.

"Kick it away from you," he ordered, not bothering

to answer him.

Lance did as he was told, but remained tense and watchful, ready to spring at him if he got the chance.

Striking Snake could not believe that everything had worked out so well, and he edged backward, dragging Trista with him. He needed the rifle to carry out the rest of his plan, and he kept moving until he had it in sight. When he'd moved within reach of the gun, he loosened his hold on Trista for just an instant so he could snatch up the rifle.

Trista had been biding her time as she tried to figure out what Striking Snake was going to do. She realized he was after the gun when he started forcing her to move backward with him. When he eased his grip on her, she made her move, pushing away from him with all her might.

Striking Snake cursed her for her action as he managed to grab the gun, and he fired it quickly at Lance.

"The gun, Lance!" Trista cried as she broke free and darted away, throwing herself in front of him.

"Trista! NO!!!" Lance's cry was agonized as he saw the bullet meant for him hit Trista. She crumpled to the ground before him.

Striking Snake was stunned to see that it was Trista he'd hit. He took aim again, meaning to shoot Lance next, but Lance gave him no time. Lance gave no thought to his own safety as he lunged at him. This man had just shot the woman he loved. He would die! Rage pounded through his veins, and the desire for blood lust surged through him.

Striking Snake saw the deadly determination in Lance's eyes and nervously fired another round. Lance knocked the weapon aside just as he squeezed the trigger, and the bullet went wide. A cry of fear erupted from the cowardly warrior as the force of Lance's assault hurled him to the ground. Over and over Lance pummeled him with his fists, hammering away at him, giving him no time to fight back.

Trying to defend himself, Striking Snake attempted to block Lance's vicious, punishing blows, but to little avail. Blindly reaching out beside him with one hand, he tried to locate the knife he had dropped when he'd gone for the rifle. He was relieved when his hand closed over the hilt of the weapon, and with what strength he had left, he swung his arm up, intending to stab Lance.

Lance saw the blow coming, and he gripped the brave's wrist to force it away. Striking Snake let out a scream of pure fury as Lance foiled his last hope. Brute force battling brute force, they struggled to control the knife. Sweat beaded their brows as they fought over it, their muscles bulging in their final efforts to win the lethal encounter.

It happened in a blinding flash. One moment Striking Snake held the knife poised between them, and the next, his strength failed him and the blade plunged deep into his chest. He stared up at Lance in painful surprise.

'You think *you* have won, but this time *I* did," he seethed as his life ebbed from him. "Your woman is dead. . . ." With that, sprawled in the dirt like the merciless creature he was named for, he died.

The feeling of triumph that washed over him at the certainty of Striking Snake's death was quickly quelled as he remembered Trista. Agony tortured his soul, and he murmured a silent prayer as he ran to where Trista lay and dropped to his knees beside her. The wound in her side was an ugly one, and he feared she was already dead.

"Trista . . ." He breathed her name in a sigh of wretched despair. An anguish greater than any he'd ever known gripped him as he realized she might die because she was trying to protect him.

Trista's world was suffused in a red haze of excruciating pain as she lay unmoving where she'd fallen. She longed to know if Lance was safe, but for some reason she couldn't fathom, she couldn't get her eyes open or make her limbs move. A burning, searing agony tormented her side, and she realized vaguely that she must have been shot. Still, her own condition did not concern her. All she could think about was Lance.

The sound of his voice came to her then, distant and grieving, and she mustered all her flagging strength to answer him. "Lance?" His name was a faint, hushed whisper.

Lance knew a dramatic surge of joy at the sound of her voice. "Trista . . . darling . . ." He hovered over her, his hands gentle as he stroked her hair back from her forehead. "I'm here. . . . I'll take care of you. . . ."

"You're all right?" The question was barely audible, and Lance had to bend closer to hear her.

"I'm fine, Trista, and you're going to be fine, too. I promise . . ."

With a careful touch, he probed the nasty wound. He was somewhat comforted to discover that the bullet had passed through her body, knowing that there would be fewer complications since he didn't have to dig it out.

"I'll be right back," he told her huskily. He didn't know if she could hear him or not, and he didn't care. All that concerned him was that she was still alive and that he had to save her.

Lance searched through Striking Snake's things to

find what he needed to dress Trista's wound. He returned to her then and used his knife to cut her blouse so he could tend her more easily. After cleansing the injury as best he could, he cut strips of material from the hem of her skirt and bound it tightly to keep the bleeding under control.

Assured that Lance was alive, Trista had drifted in and out of consciousness. She seemed aware of the fact that he was ministering to her, but she had no strength left to do more than lay passively as he worked to stop the bleeding. The pain never lessened despite Lance's efforts to ease her torment, and finally the peaceful darkness of unconsciousness that beckoned comfortingly took her.

For a moment Lance feared that he'd lost Trista, but an instant later he realized that she was still breathing and had merely fainted. Though it worried him that she was that weak, in another way he was relieved that she had lost consciousness. Lance knew he had to get help if he was to save her life. The trip to Lone Elk's village could be made by travois, but if she had remained awake, the agony might have proved too great for her.

Leaving her for a moment, Lance rushed off down the creek bank to get Fuego. He was greatly disturbed to find that the stallion was gone, but when he remembered the direction from which Striking Snake had reentered the camp, he had no doubt that the warrior had released the stallion before coming after him.

It troubled Lance deeply that Fuego was gone, not only because he had counted on the rogue's stamina to get Trista to Lone Elk quickly, but because he feared the golden one was now lost to him forever. A parallel occurred to him of how Fuego and Trista had played similar roles in his life and how losing one might precipitate losing the other, but he forced it from his mind. He would not lose Trista. He couldn't. She meant everything to him.

Determined to get her to help as fast as he could, Lance set about making a travois. In less than an hour, he had hitched the rough-hewn conveyance to Striking Snake's own mount and carefully placed Trista on it. Starting off at a measured pace, he headed from the canyon, resolved to reach the village sometime that night.

Chapter Thirty

Night Lark had finished her work for the day and was heading through the camp toward Wind Rider's lodge. She ignored the idle warriors who called out to her. Though many were wealthy and some quite handsome, she disdained them all and paid no attention to their comments. She would not waste her time on any of them. Lance was the man who held her thoughts and her heart — only Lance.

It had been weeks since he'd left the camp to track down his runaway wife and the horse she had stolen, and in all that time there had been no word from him. Night Lark found herself thinking about him constantly and worrying about his safety. She dreaded the thought he might actually find Trista and return with her, but she also knew that she would rather have him back that way than not at all.

Night Lark glanced up to see Wind Rider sitting comfortably outside his tipi. She was glad that he was at home, for she felt sure that if anyone had heard news of Lance, it would be him. She quickened her pace at the thought.

Wind Rider watched Night Lark's approach and struggled to keep from smiling. He knew why she was coming to visit him, and he also knew she would soon be leaving, disappointed. He had heard nothing from Lance since he'd left the village.

"Wind Rider . . ." Night Lark greeted him as casually as she could though her dark eyes were wide and shining with the hope that he knew something about Lance's whereabouts.

"Hello, Night Lark," he returned just as easily.

"I need to talk with you. . . ." she began.

"Oh?" Wind Rider asked, feigning mild surprise. "Is there a problem with my aunt?"

"No . . . nothing like that." She dismissed his concern as she sat down beside him. Night Lark lowered her voice and spoke in a more confiding tone. "I wanted to know if you've heard anything from Lance."

"I've heard nothing," Wind Rider responded, shrugging.

His nonchalant attitude frustrated Night Lark, and she glared at him angrily. "You don't have any idea where he is or when he'll be back?"

"I know that he went to find Trista and the stallion. I know that he will be back when he finds them."

Night Lark made a sound of annoyance at his reply.

"Night Lark," Wind Rider counseled, "you do yourself no favor by waiting for Lance. You would do better to choose one of the other warriors for your husband. Many would have you, and many could give you everything you want."

"I want Lance!" she hissed. "Lance will be mine and he'll marry me; you'll see."

"If and when Lance returns to us, we will see. . . ." Wind Rider taunted, tired of her foolish confidence. He knew that Lance had treated her with indifference through the years and that his friend had no plans to take her as a wife.

"What do you mean, 'if?'" Night Lark challenged, suddenly even more deeply concerned over his well-being. "Do you think something's happened to him?"

"No. Lance can more than take care of himself. Besides, it's not all that unusual for him to be gone for weeks."

"Then I don't understand. . . ."

"There is nothing to understand," he answered sharply. He was weary of her questions. "Lance will return when he is ready, not before. Think about that, Night Lark. If he loved you as you believe he does, then don't you think he would be in a hurry to return to you?"

She bristled at his words and got angrily to her feet. "Lance does love me! When he returns, I will be eagerly waiting for him. I will be his wife, not that stupid white woman!"

Wind Rider said no more as he watched her stalk away in a huff. Though he knew Night Lark was a beautiful maiden, he thought her the stupid one, and not Trista. He knew she was deluding herself if she really thought that Lance cared for her in that way.

He let his gaze wander to the distant hills, and he wondered again at Lance's continued absence. What he had told Night Lark was true. It was not unusual for Lance to be gone for many days. But still, as determined as Lance had been when he'd left, he had not expected it to take this long for him to catch up with Trista and bring her back. Something unexpected must have happened—but what?

Restless at the thought, Wind Rider left the comfort of his lodge and headed for the corral to get his pony. He knew he wouldn't be needed in camp, so he decided to ride a short way from the village to see if he could find any sign of Lance.

Lone Elk stood in the doorway of his lodge, his

459

arms folded across the broad width of his chest. Though his expression was outwardly mild, he was in truth, deeply troubled. It had been weeks since Lance had left, and he found himself growing concerned about him. Though Lance had often been gone from the village in the past, this time he found himself haunted by his absence.

Lone Elk wanted to deny the real reason for his worry. Yet as the days had passed and Lance had not returned with his captive wife, he had been forced to face up to his own personal fear — the fear that somehow he might have been reunited with his white father. The thought angered Lone Elk. He hated Barrett and everything the white man represented. Still, he knew he could not force his own feelings onto Lance. If they had come in contact, then Lance would have to judge for himself what kind of man his father really was.

Lone Elk realized that there was no way to find out what had happened to Lance. He knew he would just have to wait and be patient until his nephew sent word or until he returned. Restless, but knowing there was nothing else he could do, the chief turned away from the sight of the thriving village spread out before him and moved inside to the privacy of his lodge. He would try to direct his thoughts to other things and hope that Lance would soon come back.

Michael and his companions from the Diamond had little trouble tracking Lance, for this time Lance had not wanted to try to cover his trail. Since leaving the ranch, they had been riding long and hard in their effort to catch up with him. Though they had gained ground on him and expected to rendezvous with him soon, they were puzzled by the general direction they were heading.

"What's up ahead, Tom? You got any idea?" Michael asked as they settled into their cold camp that night.

Tom shook his head in consternation. "I've never been up this way before," he replied. "It always seemed too desolate . . . too hostile. . . ."

It bothered Michael that they did not know what they were riding into, but his concern for Lance and Trista was foremost in his mind. They would go on. He had promised his father that he would bring them back safely, and he intended to do just that.

Sukie stood on the front porch of the Barrett home, staring out across the countryside. Though Michael had only been gone a short while, she already missed him terribly. Fear for his safety threatened to consume her, but she refused to dwell on it. Michael was a strong, brave man. He would return to her and they would be married. She would not allow her belief in that to waver.

Her mother came out of the house to join her, and Sukie managed a slight smile in greeting. Mary Lou was sensitive to her daughter's moods, and she slipped a comforting arm about her shoulders.

"Out here all alone worrying about Michael?"

"No. I'm trying not to worry about Michael," she countered, her smile fading at her mother's perceptiveness.

"Good," Mary Lou responded. "He'll be fine; you'll see."

"I know. I just hope Lance and Trista are, too." Sukie let her gaze drift out across the land again. They were quiet for a moment before she asked, "How's George?"

"Rosalie just relieved me. He was resting quietly when I came down."

"Any sign of a fever?"

"No, thank goodness. If no infection sets in, he's going to make a remarkable recovery."

"When will the doctor be here again?"

"He said he'd check back in a week, if we didn't contact him first."

"Well, maybe by then Michael and Lance will have returned with Trista." Even as she said that, Sukie knew the chance of their returning so quickly was remote. Again, with a fierce determination, she fought off the fear that was creeping back into her thoughts.

"Yes." Mary Lou agreed with her, wanting to keep her spirits up. "Maybe they will be back by then. . . ."

Trista was floating in a fog of pain. Excruciating agony radiated from her side, and with each bump she was forced to endure, it grew steadily worse. She had lost track of where she was and how she got there; all she could recall, as she suffered the seemingly unending torment, was that Lance was nearby. A particularly violent jolt brought a weak cry of protest from her, and she was surprised when all motion suddenly stopped.

"Trista?" Lance had heard her call out in distress, and he had stopped immediately and rushed back to her side. "Trista, what is it?"

"Lance?" she whispered in a strained voice, managing to focus on him only with a herculean effort.

"Yes, darling . . . I'm here," he assured her as he carefully checked her side to make sure that the gunshot wound had not reopened and that the bleeding had not started up again.

"Lance . . . it hurts so bad. . . ." Trista gasped as she felt his hands upon her.

For the first time in his life, Lance felt helpless. Selflessly, he wished that he was the one who'd been wounded. He wished that he could take her pain upon himself and suffer in her place, but he knew it could not be. All he could do for her was to make her as comfortable as possible and try to get her to help as quickly as he could.

"I know, love," he agonized. "Just hang on a little longer. . . ."

"Lance . . ." Trista saw the worry etched into his handsome features and tried to lift a hand to caress the hard leanness of his cheek. But she was too weak to manage it, and her arm fell back to her side.

Lance stared down at her gray-tinged features, his heart frozen in his chest. Since he'd begun the trip to the village, he had refused to even think that she might die on the journey, but as he gazed down at her now, he realized just how deathly ill she really was.

"I love you, Trista, and I won't let you die," he swore out loud, but she had drifted off into unconsciousness again and did not hear him.

After checking to make sure that she was still securely bound on the travois, he mounted Striking Snake's pony again and headed off once more in the direction of the village.

Wind Rider sat atop the hill, his manly form silhouetted against the fading brightness of the twilight sky. He had ridden a considerable distance in his search for some sign of Lance, but his travels had revealed nothing. The lateness of the hour discouraged him from venturing any farther, and he was about to turn back when he caught sight of a movement on the distant horizon.

His black-eyed gaze focused keenly on the single horse and rider heading slowly in his general direction pulling what appeared to be a travois. As he followed their progress, he recognized the pony as Striking Snake's and grew puzzled. He knew the banished warrior was forbidden from returning to the village.

Only as they drew nearer and Wind Rider was able to make out the short-cropped hair on the rider did he realize that it was Lance riding Striking Snake's mount. With that recognition, a sense of urgency possessed him, and he kneed his own pony into action. Charging down the hillside, he raced toward his friend at top speed.

Striking Snake's pony was near exhaustion, yet Lance refused to stop and rest. Prodding him ever onward, he kept heading for the Comanche camp and help for Trista.

The sight of the lone warrior riding so quickly toward him worried Lance. Lifting his rifle, he prepared to defend himself should the need arise. Only when he heard Wind Rider's shouted greeting did he relax.

"Lance!" he called out as he galloped up beside him and reined in tightly.

"Wind Rider . . ." he greeted his friend in relief. "It is good to see you. . . ."

Wind Rider's horse protested as he sawed back on the reins, and he fought to control him as he gazed down at Trista. "Trista was injured?"

Lance nodded. "She's been shot. I have to get her to the village."

"How did it happen?"

"I'll explain as we ride," Lance told him as he kept up the grueling pace despite his mount's weariness. As they crossed the long miles, he explained to his friend all that had happened. Wind Rider listened but said nothing as he sensed the anguish within Lance and his need to talk about what he had been through.

"So you have come to admit your love for her," Wind Rider finally remarked when Lance had finished.

Lance was surprised by his statement. "You knew?"

"I could think of no other reason for your reaction to her. You fought her too hard not to care," he answered simply.

"I didn't want to care . . . not in the beginning," Lance said thoughtfully. "All I wanted to do then was hurt her and Michael. But now . . ." He turned a tortured gaze to Wind Rider. "She was shot saving me. . . . If she—"

"We'll be at the village soon," Wind Rider cut him off. "Then everything will be fine."

"I hope so. . . ." He turned away from him then and schooled his features into a mask devoid of emotion. He did not want anyone to guess that he was haunted by the possibility that Trista might die.

"Lone Elk!" the messenger called to the chief. "Lone Elk! Wind Rider is returning, and Lance is with him!"

At hearing the news that his nephew had finally made it back, Lone Elk left his lodge and went forth quickly to greet him. He had expected a warm homecoming, but the sight of Lance riding Striking Snake's pony surprised him. When he saw the travois Lance was pulling, he was even more stunned.

"What has happened?" he asked as Lance dismounted.

"It's Trista. She's been shot," he answered solemnly as he hurried to free her from the conveyance. Trista was still unconscious as he loosened the bonds that had held her safely upon the travois, and she made no sound as he lifted her gently into his arms.

"Let me help you," Wind Rider offered, coming to his side, but Lance refused his aid.

"No. I'll take her to my tipi myself. Go get the medicine man and tell him I need him," Lance directed as he started off toward his own lodge.

As Wind Rider went to get help, Lone Elk stayed with Lance. "Did the whites do this?" he demanded. He knew his nephew well and was able to see through the steely mask he was presenting to the world.

Lance was startled by his unexpected question and glanced at him, frowning. "No, uncle. It was not the whites. It was Striking Snake."

"Striking Snake?" The chief was taken aback by this news. "I thought he had gone. How did he find you?"

Lance entered his lodge and lay Trista upon his bed. "He wanted Trista, and I guess he followed her to the ranch."

Lone Elk was surprised that Trista had managed to find her way home, and his respect for her grew. Still, the discovery that Lance had been there troubled him. "You were with the whites?"

"I was with my father and my brother at the Royal Diamond," he answered honestly as he loosened Trista's clothing. "Striking Snake attacked the ranchhouse one night and took Trista."

"It was a bold move," Lone Elk observed.

"And it almost worked. My father was shot, his wife killed. . . . I was lucky to escape with just a graze." Lance touched the bandage he still wore as he glanced at his uncle. "I tracked him down, and I killed him," he went on coldly. "The trouble is, I didn't kill him in time. . . ."

Before Lone Elk could say any more, Bluff Owl,

the most powerful medicine man of the tribe, called out to them.

"Enter, Bluff Owl." Lance bid him to come into his tipi.

The older man moved inside to join Lance and Lone Elk. "Wind Rider said that you have need of me."

"It is my wife, Bluff Owl. She has been shot. . . ." Lance moved slightly away from Trista so the medicine man could go to her.

Bluff Owl examined Trista's wound and then turned to them. "Leave me. It will take much strong medicine."

Lance was reluctant to leave Trista, but he knew he could not argue with the medicine man. He was a great healer, his powers having been proven effective many times.

"I will be outside," Lance said as he forced himself to follow Lone Elk from the lodge.

"Come back to my lodge," his uncle offered. "We can wait there for word from Bluff Owl."

"No. I can't leave her. I will stay here and wait." Lance was firm, refusing to be drawn away. He was fearful that she would awaken and call out for him, and he wouldn't be there.

Lone Elk studied him for a long moment. He realized now that Lance truly loved Trista. It disturbed him, but he knew he would not make the same mistake twice. He had been separated from Shining Star because of his hatred for Barrett. He would not lose Lance in the same way.

"You have not told me of your time with your father." He encouraged him to speak of other things.

Lance faced him squarely. He knew he had to be truthful with his uncle, yet he knew the truth would hurt him. "I stayed at the ranch."

"Barrett has accepted you?" Lone Elk probed.

Lance nodded. "My father and I talked. I learned that there were many misunderstandings between us. He wants me to live with him on the Diamond. He wants me to return and take my place as his son."

"Will you do this?"

Lance glanced toward his lodge, thinking of Trista and their future together. "It is the life that Trista knows."

"And you would do this for your woman?"

"I love her, Lone Elk," he answered forthrightly, "but I love you, too. I do not want to make a choice."

"You are very much like your mother, Lance." The chief could not help but remember a conversation similar to this one many years before. He thought of Shining Star's death, and he was tempted to try to force Lance to stay with him. Still, he realized that had he forced his sister to give up her love and live with the tribe, she would have been unhappy for the rest of her days. Years of learned wisdom tempered his need to grasp Lance's love and hold him firmly to him. As a bird freed to fly from its nest for the first time always returns to that nest, Lone Elk knew that Lance would always return to him. "And that is good."

Within the tipi, Bluff Owl began to work to heal Trista. Stripping away her clothing, he cleansed the wound and then placed his medicine bone over the injury. To draw out the poison he chanted his ritual song and shook his gourd rattle over her still form. That done, he packed the gunshot wound with the mixture of grasses, herbs, and roots that he knew would help prevent further bleeding and keep down the risk of infection. Bluff Owl had doctored many bullet wounds before, and he knew how dangerous and ultimately deadly they could be if a fever set in.

Beginning his prayerful chant again, Bluff Owl hovered watchfully over Trista. He had done all he could. Her fate rested in the hands of the gods, and only time would tell whether she would live or die.

Dawn Blossom had been near the center of the camp when Lance and Wind Rider had returned. She had seen all that had taken place and had been surprised that Night Lark was nowhere around. Everyone knew that Night Lark loved Lance and that she had been waiting impatiently for his return.

Remembering that she had caught sight of the other maiden heading toward the creek earlier, Dawn Blossom went in search of her, eager to tell her the news that Lance had returned and that he had brought his wife back with him. Though it was dark, the moon provided enough light for her to spot Night Lark where she sat sullenly on the bank of the stream.

"Night Lark!" she called out as she went to join her.

Night Lark was annoyed to find that Dawn Blossom was seeking her out. She didn't know what the other woman wanted, and she didn't care. All she wanted was to be left alone with her thoughts of Lance and her dreams of when he returned to her.

"Yes, Dawn Blossom, I'm here," she replied with little enthusiasm.

"Good, I was looking for you."

"Why? Could you not tell that I wanted to be alone?"

Dawn Blossom was stung by her unfriendliness. "I will leave you alone then, since you do not want to hear the news I came to bring you." She turned away from the other maiden and started back up the bank.

Night Lark was surprised by her move, and quickly

spoke up. "What news do you have, Dawn Blossom? I'm sure it must be important for you to come all the way out here to tell me."

Dawn Blossom cast her a cold look and kept on walking.

"Dawn Blossom, wait. I'm sorry I was short with you."

Pleased that the other woman realized the message she was important, she paused in her retreat and turned to her. "I came out here to tell you that Lance has returned."

"What?!" Night Lark was immediately on her feet.

"Lance has returned," she repeated a bit smugly.

"When?!"

"Just a short while ago."

"Did he come alone?"

"No. He found Trista and brought her back with him."

The excitement she'd been feeling over his return faded a bit with the discovery that he'd brought his wife with him, but she did not let it bother her too much.

"Is he looking for me?"

"I don't know. All I do know is that Trista was wounded, and he called for Bluff Owl."

"Lance had to shoot her to bring her back?" Night Lark was thrilled at the thought. She would not have to wait for him to sell Trista to another tribe. . . . Perhaps she would die right away, and he'd be rid of her even sooner.

She shrugged. "I do not know how it happened. All I know is what I told you."

"Thank you, Dawn Blossom. I must go to Lance now. I'm sure he is looking for me. . . ."

Dawn Blossom watched with interest as the other maiden hurried off toward the camp. With idle malice, she wondered what Night Lark's reaction would be when she discovered that, contrary to what she thought, Lance was very concerned about his wife's condition. She started after her, eager to eavesdrop and see what she could find out.

Chapter Thirty-one

"Night Lark? What are you doing?" She Who Speaks the Truth demanded as she awoke from a deep sleep in the middle of the night to find her daughter leaving the tipi.

Night Lark had stopped at their lodge to freshen up a bit before going to find Lance. She had hoped to sneak in and out without being detected, and she cursed under her breath as she turned to her mother. "I'm sorry I woke you."

"I did not ask for an apology, daughter. I asked for an answer. Where is it you're creeping off to at this hour?" Her tone was sharp as she sat up and eyed her suspiciously.

Knowing that her mother would stand for nothing less than the truth, she was honest with her. "Lance has returned, and I'm on my way to see him."

"Lance is back?" This surprised She Who Speaks the Truth. "What of his wife? Did he bring her with him?"

"Yes," she answered in annoyance, "but Trista has been shot. I guess Lance had to shoot her to force her to return with him."

She Who Speaks the Truth found it hard to believe that Lance would shoot the white woman. "Who has told you this? Who told you Lance shot her?"

"No one. I just know he must have done it. He was angry with her when he left." She explained how she'd reached her conclusions.

"I would not repeat that story until you know the truth of what has happened. They have been gone a long time, daughter. Much could have happened between them."

Night Lark grew impatient with her mother's preaching. "Yes, Mother. I will hold my tongue until I have heard the truth of it from Lance, but I'm sure his tale will be no different. Trista has caused him nothing but trouble from the beginning. He will be well rid of her if she dies, and if she doesn't, he will probably just end up selling her to the Kiowas anyway."

She Who Speaks the Truth stared at her incredulously, wondering how her daughter could be so blind to the truth of Lance's feelings. She had sensed herself that he wasn't going after Trista merely to get his horse back.

"I find it hard to believe that Lance would have bothered to bring Trista all the way back to our village if he didn't plan to keep her."

Night Lark refused to listen to the warning tone of her mother's words as she started from their home. "He will be mine soon now, Mother. I know it."

"Night Lark . . ." She Who Speaks the Truth started to caution her, but she had already disappeared out of the lodge in search of the man she loved. She was unable to go back to sleep after her daughter had gone, and she tossed and turned restlessly, worried that Night Lark might be devastated when she learned the truth of Lance's feelings for the white woman.

Lance stood alone near the edge of the village. He

473

knew he was tired, but he was so concerned about Trista that he couldn't rest. When Lone Elk had suggested that they return to his lodge and try to sleep, he had declined, preferring to stay near his own tipi and await word from Bluff Owl on Trista's condition. Though the night would be exhausting and seemingly endless, he would not leave. Lance had sent Lone Elk on by himself to rest, promising to call him if he needed him.

Nervously, he raked a hand through the short, dark thickness of his hair. Again he wished that he was the one who had been shot instead of Trista. Striking Snake's bullet had been meant for him. He was the one the other warrior had hated, yet Trista was the one suffering because of that hatred.

Lance thought of all the times he had hurt her himself, and guilt swept over him. He remembered the first time they'd made love at the ranch and how he'd felt when he'd seen the bruises on her back where Night Lark had beaten her. A sense of outrage filled him at the way the other woman had dared to treat Trista. He vowed to himself that, if she lived through this, he would never allow anyone to hurt her again.

Night Lark hurried eagerly toward Lance's tipi, for she was anxious to see him again and to tell him just how much she had missed him while he was away. She felt confident that he would be glad to see her, too. Obviously Trista had given him much trouble, and she believed that he would be glad to be with a woman who was more willing to please him.

When she reached his lodge she was puzzled to find that he was not there. She could hear Bluff Owl chanting in the tipi and knew that Lance would not be inside, for no one was ever permitted to enter while the medicine man was working his powerful healing. She searched about the area in the dim glow from the low-burning campfires and finally found him near the edge of the village staring out across the night-shrouded land. She was glad for the chance to be alone with him and slowed her pace, not wanting him to know the complete extent of her eagerness for his company.

"Lance?" Night Lark kept her voice soft and sensual as she drew closer.

Lance had been lost deep in thought and was startled by the interruption. He did not immediately recognize Night Lark in the darkness, and thought it was one of the village women bringing him word of Trista. He turned quickly, anxiously, toward the approaching female.

"You bring word of Trista?" he asked, trying to identify the woman who came toward him in the semidarkness.

"No, Lance. I have come to see how you are," Night Lark crooned in her most endearing tone.

"Night Lark?" Lance was stunned to think that she would be bold enough to come to him after all that had happened.

"Yes," she answered, overjoyed that he'd recognized her. "I was so glad to hear that you'd returned." She sidled up to him, hoping to encourage him.

Lance was filled with outrage at all of Night Lark's brazen maneuverings. He had meant to confront her later, when things had settled down, but her presence here with him now pushed him to the brink.

"Were you?" He could barely control the violence that threatened to take him.

"Of course, Lance. You must know how I feel about you. I love you, and I missed you while you were gone."

At that, he grabbed her by the upper arms. Night Lark thought he was going to take her in an embrace and kiss her, but to her surprise, rather than kiss her, he tightened his grip painfully upon her.

"You don't know the meaning of the word 'love,' Night Lark. You make a mockery of the very idea," Lance snarled as he glared down at her.

Only then did she begin to understand that rather than welcome her, he was furious with her. "I don't know what you mean. . . ."

"I don't love you, Night Lark. I've told you that before, but you refused to believe me. Now I will tell you again, and this time you will listen!"

"But Lance—"

"Listen to me, Night Lark. . . ." he seethed as he recalled what Trista had told him had happened while he was gone. He thought of the lies Night Lark had told her about their plans to marry, the work she had forced Trista to do, and the beatings that had accompanied it. Had Night Lark minded her own business, Trista might not have run from him and might not be lying near death now. Lance's heart hardened completely against Night Lark. "I despise liars," he stated tersely, and he heard her sharp intake of breath.

"What are you talking about, Lance? I have never lied to you," Night Lark protested in confusion.

"You may not have lied to me, but you lied to Trista."

"Trista?"

"You told her that I was going to marry you, didn't you?"

"I love you, Lance, and I always thought that you cared for me." Night Lark suddenly feared that her world was about to crumble.

"I cared for you only as a friend, nothing more. I

476

have never professed to love you, Night Lark, and I never encouraged you to believe that one day we would marry."

"But—"

"Say no more, woman," he commanded harshly, giving her a rough shake as his temper flared. "Trista is the woman I love."

"If you love her so much, why did you have to shoot her to bring her back?"

"I did not shoot Trista," Lance ground out, infuriated by her assumption. "Trista was shot by Striking Snake as she tried to save my life. He is the one who shot her!"

She realized in heartrending disillusionment that all her perceptions about Lance and Trista had been wrong. Tears of humiliation stung her eyes, and she grew bitter in her jealousy of the other woman.

"I do not know why you care about her. She is nothing but a stupid, clumsy white woman. She has caused you nothing but trouble since you brought her here! She defied you at every turn, yet you claim to love her! What about me? I have loved you for as long as I can remember. I have always wanted to please you in any way I could," she told him angrily.

"Shut up, Night Lark. Don't ever let me hear you speak of Trista again! I do not love you, and I never will. Know that and leave me now!" He shoved her almost brutally away from him.

"Lance. . . ." Night Lark pleaded in a last, desperate attempt to make him understand the depth of her love for him. She took a step toward him with her hands outstretched before her. "Make love to me now. Let me show you just how perfect it can be between us. I can give you more pleasure than your pasty-faced wife! I don't understand why you care about her! I hope she dies. Then we could be happy together. I know the ways of the Comanche. She would never fit in. . . ."

His hands clinched into fists of useless rage against this woman who refused to accept the truth. "I said leave me, Night Lark! Trista is my wife, and if anything happens to her. . . ."

Night Lark saw the fury mirrored in his eyes along with his agonized concern over Trista and knew then, finally, that the white woman had won his love. He was lost to her forever. Sobbing her heartbreak, she rushed away into the night.

Suddenly alone, Lance felt his anger slowly drain from him. He glanced toward his lodge, hoping to see Bluff Owl emerging to tell him Trista was better, but the sound of the medicine man's unending chant told him that his power had not yet worked its miracle.

He thought of Trista's suffering, and memories he had long suppressed slipped through the protective barriers in his mind. Held in the grip of the childish recollections of his mother's death, Lance was filled with the need to go to Trista and stay with her. He could vaguely remember his father tirelessly remaining at his mother's side as she fought for her life against the deadly fever that had claimed her. Lance was torn between the need to be with her and the need to respect the secret workings of Bluff Owl's medicine. He had just resigned himself to passing more hours alone when he heard Trista call out in terror. The sound of her strangled cry jolted Lance, and there was no stopping him as he raced back to his lodge and threw wide its opening.

Trista tossed uncomfortably in the heat and pain that threatened to consume her. Distantly, she heard the sound of an unearthly song, and the throbbing

478

beat of it seemed to echo through her to the depths of her very soul. Her thoughts were jumbled in feverish confusion, and she opened her eyes, wanting to understand where she was and why she was in such agony. She had just shifted her weight, intending to look about the dimly lighted enclosure, when a strange Comanche suddenly loomed over her. His face was painted in the most hideous of designs, and Trista cried out in terror at the sight of him, and threw her arms up in a feeble effort to defend herself.

"Lance . . . no, don't hurt me!" Her eyes were wild as the fever raged through her.

Bluff Owl looked up angrily as Lance threw the flap open and strode inside. "Get out!" he ordered in the Comanche tongue.

Lance needed only a quick look at Trista to understand that she had a high fever, and he glared at the medicine man fiercely.

"I am staying," he stated, not caring anymore about Bluff Owl's power or lack of it. All that mattered was that he stay by Trista. He had to be with her. Somehow he had to help her.

"My powers will not work if you remain," he charged.

Lance was beyond caring about anything but his wife. He moved to kneel beside Trista, who now lay quietly, her eyes closed, her features flushed with the killing heat that possessed her.

"Your powers have done nothing for her so far while I've stayed away. She's gotten worse. I'm not leaving her," he challenged. "She needs me, and I am going to stay with her."

Bluff Owl drew himself up to his full height as he returned Lance's glare. "My medicine is strong. It will work." He was not about to lose his standing in the tribe. He would stay and make certain that she recovered.

Lance turned back to Trista, murmuring her name as he brushed back her hair from her forehead. Her skin felt hot to his touch, and he left her momentarily to get a wet cloth. With slow, steady strokes, he bathed her with the cooling water, hoping that it would somehow reduce the fever that held her mercilessly in its grasp.

Trista stirred restively. Caught up in the midst of her delirium, she thought herself back at the Diamond with Michael.

"Michael . . ." Her voice was a hoarse croak as she called his name. "Michael . . . I love him, yet I'm hurting him. . . ."

Lance's expression grew grim as he listened to her profess her love for Michael, and he felt as if his whole world had just come crashing down around him. He thought back to what Michael had told him before he'd left the ranch and Lance concluded that Trista must have realized Michael loved Sukie, and had made up the story of loving him in order to set Michael free to claim his own happiness. Lance knew for a fact that she didn't want to marry him. She had made that perfectly clear during the last night they had spent together.

"Michael . . ." Trista opened her eyes and looked straight at Lance. "What should I do? He claims we're married already. . . ."

Though Lance knew that she was not actually seeing him, trapped in her delirium as she was, he still cringed at the heartfelt misery in her tone. He felt angry over all that had happened to her because of him, and he silently prayed that he would have the opportunity to make it all up to her.

480

"Easy, love," Lance crooned as he continued to stroke her with the wet cloth. "Everything will be all right. Trust me, Trista. . . ."

In Trista's mind, she saw Striking Snake leering at her, and she screamed in horror as she thrashed about the bed trying to escape the evil warrior. Whimpers of terror escaped her as, in her mind's eye, she tried to flee him.

"No! Please don't hurt me . . . please let me go. . . ."

To Lance her words were almost a physical blow as he believed she was reliving the time when he had kidnapped her and held her as his prisoner.

"God, love, I'm sorry . . . so sorry. . . ." Fighting to keep control over his chaotic emotions, he concentrated only on trying to lower her body temperature.

Trista felt something cool and wet stroking her neck and shoulders, easing the heat and the aching pain that possessed her. She sighed as the image of Striking Snake faded, and the blackness and comfort of unconsciousness took her again.

As she went limp beneath his ministrations, Lance feared for a moment that she had gone from him. His breath caught in his throat, and he waited in agonizing uncertainty until he was sure that she was still breathing. A measure of relief washed over him, but he knew he could not relax his vigil. The only way to save her was to get the fever down. He passed the balance of the night in tense silence as he worked to keep her as cool and as comfortable as possible, while Bluff Owl continued his ritual works in an effort to prove that his powers were as great as everyone believed.

It was only when the first rays of the morning sun stained the eastern horizon in softly graded shades of pink, gold, and yellow that Lance took a break from his constant tending of her. Setting the cloth aside, he stood up to stretch his cramped limbs and moved over to the doorway of the lodge to watch the sunrise. He hoped that the clear sky promising a bright day was a portent of what was to come, but glancing back at Trista's ominously still form gave him little hope.

It was then, as Lance looked on, that Trista began to toss restlessly about once more. The infection had not lessened with the passing of the night, and her temperature threatened to soar to even greater heights.

Trista felt as if she were burning up, and she turned fitfully on Lance's bed, seeking relief from the fire that raged within her. Her tortured senses created teasing, vicious hallucinations as she fought to overcome the wound and the infection. In her sick, fevered thoughts, she was making love with Lance much as they had that last time they'd been together at the ranch. His every touch and every caress was tender and gentle, and she was cherishing his nearness as she lifted her face to his to accept his kiss. It was then, as she opened her eyes in the dreamlike state, that he changed. One moment it had been Lance, holding her and loving her, and the next moment her dream lover was transformed into Striking Snake. In nightmarish reality, his cruel visage seemed to hover above her, and his smile was brutally sensual and threatening.

"Lance . . . I want Lance. . . ." she cried, physically fighting off the illusion of the hated warrior.

Lance was surprised to hear her call out for him, and he rushed back to her side to speak to her quietly and reassuringly. "Trista . . . darling, I'm right here. . . ." He bent over her and pressed a soft kiss on her lips as he tried to calm her. He didn't know if she would recognize him or not, and at this point, he didn't care. He only wanted to comfort her and to let her know that he was there, with her, loving her, no matter what.

"Please . . . get Lance for me . . . I have to tell him . . . I didn't get the chance to tell him. . . ."

"I'm here, Trista. Please, darling . . . I'm here. . . ."

"I need to tell him I love him," she explained softly in abject misery as tears traced down her cheeks. "He doesn't know that I love him, Michael. . . ." Trista went on as if it were Michael who sat by her side and not Lance. "He doesn't know, Michael," she sighed, shaking her head in confusion. "Have to tell him that he was wrong . . . doesn't matter that he's part Indian . . . but he wouldn't listen. . . . He hates me now, Michael. . . ." Her voice drifted off as the moment of intense emotion passed, and she quieted.

"She sleeps," Bluff Owl pronounced unexpectedly from behind Lance.

Lance was startled. In listening to Trista, he had completely forgotten the old man's presence in the lodge. His eyes were glistening strangely as he glanced back over his shoulder toward where the medicine man stood.

"This is good," Bluff Owl went on. "The fever may break soon. We will keep watch." He dropped down to sit slightly behind Lance and immediately started to chant again.

Lance didn't speak. He was so choked with emotion over what Trista had just told him in her delirium that he could only nod in response. His spirits, so low only moments before, were now reaching heights of joy he'd never known existed. *She loved him, not Michael.*

She had really meant what she'd said that night at the Diamond. She loved him. . . .

The understanding of what Bluff Owl had told him began to sink in. Trista was sleeping now. That meant she was showing some progress. He breathed a deep sigh of relief and then redoubled his efforts to lower her soaring temperature.

Michael and his men broke camp before dawn and were in the saddle by first light. For several hours they followed Lance's trail through the rugged terrain, and they were amazed when they came upon the isolated box canyon. They managed to locate the campsite without any difficulty and were stunned when they found Striking Snake's remains.

Combing the camp for clues to Trista and Lance's whereabouts, they found a bloodied piece of cloth that Michael identified as having been torn from Trista's dress. Tormented by the thought that one of them had been injured, they continued to search for some sign of them. Tom was the one who finally located the trail leading back out away from the encampment. A check of the tracks revealed that only a single mount had been ridden and that it had been dragging some kind of travois behind it. Whoever the rider was, he'd headed to the north in the opposite direction of the ranch.

"Where the hell were they going?" Tom asked Michael as he stared off after the trail.

"Espada Canyon," Michael answered, understanding what his brother had done and realizing that it must have been Trista who'd been injured.

"Why would they be riding away from the ranch?" one of the men asked.

"Lance's village is in Espada Canyon. He must be heading there because it's closer."

"You think Trista was the one who was hurt?" Tom ventured as he studied Michael's closed expression.

Michael nodded curtly. "Let's ride. Maybe we can find him and help. . . ."

They hastened to mount up and then rode out at top speed following the path of the single rider.

Black Water had been watching the group of white men for some time as they had been riding in the direction of his camp. He wanted to rush back and alert Lone Elk to their presence, yet he knew there was no time. He was tempted to lead an attack against the intruders. He knew he had the element of surprise on his side, but he remembered his chief's orders to Lance the last time whites had dared to enter their territory. Signaling his companions, they prepared to confront the intruders.

"Michael . . ." Tom called out his name in a strangled voice, and Michael looked over at him questioningly. "Look . . ." The ranchhand nodded toward the hilltop ahead and to their right.

Michael followed the direction of his gaze and saw what had caused him such distress. There at the crest of the rise sat a gathering of Comanche warriors. He could count no more than three, but Michael knew that meant nothing. There could be a hundred more of them in the rocks, waiting and watching. He swallowed nervously as he fought to keep his voice level.

"If they'd wanted us dead, they'd have attacked us by now," he remarked as coolly as he could. "We'll just keep riding. The last time Pa and I came this way, all they wanted to do was parlay. Maybe once I tell them who I am, they'll help us."

The men tensed as they continued to follow Lance's tracks, but they made no move for their guns.

When Black Water knew that the whites had spotted them, he put his heels to his horse and raced down the hillside to confront them before they managed to get any closer to the tribe's camp. Though the Comanche warriors screamed their usual unnerving cries as they swarmed down the incline toward the white men, no one drew a weapon and no shots were exchanged.

Unnerved, but determined not to reveal it to his adversaries, Michael reined in and kept his expression cool and steady as he faced the leader of the group of warriors. "I am Michael Barrett. I have come in search of my brother, Lance."

Black Water regarded him levelly in silence for some time, his eyes cold, black, and expressionless. Michael marveled at the man's ability to disguise his thoughts, and he thought, with some tempered amusement, that this Comanche would make a great poker player. At long last, the warrior nodded.

"Come," he said brusquely.

Michael glanced quickly at his men and then led the way, following Black Water on toward Espada Canyon.

Chapter Thirty-two

Wind Rider was striding through the village on his way toward Lance's tipi to see about Trista when he noticed the group of riders in the distance heading their way. He paused to study the group, trying to identify them. He knew that Black Water had ridden out the day before with some warriors, and he recognized him now in the lead as they drew nearer. Along with that recognition, though, came the realization that there were white men riding in with him. Wind Rider knew that Lone Elk had to be informed, and he hurried off to warn his chief of the impending, unexpected arrival of whites in their camp.

"Come . . ." Lone Elk responded to Wind Rider's called-out greeting as he reached his lodge.

Brushing open the entrance, he came in and stood respectfully before his chief.

"What is it?" he asked, looking up from where he sat.

"Black Water is returning, Lone Elk, and he is bringing white men with him."

"He's bringing whites into the village?" The news startled him, and when Wind Rider answered positively, he rose quickly and went outside. Standing before his tipi, his black eyes flashing in anger at the warrior's daring, he waited for Black Water to come to him.

Word spread quickly through the tribe that Black

Water was returning with whites, and all activities ceased as the people gathered to watch them approach. When they actually entered the encampment, the villagers stared with open interest at the well-armed white men who rode quietly past them.

"Chief Lone Elk," Black Water greeted him as he reined in before him.

Lone Elk nodded only once in greeting as he eyed the whites suspiciously. His general hatred of them was well known, and it reflected plainly on his sternly set features.

"Why have you brought these men into our midst?" he demanded in the Comanche tongue.

"One claims to be the brother of Lance," Black Water explained.

The chief grunted disparagingly as he glared up at Michael and the others. "Which of you is Barrett?" he asked in English.

"I am Michael Barrett," Michael was quick to answer him. "You are Chief Lone Elk, uncle to my brother?"

Lone Elk nodded.

"It is good to finally meet the man who means so much to Lance. He has spoken of you often and always with great praise."

The chief regarded him coldly, and Michael sensed that he would never be able to breach the differences that existed between them. Still, he had wanted Lone Elk to know that he felt nothing but respect for him.

"There was evidence in Striking Snake's camp that either Lance or Trista was injured in their fight with him. We were tracking them in this direction when your warriors found us. Are they here? Are they well?"

"Come." He gestured toward his lodge. "We will speak of this in private."

Michael and the others dismounted. Only Michael was allowed entrance to the chief's home. The rest were made to wait outside.

Lone Elk turned to Wind Rider. "Go to Lance. Tell him of this," he instructed in their native tongue.

As Wind Rider moved off to tell Lance of his brother's arrival in camp, Lone Elk followed Michael into the lodge.

Though Trista had not stirred again, Lance had remained vigilant at her side throughout the day. Occasionally, while she lay resting so quietly, he'd managed to catch a few minutes of sleep, but generally he'd stayed alert, watching and waiting for some sign of improvement in her condition. Lance knew that her injury was serious, but he was growing concerned over the fact that Trista did not seem to be getting any better. Frustrated though he might be, Lance understood that it might take some time for her to pull through. At least, he consoled himself, she hadn't gotten any worse.

Bluff Owl had rested for only a short time since the ordeal had begun. At midmorning he cleansed her wound again and packed it once more with the healing concoction. He continued to chant unceasingly, invoking his powers to save her life as she lay in the merciless grip of the dangerously high fever.

Wind Rider's call drew Lance from her bedside, and reluctantly he went outside to see what his friend wanted. Lance's haggard appearance surprised his friend, and he realized then just how deeply Lance was being affected by Trista's pain.

"Why have you come?" Lance asked bluntly, not wanting to be away from his love in case she needed him.

"It is important," he answered. "Your white brother has come to the village."

"Michael?" Lance was stunned.

"He rode in with Black Water, and there are other men with him. He is with Lone Elk now. The chief sent me to tell you of his presence."

Lance did not want to leave Trista, but he knew he had to go to see Michael. It had been a brave act on his brother's part to follow him, and though he didn't outwardly show it, Lance was deeply touched by his effort. He hurried off toward his uncle's home.

Lance entered at Lone Elk's call and stepped inside the tipi to find Michael seated opposite his uncle. Michael got quickly to his feet to greet Lance. He noticed immediately the strained look about him, and knew a moment of dread.

"Lance . . ." Their hands clasped in a warm expression of their friendship as their gazes met. "It was Trista?" Michael said in a strangled voice.

"Yes," he replied tautly.

"Is she . . .?" Michael ventured.

"No."

"It's bad?"

"Striking Snake shot her. The bullet took her in the side. I think she's better, but it's hard to tell with the fever. . . ." Lance explained. "How's Father?"

"He's going to make it."

"Good. I only hope Trista does. . . ." Lance openly voiced his worry.

"How did it happen?"

Lance told him of how he'd located Striking Snake's camp. He went on to explain how he'd freed Trista and tried to convince her to flee while she had the chance, but then she'd refused and stayed behind with him.

"I should have killed Striking Snake years ago. Then none of this would have happened," he swore vehemently, after telling Michael how she'd been shot

490

saving him.

"I wish I could have caught up with you sooner. I might have been able to help," Michael told him with deep regret.

"It's too late to worry about what might have been. . . ." Lance said slowly, realizing that he had to accept the present and live with it as best he could.

"She'll be all right. She has to be. . . ." He wanted to reassure him.

"God, I hope so. . . ."

"Is she conscious? Can I talk with her?"

"No. She's been delirious off and on since we arrived . . . I've got to get back to her. . . ."

"Is there anything I can do?" he asked in earnest.

"Not unless you can work miracles. It's just a matter of time, of waiting, until we know whether she's going to make it or not. . . ."

"I want to stay, Lance, to help you in any way I can," Michael offered, knowing that he needed his support.

"Uncle?" Lance turned to Lone Elk in deference. He knew that whites were not welcome in their village, and he hesitated before encouraging Michael to remain.

Lone Elk had been silently observing the two men together, and he had been surprised to discover how much alike the two half brothers were. He could see the family resemblance, though he didn't want to admit it, and he could also see the depth of caring Michael and Lance felt for each other. The revelation pained him, for he feared that he would be replaced in Lance's heart. Only when Lance turned to him in respect and obedience did he realize that his place in his nephew's affections was not in jeopardy.

"They may remain," Lone Elk pronounced, and Lance nodded his thanks. "Your brother may lodge with me, and I will send Wind Rider to find a place for the other men to stay."

"Thank you, my uncle." He returned to Trista then, leaving Michael with Lone Elk.

Whitey and a group of men from the ranch had been out riding the range all day hoping to pick up any strays that might have remained in the area after the Comanche raid the other night. But as the day had progressed, they'd met with little success. They had spread out now to comb a wider area. Whitey and several riders stayed atop the ridge of the low-rising hill, while Jack Myer, one of the seasoned ranchhands from the Diamond, rode directly down into the valley to drive any recalcitrant horses from the relative safety of the brushy cover. It was then that he accidentally stumbled across the remains of Poker's campsite.

"Whitey!" Jack called out to the foreman.

Whitey heard his call and the panic reflected in his tone, and urged his mount down into the valley to investigate. He found Jack as he was riding away from the gory scene at top speed. Upon seeing his boss, Jack immediately reined in. His face was ashen, and his eyes were wide and dilated in shock.

"What is it, Jack?" Whitey demanded.

"It musta been the Comanche when they were on their way into the ranch . . . but I don't understand . . ."

"Don't understand what? What are you talking about?"

"Back there . . . it's Poker—or what's left of him. . . ." He turned away from Whitey and was violently ill.

Whitey grimly rode on alone. He had witnessed the

remains of a Comanche massacre before, so he thought he was prepared for whatever it was that had sickened Jack, but as he rode into the grisly scene, even he was shocked. It was easy for Whitey to decipher what had happened as he looked about the campsite. He could tell that the white men had been taken by surprise by the Indians and that the Comanche had ridden them down and killed them on the spot. Only Poker had suffered their devilish torture, and Whitey found himself tensing in an effort to keep down the bile that threatened to rise in his throat.

When he'd gotten himself back under control, he looked about a little more critically, and it was then that he knew what had confused Jack. Poker and all the others whose bodies were strewn about the area were dressed as Indians themselves. Puzzled, he was driven to discover what they had been doing out here in the middle of Barrett land dressed as warriors, but first he knew he had to bury them. He couldn't just leave them out here as food for the coyotes and the buzzards.

He drew his gun and fired two shots in rapid succession as a signal to his men to come to him. Dismounting in the midst of the carnage, he started to examine the remains of the camp, searching for clues as to their activities. A quick check through the saddlebags revealed nothing. It was only when he started to go through the pockets of the men's discarded clothing that he came across the letter. Poker's name was clearly written upon the envelope in a script Whitey recognized immediately. Troubled by the discovery, he wondered why Poker, of all people, would have had a letter from Eleanor Barrett. Then he remembered that Eleanor had been trying to contact Poker right after he'd left the Diamond to give him his parting wages. Whitey opened the letter, expecting it to be Poker's back pay. What he found instead left him more shaken than he'd ever been in his life.

Poker—

The raid is set for tomorrow night. I expect you to be on time and to dressed as we agreed. Should everything go as planned, and Lance and my husband are killed, I will meet you in two days at Black Rock to make my final payment to you for your services. You must remember that secrecy in this matter is vital. No one, and I repeat, no one, must know of the connection between us.

E. Barrett

Whitey stared down at the missive in horrified disbelief, and he shook his head in confusion. Evidently Eleanor had hired Poker and some other men to dress as warriors, raid the ranch; and kill both George and Lance. He realized now that the whole thing had played out much as she'd planned, except that George and Lance hadn't been the ones to pay the price with their lives, she had. As he heard the rest of his men coming up the valley to join him, he quickly stuffed the incriminating letter inside his shirt.

Without betraying any of what he'd discovered, Whitey directed the ranchhands to help him bury the men. In silence, they gathered up the personal possessions left in the camp and then headed back to the ranch to spread the word of the men's deaths.

Trista sighed and remained perfectly still, fearful that any sudden movement on her part might bring back the unending heat that had possessed her and the searing pain that had throbbed ceaselessly in her side. She tried vaguely to remember all that had happened. She realized that she'd been sick, but for the moment she couldn't recall just why. The protective haze that had buffered her vanished as Bluff Owl began to chant again, and with that foreign sound, reality rushed in. Her eyes flew open and went wide with fright as the memory of Striking Snake taking aim at Lance filled her with terror. *Lance . . . dear God, Lance! Had the other warrior killed him?*

"Lance!" Trista cried. She tried desperately to push herself into an upright position, but the sudden movement sent pain jarring through her, and she was forced to fall back.

Lance had moved away from her side to stand by the door of the lodge when she came awake. At the sound of her call, he dashed back to her and dropped to his knees beside the bed.

"Trista . . ." Lance was hoping and praying that she was coherent and not merely calling out for him in her delirium. As he stared down into her clear eyes and saw the sanity reflected there, he felt a burst of joy swell within him. "Thank God! You're better!"

"Oh, Lance . . ." Trista breathed. Seeing him looming above her, alive and obviously well, eased her trauma, and she relaxed back against the softness of his bed.

"Easy, love," he told her softly as he gently touched her forehead to judge the power of her fever. To his relief, she was cooler. The fever had broken. She would recover. "Bluff Owl . . ." Lance called the medicine man to him.

The older man ceased his chanting and came to them. Lifting the blanket that Lance had covered her with earlier, he probed the wound with knowing hands. After long minutes, he drew back, and there was a self-satisfied smile upon his features.

"It is good," he announced. "The fever has gone. She will get well quickly now."

Trista looked nervously from Lance to the stranger and then back, and Lance easily read her confusion.

"Trista, this is Bluff Owl, our wisest medicine man. His healing powers have once again been proven true. He has tended you since I brought you back here."

"Thank you, Bluff Owl," she managed.

The old man stood up straight and tall. His fathomless black eyes studied Trista in silence for a while before he gave her a slight nod. "I will go now. Tomorrow I will come and change the wrapping." With that he was gone.

"Lance . . ." There was uncertainty in her voice. "Lance, tell me everything. What happened? All I remember was that Striking Snake was going to shoot you. . . ."

"You'll never have to worry about him again, love," Lance assured her fiercely.

"He's dead?"

"Yes. He's dead." The finality of his tone told her that it was something he didn't want to discuss any further.

"You're all right?"

"Yes. Now that I know you're going to get well, I'm just fine." He smiled for the first time in days. Then, unable to resist any longer, he bent over her and pressed a soft, cherishing kiss upon her lips.

More than anything Trista wanted to lose herself in his embrace, but first she had to let him know the truth of all she was feeling. She loved him, not Michael, and she wanted him to know that now.

"Lance . . ." She hated to interrupt his kiss, but she needed his undivided attention.

The seriousness of her tone gave him pause, and he

drew back worriedly. "What is it, Trista?"

"I need to talk with you."

"We can talk later." He did not want her to overexert herself, and he thought if he discouraged her from talking, she would conserve her strength.

"No, Lance . . . this has to be said, and it has to be said right now." Though her voice was weak, her meaning was clear. She would not be deterred.

"What is it?" He was frowning as he gazed down at her pale features. She looked so weak and so delicately fragile that he was afraid that she might make her condition worse if she became too overwrought.

"I love you, Lance," she told him solemnly, her gaze meeting and holding his. "I've already told Michael, and we've mutually agreed to call off our engagement."

Lance kissed her again, this time more slowly and with infinitely more tenderness. "I love you, too, Trista, and I know all about what happened between you and Michael."

"You know?"

He nodded, his blue eyes warm upon her. "Michael told me on the night of the raid after Striking Snake had taken you."

"You know that your heritage doesn't affect the way I feel about you?" She needed to hear him say that he believed her. She couldn't live with him if he doubted the truth of her feelings for him.

"I know," he responded firmly, removing all her doubts and his own. "You are my wife, Trista. We are bound as one."

"I love you, darling," she whispered just before his mouth sought hers again in a gentle exploration.

"And I love you."

Michael was sitting with his men near Lone Elk's lodge. The day had passed slowly for him, but he did not even consider leaving. He was worried about Trista, and he wanted to be there for Lance, if he should need him. Michael longed to learn more of Trista's condition, but as the hours passed and Lance did not return, he could only assume that she had made no progress either way.

As the sun sank slowly in the west, Tom alerted him to the fact that Lance was coming. Michael stood up and went to meet him. He could tell little by Lance's expression, and he knew a moment of fear as he considered the possibility that Trista might have died. Only when Lance drew near did he smile, and relief flooded through Michael.

"She's better?" he asked as Lance joined him.

"She's better," he answered, his relief as obvious as his happiness.

Without thought or hesitation, the brothers embraced, sharing the joy of knowing that the woman they both loved and cared for would recover.

"I told her that you had come to the village, and she asked to see you," Lance told Michael.

Michael was pleased, and after relaying the good news to his men, he set out with Lance to visit Trista.

Lance had helped Trista to don one of his own buckskin shirts to afford her some modesty before Michael. Though she was weak, she was eager to see Michael. She wanted to tell him how sorry she was about his mother and let him know that everything had worked out for her and Lance. Trista was lying quietly, waiting for them when they entered the lodge.

"Michael . . ." Trista smiled up at him, and the smile seemed to light up her features.

"Trista, I am so glad that you're going to be all right," he told her earnestly as he sat beside her.

"I'll be fine now," she assured him confidently as her gaze lingered lovingly on Lance, who was standing near the doorway. "Lance told me about your mother, Michael, and I'm so sorry."

"So am I," Michael responded gruffly "Pa's going to be fine, though, and your father wasn't injured."

"That's good to know. As soon as I can travel, we'll be heading back to the Diamond," Trista remarked.

"You've discussed this? You'll really be going back?" Michael was glad to hear it. He didn't know why, but when Lance had taken Trista to Lone Elk's village, he had expected him to want to remain.

Lance came to Trista then and took her hand. Gazing down at her adoringly, he answered, "Yes, we've talked about it, and we've decided to make our permanent home at the ranch. I haven't told Lone Elk yet, but I'm sure he'll have no objection to our visiting him regularly."

"Then you've worked everything out between you?"

"Everything," Trista confided. "We'll be married in a traditional ceremony at the ranch as soon as it can be arranged, but in my heart I am already Lance's wife."

"I'll head back to the Diamond first thing in the morning," Michael said. Now that he was sure that Trista was going to recover fully, there was no reason for him to remain in the village. "I'm sure Pa's worrying about the both of you, and . . ."—his eyes were sparkling in reflection of his own excitement— "Sukie is waiting."

"Does she know how you feel yet?"

"We got it all straightened out before I left. All I have to do now is get her to the altar."

"From what you've already told me, I don't think you'll have much trouble," Trista teased.

"I hope not. As far as I'm concerned, Sukie could be waiting for me with a preacher when I get back."

499

Trista reached out with her other hand to take Michael's. "I'm excited for you, Michael. I hope you and Sukie will be happy together."

"We will, Trista," he pledged, "just as you and Lance will." Seeing that she appeared to be tiring, he knew it was time to take his leave. "I've got to go tell the men how you're doing. I'll see you again when you get back to the ranch." He kissed her cheek softly.

She smiled softly at the tenderness of his action. "Tell my father that I'll see him soon."

"I will."

"And Michael . . ."

He turned back to look at her questioningly. "Yes?"

"Thank you . . . thank you for everything."

Michael flashed her a quick, affectionate grin. "You're welcome." Then he was gone.

Chapter Thirty-three

Shortly before sunrise the next day, Lance awoke. Trista was still slumbering peacefully beside him, so he was careful as he rose and left her. Making his way silently from their lodge, he hurried through the quiet village to where Michael and his men were making ready to depart.

Michael had hoped to see his brother one more time before he left, and he was glad when he saw him coming to join them. He finished tightening the cinch on his saddle, then turned to bid him a temporary farewell.

"I am glad that you're up. I didn't want to leave without telling you goodbye," Michael told him as they shook hands.

"Be careful on your journey back," Lance cautioned.

"I will. I'll tell Pa and Randolph that you're both all right and that you'll be coming home just as soon as Trista's well enough to travel."

The words "coming home" struck Lance deeply. He was indeed going home. He and Trista had made the choice. The Royal Diamond had been his home long ago, and it would be again soon. "Good. I'm not sure when she'll be up to it, but we'll make the trip just as soon as it's safe for her."

"We'll be waiting for you . . . all of us."

They shook hands one more time, and then the

men of the Diamond mounted up and headed away from the camp. Lance watched them until they'd gone from sight before returning to his lodge and Trista.

George sat in his bed staring morosely out his bedroom window. Though his physical condition was vastly improved and he was gaining back some of his mobility, his mood was somber. It had been many long days and nights since his sons had gone after the Indians responsible for the raid, and with each passing hour he was growing more and more worried about them. He mourned the loss of his dear wife, but if Lance or Michael were to be taken from him, too, he just didn't know if he could go on. The knock at his bedroom door interrupted his gloomy musings, and he called out for whoever it was to enter.

"Come on in," he thundered, impatient with the way things were. He had expected Sukie or Rosalie, and he was caught by surprise when it was Whitey who entered. "Whitey! Good to see you."

"Yes, sir. It's good to see you lookin' better," the foreman told him.

"I'm feeling more like myself today. Rosalie might even let me go downstairs tomorrow.

"That's good news, boss," Whitey agreed.

"Well, is there something I can do for you?" George was eager for a distraction.

Whitey swallowed nervously. He knew he had to tell George about what they'd found out on the range. Still, it bothered Whitey to think that what he had to say was going to hurt him.

George noticed the play of troubled emotions on his foreman's features, and he immediately suspected that they'd just received bad news. "Whitey? What is it? Has Trista found? Has Lance or Michael been injured?"

"No, George," he hastened to reassure him, "it has nothing to do with the boys or Trista. . . ."

"Then what is it? You look worried. Is there some kind of trouble?"

Whitey braced himself and began to explain. "Yesterday me and some of the boys were out checking the north range hoping to find some strays from the raid the other night."

"Yes, so?"

"So we came across the camp of some white men who'd been massacred by the Comanche."

"These men were camped on our land?" At Whitey's confirming nod, he asked, "Did we know them?"

"Yes. It was Poker and a few of his friends. I didn't know the other men with them, but I'd seen 'em in town a couple of times in the past."

"I wonder why they were on our land. . . ." George was puzzled.

"Boss, there's more to this than just the massacre," he blurted out after hesitating.

"What are you talking about?"

"These men were dressed like Indians."

Now George was truly puzzled. "Why would they have been on Barrett land dressed like Comanche?"

"Here." Whitey shoved the note toward George. He regretted having to do it, but he knew his boss had to know the truth of it.

George studied the envelope for a moment and, recognizing the handwriting, looked up at his foreman questioningly. "I don't understand. . . ."

"Read it" was all Whitey could say.

With unsteady hands, George opened the crumpled letter and scanned the page. He paled at what he read there, and he looked up at Whitey, aghast. "Where did you find this?"

"I found it in with Poker's things when I was going through their belongings."

George let his hands drop to his lap, and the missive slipped unheeded from his fingers. "Dear God . . . I had no idea her hatred was so vindictive. . . ," he muttered more to himself than to Whitey. "Who else knows about this?" George demanded sharply as he realized the implications of what he'd just learned.

"No one," his foreman informed him. "I kept it hidden until now. I figured you were the only one who should see that."

"Thank you." He breathed a small sigh of relief to know that the knowledge of Eleanor's murderous deceit would go no further. "I want your word that you'll never say anything to anyone about this. It's bad enough that the two of us had to find out. Eleanor paid the full price for her own betrayal, and I don't want Michael to ever learn of it. He loved his mother dearly. I will not tarnish that memory."

"You have my word, boss."

George nodded grimly in acceptance of his pledge. Whitey watched as George got a match from his night table and lit it. With great care, he set the letter and envelope on fire and then let the ashes drop harmlessly onto a small dish on the tabletop.

"Any word from Michael or Lance?"

"No. Nobody's heard or seen anything."

"Let me know as soon as you do."

"I will," Whitey promised. "I'll be going now. If you need anything, just send word."

"I'll do that, but all I really need right now is to have my sons and Trista back here safe and sound."

"It'll happen. They'll be back just as soon as they can."

When Whitey had gone from his bedroom, closing

the door tightly behind him, George sat perfectly still, staring at the black remnant of the letter in disgust. Eleanor had hated him and Lance enough to plan their deaths. . . . Despite the show of equanimity he'd put on for his foreman, George found it completely devastating. He'd never guessed that she could have harbored such savagery within her. Though he had known she disliked Lance and didn't want him at the ranch, he'd never suspected that she would resort to cold-blooded murder to be rid of him. He shook his head in disbelief, and then said a short prayer of thanks that the raid had gone awry. Had Eleanor's plan succeeded as she'd hoped it would, he would be dead now and she would be sole owner of the vast Barrett holdings.

Tears of disillusionment clouded his vision, but he fought them back easily. Eleanor was not worthy of any sentiment from him except contempt. She had been a greedy, obsessed woman, who'd imagined a threat to her own wealth and security where there was none. Never again would he think of her with any of the warmer emotions. George thrust the thought of her from him and vowed never to mourn her again. He would play out the charade of loving husband for Michael's sake, but that would be the end of it. To George, Eleanor was dead; and knowing what he knew now, he was glad.

The days passed in painful slow motion for all at the Royal Diamond as they waited, nerves stretched taut, for word from Michael. Confident that George was well on his way to recovery, Mary Lou returned to her own home to see to things there, but allowed Sukie to stay on to help Rosalie with the nursing duties that remained. Sukie kept herself busy helping to take care of George and visiting with Randolph, but as George's condition improved, there was less and less for her to do. She grew continually more restless and worried, frustrated by the fact that there was no other place she wanted to be but there at the ranch, waiting for him to return.

Randolph, too, was beside himself with worry, and he cursed the day he'd given Trista and Michael his blessing on their marriage. If he'd stood firm and forced her to wed one of the men of his choice, none of this would ever have happened. She would still be alive and well and safely at home with him. Even as he agonized over her coming to Texas, though, he realized that, had he forbidden the marriage, Trista was so headstrong she probably would have run away with Michael anyway. Randolph resigned himself to passing the hours in tormented uncertainty as he waited, hoped, and prayed for some news of his daughter's fate.

George saw them first. He was slowly regaining his mobility and had been moving carefully about his room when he glanced out the window and noticed the cloud of dust rising on the horizon. Intrigued, his spirits soaring at the thought that it might be his sons returning with Trista, he leaned against the window-sill to try to get a better view. The minutes dragged by like hours as he watched and waited. When he was finally able to make out the number of horsemen heading their way, the sound of his bellow filled the house.

"Randolph! Sukie! Rosalie! They're back! They're riding in right now!" As quickly as he could, he edged about the room and threw wide the door. His gait reflected the pain he was still experiencing from the wound, but the joy he was feeling more than countered the discomfort. "Sukie! Randolph!" He made his way slowly down the hall and was just starting down the steps as the others came racing out of the parlor to see what was happening.

"George . . . what is it?" Randolph asked worriedly as he hurried up the steps to assist him.

"They're back," he related happily. "I saw them coming from my bedroom window."

"Is Trista with them?" he asked tentatively, not knowing whether to allow himself to hope or to prepare himself for the worst.

"From this distance I couldn't tell," he replied as they reached the bottom of the staircase.

Sukie was thrilled at the thought of Michael's return, and she ran outside, leaving the door standing wide open for the others to follow. Shielding her eyes from the sun, she stared off toward the group of riders coming their way. Her heart stirred wildly in her breast as she recognized Michael's mount, and she charged off the porch, unmindful of anything except that he had come back.

Michael and his men had been riding almost non-stop since leaving Lone Elk's village. Exhausted, yet pleased to be the bearers of good tidings, they rode full speed into the ranch. He saw Sukie immediately and sawed back on the reins to slow as he neared her. Leaning low, he scooped her up into his arms and drew her across his lap.

"Ah, love, I missed you so. . . ." Michael told her just before he kissed her. It was a quick, breathless exchange, and then he kneed his horse onward toward the house.

"Oh, Michael, I'm so glad you're back. . . ." Sukie told him, her arms locked tightly about him. But as she glanced back at the other riders, she realized with a jolt that Lance and Trista were not with them. The sudden change in her expression mirrored her fear that something terrible had happened to them, and she looked up at Michael, her eyes wide with fright. "Where are Lance and Trista?"

"They're back with Lone Elk at the Comanche village right now."

"They're alive?!" Sukie let the good news wash through her in relief.

"Yes, darling. They alive."

Randolph was standing in the shadows of the porch filled with misery. When the riders had entered the yard area, he had seen immediately that Trista was not with them, and he knew a moment of true sorry and grief. He thought his daughter lost to him forever. He thought her dead . . . or worse . . . and his torment was inconsolable.

George was watching Michael's approach, his heart heavy with despair. He was thrilled that Michael was back, but he feared that his younger son's returning without Lance and Trista meant that the other two were . . .

"They're alive!" Sukie called out joyously to Randolph and George as they drew to a stop before the house, and it was that happy cry that dragged the two fathers back from the depths of their private agonies.

"They're alive?" George asked, surging forward to speak with Michael.

"Yes, sir." Michael helped Sukie down and then dismounted himself as the other men dispersed to see to their own business.

"Thank God," he claimed. "But where are they, son? Why didn't they come back with you?"

"Trista's been hurt —" Michael started to explain as he joined George, Randolph, and Rosalie on the porch. He kept his arm firmly around Sukie's waist as he spoke.

"Hurt? What happened? How is she?" Randolph

interrupted.

"Trista was shot, but—"

"Shot!" He was outraged.

"Randolph," Michael told him comfortingly, "they're staying on with Lone Elk until she's strong enough to make the trip back."

"Who's this Lone Elk?" Randolph wondered.

"He's a Comanche chief and he's Lance's uncle. His village is several days ride from here, and that's where they're staying."

They made their way inside, and as they settled in the parlor, Rosalie hurried off to bring refreshments. She was excited to know that Lance was safe and that both he and Trista would soon be returning to the ranch. The mood of those gathered there was one of thanksgiving and celebration as they learned from Michael all that had happened while he was gone.

It was much later that evening, as George made ready to retire for the night, that he summoned Michael to him in the privacy of his bedroom. Although he'd put on a cheerful front during their reunion, his mood had really been solemn. There was something troubling him deeply, and he needed to know the truth from Michael. It was a truth that would either break his heart or make him a happy man. At the sound of Michael's knock, he called out for him to come in.

"You wanted to see me, Pa?" Michael asked as he closed the door behind him. When he'd been called to George's room, he'd been afraid that the excitement might have proved too much for his father and that George had suffered a relapse. "Are you feeling all right?"

George stood near the window staring out across

509

the vastness of his holdings. He had long thought that the Royal Diamond was the source of his happiness, but he knew now that it was only a small part of it. His true joy was in his sons, and he needed to know if Lance was really planning to stay when he returned to the ranch. George held the deep-seated fear that his older son would be forsaking his white heritage now and going back to live permanently with Lone Elk and the Comanche.

"Yes, son, I'm fine," he said in a voice gruff with emotion. He didn't think he could bear to lose Lance twice. He loved Lance and he wanted him home with him.

"Is there something wrong?"

"That's what I need to find out. . . ."

"I don't understand."

"It's Lance."

"What about him?" Michael wondered.

"Is he going to stay with us when he comes back? Is he going to make the Diamond his home?"

Michael sensed his father's insecurity and answered him quickly. "Lance told me that he and Trista were coming back and that they were planning to make their home here, with you."

George felt as if a great weight had been lifted off his shoulders, but he couldn't help but wonder about his rival for Lance's affections. "What about Lone Elk?"

"When we left Lance hadn't talked with Lone Elk yet, but he had every intention of continuing to visit him. He loves his uncle very much, and I could tell that Lone Elk loves him."

"He's really coming back. . . ."

"As soon as he can, Pa," Michael responded.

George felt his heart swell with emotion. Lance was home. His sons would be with him. His dream had come true. He knew then that, despite Eleanor's vicious betrayal, everything was going to work out.

Sukie stood on the porch gazing up at the starry night sky, her heart filled with love and contentment. *Michael was safe . . . Michael was home.* She heard the door to the house open behind her, and she instinctively knew that it was him, coming to seek her out.

"I had a feeling I'd find you out here." The deep, rich tone of his voice sent shivers of sensual appreciation up her spine, and Sukie turned to welcome him.

"I needed to be alone for a moment, and it's such a pretty night. . . ."

"I haven't noticed the night yet," Michael told her seductively as he moved closer to take her in his arms. "I've been too busy looking at you."

Sukie went delightedly into his embrace. "I missed you so much." She gazed up at him with all the love she felt clearly reflected in her eyes.

Michael felt his desire for her flare heatedly to life as he stared down at her. "I love you with all my heart, Sukie, and I'll never be away from you again if I can help it."

"Oh, Michael . . ." she sighed as she lifted her arms about his neck and drew him down to her for a passionate kiss.

Their lips met, tested, tasted, and then parted in want of a more sensual exploration. As they were clasped in each other's arms, the worry and trouble of the past weeks vanished. All that mattered was that they were together and that they would stay that way forever.

Kiss followed exciting kiss, each touch led to more thrilling caresses until Michael's driving need for her threatened his control. Breaking off the kiss, he shifted slightly away from Sukie's intoxicating nearness. She wondered at his actions and looked up at him, puzzled.

"What is it? Is something wrong?"

Michael gave a short laugh at her query. "No, love. Absolutely nothing is wrong. As a matter of fact, everything is right, very right."

"Then why did you stop kissing me?"

"Not because I wanted to, love, but because I had to."

"I don't understand." Her confusion was obvious, and he bent to kiss her once more quickly and softly.

"I love you, Sukie, and I want you, but this" — he glanced around in frustration — "is not the time or the place."

A daring smile curved her lips as she realized the reason for his withdrawal from her. "When will it be the time and the place?" A flicker of invitation shone in her eyes.

Michael bit back a groan as he considered the risk of slipping into her room later. The idea was tempting, but he reasoned it would be too dangerous. "How soon can we get married?"

"Tonight wouldn't be soon enough for me," Sukie told him.

"Me either," he agreed, pulling her close and kissing her tenderly once more, "but I think it'd be best if we wait until Lance and Trista get back. I would like to have them at the wedding."

"All right, it's settled then. The week after they get here, we'll be married."

"Fine."

Several hours later Sukie lay in her solitary bed tossing restlessly. She remembered the glory of Michael's lovemaking that day by the creek, and she ached with the need to know the strength of his embrace again. Her desires had been stoked to a fever pitch by their earlier caresses, and they still had not abated, even after all this time. Driven by the overwhelming excitement that filled her, Sukie crept from her bed and wrapped her dressing gown about her. Silently, knowing that discretion was essential, she left her room and hurried quietly down the hall to Michael's.

Michael lay facedown on his bed, his body throbbing with unsated desire. The passionate encounter with Sukie on the porch had awakened his need for her to the fullest, and he was having difficulty banishing the memory of her enticing embrace. The thought that she was sleeping just two doors down the hall had driven him even further to distraction, and he wondered in annoyance if he would get any rest at all.

The sound of his door opening startled him, and he rolled over quickly to see who was entering his room. The sight of Sukie wearing only her dressing gown standing just inside his bedroom door sent a jolt of excitement through him. Without speaking, he left the bed and moved to close the door behind her. He took care to make certain it was locked before turning to Sukie and taking her in his arms.

"I'm glad you came . . ." was all he murmured before he kissed her with rapturous delight.

Michael carried her to the welcoming width of his bed, and they lay together upon its softness totally enthralled in the joy of their coming together. In a celebration of their love, they cherished each other's bodies. Each touch, each kiss took on a deeper, more beautiful meaning as they stripped away the barrier of their nightclothes and joined in love's most intimate union.

Sukie was in ecstasy as she clung to Michael, reveling in his possession. He was all she'd ever wanted or needed, and now she knew he was hers, and hers alone. The wanton glory of their lovemaking sent them soaring to rapture and beyond. Lost in the splendor of their closeness, they reached the heights and crested, each calling out the other's name in hushed tones. Replete and content, they rested, exulting in the love they'd discovered and the future that promised them untold happiness.

Only as the eastern horizon brightened with the dawn of the new day did Sukie force herself to leave Michael's bed. They shared one last, soul-stirring kiss before she donned her dressing gown and fled down the hall to her own chamber.

Michael watched her disappear safely into the haven of her own room. As he returned to his now lonely bed, he found himself hoping that Trista and Lance would return soon. He wanted to marry Sukie as quickly as possible, for he loved her deeply and never wanted to be apart from her, not even for a moment.

Chapter Thirty-four

Though Night Lark acted outwardly as if nothing unusual had happened between her and Lance, she had silently been seething over his cold rejection. She knew now and had painfully accepted the fact that he didn't love her. It was that knowledge that had festered deep within her since the night over a week before when he'd cast her aside. Her once loving heart had turned into a jealous, vengeful one now, and she was intent only on wreaking whatever havoc she could between Trista and Lance.

Night Lark knew that as soon as Trista had recovered from her wound, Lance would be taking her back to his white father's ranch, where they would make their permanent home. She had seen Trista moving about the village with Lance and knew that they would be departing soon.

Her hatred for Trista consumed her. If Night Lark couldn't have Lance herself, she surely didn't want the stupid white woman to have him. She longed for a way to cause trouble between them. It was the memory of Trista's arrival in the village and her continued profession of love for Lance's half brother, Michael, that provided Night Lark with a possible way of creating doubt in Trista's mind. Night Lark knew that

Lance had only taken Trista captive because she'd belonged to Michael. She decided to use that now as a way to torment her, to try to make her wonder about the truth of Lance's love and the real reason he'd married her.

From across the encampment, Night Lark waited for her chance. She kept close observation over Lance and Trista's movements, for she wanted to speak with Trista alone. It seemed that they were together every moment of every day, and she cursed Lance for never leaving his wife's side. It infuriated Night Lark to see Lance constantly touching her and kissing her. Night Lark wished with all her heart that Striking Snake had been a better shot.

To Night Lark's vast relief, Wind Rider finally sought Lance out late one afternoon. She was thrilled as she watched the two men disappear out of the village toward the corral, and she made her move. Night Lark kept her actions casual, and though she seemed to be moving in no particular direction or hurry, her course had long ago been set. In her heart and mind, her motive was clear.

Trista was sitting in unsuspecting comfort just outside Lance's lodge. Now that the infection was completely gone, her strength was returning quickly. She felt sure that within a few days she would feel more like herself again. Trista closed her eyes against the brilliance of the sunshine and lounged there, enjoying the peace of the moment and soothing warmth of the sun. It seemed to her that her life had never been more perfect than it was at that moment.

When the warmth of the sun was suddenly blocked from her, Trista opened her eyes to discover Night Lark standing over her.

"Night Lark . . . hello," she greeted her easily. Trista knew this woman no longer posed a threat to her. She was firm in her love for Lance and confident of his love for her.

"You seem very satisfied with yourself, Trista," Night Lark snapped, resenting her obvious happiness.

"I'm satisfied *and* I'm happy," she replied. "I love my husband and he loves me."

Night Lark snorted in derision. "You are a fool if you think so, white woman." Her tone was scathing, but Trista paid little attention to her. When Trista didn't respond to her deliberate baiting, she went on snidely, "Lance does not love you, Trista; he is only using you."

"Using me?" Trista was incredulous as she stared at the Comanche maiden.

Night Lark nodded. "He only took you for his wife because you were his brother's woman. He wanted to seek revenge against the Barretts."

"I see."

"It is true. He only married you to keep his half brother from having you. There is no love in your marriage, Trista. There is only hate."

"You're very right, Night Lark, in part of what you told my wife." The sound of Lance's voice so close behind her sent a chill of fear up her spine.

"See, I told you. . . ." Night Lark tried to sound haughty before Trista, but Lance's next words put an end to any hopes she'd ever had of coming between them.

"Only part of it, woman, not all of it." His words were cold and his tone was dangerous.

"Lance?" Trista's firm belief in their devotion to each other had not been seriously shaken by Night Lark's revelation, but Lance's statement roused her curiosity.

Lance gave her a meaningful look as he faced down the woman who dared to torment Trista with her half-truths and outright lies. "You didn't tell Trista how I fell in love with her even before the wedding ceremony, but how I refused to admit it to myself."

Trista's expression turned rapturous at his open confession.

Lance continued. "You didn't explain to her how I've repeatedly told you that I don't love you and how I've never proposed to you in all the years I've known you. There was never any chance of your being my wife, Night Lark. Did you tell Trista that?" He cornered her viciously, and the maiden grew ashen at the cruel, but well-deserved, tongue-lashing. "You also didn't tell her how I sent you away from me the other night when you blatantly offered yourself to me. Have no doubt, Night Lark, Trista is the only woman I will ever love."

Caught in her own trap, the chance to save face gone, Night Lark raced away from them, realizing once and for all that Trista had won and she had lost.

Lance watched her go for a moment and then looked down at his wife. "Are you all right?"

"I'm fine." She smiled at him brightly. "Thank you."

"Don't thank me, love. I only told the truth." He extended a hand to help her up. When she got to her feet, he drew her inside the lodge and pulled the door closed behind them.

"What she said . . . was that true? Did you take me captive because of Michael?"

Lance smiled wryly. "I thought so at first, Trista, but you played well upon my heart, woman. I became the captive, not you."

A soft smile curved the corner of her mouth, and she went into his arms. "I will hold you captive forever, Lance Barrett."

"There is no need for bonds between us, Trista. It is my heart that is your captive, and it would not dare

518

escape you," he murmured as he lowered his head to hers and claimed her lips in a gentle exchange.

What began as a tender embrace suddenly threatened to explode into fiery passion. Lance pulled away.

"Trista?"

"What, Lance?" she asked as she moved toward their bed, discarding her loose Indian clothing as she went.

"Trista . . ." He cleared his throat nervously. "Are you sure this is all right?"

They had been sleeping together every night, but he had not attempted to make love to her during this time, for he was afraid of hurting her in some way. Now, as he watched her teasingly disrobing before him, his long-denied desires surged almost painfully to life. He wanted her badly, but he would not take her unless he was certain he would not harm her.

"Lance, there is nothing that would make me feel better right now than to make love to you. Please, Lance . . . love me. . . ." She whispered the last seductively as she dropped the final article of her clothing and reclined in blatant sensual invitation on the bed.

All his logical reasons for not taking her were swept from Lance's mind at the sight of her waiting for him so eagerly on his bed. Needing her, wanting her, craving the closeness of union with her, he quickly stripped off his clothing and joined her there. Their lips met and parted as his tongue thrust boldly within the honeyed sweetness of her mouth. His hands skimmed over her satiny curves, bringing her passion to blossom.

Trista, too, felt the need to touch him, and her hands restlessly traced the muscle-ridged width of his back down to the slim, driving potency of his hips. He taunted her with knowing caresses even as he explored the silken cords of her throat with heated kisses. Ecstasy flooded through Trista at his arousing exploration, and she arched up into his male hardness, needing more from him . . . needing oneness with him.

Lance sensed the urgency of her desire, but tempered his pace. He wanted her just as much as she wanted him, yet he didn't want to rush. He sought to slow their ascent.

"Easy, darling. There's no need to hurry. . . ."

"But I've missed you, Lance. I want you inside me so much. Please, love me now. Don't make me wait any longer to have you."

Her words almost broke his will to restrain himself, and his mouth sought hers with a fierce urgency. "I want to go slowly. . . . I don't want to hurt you. . . ."

"You won't hurt me. The only thing that hurts is the emptiness I feel. . . ." She moaned as his mouth descended to her breasts to kiss that sensitive flesh. Eagerly, she began to move rhythmically against the hard press of his hips. Trista understood his hesitancy, but she wanted to assure him that it was all right, that making love to her wouldn't disturb her wound.

A quiver of excitement shook Lance as she wrapped her legs around his, and his firm resolve to love her gently was lost. Positioning himself against the portals of her womanhood, he thrust forward and buried himself deep within her. Trista boldly moved against him, urging him to take her, and take her quickly.

"Now, Lance . . . now," she commanded, and he was her willing sensual captive as he began the driving motion that would take them both to rapture and beyond.

Wanton splendor pulsed through her with each of his exciting thrusts, and she moved restlessly beneath him, searching for that fevered pinnacle that she knew awaited her. Lance continued to caress her, seeking out and finding her most erotic places. A rush of breathtaking abandon came over her quickly, and she reached the heights in throbbing glory, crying out to him of her love as she crested the peak of pleasure.

At the sound of her rapturous cries, Lance, too, achieved his release. Shuddering in excitement, his own ecstasy lifted him to rapture's delight. Their desires temporarily satisfied, they lay together, bodies still as one, limbs lazily intertwined, enjoying the peace of their love. Lance started to shift his weight from her, for he was fearful of lying too heavily upon her, but she held tightly to him.

"Stay," she murmured huskily.

Being a captive of her love, he complied.

It was three days later that Lone Elk stood tall and proud before Lance and Trista. The time had come for them to return to Barrett, and his heart was aching over the impending separation. Even so, he knew some measure of contentment because of Lance's obvious happiness.

"We will return to you often, my uncle," Lance promised, feeling the pain of their parting as deeply as Lone Elk."

"I will look forward to your visits, Lance," he replied solemnly. "May your journey be a safe one."

"We will be careful."

Lance helped Trista to mount the pony she was to ride, and then he swung up onto his own horse's back. His gaze locked with his uncle's, and a moment of silent understanding passed between the men. He put his heels to his mount's flanks and started from the village with Trista riding at his side. They paused as they reached the edge of the encampment and turned

521

back to wave one final time before moving off out of sight in the direction of the Diamond.

It took them several days to reach Diamond land, and they paused and dismounted on the hilltop overlooking the house to savor the joy of their homecoming. Lance stood in silence, staring down at the scene before them and remembering all that had occurred since that night so long ago when he'd first seen Trista on the porch with Michael.

"I fell in love with you the first time I saw you," he told her.

"Out there on the range?"

"No, it was here. I was watching the house, and I saw you on the porch with Michael. I thought you were unbelievably beautiful then, and I still think so."

"Why were you watching the house?" She was puzzled at his confession.

"I had made camp nearby and I heard the music. I wanted to see what was happening."

"Did you miss your father and living on the ranch?"

"By then I had hardened myself not to miss it, but I have to admit that there were times when I longed to come back."

"And now you are back." Her eyes met his in tender devotion. "We'll be happy here, Lance."

"I know," he said huskily.

Trista went to him and kissed him, wrapping her arms about his waist. When the kiss ended, they remained standing there, locked in a cherishing embrace.

Trista whispered, "I love you, Lance Barrett."

She rested her head against his chest and thrilled to the powerful, steady rhythm of his heartbeat as she held him close. Lance was her love and her life.

"And I love you, Trista," he vowed. "Let's go home. . . ."

They broke apart then and mounted their horses. The sun was at its zenith above them as they started down to the ranch, eager to return to their families and begin their new life together.

Epilogue

Three Weeks Later on the Royal Diamond

"Where are we going, Lance?" Trista asked as they rode away from the ranch early one morning, two weeks after their marriage by the minister from town.

"You'll see," Lance told her teasingly, not giving away their destination. "Come on," he encouraged as he spurred his mount to a quicker pace, and Trista followed suit.

When Lance led her to the stream with its border of shady cottonwoods, she was thrilled. "I haven't been here since . . ."

"Since when?" he asked as they dismounted and led their horses to drink of the clear, sparkling water.

"Since the first day I saw you chasing Fuego," Trista explained. "It seems so long ago."

"It really does," he agreed, thinking of all that had happened since their first encounter. "Trista . . ."

"Yes?" She looked up questioningly.

"I was thinking . . . what would you say about building our own home here by the stream?" The stream was a place of many warm and loving memories for Lance, and he wanted to make more of those here in the future.

"I think it's a wonderful idea," she exclaimed, thrilled at his suggestion.

Lance caressed her cheek with a gentle hand. "You could be happy here?"

"I could be ecstatic here." Trista remembered her first visit there and how she had seen Fuego come charging over the rocky ridge across the valley, with Lance in pursuit. "I only wish . . ."

"What?"

"I was just thinking of Fuego. I'm sorry you lost him, Lance. I know how hard you worked to capture him."

"He's a beautiful stallion, but I think he was just meant to be free," Lance responded as he let his gaze drift across the loveliness of their future home site. It was then that he saw Fuego, standing in regal magnificence on the hill behind them. "Trista . . ." he spoke her name in a hushed, anxious whisper.

"What?" She was puzzled by the strange tone in this voice.

"Look!" Lance pointed to where the rogue remained poised, watching them.

"Fuego!" Trista was excited at the sight of the golden stallion, and took several steps toward him as she called out his name again. "Fuego! Come! Come to me!"

Fuego studied Trista and Lance for a moment and then moved cautiously in their direction. He came to stand before Trista, and he whickered low in recognition as she reached out to stroke his powerful neck.

"How are you, big fella?" she asked as she continued to pet him, and he nuzzled her gently with his velvet nose.

The sound of another horse's whinny brought Fuego's head up, and he turned quickly to glance back the way he'd come. A dainty, black mare was standing on the ridge waiting for him. Fuego gave Trista and Lance one last look before turning up his heels and racing off to rejoin the female. He paused there on the rise to look back at them once more and then disappeared down the slope beyond, with the mare sedately following his lead.

Trista and Lance shared amazed looks as they watched him go.

"He's everything you ever thought he was and more," Trista murmured, sorry that he was gone from her, but understanding his need to be free.

"That he is, love, and I think this time he's found a captive of his own." Lance chuckled as he thought of the mare. He slipped his arms about his wife then and drew her to him. "He brought us together, and for that I'll always be grateful." Lance kissed her then, and it was a breathtaking kiss that promised of the untold delights the future held for them.

SHE FEARED HER RED CAPTOR

Roping the wild stallion that roamed the Texas range was all that Trista Sinclair had on her mind when suddenly she felt a lasso binding her own arms. The golden-haired beauty was indignant when she faced her Comanche abductor...then she became even more furious when he took outrageous liberties with her. Just because he was handsome, virile and strong gave him no right to inflame her passions so scandalously! But before the blue-eyed prisoner could think to repel him, she was clinging to him with a fierce craving she'd never experienced before!

HE DESIRED HIS WHITE PRIZE

Having sworn to hate the paleface father who'd deserted him, half-breed Lance Barrett took particular pleasure in taking white captives...though none compared to the ivory-skinned spitfire now trapped in his embrace. The hot-blooded brave planned to ignite her womanly senses, then shame her with her ardor. But even as he plotted the alluring wench's humiliation, the Indian warrior couldn't think of living without her. He'd claim her as the spoils of war, then make her submit time and again in rapturous

02273

0 71268 00395 9

ISBN 0-8217-2273-5